THE DRAGON PORTAL SERIES

BY BLOOD AND MAGIC

BOOK 2

JAMIE A. WATERS

By Blood and Magic © 2020 by Jamie A. Waters

Cover Art: Deranged Doctor Design
Editor: Novel Nurse Editing

ISBN: 978-1-949524-21-5 (Hardback Edition)
ISBN: 978-1-949524-19-2 (Paperback Edition)
ISBN: 978-1-949524-18-5 (eBook Edition)

Library of Congress Control Number: 2020903190
First Edition *March 2020

Chapter One

An explosion rocked the ship.

Sabine was thrown off the bed and slammed hard against the wooden floor of the cabin. A second later, someone landed on top of her. She groaned and shoved her friend in an entreaty to move.

"Esme! Can't breathe!" She gasped, wondering if she'd managed to survive the Wild Hunt only to be smothered by a witch who was still half asleep.

"Ugh," Esmelle muttered and shifted enough to allow Sabine to escape. "Consider it payback for stealing the blankets last night."

Sabine snickered and tossed her silver braids out of her face. Crawling away, she looked up at the small shelf where she usually kept her knives, but it was empty. They'd likely fallen, probably from whatever had jarred them awake. At least she'd learned her lesson about keeping them near the bed. The first time the seas had been a little rough and she'd gotten knocked out of bed, Sabine had managed to cut her leg. Traveling on board a ship was more perilous than she'd realized.

Once she spotted the weapons under the desk, she flattened herself against the floor and reached for them. "Aha. Got you."

"Don't think your knives are going to help you much in the middle of the ocean," Esmelle said with a yawn and climbed back on the bed they'd been sharing.

Sabine made a noncommittal noise, unable to argue the point. She quickly equipped her daggers by feel alone, their familiar weight a small comfort. She'd feel better if her magic were back to full power, but she'd take what she could get.

Esmelle brushed her wayward red curls away from her face and blinked the sleep out of her eyes. She leaned toward the small round cabin window and frowned. "What woke us? Do you think we hit something?"

"Not sure, but I think we need to find out," Sabine said, pushing up from the floor rather unsteadily. The contents of the desk and bookshelves had all fallen to the floor in a crumpled heap of papers, books, and other trinkets. They'd hit some rough seas since they'd left Akros, but nothing like this. The entire ship was rocking precariously as though even the heavens were determined to capsize them.

Another explosion jerked the ship and Sabine tripped, landing hard on her backside. She winced and then froze, catching sight of a tiny pink-haired pixie banging her fists against a glass jar. The captive was shrieking silently, her words muffled by the glass. Sabine crawled closer to lift the jar and freed the pixie from her makeshift prison.

"We're under attack!" Blossom yelled, fluttering her wings fast enough to scatter glittering pixie dust all over the floor.

Sabine frowned, searching for any sign of damage to the pixie's fragile wings. She didn't see anything, but it would be impossible to see a small tear while Blossom was zipping around. "Calm down, Blossom. Are you hurt?"

The pixie continued to dart around the cabin and wailed,

"We're all going to die! I don't want to die without seeing a garden again!"

Sabine blew out a breath and pushed herself upright. Blossom wouldn't be making quite so much noise if she were truly hurt. Unfortunately, Sabine couldn't take the time to console the hysterical pixie. She needed to hurry and get out onto the deck. "Blossom, stay close to me. We need to find out what's going on, and I don't want to leave you in here."

Blossom immediately stopped with the hysterics, proving Sabine's theory she was fine. She dove into Sabine's hair and clung to her silvery braids tightly. Something hit the ship again, and Sabine grabbed the edge of the wall to steady herself before she fell. Blossom might be right about an attack. This was more than rough seas.

Picking her way carefully over the fallen debris, Sabine headed toward the door with Esmelle following right behind her.

"Is Blossom okay?"

"Yes, she's just a little freaked out," Sabine said, bracing herself as something hit the ship again. Esmelle fell over and muttered a curse. Sabine reached down to help her friend stand.

"I'm more than a little freaked out! It's the end of the world!" Blossom shouted, tugging on Sabine's braids hard enough to make her wince.

"Ow, watch it," Sabine muttered, a little surprised by Blossom's strength. "My head's still attached."

"Oops. Sorry, Sabine," Blossom said and immediately relaxed her grip.

Sabine harrumphed but managed to make her way to the door. She flung it open and stepped out into chaos.

Lightning streaked across the sky, followed almost imme- diately by a sharp clap of thunder. Waves crashed upon the deck, the salt spray making the surface slippery and wet. It combined with the rain beating down and plastered Sabine's clothing to her skin.

The wind whipped Sabine's braids away from her face, and Blossom slipped inside her shirt to hide from the elements. Reassured the pixie was as secure as possible, Sabine made her way to the railing of the upper deck. The rain from the storm made it difficult to see more than a short distance in front of her. Down below, the crew was rushing around, trying to keep the ship safeguarded.

She caught sight of Malek standing on the quarterdeck, issuing commands over the din of the storm. Sabine swallowed, feeling that familiar flutter in her stomach every time she caught sight of the charismatic dragon shapeshifter. He was a powerful and imposing figure, and not even the storm appeared to affect his bearing. If anything, his command of the ship under the current conditions made her admire him more.

"Get your ass back up in the rigging, Joshen," Malek shouted, gesturing to the ropes and cables overhead. "Levin and Kristof, arm the port-side catapults. Prepare to fire on my orders."

Sabine gripped the railing of the deck tightly, trying to figure out what was happening. Blossom was right about an attack. They wouldn't be arming the weapons if it was just a storm. She watched the crew members lift a dwarven-crafted crystal lance and fit it into the large wooden catapults on the deck.

"Someone's attacking the ship?" Esmelle asked, staggering toward the railing.

Before Sabine could respond, a large demon with skin the color of pitch leaped over the railing and landed beside her. Sabine started and tried to shield the rain from her eyes to better see Bane.

Her demon protector scanned her over and demanded, "Are you hurt?"

She shook her head and yelled loud enough to be heard over the commotion, "I'm fine. What's happening?"

"It's the Merfolk," Bane shouted, gesturing over the side of the ship. "They're attacking. You should get back inside."

Sabine frowned, searching for any sign of the maritime race who lived within the Endless Sea. Another wave crashed over the deck, pitching the ship violently. Sabine gasped and tightened her grip on the railing. Lightning streaked across the sky, its silvery glow resonating with her magic. She took a deep breath, and the sharp, metallic scent of foreign magic filled her nose. Her eyes widened when realization hit her. She'd written it off as bad weather, but this storm was magically wrought.

Leaning closer toward Bane, she placed her hand against his chest and urged, "I need to speak with Malek. We need to negotiate safe passage, or they'll capsize us. The weapons will only anger them."

Bane frowned, turning his horned head toward the front of the ship where they were arming the giant weapons. Gesturing to the catapults, he said, "We're beyond talk, little one. Decisive action is necessary, or all is lost."

Sabine shook her head. She'd never met one of the Merfolk before, but she recalled her childhood lessons. The Merfolk's dominion was the sea, and Malek's ship didn't have a hope to outrun them. The storm was intended to blind and disorient while the Merfolk attacked from below. Once the ship capsized, the crew would be taken as hostages and either enslaved or executed. They must have somehow offended the sea-dwellers or given them some cause to attack. It was imperative she try to communicate with them. The Merfolk and Fae shared a complicated history, but they'd never been at odds. Negotiating with them might be their only chance to get through this situation unscathed.

Turning to Esmelle, she gestured to where Malek was standing on the far side of the quarterdeck. He was busy issuing instructions to those on the deck below him and hadn't noticed her yet. "Esme, I'm going to speak with Malek and warn him."

Esmelle waved her off and yelled, "Go! I'll stay here. If it gets too bad, I'll head back inside."

Sabine nodded and slowly headed toward the stairs near where the captain was standing. Between the wind, rain, and furious waves repeatedly crashing over the ship, it was almost impossible to find any traction. She started to slip several times, but Bane wrapped his arm around her waist to steady her. Unfortunately, the demon wasn't faring much better in these conditions. Holding tightly to the railing, she carefully made her way to where the ship captain was issuing orders.

As though sensing her approach, Malek turned toward her and frowned. His drenched shirt was plastered against his skin, emphasizing the corded muscles in his arms. She'd had more than a few occasions to see him without a shirt over the past week, and each time caused her breath to catch. A pity she couldn't take the time to appreciate the sight.

"Malek, tell your men to hold off their attack," she urged, pointing toward the crew who were preparing to launch the crystal lances. The dwarves infused a special type of magic into the crystal tips, which would fracture under the water. It was designed to release the equivalent of poison to any living creatures in the vicinity. It was an effective deterrent against some of the giant underwater creatures who might try to attack the ship. However, an assault against the Merfolk would only renew their efforts to destroy the ship and kill everyone aboard the vessel.

Malek ordered his men to hold and closed the distance between them. "If you have a solution to our current situation, I'm willing to hear it. But if we don't do something soon, we'll all be taking a swim."

Bane leaned over the railing and frowned. "Talk if you must, but the Merfolk are changing positions. I'm going get a better vantage point from up in the rigging. I'll call out their location when I sense a group of them close enough for the lances to make an impact."

Malek gave him a curt nod. Sabine looked over the side of the ship, catching sight of a flash of silver beneath the waves. Demons had the ability to sense someone's life force and manipulate it under certain conditions. Bane must have agreed to act as a spotter to help target the crystal lances.

Turning back to Malek, she leaned in close so he could hear her over the storm. "We need to convince the Merfolk to negotiate with us. Killing or attacking them outright will only anger them further. We're the intruders here, and they won't back down. They'll summon others of their kind if they believe us to be a credible threat. We can't defeat all of them, especially not like this."

Malek's frown deepened, fingering the warding medallion around his neck. The jewelry was no simple adornment; it masked his draconic powers and allowed him to appear much like a human. He shook his head and said, "They aren't responding to any efforts for a dialogue. I have two crew members stationed at both sides of the ship trying to get their attention."

Another wave crashed over the side of the ship, drenching her hair and clothing. Blossom shivered against her neck, and the tiny pixie clung tightly to her. Sabine sent a trace of her magic outward to help stabilize and warm Blossom.

Pushing her wet braids away from her face, Sabine said, "I

might be able to help get their attention. The Merfolk aren't allies with the Fae, but we're not at odds either. A treaty has stood between our people for generations, ever since the portal was closed."

Before Malek could respond, another explosion rocked the ship and Sabine was thrown backward. A scream ripped from her throat as she slid across the deck and slipped over the edge where the railing had broken. Malek dove toward her and wrapped his hand around her wrist before she could fall into the ocean. She hit the side of the ship and winced as pain lanced through her side.

"I've got you," Malek shouted, pulling her back onto the deck. He wrapped his arms around her, drawing her close. His concerned gaze roamed over her face. "Are you all right?"

She nodded, her heart hammering in her chest. Her side hurt, but she didn't think it had caused too much damage. If necessary, Bane could always heal her.

Turning her head, she yelled, "Blossom? Are you okay?"

A tiny voice squeaked out an affirmative from beneath her shirt. Sabine's shoulders slumped in relief. She needed to get Blossom back inside soon before the little pixie was harmed. As dangerous as it was for her and the rest of the ship's crew, Blossom could easily get swept away by the waves or wind.

Malek climbed to his feet and helped her stand. While she might normally be graceful on land, the same couldn't be said about being on the sea. Malek had claimed she'd eventually find her sea legs, but she didn't believe it, especially not in this weather.

Bane rushed over and said, "Esmelle's gone. She went over the side. I couldn't get to her in time."

Sabine blanched and leaned over the railing, panic welling inside her. She couldn't lose her closest friend—not like this.

"Esme!" she yelled, searching for any sign of Esmelle's colorful clothing amid the treacherous waves. The sea thrashed in anger, the salt spraying her and the deck, but all she could see were the same flashes of silver swirling beneath the surface. There had to be dozens of Merfolk surrounding the ship, but they weren't anywhere near the surface.

She spun around to face Bane. "Dammit. We need to get her back. I will *not* allow them to harm her."

Bane's eyes flashed silver. "On your word, we'll destroy every last one of them."

Malek turned at the sound of someone shouting up from the lower deck, and his jaw clenched. He slammed his fist against the wooden railing. "Fucking bastards. Levin's gone too, along with another dozen of the crew."

Sabine scanned the sea, but she couldn't see any sign of the missing crew. If the Merfolk were already taking prisoners, they were running out of time. A few more hits like the last one, and the ship would capsize.

"If you have any suggestions, Sabine, now is the time. Otherwise, I agree with Bane. I'll destroy every last one of these Merfolk for harming those under my protection."

Without waiting for a response, Malek leaned over the railing toward the lower deck and called out more orders to ready the catapults. Sabine swallowed and tried to bury the sick fear threatening to overwhelm her. Esmelle wouldn't even have been on this ship if it weren't for her. The thought of losing one of her closest friends was unfathomable.

Sabine's hands tightened on the railing as she stared at the angry sea. "They'll keep Esme and the rest of the hostages alive until they manage to capsize the ship. Those who aren't enslaved are usually fed to their underwater pets. If they take all of us down below, we'll lose any negotiating power we might have while still under the sky."

"I've heard the stories," Bane admitted, caging her with

his arms. She leaned back against his heated skin, thankful for the warmth he offered against the chill from the elements. Bane might have difficulties tapping into softer emotions, but he'd made it no secret he admired and respected the spunky witch who was now an unwilling hostage.

"They aren't just stories," she said as a daring plan began to form in her mind.

Bane squeezed her midsection and murmured, "You are my priority, Sabine. If we must lose Esme, she will be mourned, but we cannot allow you to fall. We need to get you and this ship out of here."

Sabine turned and glared up at him. "We won't be mourning anyone. I *will* get them back—all of them. And you're going to help me do it."

Chapter Two

Lightning flashed, and Sabine lifted her gaze to stare at the dark clouds overhead. Between the magical storm above and the Merfolk attacking from underneath, it was only a matter of minutes before they were successful in destroying the ship. Her fingers curved into fists in frustration. Her magic still hadn't fully replenished itself since she'd managed to escape the Wild Hunt. She had enough for small magic but not enough to help extricate themselves from their situation.

Turning to Malek, she said, "I need you to combine magic with me."

Malek's head whipped toward her. "What? Now? Are you sure about this?"

Bane frowned and asked, "What are you thinking, little one? He'll need to remove his warding necklace to share magic with you. The Merfolk will redouble their efforts to attack if they know a dragon's on board."

Sabine straightened her shoulders and flung a hand toward the waves. "I'm aware, but this may be our only chance to recover our friends. With Malek's help, I can get their attention. At the very least, I can get rid of this damned storm. It'll buy us a bit more time."

Malek's brow furrowed, and he cocked his head. "You can control the weather?"

Sabine nodded, abandoning any thoughts of keeping her powers secret from the crew. "It's major magic, but yes. Bane can try to shield my magic through our mark, but we still run the risk of alerting my duplicitous family to my presence. I don't see an alternative. If the Merfolk destroy this ship and kill us, then it won't matter anyway. I'd rather go down fighting."

"A fight it is then." Malek squared his shoulders, and determination filled his eyes. "I can infuse you with dragon-fire. That should give your magic a boost to help with the storm, but it won't do anything to stop them from attacking beneath the ship."

"I have a plan, but we need to hurry." She pulled out her knife and sliced downward across her palm. The pain was sharp and biting, a suitable sacrifice for the magic she was about to attempt. Blood welled to the surface, and she allowed it to fall upon the deck of the ship. The huge vessel seemed to shudder in response to her offering, and even the rain paused briefly before falling again.

"I hope you know what you're doing," Malek muttered and unfastened the warding medallion around his neck. Dragon magic, both terrible and powerful, swirled around her and caressed her skin in a heated embrace. She inhaled sharply, trying to ignore the dredges of fear his magic evoked. Dragons might be her people's sworn enemy, but she'd already placed her life in Malek's hands several times. If it came down to trusting their lives to either the Merfolk or this dragon, she'd choose Malek.

He shoved the warding medallion into his pocket and took the knife from her. He flipped the blade around and repeated her action on his hand. Pushing aside her reservations about sharing blood and magic with a dragon, Sabine reached out and clasped her hand with his. She gasped and swayed at the sudden rush of power trailing upon her skin as their blood intermingled.

That gift of blood and magic would allow her the immunity to withstand the potentially devastating effects of his dragonfire, but it also stirred a suppressed need to share magic with him in a much more intimate setting. She lifted her head to meet his eyes, staggered by the longing and tenderness in his gaze. The chaos from the Merfolk's attack faded away as she got lost in the impossible depths of his blue eyes.

"Sabine," Malek said, his voice husky as he took a step closer to her. He cupped her face with his free hand and trailed his thumb across her cheek. "One day soon, I intend to do this again without the threat of enemies hanging over our heads."

He leaned down and brushed his lips against hers. The pressure was featherlight, more an offering of power than a show of force. Recognizing his unspoken question, Sabine parted her lips and closed her eyes. This was necessary, even if she also wanted him beyond the confines of this task.

She reached up and placed her palm against his chest. His heart beat faster beneath her touch, a mirrored echo of her own. Malek swept in closer, his taste and feel surrounding her as she explored his kiss and the nuances of his magic. From all outward appearances, it was nothing more than a kiss. But Malek's touch and power was more consuming than anything she'd ever experienced.

Malek breathed his dragonfire into her, and she gasped. An indescribable heat rushed through her, burning away all her subterfuge. She was vaguely aware of her glamour falling away as she was swept along on the wave of Malek's power.

The silver markings etched into her skin glowed with an unearthly light as he fueled her power and passion to greater heights. The tiny embers of her magic flared to life, charged by the force contained with Malek's dragonfire.

Sabine leaned into him, desperately wanting more, and Malek willingly provided it. Her fingers curled into his wet shirt, pulling him even closer. Gods. He was even more powerful than she'd realized. If his magic was typical of other dragons, it was no small wonder why the battle between their people had nearly decimated the world. Malek *was* power, and more than a match for everything at her command.

"That's enough," Bane snapped, jerking Malek away from her. "We don't know how this will affect her."

Sabine swayed slightly, trying to get her bearings while Malek's warmth faded from her skin. She laughed, both in delight and exultation. Leaning against the railing, she touched her lips, which were still swollen from his kiss. If that was a hint of what it could be like between them, she wasn't sure how long she could keep trying to deny her attraction to him. Malek gazed at her in return with a hungry and predatory gleam in his eyes, and her body immediately responded. She knew he was equally affected by her.

Bane turned toward her. "Do you have enough?"

She nodded, and another explosion rocked the boat. This time she was more prepared and didn't lose her footing.

Malek frowned and stared hard at the waves. "If they haven't figured out who I am yet, they will soon enough. Our catapults may create enough commotion to interrupt their attack once they sense me. If you can manage to turn the storm away, that should also help get their attention." He paused and then turned his gaze back on her, causing her skin to prickle in awareness. "Levin is practically a brother to me, and I'd rather not leave him to his fate if there's a chance to save his life. The world will be a poorer place without him in it."

Touched by the conflicted emotions in his eyes, Sabine reached over and placed her hand onto his. "I feel the same way about Esme. We'll do whatever's necessary to save them. If you can, focus on using the crystal lances to break the Merfolk's ranks. We need them closer to the surface for what I have planned."

Malek lifted her hand and brushed a light kiss against her knuckles. "I only hope the Merfolk are as equally charmed by you as I am, Sabine."

Bane snorted in amusement. "If you two are finished, I'd like to draw your attention back to the damned Merfolk trying to kill us."

Malek frowned at him, but Bane merely smirked and continued, "Once Sabine gets rid of the storm, I'll return to the rigging and call out directions as I sense them. This should enable the crew to target the Merfolk with the catapults more efficiently."

"No," Sabine said, interrupting. She put her hand over the mark on Bane's arm symbolizing his sworn oath to her. "The lances will buy us time by causing commotion among the Merfolk, but our intention isn't to kill them. We need to stop them from trying to capsize the ship. I think I know how we can achieve our goals, but I'll need your help to do it."

Bane cocked his head. "Very well, little one. What do you have in mind?"

"We're going to force them to negotiate with us, even if we have to turn the tables on them and take our own hostages."

Malek pressed his lips together and then gave her a curt nod. "You alone may hold sway over the Merfolk. I'll defer to your lead in this, but only up to a point. My priority is to keep the portal sealed, even should I lose my friend in the process. I won't allow the Merfolk to harm you or jeopardize our purpose, Sabine. I need you."

She didn't respond. There wasn't anything she could say. It was painful to think about, but Malek was right. If they didn't ensure the portal remained closed to the absent gods, their entire world would be at risk. She couldn't afford to put the lives of the crew above the millions inhabiting this world, even if it broke her heart in the process.

While Malek went back to issuing orders to ready the weapons, Sabine closed her eyes and centered herself in preparation for what she was about to attempt. Bane placed his hand against the back of her neck. The skin-to-skin contact would allow her to perform the magic without fear of alerting the Wild Hunt to her presence. After she'd expelled most of her magic back in Akros, the Wild Hunt had abandoned their pursuit. It was only a matter of time before they began searching for her again.

Pushing these thoughts aside, she focused on what needed to be done to save Esmelle. Thanks to Malek's dragonfire, her magic once again strummed steadily within her. She'd missed being able to use it without fear of being hunted, but desperation had made it necessary.

Tapping into the reserves of power within her, she gathered both the Unseelie and Seelie magic coursing through her. Her bleeding hand curled into a fist, but she didn't stanch the blood. Instead, she allowed it to continue dripping onto the deck of the ship. Lifting her gaze upward toward the heavens and the storm clouds hovering overhead, she drew her magic closer to the surface. Her entire body glowed with power, a staggering beacon penetrating the darkness from the storm. She heard a few gasps from the crew nearby, but she ignored them and instead concentrated on her task.

In a shocking blast, she expelled the built-up force within

her. Ripping through the magical storm clouds, Sabine reached for the sun. Her Seelie magic sliced through the darkness forged by more than a dozen Merfolk and allowed the light of day to shine through. A cheer went up through the crew at the sight of the sun, but she couldn't pay any attention to them. She needed to focus on the magical workings of the Merfolk.

Their power was similar in some ways to the Fae, but it was sorely lacking the strength possessed by her people. Her magic was ancient in origin, for the Fae were the first children of the gods. Her power was the same as what originally shaped this world, creating forests and lakes where none previously existed. While the Merfolk were the caretakers of the sea, the Fae would always be the victors in commanding the heavens and earth to obey.

With the magical storm temporarily abated, Sabine turned her attention back toward the sea. Another explosion rocked the ship, and her eyes narrowed. She might not be able to force the Merfolk to a reckoning while they resided in their seat of power, but she'd damned well make sure they had a challenge if they intended to try to keep Esmelle and the others.

"Bane," she said, her voice infused with the power of her ancestors as her magic pulsed wildly within her. She looked up into his amber eyes, grateful this demon had chosen to serve her willingly. "Shall we give the Merfolk further reason to hesitate?"

His eyes flashed to silver, and his mouth curved in a wicked smile. He inclined his head and said, "Absolutely. What's your plan, little one?"

"To bring the memory of life to a place of death."

Bane's brow furrowed. He followed her gaze to the front of the ship where the wooden figurehead of a woman stood in defiance against the ocean waves. Bane's eyes widened, and his gaze flew back to her. "You intend to try to awaken the ship?"

Sabine gave him a curt nod. "Demonic magic shares some similarities with necromancy. Once you bring the ship to phantom awareness, I can temporarily give it life and purpose. Between the catapults and the ship helping to defend us, the Merfolk will be forced to negotiate or back down. They can't kill what's already dead."

"A bold plan, but we will only have as much time as the magic lasts." He paused, and his expression became grim. "I'm no small power, but I won't be able to shield you from detection while we undertake this task."

Sabine nodded. "I know, but my magic will be combined with yours. This working is close enough to necromancy that it should confuse anyone searching for me. We have to take the chance."

"Very well." Bane's mouth twisted in concentration as he gathered his magic. His nearly black skin glowed midnight blue when his power surged to the surface. Even his horns, with their razor-sharp tips, shifted in color, becoming an almost iridescent silver.

Blossom wriggled out of Sabine's shirt and fluttered in front of them, her eyes wide with excitement. "I've never seen a dead tree brought back to life. Can you really do it?"

"We're about to find out," Sabine said and lowered her gaze to the mark of the goddess on her wrist. It was shaped like a chalice, a reminder of the power now residing within her. To her knowledge, no one except a necromancer had ever attempted to infuse the memory of life into the dead. In truth, she wouldn't have ever considered it until recently.

Dax, Bane's brother, had asked for her help in stealing a chalice back in Akros. Granted, they didn't know it was a relic of power and contained the essence of a long-absent goddess. A lich ward had been embedded over the top of the chalice, using demonic blood as a way to attack Dax. The idea of what she was about to attempt was distasteful, but she'd risk much to save Esmelle's life.

Sabine placed her hand on Bane's arm, using the connection between them to help fuel his magic. Demons weren't as powerful above ground as they were in the caverns deep below the earth. The pact she'd formed with Bane years earlier allowed him access to his same level of power. He was one of the few day-walking demons in the world, which alone caused him to be something feared.

Bane shouted a word of power, the demonic language harsh even to her ears. The ship trembled, and Sabine sensed the moment the vessel began to awaken. It creaked and groaned, shuddering beneath her feet. Hundreds of trees had been used in its construction, and they all simultaneously turned their attention toward the demon standing upon the bones of their lifeforce.

Bane's eyes were completely silvered. She offered him her hand, and he brought it to his mouth to accept her blood sacrifice. She hoped it would supply Bane with enough strength to do what she needed. Even with her offering, they'd still need to hurry. Embracing this type of death magic and holding the ship in his thrall would weaken Bane significantly. With her heart hammering in her chest, Sabine bent down and pressed her bleeding palm against the slippery deck.

"Awaken and obey!" she shouted, using her connection with Bane to bind her commands to the phantom ship.

The figurehead's wooden curls shifted and curved as though the wind caressed her hair. She slowly turned her head in Sabine's direction, her painted wooden eyes giving the illusion of sight. The figurehead inclined her head in acknowledgement of Sabine's command. The booms of the masts spread like arms, curving and swaying in the air as though stretching from a long slumber.

The mostly human crew shrieked prayers at the sky and others collapsed on the ground, trembling in fear. Sabine ignored them, intent on infusing the ship with her dwindling strength. Bane was right; the magic wouldn't last long, and Malek couldn't afford to give her more. Should their efforts fail in this endeavor, they'd have to trust Malek had the strength to get them safely away.

Another explosion rocked the ship, this one with far more force than any of the Merfolk's previous efforts. Sabine stumbled but grabbed a nearby railing to keep from falling overboard. Nearby splashes indicated more of the crew had been claimed by the watery clutches of the Merfolk. The ship's mind touched hers, and Sabine mentally instructed it to defend and capture.

"The catapults, Malek. Now!" she yelled toward the captain standing on the lower deck overseeing the weapons.

Malek shouted, "Fire!"

The crystal-tipped lances glowed red in the sunlight, and they shot downward into the water's depths. A high-pitched keeling noise indicated the magic contained within the crystals had done at least some damage. Sabine prayed the Merfolk wouldn't take out their rage on their existing captives.

Their gambit worked. The flash of silver that surrounded the boat close to the surface indicated the lances had forced the Merfolk into breaking ranks. The ship gave the illusion of stretching, and one of the spars unfurled away from the mast. It reached down and plucked one of the Merfolk from beneath the waves. Branches grew outward from the boom as it wrapped its wooden fingers tightly around the sea-dweller to contain it.

A piercing screech ripped through the air, and the creature thrashed wildly in the ship's grip. Some of the humans cried out, clenching their ears from the pain of the Merfolk's scream. Like the Fae, the Merfolk had the ability to infuse their words with their power. Some sailors had been known to succumb to their songs, willingly throwing themselves overboard only to embrace a watery grave.

Sabine waved her hand to negate the Merfolk's cries and took a step closer to study the creature. It appeared decidedly humanoid, with some very distinctive differences. Its skin was a silvery blue, and the sunlight created a striking shimmering effect. Where legs should have been was a tail, and it flicked its fins as it tried to wrestle out of the ship's hold.

Blossom fluttered down and landed on Sabine's shoulder. She gripped Sabine's braids and whispered, "It's shiny. It wears shells in its hair like you wear flowers."

Sabine made a noise of agreement as she stared up at the creature, recognizing it was a male of its species. His top portion appeared similar to humans, but the bottom was more fish. Its long blue-green hair more closely resembled seaweed than actual hair, with a collection of shells and other items attached by some unknown means. Sabine had heard the Merfolk had the ability to shapeshift into more of a humanoid form, but only the spellcasters of their race possessed the ability.

Sabine threw out her hand in a silent command, and the ship unceremoniously dropped the Merman on the deck of the ship. Malek withdrew his sword and ordered several of the other sailors to surround their captive. The crew appeared wary, but they immediately jumped to obey their captain. The Merman snarled at his assailants, but Sabine ignored him and walked down the stairs to the lower deck.

Aware her glamour hadn't been reapplied, she sent a pulse of her magic along the etchings on her skin. If the

Merman was familiar with the Fae, he would be able to identify her markings in accordance with her rank and level of power. Unfortunately, everyone on board the ship was now aware of her true heritage. The crew would either need to be blood sworn to keep her secret or permanently silenced, but that would be something to worry about later—if they survived the next few minutes.

As she approached the Merman, Sabine realized the shimmering effect was from the sunlight hitting his scales. It was strangely beautiful, but it also served as a reminder his ways were alien compared to her own. His eyes narrowed on her, the false eyelids sliding over his eyes as he blinked.

"You dare much, Fae Royal," the Merman hissed at her in the ancient language of the gods. "You, who would treat with our enemies, now attack the home of the True Folk?"

Sabine held her head high, refusing to be cowed by his accusations. Any sign of weakness would only hinder her position. They were already at a disadvantage, but she might be able to convince this Merman she possessed hidden reserves of strength. She hoped he wouldn't call her bluff.

Infusing her voice with power she couldn't afford to spare, she said in the language of her birth, "There is no True Folk beyond the will of the gods. Order a ceasefire so we might speak, and you *will* be returned safely to the sea's embrace once our business is concluded. If you refuse, I shall instruct the ship to capture another of your people. Perhaps one of them might be more cooperative."

The Merman flicked his tail, spattering nearby sailors with a salty spray. Sabine waited, and he held her gaze for a long time in silent challenge. The rays of the sun had to be uncomfortable for him, given the Merfolk's preference for the cool depths of the oceans. On occasion, they enjoyed sunning themselves on large flat rocks but only in limited amounts. As they grew older and embraced the magic of the sea, their tolerance for the sun faded. The one in front of her was considerably older than she'd expected, and he was likely a powerful opponent. She'd heard the storms summoned by the Merfolk were designed to shield them from the harmful effects of the sun's rays. She suspected it was why so many of them were able to attack the ship at once. By negating the storm, she'd stripped them of the ability to venture close to the surface without grave risk.

"Very well." She inclined her head in acknowledgement of his refusal and lifted her hand to command the ship.

The Merman hissed at her.

She arched her brow expectantly and said, "I wish none of the True Folk harm, unless you force my hand. The choice is yours."

He studied her for a long time before lifting his head and releasing a long bellow. The noise resounded through the wooden deck of the ship. Immediately, the waves calmed and the ship stopped rocking precariously. Only the gentle slap of the waves against the hull filled the air. Inwardly, Sabine breathed a sigh of relief. At least they'd have a brief reprieve.

He turned his gaze back on her and spat, "Speak, Fae."

"Careful," Malek warned, angling his sword in the Merman's direction.

Sabine held up her hand to stop Malek. The Merman likely knew Malek was a dragon, and his presence would only make things worse. She approached the Merman, noting other details that had previously escaped her notice.

He wore jewelry around his neck and wrists, in the form of shells and colorful pieces of coral. Delicate webbing stretched between his fingers, but it was his pointed ears which surprised her the most. They had the same curve and shape of hers, but such a feature was lacking among the dwarves and demons. It was one more similarity the Fae shared with the Merfolk.

Choosing her words carefully, Sabine said, "Despite our current situation, we mean you nor your people any harm. We simply seek passage to the southern lands. You have attacked my ship, in direct violation of the treaty formed between my people and yours ages ago."

"The treaty does not include the messengers from the underworld," the Merman hissed, indicating Bane's presence, and then he glared at Malek. "Nor does it include the enemies of our world."

Sabine paused, unaware of any contention between the demons and Merfolk. She glanced over at Bane, but he was heavily perspiring from holding the death magic over the ship. She didn't dare have him release it just yet, or all their efforts would fail. Blossom tugged on Sabine's braids, but she couldn't take the time to speak with the tiny pixie. She needed to hurry before the magic crumbled. Already, she could feel herself losing a bit of control over the ship.

Turning back toward the Merman, she said, "That may be, but the demon and dragon are under my protection. By attacking them, you also attack *me*. Order your people to release those you've stolen from me, and we will depart in peace."

"There shall be no peace," the Merman snapped, swishing his tail in fury. "You have betrayed your kind and the gods if you protect our enemies. Once you kill me, my people will rejoice in the destruction of your ship and ripping your lives from the fabric of this world."

Chapter Three

Sabine's hands curled into fists, her nails biting into her palms. She wanted to lash out and punish this Merman, but it probably wouldn't do much good. He was as arrogant as the Fae, believing his people's supremacy was their gods-given right. The idea she'd be unable to save her friends was a bitter drought to swallow.

Esmelle deserved so much better. Her witch friend had a caring and compassionate nature that had touched Sabine from almost the first moment they'd met. In one fell swoop, these sea-dwellers threatened to destroy one of the most beautiful souls Sabine had ever encountered.

Blossom tugged on her braids frantically. "Don't kill him, Sabine. We can fix this."

In a low voice, Sabine asked, "How?"

"The chalice," Blossom whispered in her ear. "The goddess says she'll make them obey you."

Sabine froze. The chalice? She looked down at the image of the chalice etched onto the inside of her wrist. It was a symbol of her pact with the goddess Lachlina. The goddess should have no reason to aid them in this matter, but it would be foolish to discount her offer.

Keeping her voice quiet so the Merman couldn't hear them, she asked, "At what cost?"

Blossom fell silent. When she spoke, she sounded somewhat uneasy. "The goddess has her reasons for making this offer, but she won't elaborate. I don't think she likes being questioned."

Sabine weighed the decision carefully. It was impossible to know what could motivate Lachlina, but she'd already helped them several times back in Akros. If Sabine refused the offer, such a thing might never come again. Besides, she didn't have any hope of saving Esmelle's life without the goddess's help.

Sabine took a steadying breath and nodded her agreement.

Power, sudden and surprising in its intensity, rushed through her. Her hair lifted, and the wind whipped wildly around her. Sabine lifted her arms as the goddess's magic filled her and traveled along her skin. Her marks pulsed even more vividly, shifting colors from silver to gold and then back again.

The Merman's eyes widened in shock, and he threw himself down on the deck in obeisance. Several of the remaining crew also fell to their knees, pleading for mercy. Even Malek appeared taken aback by her appearance. Sabine swallowed and forced her attention back on the Merman.

"Forgiveness, Shining One," the Merman pleaded from his prone position, stretching out his webbed fingers in supplication. "We were unaware the gods still speak through your kind."

Sabine lowered her arms and took a step toward the sea-dweller. "What is your name?"

He lifted his head enough to meet her gaze. "I am Ilwan."

"Well met, Ilwan. Please rise," she stated, closing the distance between them. She wasn't trusting enough to get within touching distance, but the Merfolk were a proud race and deserving of respect. "You may call me Sabine."

Ilwan sat up, regarding her with wariness. "What is it you wish to discuss?"

Sabine clasped her hands together and said, "I would ask you to release my people. As long as our passage isn't impeded in any way, we will trouble the True Folk no more. You will be returned to the sea, unharmed."

The false eyelids slid over the Merman's silvery eyes. "Regretfully, I may not return your people without compensation. You have invaded our territory, and they are no longer your subjects."

Sabine paused in surprise and then tilted her head to study him. Like the Fae, the Merfolk couldn't lie. She didn't believe he would disregard such a request, especially with the goddess's power riding through her.

Blossom tugged on Sabine's braids again and whispered, "The goddess says their people *will* negotiate a release, but their honor requires something of equal or greater value in exchange. They reject the concept of gifts or returning property rightfully stolen."

Sabine's entire body went rigid. "Esmelle is *not* property."

"She's considered spoils of war by the Merfolk," Blossom explained, her wings brushing against Sabine's neck.

Ilwan narrowed his eyes on Blossom, but he remained silent.

Sabine considered the Merman for a long time. She had no idea what would appeal to them or what they'd consider suitable in trade. Her knowledge of the Merfolk was cursory at best. Sabine wasn't sure she was up to the task of maneuvering this new set of rules. Unfortunately, everyone else on board had even less insight than her.

"You must hurry, little one," Bane said in a voice barely above a whisper. His shoulders were tense as though struggling under the weight of the magic he was wielding. Sabine frowned and sent a small wave of her magic toward him to strengthen his resolve. Her own was quickly nearing depletion, and only the goddess's power continued to sustain her.

Sabine took a steadying breath, determined to end this quickly. Holding out her hands in a peaceable gesture, she decided upon honesty. "I regret to admit I know very little of your ways, Ilwan. My pixie companion has informed me you would be willing to negotiate a trade, but I'm unfamiliar with the normal procedure for such matters."

Ilwan straightened, sweeping his gaze over the ship and the mostly human crew that surrounded him. "I have never known one of your kind to admit to such a flaw. Nor have I heard of your people traveling with such... unusual companions."

Sabine gave a half-hearted shrug. "Necessity leads to strange alliances. What do you wish in exchange for the lives of my friends?"

Ilwan studied her thoughtfully. "A trade. Your companions shall be returned, unharmed and in the same condition in which they were given over to the sea. In exchange, you will return our Pearl to us."

Sabine's brow furrowed. "Where can I find this pearl?"

Ilwan pursed his lips together, and his ears twitched as though listening for something. "Pearl was sent as an emissary to trade with one of the human cities. She did not return at the appointed time. If she fails to return to the sea by the next full moon, she will be lost to us forever."

Sabine's eyes widened in surprise. She'd thought he'd meant an actual pearl, not one of the Merfolk. "She's one of your spellcasters?"

Ilwan inclined his head. "And a beloved mate to one of our leaders."

Malek lowered his sword and asked, "Do you know which city she intended to trade with?"

Ilwan didn't spare Malek a glance. Instead, he kept his attention on Sabine as he answered. "The humans call the city Karga, but none know what path she took once she arrived on land. Our efforts to contact her through arcane means have failed. We sent another one of our people to search for her, but he could not find any trace of her. All I know is Pearl still lives, but her whereabouts are unknown. She's not the first to go missing, but she is the most powerful."

Sabine frowned. Only a handful of races would have the ability to hide one of the Merfolk, unless something else was going on. The Fae could do it, but they wouldn't leave Faerie. "The magic of the True Folk is legendary. Who among your enemies would have the means of thwarting your magic?"

Ilwan's mouth formed a thin line. "It matters not that the gods deign to speak through you. Such knowledge is forbidden to outsiders."

Sabine nodded. Trust was a fragile thing, and if she were in Ilwan's position, she wouldn't confide in her either. "I understand, and I hope my question hasn't caused any offense."

He waved his hand, dismissing her concerns. "It is a small thing. I will provide you one last piece of information. Your purpose here must be important if the gods have decided to aid you." He paused and darted a glance at Malek and Bane. "Regardless of your choice in companions."

Sabine smiled. "I'd gladly hear any advice that might better aid our cause."

Ilwan reached up, unfastened a necklace, and held it out to Sabine. She accepted the unusual piece of jewelry, surprised and intrigued by both the craftsmanship and design. The pearls shimmered with the same sheen of Ilwan's skin, shifting to various shades of white, pink, and blue, depending on how the light caught it. The effect was rather hypnotizing.

"Wear this necklace, and Pearl will know you have been sent to aid her," he instructed, gesturing for Sabine to fasten it around her neck. "Once you have located her and are ready to make the trade for your companions, simply clasp the necklace in your hand and infuse your magic into it. As long as you are near the sea, we will heed the call and come to you."

Sabine dipped her head in a gesture of appreciation. Like most of the original races, words of gratitude were an acknowledgment of a debt to be called due at a later date.

She fastened the necklace, its weight a reminder of her oath and purpose. "I will do as you instruct. Do you need any assistance returning to the sea?"

Ilwan looked upward at the wooden masts of the ship. "In truth, I have never heard of anyone bringing life to dead wood. If I hadn't seen it for myself, I would not have imagined such a thing was possible. It appears the Fae have more secrets than we believed." He frowned and shook his head as though to clear it. "I will return to the sea on my own power or not at all. I wish you good fortune in your efforts. Your people will be kept safe and comfortable until the next full moon."

Sabine watched Ilwan use his arms and tail to pull himself toward the edge of the ship. Without another word, he dove over the side and disappeared from sight.

Chapter Four

Malek sheathed his blade and moved to stand beside Sabine. Her accomplishment in forcing the Merfolk to negotiate was no small feat, but he wasn't sure what it had cost her. He studied her in the sunlight as she stared at the sea, absently fingering Ilwan's pearl necklace. She hadn't yet reapplied her glamour, and her skin still glowed faintly with the vestiges of her power.

"You managed to buy us enough time to try to save them," he said quietly, wishing he had more insight into this intriguing woman. He was hesitant to pry too much, lest she reject the invasion outright and push him away. But the memory of the kiss and power they'd shared would likely haunt him for a long time.

"I just hope it's enough," she murmured, still staring at the waves where Ilwan had disappeared. With a sigh, she slipped the necklace under her shirt to hide it from view. "I'm sorely out of my element. I don't know enough about the Merfolk to guess where this Pearl could be hiding. We don't even know if she's left her people voluntarily. If she doesn't want to be found, what hope do we have?"

He frowned. Before he'd left the Sky Cities, both he and Levin had come to terms with the possibility they might never return home. If one of them should fall, the other had agreed to see their purpose through. He hadn't lied to Sabine; it would pain him to lose Levin, but it was worse for her. Her companions hadn't necessarily agreed to the same risks. If Malek hadn't coerced Sabine into finding the artifacts needed to seal the portal, Sabine and her companions would be safely back in Akros.

He sighed, knowing there was no way to offer her reassurance, but he couldn't leave her without hope. "Your knowledge of the Merfolk is greater than mine. They're more secretive than the Fae in some respects. I have a few contacts in Karga we can call upon for information. If anyone's heard anything about this missing woman, we'll find out."

Sabine turned and looked up at him with her lavender eyes. With her silvery hair and softly glowing skin, the effect in the sunlight was staggering. It was never more apparent this woman didn't belong on a ship but in a forest among the silver trees. She might be attractive in human form, but without her glamour, she was utterly breathtaking. But he was drawn to more than her appearance, which could be altered as easily as the wind changed course. Sabine possessed a quality he'd never encountered in any other woman, and he'd been captivated by her since the moment they met.

Unable to resist, he reached up and tucked one of her silvery braids behind her pointed ear. She gave him a small smile and said, "I'm glad you're here, Malek. If you didn't agree to share your magic with me, we wouldn't even have a chance to save them."

He reached down and took her hand, then lifted it and kissed her knuckles. "All you ever have to do is ask."

Her gaze softened, and she gave him a small smile. "I'll keep that in mind." She glanced at Bane and frowned. "If you'll excuse me, Bane and I need to put the ship to rest. I wanted to make sure the Merfolk would honor their agreement to leave us in peace, but the seas are still calm. We should be able to sail peacefully enough, but we'll need to make haste. The next full moon is less than a week away."

He nodded and released her hand just as one of his crew came running up. The bedraggled sailor staggered to a halt in front of them, breathing heavily from the exertion.

"Apologies for the interruption, Captain," Eshon said, shifting from foot to foot. "The hull's been damaged. We're taking on water. The Merfolk took out our bilge pump in the first attack, and we can't get it working."

"Dammit," he muttered, scanning the horizon and the endless sea in front of them. Karga was the nearest port, but they were still several days away. "Get Joshen working on it. He's a wizard when it comes to mechanics."

Eshon shook his head. "Joshen's gone. Ryley too. They went overboard. We've lost everyone who could fix the damned thing. The chain completely snapped, and the handle's gone missing."

Muttering a curse, Malek ran to the center mast where the bilge pump passed through the deck. It was designed from felled trees, with cups mounted on a chain. At least two crew members manned the pump, turning the handles to drain water from the bilge. Without it, they didn't have a chance in keeping the ship afloat. With almost half the crew taken captive, their options to repair it were limited.

Blossom flew off Sabine's shoulder to inspect the damaged pump. "Wow! They blew that sucker up! I bet it's even worse down below."

Sabine put her hand on his arm to get his attention.

"Before we put the ship to rest, I can swell the wood to seal the holes temporarily."

He arched his brow. "How long will that last?"

She frowned. "A few hours, but no more than that."

Malek covered her hand with his and shook his head. "I'm afraid a few hours won't give us enough time." He considered the bilge pump a moment, debating his options. With Levin gone, they'd lost their navigator too. They didn't even have enough people to work the sails.

He squeezed Sabine's hand and asked, "How skilled are you at glamour?"

Blossom fluttered her wings and clapped her hands excitedly. "Sabine's the best at glamour! She once made me look like a giant pixie."

Sabine frowned at Blossom before turning back toward him. "I don't think you're interested in looking like a giant pixie. Why are you asking?"

"Can you shield the entire ship from view?"

Her brow furrowed as she swept her gaze over the ship. "Glamour doesn't work like that. I can't make something invisible. I can change appearances or plant a suggestion for people not to notice something, but I've never tried it on anything this large. Why? What are you thinking?"

"Even if the weather holds, we're too far away from the nearest port. Given our time constraints with the Merfolk's demand, I think our only option is for me to try to fly the boat out of here. I'd rather no one see me in dragon form, or rumors will spread all along the coast."

Sabine's eyes widened, and she pulled her hand away. "You can't be serious. You want to fly with the ship? While we're still on it?"

He gave her a grim nod. "I don't see an alternative, and this isn't ideal. The ship will likely take more damage if I have to fly with it, and it'll drain my remaining power significantly."

"Can you even do it? You're a large dragon, but this ship is huge."

Malek grimaced. "It won't be an easy feat. I'll likely need at least a full day to rest after it's done. I won't be able to shift again for a few days."

Sabine frowned. "How much of your magic is required to change forms?"

He hesitated and then shook his head. "My magic is different from yours. My dragon form is a physical manifestation, not true magic in the conventional sense. I suppose you could say it's just another facet of my power. But my magic *will* give me enough strength in dragon form to pick up the ship and take it to safety." He paused, sweeping his gaze over his remaining crew. "I'm more concerned about the crew. We'll have to replace all of them when they find out what I am. As it is, they already know you're Fae."

Sabine bit her lip. "I might not be able to hide the ship completely, but I can help with the crew."

He arched his brow. "How?"

"You have some Faerie wine in your hold, correct?"

When he nodded, Sabine gave him a mysterious smile. "If you can bring up a few bottles from the hold, I'll take care of the crew. In the meantime, I need to help Bane. Ilwan's departure eased some of his burden, but the connection with the ship is still draining him."

Without waiting for a response, she walked toward Bane. Malek would be damned if he could figure out what Sabine saw in the demon. For whatever reason, she trusted him. The same could be said for Bane and his trust in her, which was surprising given what he knew of demons.

Malek waved Eshon back over and said, "Have the remaining men manually haul buckets out of the bilge for the time being. We have a plan in place, but it'll take a bit of time before we're back under way."

Eshon nodded and scampered away to round up the necessary crew. Malek headed over to the ladder leading to the hold of the ship.

Blossom landed on his shoulder and asked, "Can I come too?"

"All right. Just be careful," he said, climbing down the rungs. "I don't know what condition everything's in down here."

"Aye, aye, Captain," Blossom said, giving him a salute.

He chuckled and climbed down to the floor of the hold. The strong scent of salt and fish filled his nose, but it was impossible to see anything. The only illumination was close to the entrance, provided by the sunlight streaming from the open hatch.

He reached over and activated the dwarven crystalline lantern hanging nearby. The magic contained within the crystals began to glow brightly, chasing away the shadows and casting some light throughout the hold.

"Dammit," he muttered, stepping over destroyed containers of merchandise he'd planned on selling to help fund their mission. Crates had been toppled, shattering glass and spilling rare herbs and other items onto the floor of the hold. The gems and gold he'd hidden were likely safe enough in his cabin, but the more delicate items probably couldn't be salvaged.

His men had secured the crates before they left Akros, but the Merfolk's attack had negated their efforts. Now he'd be lucky if he was able to salvage even a small portion of the items he'd acquired over the last several months. Malek carefully picked his way around the fallen debris, trying to locate the crate containing the bottles of wine.

Blossom fluttered around. "Oh no! I hope the wine wasn't destroyed."

Malek didn't reply, worried about the same possibility, especially when he caught sight of where it had been stored. The wooden box containing the last of the wine had tipped over and the lid had fallen off. With another curse, he knelt beside it to assess the damage. At least a dozen bottles were broken, the expensive wine pooling on the floor of the hold.

Blossom landed on his arm and said, "Sabine's going to be sad. She loves Faerie wine."

Malek made a noncommittal noise, remembering the evening they'd shared the magical wine together. Since Sabine had learned he was a dragon, she'd been wary of him. Traveling together over the past week had softened some of her resistance. He'd hoped to convince her to share wine again while they sailed to Razadon, but that possibility had been shattered, along with the glass bottles under his feet.

He sighed. "We'll have to get her more when we arrive in the dwarven city. They still trade with Faerie periodically. That's where I got the last shipment."

"You like her a lot, don't you?"

Malek lifted his gaze to meet Blossom's inquisitive stare. He chuckled and said, "I don't think I've made any effort to hide my interest."

"She likes you too."

Malek winced when he cut himself on a jagged piece of glass. "I'd like to think that, but she's been avoiding me. I think she's still coming to terms with me being a dragon."

Blossom shrugged and landed on top of the crate. "Yeah, but can you blame her? You could eat her for dinner if you wanted. I used to be scared of Bane and Dax because they could eat me, but Sabine promised not to let them. Maybe if she knows you'll protect her, she won't be scared of you either."

Malek moved aside another broken bottle. He suspected Blossom had the right of things, but he wasn't sure how to overcome Sabine's reservations. "Any suggestions?"

Her wings fluttered excitedly. "I bet if you help save Esme, she'll forgive you for not telling her you're a dragon. Esme's one of her favorite people. Then she'll know you won't eat her."

"I'm going to make every effort to save Esme *and* Levin," Malek promised, moving aside broken glass and packing material. Underneath were two bottles that appeared to still be intact. Lifting them up to the light, he checked for any signs of damage. "Hopefully this will be enough. I'm not sure how much wine Sabine actually needs. Any idea why she wants it?"

Blossom grinned. "Magic!"

He chuckled and stood. If Blossom wasn't going to tell him why Sabine wanted it, he'd have to find out from the intriguing woman who had captured his interest. And maybe, during their journey together to save their friends, he might also manage to soften her heart toward him too.

Sabine frowned at Bane. "I don't see any other option."

Bane's eyes flashed silver, and his voice took on a sharp edge. "And what's stopping him from flying this ship north to the Sky Cities? Both of us are now too weakened to fight him. The timing is a little convenient, Sabine."

She sighed and rubbed her temples to ward against her impending headache. The need to rest was becoming more urgent, especially with her magical reserves already low. Arguing with Bane was always exhausting, and their current situation wasn't helping.

Bane might be sworn to protect her, but they sometimes

had different views on what that entailed. She didn't argue with him as frequently as she had with Dax, but the end result was the same.

"Bane, I'm not disagreeing. Nothing about this situation is ideal. But if Malek wanted to fly the ship to the Sky Cities with us on it, he could have done it before now. He knew my magic hadn't replenished itself, which is why he agreed to share power with me. Like it or not, this is the only option we have."

Sabine frowned and stared at the waves. Somewhere below the water, Esmelle was being held prisoner. She had to trust the rest of the Merfolk would honor Ilwan's vow, but the bleakness of their task threatened to steal her resolve.

Bane took her chin in his clawed hand and forced her to meet his gaze. "Do not be foolish and trust this dragon blindly, little one. I've seen the way you look at him, but there is no future with him. Your people will never accept a dragon at your side."

"You think that's what this is about? That I'm misguided because I'm attracted to Malek?" Sabine pulled away from his grasp and flung her hand toward the sea. "Esmelle is counting on us to rescue her. Malek's people are down there too. He has just as much at stake, if not more. If he has any hope in acquiring the artifacts used to seal the portal, he won't dare betray me. We *will* do this, and we'll support Malek however possible in this endeavor. Right now, I'm more concerned about saving Esme's life."

Bane considered her for a long time. Finally, he inclined his head and said, "Very well. I see you've decided to trust him in this matter. I will raise no other objections, but I do not enjoy being at the dragon's mercy."

Sabine stood on her toes and kissed his cheek. "I know, and I'll try to avoid making such demands on you in the future. You may not think of yourself as a hero, but if it weren't for you, we wouldn't have been able to capture one of the Merfolk. You helped save all of us today, Bane."

He lowered his head and slapped his clawed hand against his chest, the gesture a sign of deep respect and loss. "I know how much the witch means to you. In truth, I've grown fond of her too. I will do what I can to help save her."

Sabine nodded at this truth and wrapped her arms around Bane. She leaned against him, grateful for his presence. They might argue now and then, but it never lasted. Holding his death magic over the ship for so long had taken its toll. Demons respected strength, and his current weakness had made him irritable. He rarely complained to her, and she needed to remember to be more cognizant of his needs. Demons may not experience grief in the same manner as other races, but in some ways, they felt things more deeply. They were just different.

"How much do you know about the Merfolk, Bane?"

He pulled her closer. Running his hand over her hair absently, she felt him siphon some of her magic away and infuse it with his aura. She had little to spare, but she couldn't begrudge him for it.

"They don't care much for my kind. When our people were forced into the underworld by the gods, we claimed some of their territories. They tried to object but could not stand against our might."

Sabine frowned and lifted her head to regard him. "But why? Demons can't live underwater."

"No, but there are caverns that exist deep below the sea. We sealed off the territory we claimed, denying it from them permanently. It allowed us more freedom of movement since we're unable to live above ground during the daylight hours without a host."

Her eyes widened. "So your people would travel in those

caves during the day and then at night, they'd go to the surface?"

Bane chuckled. "Indeed. The gods may have intended for us to be confined to areas of their choosing, but we've never been meek nor passive. The human priests of this world may have tried to discourage their sheep from making pacts with us, but we have always been… resourceful."

"Hmm," she murmured, leaning against him again. At least she had a better understanding of the contention between the demons and Merfolk, but it wouldn't get her any closer to locating this Pearl. If she'd known about their issues ahead of time, they could have taken precautions. Her lack of experience with the world outside of Faerie had led to several miscalculations over the years, but it would pain her deeply if Esmelle and the others had to pay for her mistakes.

Blossom flew toward them, her wings sending a smattering of pixie dust everywhere. It seemed to happen more often when she was overly excited. "We're back! You should have seen the mess in the hold."

Sabine straightened, catching sight of the ship captain heading their way. Bane's warning flitted again through her mind, but she pushed it aside. He was wrong about Malek. Dragon or not, he'd proven to have no small amount of integrity.

"Sadly, this is all that remains." Malek held up two bottles of wine. "I'm not sure what you have planned, but short of figuring out how to get spilled wine off the floor of the hold, this is all I can offer."

Sabine hesitated and then gave him a curt nod. "It'll have to be enough. If you can bring them into your cabin, this shouldn't take long."

Bane's eyes narrowed on Malek, but the demon didn't argue. Instead, he followed Sabine toward Malek's cabin located off the quarterdeck. Sabine pushed open the door, ignoring the belongings still strewn all over the floor. She took one of the bottles from Malek and placed it on the desk, using her knife to uncork it.

"You can open the other one," she said and lifted the bottle to take a sip. She closed her eyes as the power rushed through her and used the wine to fortify her remaining power. The bottle was affixed with a gold cap, indicating it was extremely potent for magical workings. It might be perfect for her needs, but it was a shame to give such a rare vintage to a bunch of humans who could never appreciate it.

Sabine opened her eyes. The wound on her hand she'd used to revive the ship had already healed. She suspected it was the goddess's doing, but she wasn't going to risk asking Blossom. From what Sabine was told, the goddess didn't appreciate being questioned.

She grasped her knife and pricked her finger. Sabine counted out three drops of blood, part of the recipe for most magical workings. If she were attempting to coerce other magical races without their permission, it would require a greater sacrifice. But humans were extremely susceptible to Fae magic.

After taking the other bottle from Malek, she repeated the gesture and said, "I'll need you to gather your remaining crew on the deck. They each need to take at least one swallow, but more would be better. I'm not sure how many of your crew are left."

Malek hesitated. "You don't intend to share your memories with them, do you?"

She looked up at him, somewhat surprised by his reluctance. Understanding dawned, and she bit her lip to keep from laughing. Gods. That would be awkward. What she'd shared with Malek had been extremely intimate and not something she'd dream of sharing with random strangers. "No, nothing like that. I'll use the magic in the wine to put them to sleep. I'll give them some pleasant dreams and obscure their memories of my heritage, but that's all. No harm will come to them, and they won't be aware you've shifted to dragon form. It's the best I can do without full access to my magic."

"Ah," he murmured with a trace of a smile. "It's probably for the best. I'd hate to have any more competition for your affections."

Her mouth curved in a small smile, but before she could respond, Bane picked up the bottles and shoved them in Malek's direction. "Here. You'll need to order them to drink. They know she's Fae. It's unlikely they'll take it from Sabine's hand."

"A moment," Sabine interrupted, placing her hand on Malek's arm to stop him. "I need to warn you about something before we do this."

He arched his brow. "What is it?"

She darted a quick glance at Bane, then turned back toward Malek and said, "When we were in Akros, you showed me I could trust you. If we are to be allies in truth, you need to understand this effort will consume my remaining power. Once I send the crew to sleep, I will be unable to aid you until I have sufficient time to recover."

Malek frowned. "Will this harm you in any way?"

She smiled and shook her head, his question easing the last of her fears. "No, but I may need to enter a restorative slumber. The goddess consented to aid me in the negotiations with the Merfolk, but she's now silent within me. Her power is still weaker than it was in the days of the Dragon War, and I suspect it cost her dearly to help me."

Blossom nodded and landed on the desk. "She's sleeping. The goddess thinks it's silly to spend so much energy saving humans, but she likes Sabine. She calls Sabine her little silver flower."

Sabine stared at Blossom in surprise. "What?"

Blossom grinned. "She asks questions all the time, about you, your family, and why you went to Akros. She's really curious about why you like Bane and Malek."

Bane scowled and crossed his arms over his chest. "I'm not sure it's wise to confide in this absent goddess. She already observes enough. We are giving away too much information without understanding her motivations."

Sabine frowned. "Blossom, I have to agree with Bane in this. Until we learn more about what she wants from us, it may be best to use caution." At Blossom's worried look, Sabine softened her tone and said, "I'm not saying to stop speaking with her. Continue to converse with her as you will, but I want a detailed accounting of everything that's discussed. I would like to know the reasons for her interest, and her questions may give us some insight."

Blossom nodded. Sabine turned back to Malek, who was regarding her thoughtfully.

He rubbed his chin. "I'd assumed the Fae would blindly follow the gods should they ever return to this realm. That's not the case, is it?"

Sabine hesitated and then sighed. "I can't speak for all of Faerie, but the gods have been absent for too long. Some would follow unconditionally, of that I'm certain, but others would exercise caution—especially the Unseelie." She shrugged. "Perhaps I'm too much my mother's daughter, but I have no intention of returning to the old ways."

Malek searched her expression for a long time. "You keep surprising me, Sabine." He held up the bottles and added, "I'll take the wine out to the crew, but it may be safest if you remain within the cabin while I'm flying the ship out of here. I can't promise it'll be a smooth flight. I trust Bane will keep watch over you if you need to rest?"

"She'll be protected," Bane snapped, not bothering to hide his irritation at the question.

Sabine ignored Bane's comment. "I'll join you on the deck after the crew drinks from the wine. It won't take me long to send them to sleep. Then we can move them to the other cabin."

Malek nodded and headed toward the door.

When it closed behind him, Bane muttered, "I don't like this, little one. Even if he intends you no harm, we don't know what we'll face once we land. We'll both be too weakened to do much."

Sabine turned to regard Bane. "I know, which is why we need to trust him. Our best chance of success is for all of us to work together—as allies."

Bane frowned and paced the cabin. Sabine reapplied her glamour, the task more out of habit than necessity. Until they made landfall, she would be safe enough from any spies her family had retained. Her glamour used no small amount of magic, and keeping it engaged would act as a failsafe to ensure she had enough magic left over to keep her presence hidden. If necessary, she could always remove it later.

Sitting on the edge of the bed, Sabine closed her eyes and focused on isolating the magic of the wine she'd woven into her own power. Drinking from the bottle had been part of the ritual. When each crew member drank of the foreign magic and her blood, they would be linked together for the duration of the spell.

It wouldn't do any good to express her doubts to Bane; their path was already set. The only thing left was to try to make the best out of a difficult situation. Between all of them, she had to believe they'd find a way to rescue Esmelle, Levin, and the rest of Malek's crew.

Pushing aside these distracting thoughts, she opened her

eyes and asked, "How many of the crew do you sense outside?"

Bane walked to the cabin door and pressed his hand against it. After a long moment, he said, "No more than thirty, and closer to twenty. Perhaps twenty-two or twenty-three."

Sabine nodded and closed her eyes again. The magic within the wine had already begun to spread to each crew member. Faerie wine had never been designed with humans in mind, and their psyches were different from the Fae. In some ways, they were more susceptible to her magic, but they were far more resilient and adaptable than other magical races. The trick would be to lure them to sleep without allowing them to know it was her power at work. Any resistance on their part would require more magic, which she couldn't afford.

Dimly, she was aware that almost two dozen people had drunk from the wine. If anyone else had yet to drink, they would shortly. Lifting her hands outward, palms facing upward, she focused on the magic linking her with the crew and the feelings of relaxation needed to send them to sleep.

She imagined a night sky with a smattering of stars and the moon shining brightly overhead. The ocean waves were calm, and a gentle breeze stirred the sails of the ship. She infused her own memories of the scent of the salt spray, the sound of the waves lapping against the hull, and the creak of the ship as it moved through the water.

Sabine held the image in her mind for a long moment, infusing it with as much realism as possible and a sense of calming peace. It was the same type of magic used on Fae children when they didn't want to go to bed. The phrase "sweet dreams" had been created by the Fae as they sent their offspring to dream their dreams of power. All of life was a lesson, both waking and dreaming. No one understood that more than the Fae.

After a long moment, she projected her vision outward and whispered, "*Somnia.*"

A pregnant hush fell over the ship. Her magic explored the occupants of the ship in a subtle caress, searching for those who had consented to her magic by imbibing the wine. Once upon a time, humans had been wary about accepting food and drink from the Fae, but the Fae's solitude and absence from much of the world was now to Sabine's benefit. These people either didn't remember the warnings from ages past or they'd chosen to trust in their captain. Either way, the result was the same. If Sabine were a different type of person, she could hold these humans in her thrall indefinitely.

She *should.* The humans were nothing, less than play-things. They were no match for the powers of the Fae, and they should be used as tools. If she needed an army, she would take an army. None of her enemies could stand against her might. She'd destroy anyone who might dare oppose her will.

These foreign thoughts shocked Sabine enough to bring her back to a semi-state of awareness. Struggling to break free of them, she whispered, "Bane, I need you."

He immediately came to her side and placed his hand against her shoulder. She reached up blindly and brushed against his heated skin. She grabbed his hand, needing the skin contact to help clear her head. Blinking up at Bane, the demon came into focus and then back out again.

"Something's wrong," she managed to say, gripping his hand tightly.

Bane frowned and knelt beside her. "What happened? Did the magic not work?"

Blossom flew toward her, her eyes wide with worry. "It's the goddess, Sabine. She's sleeping. You tapped into her dreams with your magic. You have to release her, or her thoughts will merge with yours."

Sabine frowned and focused again on the power of the wine. Intent was a large part of magic, and it had never been her intention to snare the goddess in her spell. It was equally worrisome she had the ability in the first place. Either the goddess was weaker than Sabine had imagined, or her magic had somehow changed.

Following the thread of power from the Faerie wine, she focused on each individual who had succumbed to the dreamlike trance she'd woven over the ship. It was the equivalent of capturing dozens of rocks in her hands and trying to find the one pebble unlike any of the others. Sabine paused in surprise, recognizing the goddess's stone in her hands. It was multi-faceted with a strange glow; however, it wasn't the differences that interested her but rather the similarities.

"Is she all right?" Malek asked from somewhere nearby, but Sabine couldn't answer him. She needed to disentangle her magic from the goddess without waking her. If the goddess ever learned Sabine had the ability to affect her, such knowledge could endanger her and everyone around her. The Wild Hunt was fearsome, but the wrath of the gods had destroyed entire worlds.

"She'll be fine," Bane snapped, still keeping his hand on her shoulder. "Are they all asleep?"

"They are. Sabine's plan worked well. I took them into Levin's cabin before I gave them the wine, and they all just drifted off to sleep. They should be safe enough in there while I fly the ship."

Sabine severed the last of the magical threads ensnaring the goddess's mind and gently eased away. It was done. With a sigh of relief, she opened her eyes. Her vision swam for a moment as the room tilted. Bane caught her before she fell backward. He wrapped his arms around her and pulled her against his chest.

She reached up, needing the touch of his skin to help keep her centered and awake. It wouldn't have been this bad if she hadn't also ensnared the goddess. The cold chill was a sharp reminder of her depleted magic, and she blinked up to meet Malek's concerned gaze.

He knelt in front of her. "Are you all right?"

She managed to nod. "Yes. Just tired. It took more out of me than I expected. Unless we find a forest soon, it'll take me a while to recover."

He reached over and took her hand. "As soon as we land, I'll share what power I can with you. If I need to fly you to a forest, so be it."

She smiled and closed her eyes again, leaning against Bane. "I might take you up on sharing power, but I don't think I'm willing to take to the skies with a dragon just yet. Maybe not ever."

Malek chuckled. "Just say the word. Until then, it looks like everything's under control here."

She heard Malek move away, and the cabin door closed with a *click*. Bane's arms tightened around her and he murmured, "Just rest, little one. We'll be on land soon enough."

"Good," she replied and cuddled against his warmth. It helped alleviate the worst of the chill from the absence of her power. Unfortunately, it couldn't ward against the fear of what might happen if the goddess discovered Sabine had the ability to manipulate her with magic.

The ship dipped suddenly as though a great weight had landed upon it. Sabine inhaled sharply and bit back a scream when the ship tilted backward. The sounds of the ocean faded away, and Sabine knew they were airborne. It wasn't a smooth flight. The ship lurched in time with the flapping of wings, and Sabine pressed her hand against her queasy stomach.

"Sabine!" Blossom fluttered her wings excitedly as she peered out the window. "We're up really high. I didn't know Malek could touch the clouds!"

Despite herself, Sabine smiled and asked, "Help me stand?"

Bane stood and helped her up. She climbed over the bed to look out the window, and her eyes widened. Blossom was right; the clouds were everywhere, and the ocean was an endless blue floor below them. At this height, she couldn't see the individual waves. Even within Faerie, where some of their homes were built within the most ancient of trees, they didn't reach these heights.

Sabine bit her lip as she stared out the window. "Do you think he'll be okay? The ship must be heavy."

"As long as the idiot dragon doesn't drop us," Bane muttered from behind her. "If he does, I'll have to kill him."

Sabine's mouth curved upward. Bane might be an extremely powerful demon, but she wasn't convinced he'd win in a fight against Malek. So far, the dragon had demonstrated he had strengths beyond anything she'd imagined. Still, she wouldn't tease Bane about it. Demons relished a challenge, and he'd find it necessary to prove himself the victor or die in his attempt.

She turned back around and sat on the bed. "I'm just glad he's on our side."

Bane grunted in response and continued staring out the window. "If you're going to rest, you should do it before we land. I'll keep watch."

Sabine nodded and curled up on Malek's bed. Bane sat beside her, but his focus was still on the dragon flying with the ship.

She yawned and said, "Don't be too hard on him, Bane.

We wouldn't have escaped Akros or the Merfolk without his help."

"Perhaps," he murmured, not tearing his gaze from the window. "Sleep, little one. We shall arrive soon enough and then I suspect you'll have little time to rest."

Chapter Five

A jolt awakened Sabine.

She flew upward into the air, and a scream ripped from her throat. Bane yanked her close and tucked her against him in a protective gesture. They slammed hard onto the bed, the force jarring enough to leave her somewhat dazed. Her heart pounded in her chest as she tried to figure out what had happened.

"I'm going to kill that damned dragon. Are you hurt?" Bane demanded, his gaze roaming over her as though assessing for any injuries.

She shook her head and tried to disentangle herself from the blanket Bane must have used to cover her. This was the second time in less than a day she'd been awakened with a start. Sleeping aboard the ship was proving to be hazardous. "No, I'm fine. Where's Blossom?"

Blossom zipped across the room. "We're here! I see land, Sabine! Now we can go save Esme."

Sabine turned to look out the window, her eyes widening at the sight. Night had fallen, but the moon cast a silvery glow over the prone figure of a dragon lying on a beach.

"Malek," she whispered, leaping up from the bed. She ran to the cabin door and flung it open, then staggered out onto the deck. They must have been traveling for hours, much farther than she'd imagined.

"Careful, Sabine," Bane warned, grabbing her arm. "We don't know what kind of condition he's in."

"We need to find out," she said, rushing to the edge of the ship. Malek had dropped them close to shore, but the ship was angled on its side in water much too shallow for sailing. She wasn't sure how they'd get back out to the deepest part of the ocean, but that was something they'd need to figure out later. Right now, she had to focus on the dragon who needed help.

Sabine frowned, scanning the length of the deck. The ship had a ladder they used to get down, but she couldn't take the time to locate it. Until Malek was back in human form, she couldn't risk waking the crew and alerting them to his identity. She gripped the railing to climb over it, but Bane stopped her.

"Not like that. Let me go first," he ordered, pulling her away from the edge. Without waiting for a response, he leaped over the side, landing amid the waves. The water was shallower than she'd thought, reaching only to halfway up his chest. He motioned for her to jump.

Sabine climbed over the railing and jumped down. Bane caught her and placed her gently on the ground. With her much shorter height, the waves threatened to knock her over, but Bane kept her steady as she navigated closer to shore. Blossom flew past them toward the dragon, but Sabine barely noticed.

She approached Malek slowly, but he still hadn't moved. Worry lessened her fear as she searched for any sign of injuries. Up close, Malek's dragon form was even larger than she'd thought when she'd seen him flying over Akros. His skin was formed by thousands of tiny scales, the moonlight making them shimmer like stars across the night sky.

"Malek?" she whispered, unsure how she could help a dragon. "Please tell me you're alive."

His head shifted a fraction and then he opened his large serpentine eyes to stare at her. She froze in fear. He blinked slowly but made no other move toward her, and she let out the breath she'd been holding. In her younger years, she'd heard stories about how some Beastpeople had to be put down when they had displayed more animalistic traits and turned rabid. She'd hoped that wasn't the case for dragons, but her experience was far too limited. Intelligence shone in Malek's eyes, and it reassured her enough to believe he was the same person even in dragon form. The magic must be different, like he'd said.

Sabine started to reach toward him but paused and clasped her hands together instead. He was magnificent to behold, but it probably wasn't wise to touch a dragon without an invitation until she was sure it was safe.

Malek closed his eyes again, and she frowned. Turning toward Bane, she asked, "I don't know what he needs or what we can do for him. Do you think he's hurt?"

"Well, if we can't figure it out, I could always use a pair of dragonskin boots," Bane said with a shrug.

Malek exhaled in a huff, sending the sand in front of his nose flying. Sabine's mouth twitched in a smile, suspecting he'd found Bane's comment amusing. Bane might stir fear in the hearts of ordinary humans, but the same couldn't be said for a dragon.

She tilted her head, still awestruck by his true form. It wasn't just his size, but there was an elegance in the lines of his body. The glimmer of moonlight across his scales reminded her of the precious and magical gems harvested only from dwarven mines. "I've never seen your equal, Malek."

Malek opened his eyes again and stared at her. He turned his head, angling it closer to where she was standing. She frowned, unsure if he wanted something from her. His tail lifted and wrapped around Sabine. She inhaled sharply, but his touch was gentle as he eased her closer to him. Malek was trusting her not to panic, and she refused to let him down.

Bane scowled and said, "You harm her, and I'll filet you for dinner, worm."

Malek's eyes narrowed on Bane, but the dragon made no other aggressive moves toward the demon.

She smiled. "He won't hurt me, Bane. But I *am* worried about why he's lying like this and not moving. Would you mind checking for any injuries?"

Bane frowned but moved away. Since Malek had essentially given her permission, Sabine slowly reached out and brushed her fingertips over the dragon's snout. His scaled skin was smooth with the tiniest ridges, yet each scale was nearly diamondlike in hardness. He closed his eyes as she ran her hand downward, still marveling at his sheer magnificence.

Her hand started vibrating, and she laughed in delight. "Are you purring?"

Bane snorted and walked away, circling the dragon and studying him from all sides. "A dragon who purrs. Fearsome, indeed."

Blossom landed on Sabine's shoulder and asked, "Isn't he pretty, Sabine?"

She nodded, even though pretty was far too tame of a word to describe him. "He's beautiful. I just wish he could talk to me and tell me how to help him."

"Maybe he can do the mind-speech thing like the Beast-people." Blossom flew closer to land on Malek's snout. She bent over to peer into one of his oversized nostrils and said, "No bats in the cave."

Sabine bit back a laugh. "I'm sure he'll appreciate hearing that."

She ran her hand up his snout and then up and over one of his prominent eye ridges. In dragon form, he had horns jutting out of the top of his head, like Bane, and then down his body. With the sharp and spiny thorns peppering along the ridge of his back and tail, he would be formidable in battle even without his dragonfire. She couldn't imagine anyone able to harm a dragon through mundane means. Most weapons would simply bounce off his scales.

"I'm surprised he managed to fly the ship all this way," Bane said and moved to stand near her again. "I don't quite understand how dragon magic works, but I'm guessing he's simply tired. I don't see any injuries."

She smiled at Malek, who was still watching her. He didn't seem to care about Bane's presence. At least, he wasn't paying any attention to the demon. Malek hadn't looked away from her, except to close his eyes. "Good. I'm not sure how long he'll need to rest, but I'll wait to awaken the crew until he's able to shift back."

Malek sighed, the gesture causing the ground to rumble under her feet. His scales shimmered even more dramatically. Sabine leaned in closer to study them. They changed to nearly iridescent and then glowed with a strange light until the effect was nearly blinding. Sabine looked away, shielding her eyes from the sight. Almost as soon as it had started, the light vanished.

Sabine blinked against the sudden darkness of the night while her eyes adjusted. When she could see again, Malek was lying on the ground in the same position where the dragon had been moments before. Somehow, he'd managed to shift back wearing all his clothing. Perhaps it was another quality of his magic.

Malek rolled onto his back and turned his head in her direction. His mouth curved upward, and he asked, "You think I'm beautiful, huh?"

She laughed and knelt beside him. "Yes, but I think you already knew that."

Blossom landed on Malek's chest. "My wings are prettier, but I wouldn't mind being as big as a dragon."

He chuckled and closed his eyes. "It has its benefits, but pixies can go plenty of places I can't."

Blossom nodded sagely. "I bet Sabine could turn you little like me. She made me big once. I got to keep my wings and everything."

When Malek didn't respond, Sabine reached over and put her hand over his. "Are you all right?"

"Mmhmm," he murmured, opening his eyes to look up at her and interlacing their fingers together. "I can't remember ever being this tired. My magic is pretty much spent. We were farther away from Karga than I thought. The Merfolk's storm must have affected our navigational instruments."

She frowned, scanning the length of the empty beach. The wind kicked up, and she shivered through her wet clothing. "Do you know how far away we are from Karga?"

"I caught a glimpse of the city before we landed. I'd say we're about a day's walk from there. I couldn't risk taking the ship any closer."

"A dragon flying with a ship in its claws would definitely be something to behold," Bane muttered, picking up a few pieces of driftwood scattered on the sand.

"Oooh, are we going to make a fire, Bane?" Blossom took flight and flew after the demon.

"That's the plan," Bane said, stopping to pick up another piece of wood.

Sabine absently rubbed her arms. The chill she felt wasn't only because of the coolness of the night or the absence of her magic. Something wasn't right, but she couldn't pinpoint it. She paused and inhaled deeply, but she couldn't detect anything except the briny sea air. "I suppose we can set out on foot in the morning. Will that give you enough time to recover?"

Malek reached over and lifted one of her many braids. He seemed to take every opportunity to touch her, but Sabine didn't mind. If anything, she found herself doing the same thing with him.

Running her braid between his fingers, Malek said, "It'll have to be enough. I'd rather leave now, but I've heard the outskirts of Karga can be dangerous for travelers. With our magic depleted, it might be best to stay on the ship tonight and then make our way there in the morning."

Bane approached them and dropped the driftwood beside Sabine. He used the motion as a distraction as he whispered, "We may need to get underway sooner. A group is gathering up on the ridge."

Sabine inclined her head to let him know she'd heard. "How many?"

"At least six, but I sense more of them farther back and rapidly approaching," Bane said quietly as he crouched and stacked the wood for a fire. "My guess is they caught a glimpse of Malek's lightshow and came to investigate."

"Damn," Malek muttered. "I'd intentionally chosen an abandoned area of the beach far away from any settlements. They must be part of a hunting caravan. I've heard they travel in numbers anywhere from twenty to thirty."

"Are they human?" Sabine asked quietly, unwilling to risk looking in the direction Bane indicated. He'd know better than anyone if any living creatures were nearby.

"It's likely," Bane replied, still appearing to be focused on his task. Sabine knew he was tracking each lifeforce of the people watching them, to see what they were going to do.

Sabine gestured for the tiny pixie to take flight. "Blossom, see what you can find out."

Blossom nodded and disappeared into the darkness.

Malek sat up. Keeping his voice low enough so only they could hear, he asked, "They won't spot her?"

Sabine shook her head. "Blossom will keep to the shadows to avoid detection. It's only a risk if they're Fae."

"Or a demon," Bane muttered as he stood.

Sabine didn't answer, not willing to divulge the truth. Blossom had spied on both Bane and Dax numerous times for Sabine over the years. Some secrets weren't hers to share.

Malek frowned and said, "If it's one of the desert tribes, don't draw your weapons under any circumstances. They may simply be curious, but the sight of weapons may incite them to violence. They deal harshly with outsiders."

"Violence is a part of life." Bane stood and flung out his hand. Flames erupted from his fingers, illuminating the night. The driftwood caught a second later in a spectacular display, its heat scorching with its intensity.

Malek narrowed his eyes at Bane and snapped, "You're a fool. If there was any doubt about who we are, it's gone now."

Sabine shook her head, understanding why Bane had used some of his remaining magic when they could least afford it. "No. They'll know the instant they see him Bane's a demon. We can't hide his physical attributes, and I don't have enough power to shield him with glamour. What Bane did just now diverted attention away from you. If we're lucky, they'll believe he's the source of the light they saw."

Malek paused, cocking his head to regard Bane. "And they may be reluctant to entangle with a powerful demon."

Bane smirked. "Perhaps you're not as stupid as you look."

Sabine sighed and scooted a bit closer to the fire. "Have they moved?"

"They're closer, but more importantly, there are now almost twenty on the ridge. A few more are farther back. I suspect they're probably deciding whether to engage us."

Sabine glanced at the ship. "The crew is still asleep. I can awaken them, but I'll need to remove my glamour to tap into my reserve magic."

Malek frowned. "Will the spell break on its own?"

Sabine hesitated. "Yes, but not until tomorrow afternoon, possibly a bit longer. Those with stronger constitutions will be the first to awaken."

"They're approaching," Bane warned, lifting his gaze to stare at the ridgeline.

"Hold off on waking the crew," Malek said quietly. "Our only option is to bluff our way out of this. Follow my lead."

Sabine nodded. A shout pierced the night a moment later. Sabine and Malek surged to their feet. More than a dozen men and women ran toward them, shrieking a battle cry. The group quickly surrounded them, waving their elongated spears in the trio's direction. They appeared human, but if any of them possessed magical ability, it was too slight for Sabine to easily detect.

Their coloring marked them as natives to the southern lands, with bronzed skin and dark hair and eyes. It was their unusual orange clothing with distinctive black stripes that caught and held Sabine's attention. Only one creature she knew had similar markings, the six-legged squarvo. The squarvo was a large creature with the ability to spit acid in a wide arc to decimate its enemies or crush them with its significant weight. It was said they could grow to reach the size of a small house. The fact that these humans could bring one of these creatures down was a testament to their ferocity.

Malek held up his hands in a peaceable gesture. "We mean you no harm."

One of the men stepped forward, brandishing an unusual pole weapon. It had a crystal tip at one end, while the blade on the other end was curved in a half-moon shape. His clothing possessed more decoration than the others, with beads and feathers woven into the design, leading Sabine to think he might be one of their leaders or even a spokesman for the group. Sabine studied the others, but most of them appeared more concerned with Bane's presence than her or Malek.

"Who are you to summon one of the horned devils to attack our land?" the stranger demanded, gesturing with his weapon toward Bane.

"I have no interest in your lands," Bane snapped, his eyes flashing silver in warning.

Sabine tensed, recognizing this had the potential to go bad very quickly. If these people had the tenacity to attack and kill a squarvo, they might not think twice about attacking a demon. She opened her mouth to intervene, but Malek shook his head in warning.

He stepped forward, still keeping his hands raised, and said, "My name is Captain Malek Rish'dan of Obsidian's Storm, the merchant ship you see behind me. On my word, we mean none of you any harm. The demon with me was a passenger on my ship. We were attacked by the Merfolk and barely made it to shore with our lives. Most of my crew were lost at sea during the attack, and as you can tell, we sustained a significant amount of damage."

One of the women, an attractive dark-haired woman, stepped close to their leader and whispered something in his ear. She was wearing similar attire as the leader, which consisted of a long tunic fastened with a colorful woven belt over loose-fitting pants. The leader nodded at her, and she stepped backward.

"If you have not summoned him, by what arts is this devil standing aboveground?"

Malek frowned. "In truth, I don't know. The ways of his magic are unknown to me."

Sabine glanced over at Malek in surprise. Like the Fae, dragons couldn't lie. Technically, he didn't know the details of the pact she'd forged with Bane, but it was a near thing. Malek had very carefully maneuvered these people to draw conclusions that he was a simple ship captain. She just hoped they didn't take out their anger and fear on Bane.

"Then we shall kill him and be rid of him," the man announced and gestured toward one of his men.

"Wait," Sabine interrupted, earning a worried look from Malek. She gestured to her pointed ears and said, "We sailed from the northern cities, and mixed heritages aren't uncommon there. Some of us simply have more pronounced features than others."

Their leader frowned. He scanned her up and down before studying Bane again. "I have heard these claims, but I will not allow one of the devils from the underworld free rein in our lands. We will take you to our village and allow our elders to test the truth of your claims. Throw down your weapons. Now."

Sabine tensed. If their elders had any talent for assessing magic, they'd know immediately Bane was a full-blooded demon.

Malek's jaw clenched, but he reached down and began disarming. He leaned in close and whispered, "Put down your weapons. You've bought us time, and this is our best chance. Otherwise, they'll cut us down where we stand."

Sabine hesitated, glancing at Bane and discovering he

hadn't moved. His hand still gripped his sword, not that he needed it to slaughter these people. He wouldn't be happy with her request, but she didn't want these people to die. She caught Bane's eye and nodded at him to follow their instructions. He hesitated, and she narrowed her eyes at him in a silent warning.

With a look of disgust, Bane tossed his weapons onto the sand. Sabine removed her knives and throwing daggers and placed them carefully on the ground. The woman and another man emerged from the ranks and swept up the weapons, giving Bane a wide berth while they collected them.

Malek cleared his throat. "We appreciate your understanding and look forward to seeing your village. Is it far away?"

"A little more than a day from here," the leader said, gesturing toward one of his men. "The devil will be bound until we can determine the truthfulness of your claims."

The second man walked forward carrying a woven rope-like material. Bane huffed but put his hands in front of him so they could bind him. He held her gaze, the meaning in his eyes clear: He was only tolerating this for her benefit. Sabine inclined her head in understanding, mentally promising to make it up to him for this degradation.

Malek leaned in close and whispered, "He'll be fine. The desert tribes adhere to guesting traditions. Unless it's determined he's what they believe, they won't risk harming him for fear of angering their ancestors."

Sabine nodded, hoping Malek was right.

MALEK LEANED FORWARD, trying to catch the attention of one of the hunters. A woman with dark hair bound tightly against her head narrowed her eyes at him. She made a sign to ward against evil and turned her mount to the side.

"Superstitious fools," he muttered and leaned back in frustration. The cart carrying him and Sabine was being pulled by several thontons, the large beasts of burden used by the desert tribes. The group that had intercepted them was a hunting party, and their caravan was headed back to their village after their latest hunt. Unfortunately, as far as he could tell, they were heading north—the opposite direction of Karga.

He glanced at Sabine, who'd been quieter than usual since they'd bound Bane and led him away. While most of the hunters were riding thontons, the demon had been forced to walk in the rear of the caravan with a couple armed hunters keeping watch over him. Malek might not be overly fond of Bane, but Sabine obviously cared and was worried about him.

She sat curled up with her back against the wall of the cart, her silver braids swaying slightly every time the cart hit a bump. The moonlight filtered through the cracks in the wagon's canopy and caressed her features, making them appear even more delicate. It was a sharp contrast to the hidden strength he knew resided within her. He wished he could offer her some reassurance besides empty platitudes.

Malek sighed and shifted in the crowded cart, trying to bury his exhaustion. If he wasn't so concerned about Sabine and the direction they were traveling, he might be tempted to sleep. But it was too dangerous to take that chance.

Depending on the perception and knowledge of the desert tribe's elders, they'd not only identify Bane as a demon, but they'd also be able to tell Sabine was Fae and he was a dragon. He needed to get them out of here before anyone discovered the truth. It was impossible to know how they'd react, but he suspected it wouldn't be favorable.

Keeping his voice low, he asked, "Have you seen any sign of Blossom?"

Sabine glanced out the back of the cart and then shook her head. "No, she'll keep her distance until it's safe to approach. She's skilled at staying hidden and is more resourceful than most people believe. I'm more concerned about Bane. I don't like how they've separated us."

"They won't hurt him, but we should still make a plan to leave soon." He put his hand over hers and frowned. Sandwiching her hand in between his, he murmured, "Your hands are like ice. I'd forgotten your clothing was still wet. You didn't have a chance to dry off before they brought us with them."

She lowered her gaze. "It's a temporary side effect from being low on magic. It'll get better once I have more rest."

Malek moved closer to her and put his arm around her shoulders. "My natural temperature runs hotter than yours. It might help."

Sabine nodded and curled against him. The intoxicating scent of night-blooming flowers filled his nose. He squeezed his eyes shut and counted to ten, using the time to center himself. They were in a precarious situation, and he couldn't afford to be distracted by her closeness.

"Do you know much about these people?"

He swallowed, trying to focus on her question rather than the way she felt pressed against him. At least he wasn't in danger of falling asleep. Now a different sort of need was plaguing him. "Only a bit from my dealings in Karga. I'm not sure which group these belong to, but there are dozens of desert tribes. They're a proud and rugged people, and their culture is heavily steeped in tradition. They're not bad people, but I'm not sure how we'll fare if we can't escape before we arrive in their camp."

Sabine fell silent for several minutes and then lifted her head to regard him. "How are you feeling?"

Malek gave a half-hearted shrug. He could easily sleep for a full week, but they couldn't even afford a few hours. "I'll feel better once we're safely away. I caught sight of where they put our weapons. If we can get word to him, Bane should be able to melt through his bindings without any trouble."

Sabine frowned and glanced toward the back of the caravan. "I'm afraid that won't be possible. Holding his death magic over the ship took too much from him. The fire he summoned on the beach was likely the last of his magic. He's as weakened as I am, if not more so."

"Damn," Malek muttered, running his hand up and down Sabine's arm to warm her. He'd been counting on Bane to help with their escape, but that wasn't going to be an option. Even if they had their weapons, they were too outnumbered to be effective against the desert tribe. If Bane didn't have access to his power, it explained Sabine's worry for the demon.

He sighed. "It'll be several hours before any of us have recovered enough power to be able to escape. We need to find a way to be reunited with Bane before then. The closer we get to their village, the more difficult it will be to leave undetected."

She laid her head against his chest. "Will they travel throughout the night?"

"It's doubtful, but I can't swear to it. From what I've heard, the desert clans claim certain territories. They're forbidden from hunting or even making camp in any areas that aren't neutral or claimed by their tribe. They'll likely travel until we reach one of those areas."

She fell silent again and he settled back, enjoying having her in his arms even if circumstances weren't ideal. The cart jerked as though it had hit a hole but continued moving steadily onward. He studied the inside of the cart thoughtfully, somewhat surprised it wasn't having more trouble on these broken roads. Not only was the cart overcrowded with traveling supplies and animals still curing from their recent hunt, but the joints were somewhat corroded. If the rhythmic wobbling was any indication, the wooden wheels were beginning to warp too.

He straightened. "I have an idea how we might be reunited with Bane."

Sabine sat up to regard him. "How?"

"They put us in here so they didn't need to watch us every second. They trust us a bit more than they trust Bane."

Sabine frowned and darted another look out the back of the wagon. "None of them will speak to us. Every time we try, they make a sign of protection and move farther away." She sighed and leaned against him again. "I think it's more likely they simply view us as less threatening than a demon. With only one way in or out, it makes sense to conserve their resources. They can have one person keep an eye on the cart instead of having several guards watch over us."

He grinned. "True. But if something happens to one side of the cart, they'll have to bring us out while they repair it. They won't risk damaging their meat or the hides. Once we're out, I doubt they'll watch us too closely."

"You might be right, but they removed any tools or items we could have used to damage it." Sabine gestured toward the meat, hides, collapsed tents, and bedding around them. The cart jostled them again, knocking a few of the bedding items on their sides.

"Not exactly," Malek said quietly, keeping an eye on one of the hunters who had moved a bit closer. He waited until the hunter fell back to speak with one of his companions before continuing.

"I told you my power was different from yours. I don't *need* magic to change forms, but it helps the process. Even in this form, I can heat the metal bolts securing the wheels to the cart."

Her eyes widened. She straightened and gave him a brilliant smile, her eyes sparkling with hopeful excitement. Malek froze, unable to tear his gaze away from her. She was attractive in her glamoured form, but her smile made her positively radiant. He'd pay a small fortune to have her smile at him without the illusions she wore like armor to hide herself from the world.

Sabine placed her hand against his arm. "How will this work?"

"I was hoping you might be able to help me," he admitted, the beginning of a plan forming in his mind. "I know you don't have much magic to spare, but you can read the memories of the wood in this cart, right? Similar to what you did on the ship?"

Sabine's smile faded, and she pulled her hand away. Her expression became guarded as she asked, "What do you wish of me, Malek Rish'dan?"

He paused, searching her expression for a long time. The warmth and familiarity she'd exhibited a few moments ago had disappeared. In its place was a woman who was now regarding him with a great deal of suspicion and even wariness. The use of his full name warned him that she was treating his request with more formality than he'd intended.

The Fae were fierce when it came to favors and debts, and he suspected she was waiting for him to press his advantage. He didn't fully understand their culture, but he knew enough to understand he needed to handle the next few minutes carefully or risk losing any ground he'd established with her.

It reminded him of their first meeting when he'd killed one of the men attacking her. Then later, he'd negotiated with her again when she'd snuck into his room at the inn. Only this time, she wasn't flirting with him to set him off-balance and gain an advantage. The realization shocked him. The woman in his arms just a few minutes ago had been the true Sabine, one who had relaxed enough to curl up against a dragon.

More determined than ever to win her affections, he smiled as though unconcerned with her tone. He tucked a braid behind her ear and then trailed his thumb across her cheek. Her shoulders tensed and her eyes narrowed slightly, but she didn't pull away.

Elation rushed through him. Sabine might be wary, but she was also beginning to trust him. It was enough to give him hope. Perhaps Blossom had been right when she'd suggested Sabine cared about him too.

Malek nodded toward the opposite wall of the cart, which appeared to be formed by wooden planks. "I can't see the metal from here to breathe dragonfire directly on them, but if you can read the wood enough to help direct my dragonfire to the metal, we can loosen the bolts."

She blinked up at him, and her shoulders relaxed. "Not a favor then."

He shook his head. "No favors. A cooperative effort between allies to rescue our companions."

Her gaze softened, and she murmured, "It would seem I owe you an apology."

He pressed his finger against her lips to eliminate any need to repay a perceived slight. "Trust takes time, Sabine. We may have been through a great deal together since we met, but we haven't known each other for long. You haven't stayed alive this long by trusting easily. No apologies. Not from you."

Sabine's mouth curved in a hint of a smile, and she

nodded. She leaned forward to cup his face and brush a featherlight kiss against his mouth.

When she pulled away, Malek said, "If kissing you is my reward for not asking any favors, I'll never ask for anything again."

Sabine laughed, her eyes dancing with amusement. "I'll see what I can do." She paused, tilting her head to regard him. "Back on your ship, you said I keep surprising you. The truth is you keep surprising me too, Malek."

He took her hand and squeezed it gently. "At least our travels together won't ever be boring."

"There is that," she said in agreement and then fell silent, staring at their clasped hands. "Reading dead wood requires far more magic than living wood. It's possible to do, but I'll need to remove my glamour to access my full strength. Unfortunately, I'll be more of a liability for a time afterward until my power is replenished. We also run the risk of alerting my family to my presence since Bane isn't close enough to shield me. I don't believe they'll be able to summon the Wild Hunt again so soon, but I can't swear to it."

He frowned. "Damn. I didn't think about that. I suppose I can try heating up one side of the cart and hope it helps loosen the bolts. You may want to stay on this side and close to the exit while I try it. You should probably hold on too. Since it's wood, there's a chance it'll catch fire."

He started to move away, but she grabbed his arm. "Wait, Malek. There is… another possibility."

"Oh?"

Sabine reached over to touch the mark she'd placed on his wrist the night they met. It was a temporary marker acknowledging a minor debt or, rather, an intent to share a private dinner together. It hadn't happened yet, so the marker hadn't disappeared. "With your agreement, I can change the mark to signify a different sort of arrangement between us. Changing it won't require much magic, since the mark already exists. It should give me enough power to read the wood without making me a liability."

He arched his brow, more curious than suspicious. From what he'd seen, Sabine was both cautious and fiercely loyal. He doubted she'd make a suggestion that would endanger either of them or be anything other than fair. "What sort of arrangement are you suggesting?"

She ran her fingertips over the mark. "One that may be mutually beneficial, but it's something we both need to consider carefully. If I alter the mark and its intent, it will allow us to share power between us without the need to exchange blood. We can do far more together and with less magic than if we remain separate."

He leaned back in surprise. To his knowledge, he hadn't thought such a thing was possible. He'd assumed his dragon grandfather and Fae step-grandmother had needed to share blood to exchange power.

Intrigued by what this could mean as far as his relationship with Sabine, he asked, "I had no idea you could do that. Is this a Fae ability or just yours?"

She hesitated and lowered her gaze. "Any Fae can create a debt marker, but only some of us can alter an existing mark in such fashion. It's an ability which has been granted to certain bloodlines." She paused and then lifted her head to meet his eyes. "This type of arrangement isn't entered into lightly, but I believe I can trust you, Malek."

Taken aback, he glanced down at the triangular pattern on his skin. Bane had a similar design on his wrist, but there were some slight variations and richer colors in the demon's marker. "This change you're suggesting, is it similar to the one you've given Bane?"

"Not quite," she said with a small frown and glanced toward the rear of the caravan where Bane had been taken.

"What's between Bane and myself is a different sort of arrangement. He swore an oath to protect and serve me in exchange for certain… concessions."

Malek would be lying if he said he wasn't curious about those concessions. He didn't think she'd be willing to discuss it with him, and he wasn't about to pry now that she'd warmed up to him again. "I see. How will this new arrangement work then?"

She paused, scanning the contents of the cart. She reached over to pick up an empty bucket that had been tossed in the corner. "I suppose we can compare this new arrangement to a bucket."

His brow furrowed. "I think you're going to have to explain."

Sabine smiled. "I know it sounds strange, but let's assume this bucket belongs to both of us. It's a shared possession. It can be used for different purposes, but it falls to the person holding it to determine how they intend to use it."

When he nodded, Sabine gestured toward the bucket and said, "If you agree to allow me to use the bucket, I might decide to carry some items in it." She offered it to him. "If I agree to allow you to use it, you might decide to bail out water from your ship." She took the bucket away again. "But if I refuse to allow you to use the bucket, you won't be able to bail water. We both must agree how it shall be used and who will be directing it."

"Ah," Malek murmured as understanding filled him. "The intent must be there on both our parts for the magic to work."

The wagon hit another hole, jostling it hard enough to make a few more items topple over. Sabine tossed the bucket back in the corner and said, "Exactly, and we won't need to make a sacrifice when we share power. This arrangement is a type of sacrifice—the death of autonomy and the birth of trust. As such, it will be more difficult to dissolve than our current one."

He moved his wrist closer to her. "Go ahead and change the mark."

She lifted her gaze and frowned. "You don't want to know how to dissolve it first?"

Malek chuckled. "Sabine, I'm not in a hurry to be rid of you. I've been wanting a deeper connection with you, and I'm not foolish enough to believe I'm the only one accepting this risk." He leaned forward and added, "I trust you."

Her mouth formed a thin line. "It's dangerous to trust any Fae."

"I'm not trusting any Fae," he said gently and squeezed her hand. "I'm trusting *you*."

Sabine searched his expression. After a long moment, she nodded. "Then allow me to tell you the rest before we do this."

He waited, and she sighed. "This next part isn't shared openly with outsiders, but marks of this nature often take on a life of their own. It's wild magic, the same type that originally created the Wild Hunt and changed the Huntsman from his original form. It's why only a few royal bloodlines have this power, those families who first combined their magic to breathe life into the Hunt. It's also why the Wild Hunt still affirms the line of succession. That was once part of the Hunt's original purpose, before it forged its own path."

Malek sat back, thoroughly stunned. Blossom had shared some of what had transpired back in Akros while he'd been in dragon form, but now he was questioning everything he'd ever learned about the Fae. "Is that why the Huntsman was willing to exploit a loophole for you? Because the Wild Hunt has acknowledged your right to rule?"

Sabine nodded and stared out the back of the cart. "In

part. After the death of my mother, they declared I was the rightful leader of the Unseelie. I believe the Huntsman also views me with some… affection. Like them, I'm neither fully Seelie nor Unseelie. Although they are closer to the Unseelie, they're more independent than most Fae are willing to admit."

Malek arched his brow. "If these marks are wild magic, are you suggesting this change might turn one or both of us into something similar to the Huntsman? And create a new Wild Hunt?"

Sabine smiled and shook her head. "No. The original intent has to be similar for such a thing to occur. I'm simply saying the closer we become, the more the lines may blur. It may come to pass that one day we're able to borrow the bucket without asking the other for permission. It may not be our intent for things to develop that way, but it could happen."

Malek chuckled. "Sabine, from what you're saying, I think this is more of a risk for you than it is for me. No matter what magic we share, you won't be able to transform into a dragon. Are you sure *you* want to do this?"

Sabine was quiet for so long, he thought she might be reconsidering her suggestion to change their connection. Unwilling to push her, he opened his mouth to suggest they try his original idea when she lifted her head.

"I want a deeper connection with you too, Malek," she admitted in a soft voice. "But what's already developing between us worries me."

The vulnerability in her eyes surprised him. There were facets to her nature he hadn't even begun to discover. He squeezed her hand and said, "Talk to me, Sabine. I won't push you to do this, but I'd like to know your concerns."

She lowered her gaze to their clasped hands. "When I fled Faerie, I never imagined I'd encounter a dragon. I know very little about your ways, except what I learned in stories designed to frighten Fae children."

Malek frowned. "Are you worried I might take advantage of our connection?"

She gave him a small smile and shook her head. "No. You've already shown me you're not what I once believed, but we still don't know each other very well. It took me years of knowing Bane before I even considered our current arrangement." Sabine paused and stared out the back of the cart. "My ignorance is a liability we can't afford, Malek. That much was proven earlier today when we were attacked. I wasn't aware the Merfolk hated demons. That lack on my part was what led to Esme and your crew being taken from us. Now we're in a similar situation. I don't—"

Another hunter approached on his mount, and Sabine fell silent. Malek tensed and inwardly kicked himself. He'd been so focused on Sabine, he hadn't been paying much attention to their surroundings. The hunter peered into the cart, gave them both a curt nod, and moved aside.

Once he was out of earshot, Malek relaxed slightly and said, "Go on."

Sabine frowned. "I know virtually nothing about these desert people, except they view us as enemies. I was the one who insisted Bane deplete his magic back on the ship. Now he's facing the possibility of being banished back to the underworld or even killed. I swore to him I would never allow that to happen."

She lifted her gaze, and the despair in her eyes wounded him. Malek frowned, feeling sorely ill-equipped to alleviate her guilt. If Bane were with them, he might be able to convince Sabine she was wrong, but Malek couldn't allow Sabine to keep punishing herself over circumstances that were beyond her control. He just hoped he didn't make things worse.

Malek sighed and said, "I think you're being a little hard on yourself. You lived most of your life in Faerie. No one expects you to know everything about foreign cultures, especially with how isolated your people have been. I've been studying for years, and I've only scratched the surface."

She frowned, her lips turning to an adorable pout. "That's not an acceptable excuse. I should have known better than to allow Bane to travel on your ship without a way to mask his identity. Now Esme, Bane, Levin, and the others are all in danger because of my poor decisions."

"I see. And when were you supposed to stop Bane from boarding my ship? Back in Akros when you were carried aboard because you were too weak to walk?"

Sabine blinked at him. "No, but I could have tried to—"

He pressed his fingers against her lips to stop her objections. "No, you couldn't have done anything except what you did. The Wild Hunt was chasing us, and we couldn't even risk stopping for supplies. We all did what we had to do to survive."

Sabine wrapped her hand around his wrist, and he lowered his hand. She frowned and said, "Esme and Bane are mine to protect, just like Levin and your crew are yours. Ignorance and circumstance don't excuse that simple truth."

"You're right. They *are* yours to protect," he said gently and took her hands again. "But none of us knew the Merfolk attack was a possibility. I'm sure Bane didn't even realize it. We may not see eye to eye, but that demon would *never* put you in harm's way."

Sabine didn't answer right away, which made him hopeful she was at least considering his words. He reached up to tuck another of her silver braids behind her pointed ear and said, "When it came down to it, you alone were the one who saved my remaining crew and forced the Merfolk into a negotiation. You may not know everything, Sabine, but it's the wisest of people who admit that fact. And you, my dear, have proven to be very wise."

She swallowed, her eyes shimmering with unshed tears. "They're all I have left, Malek. I don't know how to save them."

The vulnerability in her eyes was nearly his undoing. Unable to resist, he wrapped his arms around her and pulled her closer. Running his hand over her silky hair, he marveled how this incredible woman had already found her way into the deepest recesses of his heart. "You aren't alone, Sabine. If I need to knock this damned cart over to get us out of here, so be it. We're going to liberate Bane, find Blossom, and make our way to Karga—together. Someone there will have some knowledge of Pearl. We'll get Esme back for you."

Sabine nodded. She managed a weak smile and brushed away her tears. "I'm sorry. I normally don't fall apart like this."

Malek arched his brow. "In the short time we've known each other, you've proven to be one of the strongest people I've ever met. Most would have given up after experiencing a fraction of the challenges you've faced." He chuckled. "I admire you, Sabine. I don't think anyone would begrudge you a few tears, and if so, to hell with them. I'd like to see them try to walk in your footsteps."

"I'm glad you're here with me." Her gaze lowered to the mark on his wrist and then she lifted her head to meet his eyes. "I would like to change our arrangement, Malek Rish'-dan. Will you allow me to alter your mark so we can exchange power at will?"

Malek searched her expression, but the look of determination in her eyes erased any doubts. He smiled and nodded. "I'd be honored."

"All right. First, you'll need to remove your warding medallion."

Malek looked out the back of the cart to check on the placement of their guards. Satisfied no one was paying them any attention, he removed his necklace and placed it in his pocket. The original mark Sabine had given him in Akros hadn't permanently affixed to his skin until he'd removed the warding medallion. "Now what?"

"I'll need to cut both of us to change the mark," she said, glancing around the cart for anything to use. She picked up a few items before dropping them back down.

He reached to grab one of the clasps used to fasten the hide over top of the cart. It was made of critonia, a common lightweight metal too flimsy to be used without a lacquer made from yaven trees to strengthen it.

He offered it to Sabine. "Will this work?"

She nodded, pressed the sharper edge of the clasp against her finger, and sliced downward. Closing her eyes, she traced the outline of the original mark using her injured finger. Her magic, potent and beguiling, poured over his skin and penetrated beyond his barriers. He inhaled sharply as desire rushed through him and his own magic surged to the surface.

The moonlight filtering through the cracks in the tarp cast a glow over Sabine's features as though even the night awaited her commands. Even with her glamour, he found himself wondering how he could have ever thought her to be anything other than Fae. She was magic incarnate, and as rare and exquisite as the most precious gems hidden deep within the dwarven mines. Like those precious gems, he wanted to claim her for himself.

Switching to the ancient language of Faerie, Sabine whispered, "By blood and magic, and by rights of both, I command the elements to attend me."

A sharp crack of thunder pierced the night. The hunter's mounts trumpeted, and several of the hunters called out warnings about an approaching storm. The caravan came to an abrupt halt. A sharp wind picked up, causing the treated and leathery hide affixed over the cart to shudder.

Malek darted a quick glance out the back of the caravan to ensure no one had seen anything, but no one was paying them any attention. The hunters were busy trying to calm their mounts. Malek hoped they didn't realize the wind and thunder were magically wrought, or they might be in far worse trouble than their current situation.

The mark on Malek's wrist pulsed at Sabine's touch, drawing his attention back to the woman beside him. Sabine lifted her head and he froze, too entranced to look away. Her glamour had softened, fading to reveal a glimpse of her true features. The changes were subtle, as though a fog was beginning to lift. Her skin was the color of the rarest of porcelain, with a flawlessness only marred by the silver marks of power etched into her skin.

It was her eyes, though, that captured his attention and held it. The color had deepened to a shade of lavender that could never be confused with a human, but it was more than the color that made it impossible to look away. It was the way she was looking at him, with a combination of desire and need, that threatened his weakening control. He swallowed, wrestling with his draconian instincts that urged him to steal her away and get lost in her for the remainder of his days.

Her fingers moved across his skin as she traced the mark a second time. When she finished, she cut a line straight across it. The dull metal pierced his skin without warning, and he winced. Sabine pressed her bleeding finger over his injury, and the mark glowed with a strange silver light. Her power accompanied her touch, and a need unlike anything he'd felt before filled him. He wanted this woman more than he'd ever dreamed possible. Sabine's breath caught and she stared up at him, her gaze mirroring his own emotions.

The wind grew stronger, whipping through the cart. The hide covering ripped off and flew into the night. Shouts filled the air as the caravan leader issued commands to secure their belongings, but Malek couldn't tear his gaze away from the woman in front of him.

When she spoke, Sabine's voice was infused with power, and his heart pounded in rhythm with the cadence of her words. "By blood and magic and by rights of both, what once was solely ours shall be no longer. By will and might, we merge our purposes and intents. As I will it, so mote it be."

Lightning streaked across the sky, its spidery tendrils illuminating the darkness. Repeated cracks of thunder created a cacophony of noise, and the cart shook in time with the booming sound. Sabine's magic rushed through him, and his back bowed from the sheer force. His heated power surged forward, expelling from him in a shocking blast. Sabine gasped as she gazed up at him and her glamour fell away. Her skin began to glow, a beacon of power chasing away the darkness. She was exquisite, and he no longer gave a damn about resisting his instincts.

He lowered his head and claimed her with his lips. Their magic blended together in an intricate and impassioned dance. Her fingers curved into his shirt, pulling him closer as she returned his kiss with equal fervor. Her magic wrapped around him in an erotic wave of heat, and he responded in kind. She tasted of wild magic, of forbidden ancient rites promising to deliver a glimpse of the heavens if he could only hold on to her.

The power between them continued to build, staggering in its intensity, but there was an undercurrent of foreign magic he didn't recognize. Screams sounded from somewhere in the background, but all he could focus on was

Sabine. Something wasn't right, but he couldn't seem to break free from her spell. He was drowning under waves of magic, and he was dimly aware Sabine was also struggling to break the connection between them.

"Sabine!" Bane roared, and she was yanked out of Malek's grasp a moment later.

Sabine staggered and blinked up at the demon in confusion. "Bane? What—"

Before she could finish her question, Bane's silvered eyes narrowed on Malek. The next instant, the demon pushed her aside. With a roar, Bane dove into the cart and tackled Malek, knocking him to the floor.

Bane's razor-sharp claws lashed out, and Malek struggled to grapple with the demon without causing him undue harm. Sabine would never forgive him if he killed the demon. "Dammit, Bane. Don't make me hurt you."

"Enough!" Sabine shouted, clapping her hands together with a sharp crack. The magical backlash was enough to wrest them away from each other. It took Malek a few seconds to shake off the worst of the effects from whatever Sabine had done. Bane appeared equally nonplussed and dazed, sitting on the floor of the cart. Malek slowly sat up, his eyes widening at the sight surrounding them.

Everyone was gone. The hunting party had disappeared. Clothing and weapons were strewn around the cart, all in various placements as though each person had disappeared from existence in a heartbeat.

Malek climbed out of the cart and dropped onto the sandy ground. He approached one of the bundles of clothing and picked up an abandoned spear. A sick feeling rose in the pit of his stomach as he moved aside the clothing, and he squeezed his eyes shut. It was as he feared. Nothing but smoking ash remained. Such widespread destruction shouldn't have been possible in human form, but he couldn't argue with what he had just witnessed.

"This was your doing, dragon," Bane snarled from behind him. "Only dragonfire could kill so efficiently. While I have no issue with these deaths, I'll destroy you if you ever put Sabine in harm's way again."

"This wasn't Malek's doing, nor was it mine," Sabine said, the fury in her tone causing him to turn. She hadn't yet reapplied her glamour, and her beauty was almost cruel given the circumstances. Such death and destruction should never touch someone so full of life and passion.

Malek frowned. "How? Bane's right. This was caused by dragonfire."

Sabine whistled sharply into the night and then approached him. "We are responsible, but only in that our magic was used to achieve these results. But this was done without consent and not by our hand."

Malek's eyes narrowed. "Then who?"

Sabine didn't answer right away. Instead, she knelt beside one of the piles of ash. Malek frowned and glanced at the demon, whose eyes had reverted to their normal amber color. In an effort to take advantage of their circumstances, Bane had already confiscated some of the discarded weapons and was going through the remaining supplies.

A tiny pixie flew toward them. Malek sighed in relief, thankful at least Blossom had been spared.

Sabine lifted her head, her stance regal as she regarded Blossom. "Is the goddess fully aware of what transpired here?"

Blossom winced, still hovering in midair. "I'm sorry, Sabine. I told her you'd be angry, but she wouldn't listen. She said humans should never be allowed to take one of her children captive."

"This was the goddess's doing?" Malek demanded as fury

filled him. The idea this alien goddess had declared it her right to use them in such a manner was intolerable. "She used our combined powers to murder these people?"

Sabine gave him a curt nod. She picked up a knife lying beside the pile of ash and stood. Turning back toward the pixie, she said, "You will allow her the use of your eyes and relay these words exactly as I speak them, Blossom. I would have Lachlina understand the consequences of her actions."

Blossom nodded. The tiny pixie fluttered her wings at nearly blinding speed, reminiscent of an agitated humming-bird. A high-pitched whistling noise filled the air, and Blossom glowed with a strange gold light.

Bane walked toward Sabine and asked, "The pixie has the power to summon the goddess among us?"

Sabine held up her hand to silence Bane. He scowled but remained quiet.

Sabine waited until the whistling noise stopped before she said, "You have stolen that which was not bargained nor gifted, Lachlina."

"One may not steal what they have created," Blossom said in a voice foreign and alien to Malek's ears. The cadence and inflection were similar to Sabine's voice when she spoke words of power, but Blossom sounded far away, as though she weren't truly in the present.

"Then understand this," Sabine warned, her skin glowing as she drew upon her remaining power. "The Fae shall *never* again be slaves to any of the gods."

"You seek to challenge *me*, daughter?"

Sabine's eyes narrowed, and her skin glowed with a power that rivaled the brilliance of Blossom. "I agreed to aid you in protecting this world. Not only have you violated our agreement by forcing my magic to destroy innocents, but you have also caused me to break an oath between me and my allies. You used Bane's magic to seek out their life force and Malek's dragonfire to destroy them. This will *not* stand!"

Sabine lifted the knife and pressed it against her wrist over the chalice mark that was a symbol of her pact with the goddess. "I will flay your mark from my skin should you ever attempt to bind me to your will again. Your chalice shall be melted in dragonfire, and the remnants buried in the deepest recesses of the underworld. I will see your memory shattered and destroyed before I allow this to transpire again!"

She dug the knife into her skin, causing a rivulet of blood to flow down her hand. Malek stared at Sabine with a combination of both admiration and horror. The resolve in her eyes made it clear this wasn't an idle threat.

In a sharp sting of power accompanying her words, Sabine shouted, "Acknowledge, or this ends now!"

"Very well, Sabin'theoria, daughter of Mali'theoria," Blossom intoned. "You have an agreement forged by blood and magic. Your bond shall remain yours to command."

The glow faded from Blossom, and the pixie's wings slowed. Sabine held out her hand, and Blossom landed on it. Her cheeks were streaked with tears as she said, "I'm sorry, Sabine. She thinks it's silly you want to protect humans."

"Shhh," Sabine said quietly. "This wasn't your fault. You couldn't have stopped her."

Blossom hugged Sabine's thumb. "It hurt you."

Sabine turned toward Malek, her eyes tired and sad. "You and Bane have my apology as well. You both trusted me, and I didn't ward well enough to prevent this."

Bane snorted. "The gods have always been fickle. But mark my words, Sabine, she will try to get around your agreement at the earliest opportunity."

Malek frowned. "Can she do that?"

Sabine nodded, lifting her hand so Blossom could perch on her shoulder. "Eventually, yes. I believe she wants to keep the portal sealed, but I also think there's something she's not telling us. Her callous disregard for human lives worries me. We've bought ourselves some time to figure out a solution, and I have a few ideas we can discuss later."

Sabine paused, and her gaze lowered to the many piles of ash. "This should never have happened, and I won't allow it to happen again."

Bane put his hand on Sabine's shoulder and said, "We must go. The grooves in the road indicate it is well traveled, and someone will be along soon. We can't risk getting caught here."

Malek looked down at the remnants of human lives that were now gone. It had been centuries since dragonfire was last used in such a manner. Destruction such as this had been outlawed since the portal was sealed. If any of his clan discovered his hand in this, his life would be forfeit. They couldn't risk alienating this world further than they already had. His people were trapped here and not nearly as powerful now that they were cut off from the universe's magic. For better or worse, the remaining dragons were here to stay unless the portal was reopened.

"Malek?" Sabine approached and looked up at him with a question in her eyes.

He frowned. One day he'd need to tell her everything, but her burdens already weighed too heavily upon her. "Let's go."

Chapter Six

Sabine woke to the smell of cooking meat. Rubbing her eyes, she yawned and sat up. The sun had already been up for a few hours, and the day was beginning to warm. After eliciting the agreement of the goddess, they'd managed to locate some of the hunter's mounts that had run off. They'd traveled throughout the night before finally making their way back to the beach where Malek had left the ship.

"Good. You're awake." Bane turned the meat roasting over the campfire and brought over a steaming cup to her. "The food should be ready soon. How did you sleep?"

Sabine accepted the cup, the familiar aroma of one of Esme's special tea blends filling her nose. She took a sip and said, "As well as can be expected. Did you get any rest?"

"A bit," Bane said, poking the fire with a stick to distribute the embers evenly.

She looked around, but the beach was completely empty. "Where's Malek and Blossom?"

"Malek's on the ship. He woke up an hour ago and needed

to check on some things. I told him you'd likely sleep for a while. Blossom's looking for flowers."

Bane continued to fiddle with the fire, but he didn't say anything more. He wasn't normally a huge conversationalist, but the tension in his shoulders and taciturn responses made her think something was bothering him. Prying wouldn't do any good. She'd learned a long time ago Bane had his own ways of doing things and in his own time. She just needed to wait him out.

Sabine fell silent and continued drinking her tea. She could feel the magic holding the crew asleep beginning to falter. Their sleep was changing, and they'd begin rousing in the next hour even without her interference. It was just as well. The timing worked out, especially since they'd need to head to Karga soon.

After several minutes, Bane asked, "Why didn't you tell me about the pixie?"

Sabine frowned. "What?"

"Dammit, Sabine," he said and tossed the stick onto the sand. "I know you keep secrets from me. I expect it. But you should have told me the gods could still speak through pixies. If your pixie is accompanying us, I have a right to know she could be a threat. I can't protect you if I don't know what I need to protect you from."

Ah. So that's what had been bothering him. Sabine sighed and put her tea aside. "Bane, you do protect me. Even if I had told you, you couldn't have stopped what occurred last night. This was Blossom's secret to share, not mine."

Bane frowned and sat on the blanket beside her. "You can't be sure the pixie won't betray you."

Sabine smiled. After scooting closer to him, she placed her hand on his arm. "I'm not worried. Blossom's as loyal as you, just in a different way. I tell you things I don't always share with her. You each have different perspectives, and I've come to depend upon both of you."

Bane put his hand over hers, holding her to him. He stared at the fire for a long time as though considering her words. "How long have you known they have this ability?"

"Since I was a child," she admitted, studying Bane's body language. Sometimes he was difficult to read. The tension in his shoulders had eased, but she'd obviously hurt Bane by not confiding in him. She softened her tone. "It's not common knowledge about the pixies, not even among the Fae. Many people believe them to be nothing more than noisy butterflies, a misconception that's served them well."

Bane arched his brow. "How did you find out?"

"My mother shared the truth with me after she named me her heir."

Sabine picked up her tea again and stared into the cup, remembering her mother's words. They'd gone walking through the Silver Forest that day, and her mother had taught her a great deal about her family line. In time, her mother would have shared more, but that opportunity had been forever denied thanks to her father's treachery.

Sabine took another sip of the tea, grateful for the fortifying effects of the complementary herbs. The extreme emotions over the past day and her lack of magic had been taking its toll. Bane had likely decided to brew it for her to help alleviate the worst of the effects. Normally, it would be Esme who would push her teas on Sabine. Feeling another pang of loss at the absence of her friend, Sabine cradled the cup in her hands.

Bane picked up the stick again. "Can they communicate with all of them? Even the ones who created the demons?"

Sabine frowned. "I don't know. Blossom doesn't think of the gods in terms of their alignment or past acts. The pixies assign them nicknames to keep them straight. From what

I've gathered, they have more of an affinity for those gods who possess the lighter magics. They've mentioned Sparkles, Shiny, Golden, and other similar names. I think it's why so many of the Fae disregarded the pixies as being full of nonsense."

Bane twirled the stick absently. "We don't have pixies in the underworld, but there are lesser Fae down there from the time your people still resided with us. What are the chances they could speak with them?"

"It's possible," she admitted, breathing in the comforting herbal scent of her tea. "Among the lesser Fae are those who can still hear the whispers of the gods. They can't all speak to them with the portal closed, but they've been able to glean some information from these whispers. Most of the things they overhear are related to the war between the gods and dragons that's still being waged in worlds beyond the portal."

She took another sip, considering some of the conversations she'd shared with Blossom over the years. "I believe their ability to listen is how some of the lesser Fae have retained their magic or gained new abilities. It's certainly not from my people in our tiny pocket of Faerie. Other than the pixies, few of the lesser Fae are able to penetrate our forests. We never opened our home to them after the portal closed."

"How can Blossom speak to this goddess then? Is it because she wasn't on the other side of the portal when it closed?"

Sabine frowned. "I don't think Lachlina is trapped on the other side of the portal like some of the others, but she's not part of this world either. Blossom says she's in a dark place that's part of the in-between."

Bane put down the stick, leaned forward, and removed the meat off the spit. It appeared to be meat from a karpin, a burrowing animal with leathery skin and large ears. It was considered a pest by many farmers, and most people avoided eating them. Their meat could be toxic if not properly prepared.

He placed it on a flat piece of driftwood and pulled out his knife. "When we were back in Akros, you used to move through the in-between to get to the crypt. You said the magic of the gods created that space. Is that where she's trapped?"

"I believe it's similar, possibly interconnected," Sabine admitted, watching as he cut into the meat to check to make sure it had turned from green to orange, a sign the poison had been completely cooked out of it. Her stomach rumbled in appreciation.

Bane handed her the dish and said, "Try this."

She took the plate and looked up at Bane in surprise. "You're not eating?"

"The dragon and I already ate," he said, waving off her concerns. "Malek should be back soon. He wanted to check on the damage to the ship and collect some supplies to trade in Karga."

Sabine pulled apart the food, thankful it was something other than fish. She took a bite, and the slightly sweet flavor of the karpin meat was better than she'd expected, especially with the smoke flavors from the fire. Digging in, she satisfied the worst of her hunger. "This is very good."

Bane nodded and leaned back, stretching out his legs in front of him. "I think it would be best if I remained here while you and Malek head to Karga."

Sabine swallowed the bite she'd been chewing and frowned. "Why?"

"I've been thinking about it ever since we encountered the hunters. From what I overheard while we traveled, these desert tribes are a suspicious and distrustful lot. I'd likely attract the wrong sort of attention, and it would be counter-productive to our efforts in acquiring information."

"I could glamour you," she offered, putting the half-eaten food aside. "If you appear more human, they won't know you're a demon."

"You don't eat enough," Bane stated, frowning at her abandoned plate. She huffed at his observation but picked it back up. As soon as she resumed eating, Bane continued, "Your power isn't limitless, little one. It would be better to conserve your strength for when you truly need it."

She couldn't fault Bane's logic, but she'd come to depend on the demon for more than his protection. "Bane, you have a way of looking at the world that forces me into seeing things differently. Now, more than ever, I need you with me. I'm out of my element in this place." She lifted her head. "What if your presence is the difference between us learning about this Pearl and saving Esme?"

He arched his brow. "And what if a demon's presence dissuades those who might normally be willing to speak with a beautiful woman? I think not. You can change your own appearance with ease, but two of us? We do not have a forest nearby for you to restore your magic."

Sabine wrinkled her nose at him. "It could be done. You're minimizing your value to me."

Bane chuckled and said, "Let us speak frankly, little one. You are a shrewd judge of character, and my help will be limited unless you want someone tortured. You have also now marked the dragon, which will allow you to access his magic without a blood offering. I still do not care much for him, but he *has* proven himself in his desire to protect you." Bane paused, his expression becoming calculating. "I think it's far more likely you want me there to avoid being alone with him. You don't trust yourself around the dragon."

Sabine frowned and put her plate aside again. "You've been cautioning me against trusting him. Now you're saying I should? What game are you playing, Bane?"

Bane shrugged and picked up the stick again. He moved the embers around absently and said, "That was before you marked him. This new connection will give you immunity from his dragonfire, right?"

"Yes, in theory," Sabine replied, wondering where Bane was going with this.

"Then I think you should go alone with him."

Sabine narrowed her eyes. "Stop dancing around and start explaining. Why this sudden change?"

"You marked him as an equal, little one. He has not sworn fealty to you, nor have you retained full control over the bond. In a way, you have weakened your position with the dragon."

Sabine glared at him. "We had limited magic available, and combining our strength was our best option for freeing you. I don't know him well enough to propose any other sort of arrangement. I judged it a suitable risk, and I stand by my decision."

Bane nodded. "I agree, but now you must bind him to you in another way. Malek has already displayed protective instincts when it comes to you. These need to be fostered and allowed to grow."

Sabine stood, trying to rein in her temper. "I will *not* manipulate his affection for me, nor will I whore myself for an alliance." She narrowed her eyes as a thought struck her. "Was this Balkin's suggestion or yours?"

Bane smirked, a gleam of approval in his amber eyes. "The Beastman's, but I don't disagree with your other protector. This would happen eventually, little one. The dragon's half in love with you already. I'm simply trying to speed it along by making myself absent."

Sabine looked in the direction of the ship, knowing Bane was right. She'd seen it in Malek's eyes every time he looked at her. Esmelle had pointed out Sabine'd been looking at him in the same way. The witch had been right too.

"I'm falling for him too," she admitted and lowered her gaze. "My feelings for him scare me, Bane. This was never supposed to happen. You know I can't afford any emotional entanglements, and there's so much we don't know about him."

"I know," Bane said quietly. "I'd advise you to harden your heart, but you've never been good at that. In some ways, I think he's good for you. Far better than Dax, anyway. I worry he'll hurt you before the end though."

Sabine knelt beside Bane. Taking his clawed hand in hers, she said, "Sometimes I think you know me better than I know myself. You've always told me the hard truths, even when I didn't want to hear them. I'd like to know what *you* think I should do, not what Balkin instructed you to tell me."

Bane was quiet for a long time and then he sighed. "If you've already grown to care that much for the dragon, the only thing you can do is bind him to you. We'll have to hope he doesn't betray us when he learns you'll never belong to him. I'll do what I can to protect you, but I cannot safeguard your heart, little one."

Sabine swallowed and nodded. From everything she knew about dragons, they could be extremely possessive. They hoarded treasures, secreting them away from the world. Many Fae had been taken captive by them during the Dragon War, and no one knew what had become of her stolen people. She knew Malek was different from those creatures of legend, but there was always some truth to the stories. She'd had to suppress some of her instincts while living among the humans. It stood to reason he'd done the same, but no one could deny their true nature forever.

She lifted Bane's hand, pressed it against her cheek, and

said, "I'll consider your words carefully before I decide. Will you be all right if I leave you here?"

"For a time. My magic is weaker than normal, but I should be fine aboveground for several days without your presence. If I begin to feel the call of my ancestors, I'll set out in search of you."

Sabine nodded and curled up beside him. Skin contact helped strengthen their connection and made it easier for him to fuse her magic with his. "Take what you need, Bane. I'll regain more of my magic soon enough now that we're on land. I'm already feeling stronger."

Bane wrapped his arm around her shoulders and said, "You worry too much, little one."

"Don't make me forswear my promise to you," she teased lightly, not worrying for a second he'd accuse her of such. "I'll always worry about you, just as you do with me."

He chuckled and siphoned off some of her magic. She sighed and settled against him. The sleep had helped considerably, but she'd feel much better after she found a forest. Unfortunately, their brief journey with the hunters had revealed little but a lot of sand and dirt. It was difficult to imagine this area had once been covered with lush foliage and trees.

Blossom came flying toward them carrying two unusual desert flowers. "Sabine, you have to see what I found!"

Sabine smiled as Blossom landed on her lap and offered her the flowers. She picked up the pink one with petals that appeared more like hair or fur. It was unlike anything she'd ever seen before. Sabine inhaled deeply, evaluating the nuances of the flower's energy and memorizing her impressions. "This is beautiful. Poisonous, but beautiful."

Blossom nodded, her eyes dancing with excitement. "Can you use it to make a new poison for your weapons?"

The flower was unfamiliar to her, but the memories of

her bloodline would always be hers to access. One of her ancestors could have come across this flower or a similar variation. Sabine closed her eyes and inhaled again, tapping into her locked memories. It only took her a handful of minutes to recognize it as a variation of another plant.

Opening her eyes, Sabine shook her head and said, "Sadly, no. This needs to be ingested for it to be effective."

"Drat," Blossom muttered and picked up the blue flower, which more closely resembled some species found near Akros. "What about this one?"

Sabine picked it up. She repeated the same procedure, and her eyes widened as memories rushed through her. "Where did you get this?"

Blossom pointed toward the south. "It was along the road that way. There's a whole field of them. You recognize it?"

Sabine nodded, studying the flower closer. "I've never seen it before, but this is a Fae creation. At some point, probably before the Dragon Portal was sealed, my people lived here." She stared in the direction Blossom had indicated. "Karga lies in that direction, right?"

Bane nodded and studied the flower. "Yes. You're hoping to find some trace of the Fae?"

"This flower is trace enough," Sabine said quietly, cradling the flower in her hands. "If my people were here, there may be other signs too. I know it won't be the same as returning to Faerie, but..."

"You miss your home," Bane murmured.

Sabine sighed. "Yes."

Blossom's wings drooped. "It wasn't supposed to make you sad."

Sabine smiled at Blossom. "Such a wonderful gift could never make me sad. I love it, Blossom. Truly. Not only that, but I may be able to recharge my magic more easily than I expected."

Blossom beamed at her. "When we leave, I'll show you where I found them. I bet we can find lots more! Can I put it in your hair?"

Sabine nodded and handed the flower back to the pixie. Blossom flew up to her shoulder and hummed as she started to braid. Sabine had unbound her hair the night before while they traveled back to the beach, and Blossom had been itching to play with it again. The pixie siphoned off tiny amounts of her magic through touch, but it was so slight, Sabine rarely noticed.

"The dragon comes," Bane said, nodding toward the ocean.

Sabine turned to see Malek trudging through the waves carrying two large bags. He dropped them on the beach near the fire and said, "The damage to the ship was worse than I thought, but I should be able to salvage some items stored in the hold. I brought a few things with me to sell in Karga so we can at least retain the services of the shipmaster and begin the repairs. We may need to trade for additional resources though. The crew can pitch in to help with the work. That should offset some of the expense."

Bane nodded and stood. "I'll oversee the repairs and the crew while you're gone."

"They should begin waking up soon," Sabine said, glancing toward the ship. "You may be able to convince them it was the Merfolk who sent them to sleep as part of our negotiation."

"That could work," Malek mused, glancing toward the ship. "The Merfolk's interference could also explain how the ship made it to shore with that much damage."

Bane held out his hand to her, and she accepted it. He helped her to her feet, and she brushed off the sand from her clothing. It seemed to get everywhere. "I really hope they have a place to get a bath in Karga."

Malek chuckled. "Aye, they do. Karga's about a day's travel on foot. With the mounts, we should be able to get there before nightfall. You'll be able to sleep in a bed tonight."

"I can't tell you how wonderful that sounds," she said before turning back to Bane. "Promise me you won't wait until the last minute if you need me."

Bane inclined his head. "You have my word. If you're not back within a week, I'll set out in search of you."

Sabine nodded and stood on her toes to kiss his cheek. "Be safe, my protector."

"You as well," Bane murmured. He turned toward Malek and ordered, "You will guard her with your life."

Malek gave Bane a curt nod. "I swear it."

"This is going to be fun. Maybe we'll find more flowers on the way," Blossom said, tugging lightly on her hair.

Bane gave Sabine a meaningful look, and she returned it with a weak smile. For better or worse, she was going to spend the next several days alone with a dragon with only a pixie to help run interference. She couldn't decide if she was more uneasy at the prospect or looking forward to it.

Chapter Seven

"*D*o you think we'll find any pixies in Karga?" Blossom asked from her perch on Sabine's shoulder.

Sabine tightened her grip on the reins and pulled hard to the left, forcing the thontin back onto the path they were following. The giant lumbering beasts might be beneficial in transporting heavy objects, but they were easily distracted. This one was determined to dig around in the sand for the parasites that were their primary source of food. It didn't matter he'd spent the entire morning doing the exact same thing. The creature had a one-track mind.

Riding the thontins, with their scaled, leathery skin and extremely wide torsos, was uncomfortable and somewhat hazardous. She'd nearly fallen a few times, until Malek realized her elevated seat mount had been designed for a much larger individual. He'd insisted on trading with her, but the new one wasn't much of an improvement.

"I suppose it's possible," Sabine replied, tugging again on the beast's reins. How these creatures could tolerate the oppressive heat was beyond her. She shifted in her seat, trying to keep her clothing from sticking to her skin.

Blossom grinned and clapped her hands in delight. "If the Fae used to live here, there might be enough magic still remaining to sustain a colony. They'll know all the good spots to forage."

Malek glanced at her. "Is that all it takes to attract a colony of pixies? Just a source of Fae magic?"

"Lots of plants too," Blossom said, fluttering off Sabine's shoulder and onto the top of her thontin's head. "I like sweet flower nectar best, but fruit is really good too."

Malek's brow furrowed. "Do you *eat* Fae magic?"

Sabine laughed. "I wouldn't say she eats it, but it's the same as a plant might need soil to grow. It's nourishment of a sort."

Blossom nodded, swinging her legs idly. "Yep. Sabine's magic has an extra kick to it. She offered enough magic so forty-two of my brothers and sisters could live in Esme's garden. She was even going to let me bring more of my aunts and uncles to Akros, but we had to do it in secret so no one in Faerie knew."

Malek's eyes widened. "Forty-two? You have that many siblings? Is that common?"

Sabine smirked. "You've heard how prolific rabbits can be? Pixie families put their numbers to shame."

Malek laughed. "I had no idea."

Blossom grinned. "That's not even all of them. I have sixty-seven in total." She perked up. "Hey! You could come to our next family reunion! They'd love to meet a dragon."

Malek chuckled. "I'd be honored to meet your family."

Pulling on her reins, Sabine directed her thontin to avoid a tumbleweed. On the surface, the tumbleweeds appeared harmless, but Malek had warned her they sometimes contained tiny parasitic insects which could inject toxins into anyone who came into contact with them.

There was a strange and alien beauty within the desert, but she missed the cooler forests of her home. Even Akros wasn't this bad. The novelty of seeing cacti and the large rock formations which peppered the sand dunes had waned fairly quickly, especially once the temperature started rising. If they didn't find some shade or water soon, she was inclined to cut open her hand and summon a storm. At least the Wild Hunt would bring a little shade with them when they sought her out.

"Oh, look! There are more of those blue flowers." Blossom pointed at an area off the side of the road.

Sabine turned in the direction Blossom had indicated, and her eyes widened. It was a sizable valley with dozens of dark-green plants covered with splashes of blue. She hadn't thought anything like these plants could survive in such an inhospitable climate.

"I want to check it out," Sabine called over her shoulder as she navigated her thontin off the path. She glanced back to make sure Malek was behind her. He nodded at her to let her know he would follow her lead.

They made their way down one of the ridges and into the valley area. Throwing her leg over the side of the thontin, she slid off his back. Her legs were stiff and sore from remaining in the same position for so long, and she relished the opportunity to stretch and move around.

Patting the gentle beast's neck, she stepped around him while he went back to digging in the sand. Blossom flew off, a colorful blur darting from flower to flower, collecting or feeding from the plants.

Malek tied the reins to the saddle so the animals wouldn't get tangled. "Do you think you can recharge your magic from these?"

"Not sure, but I think there's something here." Sabine walked down the ridge where several of the flowering plants were growing. She scanned the area, but there wasn't any sign of a river or spring. These plants shouldn't be able to survive without a source of water nearby.

"What are you looking for?" Malek asked, following her.

"I'll show you," Sabine said and knelt in front of one of the plants. The leaves were dark green with silver veins. Clusters of blue flowers burst at the end of each stem, and their alluring perfume filled the air. Sabine smiled and trailed her fingers over the leaves. It was just as she'd thought. These flowers were identical to some found near Faerie, but she'd only seen them in shades of purple and red. It had been more than ten years since she'd last seen their equal.

Sabine motioned for Malek to join her. He crouched next to her, and she reached over to take his hand. Carefully, she showed him how to caress the delicate leaves without causing them any harm. "Do you feel the moisture in the plant?"

Malek's brow furrowed. "How is this possible? There's no freshwater near here, and we're in the middle of the desert."

"Underground springs," Sabine said with a smile. "This area wasn't always a desert. Thousands of years ago, my people had crystal cities all over the world. These flowers are usually grown near our temples, although I've never seen any this wonderful shade of blue."

"I thought your people lived in homes built around the trees." Malek caressed the leaves of the plant, making Sabine wonder what it would be like to have him touch her the same way.

"Not exactly," she admitted, breathing in the light floral scent to help distract her from Malek's closeness. "Our forests protect the heart of Faerie, but it's not where we live.

Inside our cities, you would find wonders no longer existing anywhere else in the world." She smiled and sighed dreamily, remembering her home. "Treehouses towering up hundreds of feet, crystalline buildings so delicate they catch the sunlight and spin them into rainbows, thousands of plants and flowers of all different colors and scents… The magic is so potent, you can't walk without breathing it in."

"You miss it," Malek murmured, watching her thoughtfully.

"Sometimes," she said in agreement, looking down at the plant that represented so much of her past. She released the leaf she'd been holding and sat back with a sigh. "The dwarves designed complicated plumbing systems to draw water from underground. We still use them to supply our fountains and bathing pools. There must be an underground spring here, which is why these flowers are still thriving."

"This is incredible," Malek murmured, scanning the area. "I don't see any other signs of a settlement. If it weren't for you, I never would have guessed such a thing was once here. Is it possible for you to use these flowers to recharge your magic?"

"Not the flowers, no. If we're standing near an old temple, there might be another way. Give me a moment."

Sabine pulled off her boots and stood, the heated sand warming her feet. If it weren't for the underground spring and the traces of Fae magic still lurking in this area, the sand would have been scalding. She walked around the area, guided by instinct alone. A flicker of awareness passed through her, subtle and cloying. She paused and closed her eyes, focusing on the connection with the land and the water deep below the surface.

She crouched and dug her fingers into the sand. She sent her awareness outward and across the landscape, searching for the source of Fae magic in this area. For a second she felt something, but then it was gone. Sabine opened her eyes and muttered a curse.

"Are you all right?" Malek asked, approaching her with concern in his eyes.

She nodded. "Yes. I just don't have enough magic to connect with the land."

"Can I offer you more of my power?"

Sabine gave him a small smile and shook her head. "Using more of your magic might have the opposite effect. The land won't recognize you." She stood and brushed off her hands. "I can try to offer a blood sacrifice, but I run the risk of alerting my family to my presence. I'm not sure if they're aware the Wild Hunt was unsuccessful in killing me."

"Ah," Malek murmured, closing the distance between them. "Bane said I can probably block anyone from sensing you. That's what he and Dax did for you, right?"

Sabine tilted her head to consider him. She wasn't sure it would work, but her Beastman protector had believed it to be possible. Dax and Bane relied upon their fire magic to shield her, which was similar to Malek's power. "I suppose we can try it."

Malek nodded. "All right. What do I need to do?"

Sabine hesitated. "I'll try to explain, but the mechanics might be a bit different since you're not a demon." When he nodded, she continued, "Distance is usually a factor. We've found skin contact works better. Dax and Bane usually touch the back of my neck and surround me in a type of shield using their power. It masks most of the effects of a blood sacrifice, confusing anyone who may be searching for me."

"That sounds simple enough. Shall we try it?"

She nodded, not trusting herself to speak. Gods. This man had a way of twisting her into knots. She didn't know how she was going to manage the next several days alone with him, especially if the thought of his touch sent her heart racing.

He slipped off his warding medallion and then moved to stand close enough that she was forced to look up at him. Taking a steadying breath, she moved aside her hair and he placed his warm hand against the back of her neck. She shivered, disconcerted by his nearness and the intimacy of what they were about to attempt. No one other than Dax or Bane had ever done this with her, and it was strange to have someone else put her in such a vulnerable position.

"Is this okay?" he asked, his voice husky and almost right in her ear.

"Yes," she whispered and withdrew her knife, trying to focus on her task. "Go ahead and surround me with your power. Whatever happens, let me know before you lower the shield. If the blood sacrifice is successful, I'll break contact with you when it's safe."

Malek's heated draconic power wrapped around her, trailing over her and causing her skin to prickle in awareness. This wasn't on the same level as the magic she'd performed on the ship, but it was still a risk. She took a steadying breath and cleared her thoughts of everything except her desire to connect with the land.

Gripping the knife in her hand, she pricked her fingertip and allowed three drops of blood to fall onto the sand. Almost immediately, the blood disappeared. The sand slowly fell into itself, creating a deep hole. A second later, water bubbled up from the ground.

"Well, I'll be damned," Malek muttered.

Sabine laughed and knelt, breaking their contact and ending his magical shield. Using her hands, she moved some of the sand away as a tiny oasis formed. Malek crouched beside her and did the same. Water continued to bubble upward, growing larger by the minute.

Blossom flew toward them, her eyes wide with excitement. "Are you going to make a forest? We could grow lots of stuff here."

Sabine shook her head, wishing it were possible. "No more than I already have by summoning the water to the surface. Any forest I create with my power will act as a beacon to my family and alert them to my presence. Perhaps one day, we'll return here and see the effects of our new oasis."

With her hands cupped, she scooped up some of the cold water and took a long drink. Power flowed through her, and she closed her eyes, drinking deeply of the magic. The tiny embers of her Seelie and Unseelie magic flared to life, and she breathed a sigh of relief.

Sitting back on her heels, she said, "Blossom, go ahead."

The pixie squealed and lay down on the sand, drinking from the Fae spring. Sabine lifted her head and found Malek watching her with wonder. "Would you like to try some?"

He arched his brow and replaced the warding medallion around his neck. "Is it just water or something else?"

Sabine beamed a smile at him. "Both, but you have my word it won't harm you."

Malek nodded, and she scooped up more of the water. Holding out her hand, she offered it to him. He cupped his hands around hers and held her gaze as he took a drink. He swallowed, and his eyes widened in surprise. "That's incredible. It tastes like water but also something… more."

Sabine nodded, staring at the bubbling oasis. "Among my people, we call this the Gift of the Fae. Finding a place where the old magic still remains is usually a time of merriment and celebration." She turned back toward Malek and put her hand over his. "I'm glad you're here to share it with me."

Malek lifted her hand and kissed it. "I'm honored you trust me enough."

"So, so good," Blossom said and took another long slurp. She hiccupped and Sabine laughed.

Scooping up the pixie, she teased, "You're drunk already?"

Blossom giggled and rolled over, leaving a smear of glittering pixie dust on Sabine's hands.

Sabine looked at Malek and said, "We should probably get Blossom away from here. Between sipping flower nectar planted by the Fae and drinking from the old temple spring, she'll be out of it for a while."

Malek's lips twitched in a smile and he burst out laughing. "I didn't realize pixies could even get drunk."

Sabine laughed. "Oh, they sure can. This one used to get into honey-sipping contests with her brother, Barley. Once, I had to fish them both out of Esme's pond because they forgot they knew how to fly. Their sister thought it would be funny to push the leaf they were sitting on out in the middle of the pond."

Malek burst into laughter again, shaking his head.

"Sooo-*hic*-ooo good," Blossom slurred and gestured toward the flowers and oasis. "Bar'ley 'uld 'ike th—*hic*—is."

"What did she say?"

Sabine grinned. "She said, 'Barley would like this.' You'll begin to decipher pixieisms soon enough."

Malek stood and helped her to her feet. "You know, I feel pretty good too. Lighter and more complete somehow. Was it the water?"

Sabine nodded. "It's rejuvenating but completely harmless. The Fae who lived here infused it with power, which is why I was able to sense it. We should feel the effects for a few hours." She caught sight of her mark on Malek's wrist. "I think you may also be feeling the effects of my magic being replenished. You can sense me through the modified mark."

Malek paused and then murmured, "You're right. I hadn't

realized this would be possible, but I can feel you. It's as though you're part of me."

"It's different for everyone," she replied and bit her lip, hoping he wasn't regretting the decision. "Bane can track me through his mark or tell if I'm hurt. Part of that is the nature of his magic, combined with the binding. We won't know how your mark will work yet. It may never evolve beyond its current purpose."

Blossom rolled over in Sabine's hands and began snoring. Sabine smiled at the tiny pixie and asked, "Do you have anything I can use to carry her?"

Malek nodded and walked back to his thontin. He rummaged through one of the bags and pulled out a small decorative box encrusted with gems. "Will this work? It's one of the items I was planning on selling."

"It should. Would you hold her for a moment?"

Malek arched his brow at the sleeping pixie. "I won't hurt her?"

Sabine smiled, touched by his concern. "No. She's not nearly as fragile as she appears. Just be careful of her wings."

Sabine gently eased Blossom into his outstretched hand and walked back to the flowers. Using her knife, she cut several stalks, making sure not to cause irreparable damage to the plants. Walking back toward him, she said, "Blossom likes you quite a bit."

"I've grown rather fond of her too." Malek cradled Blossom carefully and studied her wings. "I never had a chance to take a good look at her because she's always in motion. She looks like a miniature Fae, only with wings and without the markings on her skin."

Sabine lined the cut flowers on the bottom of the jeweled box. They should give Blossom a bit of comfort and allow the pixie to speak with her family through the magic contained within them. "You should tell her when she wakes up. Some pixies might not appreciate such a comparison, but Blossom would consider it a compliment."

"Did you really make her human sized?"

"Yes, and she's been asking me to do it again ever since. One of these days, I probably will, but a giant pixie would draw too much attention." Sabine picked up Blossom and carefully placed her inside the container. The pixie mumbled something incoherent and cuddled against the flowers.

After fastening the box to the saddle of her thontin, she filled her flask with the water from the oasis. The pool was still growing larger and would likely end up forming a small lake. In a few weeks, this area would be teeming with life. It was a shame she couldn't remain to help foster and cultivate it. Her magic wanted to be used the way it was intended, but it was too dangerous.

Turning toward Malek, she said, "If you hand me your flask, I'll fill yours as well."

Malek offered it to her, and she bent down to fill his container. Brushing her loose hair away from her face, she handed it back to him. "That water will go much further than regular water. We won't need to drink nearly as much."

Malek gestured to the small oasis. "The water's still bubbling up from the ground. Should we stop it?"

Sabine shook her head. "No. This land has been parched for far too long. Animals that abandoned this area now have a chance to reclaim their homes. It won't change the rest of the desert, but in another few months, life will begin returning to this small area." She climbed onto the back on her thontin. "We only have a couple hours until nightfall. If we're going to learn anything about the Merfolk's missing Pearl tonight, we should probably make haste. We only have a few days until the new moon."

Malek nodded and nimbly mounted his beast. "Not sure how much haste we can get out of thontins, but I agree. I'd rather not chance running into more of the desert tribes. We'll need to leave our mounts outside of Karga to avoid anyone recognizing the markings on the saddles."

Sabine nodded. Clicking her tongue at the thontin, she tugged on the rein to direct it back to the path. The creature plodded along, ambling toward the city and hopefully toward some answers.

Chapter Eight

Karga was hot and dusty.

They'd left their mounts outside the city, hoping they wouldn't be noticed by anyone who might have a connection with the hunters. A tall wall surrounded the entire coastal city with spear-wielding guards manning the gates. Over top and within the ramparts, more guards peered down as the pair passed beneath the wall. Strangely, even though they'd been watched since they began their approach, no one had stopped them from entering.

Sabine had expected Karga to be similar to Akros, but the two couldn't be more different. Most of the buildings were single story with low, flat roofs. All the structures they passed appeared to be made from some sort of clay building material rather than the stone and wood commonly used in Akros. The rich smells of cooking meat and exotic spices permeated the air, making her mouth water in appreciation.

It was the people, though, who possessed the greatest differences. There was no doubt Karga was a human city. She caught sight of a few who might have some magical traces somewhere in their bloodlines, but it was nothing like Akros.

It made her grateful her magic had been completely replenished so she could blend into the shadows if the situation required it. Humans could be fearful when faced with someone who was different from them.

Most of the people they passed had deeply bronzed skin and dark hair and eyes. Sabine stood out even with her current glamoured human appearance. It wasn't simply a matter of her pointed ears and nearly white-blonde hair but also her clothing. Her belted tunic over a pair of fitted leather pants might be fairly standard attire back in Akros, but not here.

Most of these people wore colorful attire made from some sort of nearly transparent material which was much lighter than her clothing. It made sense given the warmer climate, but the differences clearly marked both her and Malek as outsiders. Since she'd spent the last ten years in hiding, the scrutiny was making her uneasy.

"Not what you expected?" Malek asked, walking close to her with his hand on his weapon. The two bags he carried were slung over his shoulder, but everyone seemed to be giving them a wide berth. She hoped it was simply because they were outsiders and not for some other nefarious reason.

"Not quite," she replied, brushing her fingers over her throwing knives. It was a nervous gesture and one she tried to avoid, but their weight gave her a small measure of reassurance. "We're attracting a lot of attention."

Malek nodded. "We're heading toward the market district. We'll pick up some clothing and find a bathhouse. We'll still stick out but not quite as much. I know an inn closer to the docks where we can make some inquiries into repairing the ship. More strangers gather down there since so many ships pass through on the way to the northern cities."

"Do you want me to snoop?" Blossom asked from her

perch on her shoulder. The pixie was keeping herself mostly out of sight, and Sabine was using a trace amount of glamour to mask Blossom's presence from the curious onlookers.

"Wait until we're in a less populated area," Sabine murmured, trusting Blossom could keep herself hidden once she was on her own. It was unlikely pixies ventured near the city, and the inhabitants had probably never seen one of her kind. Fortunately, Blossom had the ability to use minor glamour, confusing her appearance with different small winged creatures when it suited her. Since Blossom had drunk deeply of the Fae spring, her magic was also fully recharged. Blossom should be able to flit around the city for hours without being recognized.

They made their way through a number of streets until they came to a large marketplace. It was a wide-open district with numerous stalls set up. Some of them were already closing for the night, but more than a few were still open. At the sight of Sabine and Malek, a few merchants called out invitations to browse their wares.

A merchant held up several bolts of cloth and approached them. "Would the lady be interested in some of my rare and precious silks and other cloth all the way from Tarvei?"

Malek halted, glancing at Sabine with a question in his eyes. She nodded, and Malek turned back toward the merchant. "Indeed. We'll take a look."

They walked to the man's stalls filled with colorful cloth. Sabine trailed her fingers over a bolt of pale-yellow cloth, astounded by the softness. It was nearly sheer and better suited for a boudoir than walking around in public. She couldn't deny it was extraordinarily beautiful, but it wouldn't be suitable for their purposes.

With a sigh, she released the cloth and said, "I think we're going to need some clothing that's already made. We won't have time to find a seamstress."

"No need, no need," the merchant said quickly, obviously reluctant to lose a potential customer. "I have several items you can wear immediately."

He left to look around in the back of the stall and then brought over dozens of items. Laying them out in front of her, he said, "These are of the highest quality you will find anywhere. With your features and wearing one of my dresses, you shall be the envy of all of Karga."

Malek's mouth twitched in a hint of a smile. "What do you think? Do you like any of them?"

Sabine bit her lip, studying the choices. She ran her fingers along the material of a dark-blue dress that almost seemed to shimmer in the light. It was much more substantial than the last bolt of cloth but promised to be considerably cooler than her current attire.

She lifted it closer, fascinated by the intricate silver stitching that was clearly the work of a master artisan. The merchant may be trying to make a sale, but he hadn't been lying about the quality of his merchandise. It was both finer and lighter than anything she'd ever worn while she lived in Akros.

"That color suits you," Malek said, nodding toward the dress she was admiring.

"It's beautiful," she said and reluctantly placed it down so she could move on to the next dress. The vendor had laid out clothing in nearly every color, each of them extraordinary in their attention to detail. Picking up another one that was a deep forest green with gold trim, she couldn't help but think of her missing witch friend. With Esmelle's curly red hair and green eyes, she would be striking in this dress. "I wish Esme were here to see these. She'd love this one."

Malek picked up the blue one she'd been admiring and pointed at another bright red one with gold stitching and the green one she was holding. He selected two more in different colors and then haggled with the merchant. Sabine's eyes widened, surprised he intended to purchase all of them. She'd thought he'd only buy one or two, but he clearly had other intentions.

"You shall bankrupt me, good sir," the merchant pleaded after Malek suggested a paltry sum. "I will never be able to feed my children for so little!"

Malek gestured at a few items on the opposite table. "I'll give you another thumb-sized gem if you throw in a couple of those chained and beaded belts and two pairs of sandals."

The merchant's eyes widened, and he hastily nodded. "Of course, of course. Whatever you wish. Shall I wrap them?"

"Everything together except the blue dress, one pair of sandals, and the matching belt. Wrap those separately."

The merchant nodded and quickly folded up their purchases. Sabine went back to watching the crowd. The sun was beginning to set, and more people were closing their stalls for the evening.

Sabine frowned as she watched one of the nearby merchants lock his merchandise into a chest in his stall area. From what she could tell, it was a rather flimsy lock. Any of the street kids in Akros would have had it open and emptied before the merchant had made it halfway down the street. She noticed a few others doing the same thing.

Leaning close to Malek, she asked, "Aren't they worried about their belongings being stolen?"

"The laws in Karga are harsh," Malek admitted, following her gaze to the nearby stall. "The merchant's belongings are as safe here as they are in their own homes. You'll find very few thieves."

Thievery was unheard of in Faerie, but her time in Akros had made her believe it was common in human cities. In her experience, lies and deceit came to them as easily as the truth. "We've been watched since we entered the city. I thought they might be pickpockets or thieves, but they're not?"

"Thieves have no place amongst us." The merchant spit onto the sand in disgust. "Those who watch are part of the Kiervan."

"Kiervan?" Sabine questioned, unfamiliar with the word.

"They're similar to city guards," Malek explained, taking the packages the merchant offered. He placed them inside one of his bags and slung it over his shoulder. "Good fortune to you, merchant."

"To you as well," the merchant replied, pressing his thumb and forefinger to his temple in a gesture of gratitude.

Malek placed his hand against Sabine's lower back and led her away from the stall. In a quiet voice, he said, "The Kiervan are also spies. They keep watch for outsiders and report anyone suspicious to the city's leaders. Our presence has already been noted, and they'll keep an eye on us for a while. Spending coin in their marketplace is one of the quickest ways to alleviate their distrust. We still need to be careful to avoid any suspicion."

Sabine frowned, catching sight of one of the Kiervan. The man's eyes were narrowed on Malek, but they weren't paying much attention to her. Malek ignored him and continued moving through the market district.

"I bet those guys know something about Pearl," Blossom whispered from her hiding place under Sabine's hair.

"Possibly, but you heard what Malek said. Be careful when you investigate," she said low enough so only Malek and Blossom could hear.

Malek nodded. "Blossom may overhear something, but I suspect you might have better luck, Sabine. Women are deeply respected and even revered in Karga. It's considered one of their greatest offenses to harm a woman."

Sabine arched her brow. "Do women also hold a place among their leadership then?"

"Sadly, no," he admitted, leading her down a ramp away from the market. "In some cities I've visited, women are considered equals. Women in Karga are considered precious and rare, more so if they're of child-bearing age. Life in the desert is harsh, and there's always a lack of women willing to embrace that life."

Malek pointed at the high walls surrounding the city. Several archers were patrolling the top, looking toward the outside area and not paying any attention to what was happening within the city walls. "Those guards are to prevent raiders from infiltrating the city and stealing their women and supplies. If any raiders make it inside, the Kiervan will also attack them."

Sabine studied the armed guards manning the wall. They were well equipped with heavy crossbows, and their clothing was similar to what the hunting tribe had worn. Their leathers were dyed to match the same ochre color as the walls, making them blend in a bit easier.

Glancing over at Malek, she said, "They allowed us entry without any problems."

He nodded. "Your presence made it easier for us to enter, but leaving may be a bit more difficult. Outsiders are welcome if they're here to trade, but no one quits the city without being searched and questioned."

Sabine frowned. "Ilwan said they sent someone to search for Pearl and couldn't find any trace of her. If she isn't here, Pearl must have left of her own free will."

"Not necessarily," he said quietly as they passed a group of people who sounded like they were heading to a nearby tavern. "There are ways to move in and out of any city without being detected. I'll make some inquiries with some of my smuggler contacts while we're here. They might know something."

Malek stopped outside a large building. A girl on the cusp of womanhood was standing outside, leaning against the wall. Her dark hair was braided in two simple braids, with the center part painted a deep red color. It wasn't the first time Sabine had noticed such an adornment in the city, but she hadn't yet learned its significance.

The girl straightened, her eyes widening at the sight of Sabine. "Would—would the lady like to visit our bathhouse? We have the nicest hot springs anywhere in the city and perfumed oils for a massage, if that's your preference."

Malek withdrew some coins from a pouch and handed them to the girl. "That should cover everything. I'll double the amount if you have her old clothing laundered and brought to the dockside inn. She'll also need an escort to show her the way."

The girl's jaw dropped at the wealth she'd just been given. "Of-of course, good sir. My uncle can escort her once she's finished. I'll take her in right now to see my grandmother."

Malek nodded and withdrew the wrapped package containing the blue dress. He handed it to the girl and said, "Give us just a moment, and she'll be inside. That packet contains clothing for her to change into while you're laundering what she's wearing."

"I'll be right inside waiting for you, mistress." The girl bowed low and hastened inside.

Sabine smiled at Malek and teased, "You're not staying? I thought you'd be just as eager to get cleaned up."

"Tempting, but opposite sexes are not allowed in the public bathhouses." Malek chuckled and pointed at a building farther down the street. "The men's bathhouse is right over there. After I'm finished, I'll meet with the ship-builder to inquire about the repairs and leave word I need to smuggle some items out of the city. That should give us an opportunity to inquire about Pearl. I'll meet you at the inn when I'm finished."

Sabine glanced around, but the crowd was thinner in this area. No one was paying them much attention. In a low voice, she said, "Blossom, go ahead and take flight. Come find us at the inn when you're finished. I'll leave a window open for you. If you're not back by midnight, I'll go for a walk outside and find you."

"Don't worry, Sabine," Blossom said and hugged her neck. "They'll never notice me."

The tingle of pixie magic indicated Blossom had glamoured herself and then she was gone.

Malek's eyes widened, and he murmured, "She's a moth."

Sabine's mouth twitched in a smile. "Of course. It's a little hard to snoop when you stand out. During the day, she's a butterfly or a small bird, but a moth blends in better at night."

He shook his head and chuckled. "You both are full of surprises." His expression became more serious. "Be careful. They're reluctant to harm women, but you're still an outsider. They'll be suspicious if you ask too many questions."

"I understand." Sabine smiled and kissed his cheek, touched by his concern. "You should be careful too. I've started to enjoy having you around."

Without waiting for a response, she pushed aside the leather flap blocking the doorway and ducked inside. The smell of incense and smoke filled her nose, and her eyes watered. It was a little too strong, but humans didn't have the same olfactory senses as the Fae. Unfortunately, that meant she'd be nose-blind for the next several hours.

The girl grinned and rushed toward her. She took

Sabine's hand and said, "Your husband is very generous. He's a good match for you, no?"

Sabine paused, disconcerted by the girl's assumption. Until she knew more about these people, she was reluctant to correct the misconception. "He's very generous. What's your name?"

"Rika, mistress."

"Call me Sabine," she said gently and looked around the room. A few low tables with oil lamps lined the walls, while plush lounging cushions were scattered on the floor. A man leaned against the wall, scanning her up and down with interest, but he remained silent.

"That's my Uncle Ekon. He keeps everyone out, except invited guests. Don't worry. He won't come in the main part of the bathhouse. Only women are allowed." Rika tugged on Sabine's hand. "My grandmother is preparing everything for you. She's very pleased you're here. I'll take you to the scrubbing room first and then we'll go to the hot springs."

Sabine followed Rika as she pushed aside another flap and led her into a brightly lit chamber. Painted screens were set up throughout the room, offering a modicum of privacy. Rika led her to one of these areas and picked up a large clay jar. She poured some perfumed water from it into a large bowl and gestured at a brush.

Sabine's brow furrowed, but she picked up the brush. It looked similar to a hairbrush but with a much longer handle. Beside it was a tiny brush with a strap affixed to the back. "What is this?"

"You must scrub your skin before entering the springs. I can help you wash your hair," Rika said and gestured at Sabine's bag. "If you leave your possessions with me, I promise to keep them safe for you."

Sabine hesitated but allowed the girl to take her bag. She removed her weapons and started unlacing her shirt, taking care to hide the Merfolk's necklace in the bottom of her bag. She wasn't sure if Rika would recognize the jewelry, but it would be best to keep it hidden for now.

Glancing down at the small bowl of water, Sabine asked, "You want me to use this water to scrub my skin?"

Rika giggled and nodded. "You are new to Karga, no? It's different where you are from?"

Sabine nodded and gave her a small smile. "I suppose it's obvious. I hope you'll tell me if I do something wrong. I don't want to offend anyone."

Rika beamed a smile and took Sabine's shirt. "We don't get many outsiders here, especially not like you. Sometimes sailors come and visit the men's bathhouse, but they aren't welcome here. Are... Are you from far away?"

"Far from here," Sabine replied in agreement and handed the rest of her clothing to Rika. She dipped one of the brushes into the perfumed water and began brushing her skin. Rika gave her an encouraging nod and put her clothing aside.

Rika unbraided the two small braids Blossom had started and then picked up the smaller brush. She looped the handle over her hand and brushed Sabine's hair. "Your hair is so long and soft. I've never seen this color before."

Sabine turned and smiled at the girl. "It's common where I'm from, but I think your hair is a lovely shade of brown. We call the color chestnut, after the nuts gathered during harvest season. I had a friend close to your age who had hair similar to yours. I often admired it."

Rika gave her a shy smile and continued brushing. Once Sabine finished scrubbing every inch of her skin, Rika motioned for her to lean back. She did, and the girl picked up a small bowl filled with some sort of white paste. She rubbed it into Sabine's hair and poured the perfumed water over her hair, cleaning it completely. Once she finished, Rika motioned for Sabine to follow her.

Sabine hesitated, glancing at her belongings. In addition to her weapons and the Merfolk necklace, her bag also contained the Faerie water. She wasn't thrilled with the idea of leaving her possessions behind while she went to another location.

Rika took her hand and said, "Please, Sabine. All is ready for you at the springs. We can leave your clothing and belongings here. No one will touch them. We're just going downstairs. Grandmother will box Uncle Ekon's ears if he allows anyone in here."

"All right." Sabine followed the girl down an earthen staircase. The entire building had been built overtop of what appeared to be an enlarged cave. Lanterns had been set up throughout the cavern, their flickering flames dancing and casting shadows on the walls. The air was heavy and thick with moisture, a sharp cry from the dry and dusty atmosphere in the city above them.

In the center of the cave was a sizable underground spring with steam wafting up from the water. Another woman was already soaking with her nearly black hair pinned on top of her head. She opened her dark eyes briefly to assess Sabine and then closed them again.

An older woman with a lined and weathered face grinned. She wore her graying hair braided identically to Rika's, with the center part also painted dark red. Several of her teeth were missing, and the remaining ones were stained brown. Sabine recognized the signs of chebo nuts, which were frequently used as a painkiller by humans. When chewed, the juices created temporary feelings of euphoria, but they also rotted the patient's teeth and dulled the senses.

"Come in, child," the woman crooned, gesturing for Sabine to come closer. "You may call me Zaverza. Enter and be at ease. Rika will fetch you some refreshments while you soak."

Sabine nodded and stepped down into the water, pausing in surprise at the intense heat. They must be drawing the water from the underworld for it to stay this hot. It took a few moments to get used to it, but she gradually submerged herself.

Seats had been carved out from the natural stone, and Sabine sat down. The water came almost to her neck. She leaned back, finding the heat far more relaxing than she'd expected. This might not be a magic-infused spring, but there was always power in the raw elements of nature.

Zaverza sat near her on a cushion outside the spring. The woman coughed and adjusted her thin wrap around her, silently watching Sabine.

Sabine suspected the elderly woman stayed close to the spring to alleviate the worst of her pain symptoms, but the scrutiny was making her a bit uneasy. If she didn't have her magic thrumming strongly inside her, she probably wouldn't have agreed to leave her weapons in the other room.

Sabine settled back and studied the cave. It was dome shaped, which explained why they were so far underground. The smooth rock surface of her seat led her to believe these springs had been used in this capacity for a long time, possibly even centuries. She didn't know how old Karga was, but it was founded sometime after the portal closed.

Rika reappeared a few moments later, carrying a large jug and goblet. She poured wine into the goblet and handed it to Sabine before disappearing into the other room.

Sabine sniffed the beverage, but she didn't detect anything unusual. The incense might be masking her ability to detect some ingredients. Once she took a cautious sip of the spiced wine, she found herself pleasantly surprised. It had a stronger bite than Faerie wine, but it had earthy tones that were similar.

"You are not from Karga," Zaverza said, picking up some knitting that had been lying beside the cushion.

Sabine didn't respond right away. She glanced at the other woman who was soaking, but she was still sitting on the far side of the spring with her eyes closed. Zaverza, on the other hand, was still studying her with a great deal of scrutiny. It could simply be curiosity about a stranger, but Sabine wasn't fully convinced. "No. I traveled from the north by ship. Your city is much different than my home, but I've been enjoying exploring it."

Zaverza clucked her tongue in approval. "You have come at a good time then. Karga will soon participate in our annual burning festival." She paused, her eyes narrowing slightly. "Our city is closed to outsiders during that time while we rid ourselves of the taint."

Sabine frowned. "Burning festival? Taint? What do you mean?"

"We regularly purge our city from those who possess devil magic," Zaverza said matter-of-factly, clicking her knitting needles together. "The desert tribes want our women because they are free from this affliction. Their men must raid the city again soon, or they will be forced to go without wives until next season. They know we breed the toughest warriors and best hunters. Until the city is reopened, not even the desert tribes dare try to enter. It is tradition."

Sabine's brow furrowed, and she absently swirled the wine in her goblet. If they weren't already under time constraints, they would be now. This purging didn't sound good, and she had no intention of sticking around for it. As soon as she located Pearl, they could leave. At least Bane was safe back on the ship. She was thankful he'd had the foresight not to accompany them.

Deciding it would be best to change the subject, she asked, "The tribes raid for wives?"

Zaverza nodded and continued to knit. "Of course. It is the only way to ensure our daughters go to the strongest and cleverest of hunters. Is it not the same in the north?"

"Not exactly, but I suppose there's always a desire to have a strong mate," Sabine admitted thoughtfully and put her wine aside. It was a little strong, and she needed to keep a clear head. "I was under the impression women were highly valued in Karga. Does that mean they have no say in who they wed?"

Zaverza reached over and popped a chebo nut in her mouth. She chewed and then swallowed the juice. "All women need a strong husband and provider. Still, some do not wish to leave Karga. So they hide in their family's larders when the raiders come, and their brothers and fathers guard them fiercely. It has always been the way of things in Karga."

"I see," Sabine murmured, leaning back and considering the strange customs. She wished she knew more about Pearl and when she'd left her ocean home. If Pearl had arrived during one of these raids, she might have been carried off by some desert tribesman. "When was the last raid?"

Zaverza shrugged. "Perhaps a week? They raid more frequently this time of year." Zaverza's eyes narrowed on the woman still resting on the other end of the spring. "Misa, the hour grows late. Your skin shall wrinkle and prune if you remain much longer. Not as pretty then, eh?"

The other woman opened her eyes and scowled at Zaverza. With a sigh, she climbed out of the bathing pool. Unfastening the pins binding her dark hair, she sneered, "I shall always be younger and prettier than you, Zaverza. Your time will end soon, and your pretty little granddaughter shall be left without a protector."

Zaverza ignored her. The only sign of the older woman's

irritation was the louder clack as her knitting needles tapped together.

Misa approached them and studied Sabine. "You're not completely hideous, but those pointed ears are likely a sign of the devil's magic. I've heard rumors another raid is planned either tonight or tomorrow. You needn't worry about being taken. They'll likely kill you on sight." The woman wrapped a loose drying cloth around herself and smirked. "I will be the first of those captured, but this time, I intend to find an even better hunter. The last one wasn't worth my time."

Zaverza spit the chewed chebo nut into a nearby cup. After wiping her mouth with the back of her hand, she said, "Sakiu is warming the perfumed oil for you, Misa. She will massage you to prepare you for the claiming. Best you go and ready yourself."

The woman nodded and swept out of the room, retreating to another side door.

Zaverza picked up her knitting again and said, "Misa was already captured once. She was returned within a fortnight."

Sabine whipped her head back toward the old woman. "They return people?"

"When they are called Misa." Zaverza snickered, her knitting needles clicking together. "That one is both pretty *and* petty. Most men in Karga avoid her, claiming she's akin to a venomous viper. Her only hope is to find one of the desert tribesmen who will take her. When a hunter captures someone as disagreeable as Misa, they sometimes dump them in front of the city. It's considered shameful."

Sabine frowned, no longer enjoying the effects from the hot spring. Given the direction of the conversation, she was anxious to leave. Rising from the rocky bench, Sabine gripped the edge and climbed out of the water. "She's hoping to be captured again for a better match?"

Zaverza nodded and slowly rose to her feet. She picked up a nearby drying cloth and handed it to Sabine. "It will not happen. Misa will be captured again, but she will return again within a fortnight." Zaverza touched her fingers to her forehead. "My mother had the sight, as did her mother before her. I see much." She paused and gave Sabine a slow smile, revealing her missing and discolored teeth. "I also *see* you and those markings you try to hide. You're one of *them*."

Sabine froze, the heaviness in the air making it difficult to breathe. She'd heard of seers, those humans with the ability to see through glamour, but she'd never met one. The Fae always killed anyone with such a talent. It was too dangerous to allow them to live and risk having them divulge the Fae's secrets. They alone had the ability to penetrate the Silver Forests and enter Faerie without an invitation. As long as they lived, her people were at risk.

Zaverza reached out and gripped Sabine's arm tightly with surprising strength. "I foresaw your arrival, Princess. A terrible storm. A flying ship. A woman with silver hair and the royal blood of the Fae."

A cold chill rushed through her at the woman's words. In a voice infused with power, Sabine demanded, "Unhand me. Now."

"You seek something," the woman insisted, brushing off Sabine's magic as though it were inconsequential. "I would barter with one of your kind for a favor. In exchange, I will employ my gifts to set you upon the correct path."

Sabine's eyes narrowed, understanding immediately how dangerous this woman could be to her kind. She hadn't realized they could negate words of power. "Be careful, old woman. If you know who and what I am, you also know it usually doesn't end well for your kind."

Zaverza released her and clasped her gnarled hands together. "You may strike me down as your ancestors once did my people, it is true. I am old and will not be long of this world anyway. There is a weariness in my bones that promises my end is near. Yet I would still barter with you."

Sabine straightened. She didn't enjoy threatening humans, but she couldn't allow this woman to jeopardize everything. To do so would endanger everyone depending on her. "Then name your price, Zaverza of Karga, but understand the risk. If an agreement is not reached and your silence is not assured, you will not leave this room alive."

Zaverza nodded and her expression became calculating. "In my vision, I saw you were different from others of your kind. I also saw why you have come to Karga and what you hope to accomplish. In exchange for my information, you shall take my granddaughter with you when you leave. You will keep her and protect her the same way you protected the children of your last home."

Sabine studied Zaverza for a long time. Lies came easily to humans, unlike they did for Fae. There was no way to ascertain whether this seer had any reliable information to share. If their culture was so steeped in superstition, Zaverza might be inclined to provide false information to put an end to Sabine's existence. No. It was better not to trust this woman, even if she did have some knowledge of Pearl.

Sabine was about to refuse when the old woman dropped to her knees. Clasping her weathered hands together, she pleaded, "Please, Princess. I am begging you. Rika is a good girl, but she carries my same affliction. I had hoped she would be spared from this curse of sight, but her ability is now beginning to emerge. Once I am gone, she will be left without any protection."

Sabine frowned, her resolve weakening as tears streamed down Zaverza's face. With a sigh, she held out her hand to help Zaverza to her feet. "Rise, grandmother. I'm not insensitive to your plight. But even if I were to agree to take Rika with me, I cannot guarantee her safety. She'll likely be in more danger, not less."

Zaverza shook her head. "The Kiervan will kill her once they realize what she is. Even if they do not, the desert tribes will execute her once they come to claim her as a wife. It is impossible to hide our gifts without training. I will not survive long enough to show her how to protect herself."

"And what of her uncle?"

"He does not know," Zaverza whispered, her shoulders hunching in despair. "He shall be duty-bound to report her to the Kiervan once he learns the truth. Please, Princess. I swear on my honor and the lives of all my remaining family, you are Rika's best hope for survival. She will be a good servant to you if that is your wish. If you cannot keep her or if she displeases you in some way, then take her somewhere safe, but please, take her away from here."

Sabine was quiet for a long time. If Balkin, her Beastman protector, hadn't helped her escape after the death of her mother, she'd likely have met the same end as Rika. No child, human or Fae, should ever be punished simply for being what they were. She couldn't lie to Zaverza or make false promises, but she *could* offer Rika a chance to survive. In return, Rika's abilities might give Sabine an advantage in dealing with her treacherous family. It was worth taking the chance, provided Rika and Zaverza offered her some assurances.

With a sigh, Sabine said, "I will not promise to keep her safe, since that's beyond my abilities."

Zaverza's eyes filled with hope, and she clasped her hands together. "You will take her?"

"I will," Sabine replied, hoping she wasn't making a mistake. "Once my business in Karga is concluded, I will collect your granddaughter. I will ensure she is cared for until she learns to hide her gifts, but I will not risk any of my companion's lives for hers."

Zaverza nodded eagerly. She opened her mouth to speak, but Sabine held up her hand to stop her. "Before I leave here today, you will *both* swear a blood oath to keep your silence about my identity. Your granddaughter will also need to swear fealty to me."

"Of course. Anything. We will both swear."

"Then allow me to dress, and summon your granddaughter," Sabine said, wringing the excess water from her hair. "The hour grows late, and I need to meet up with a companion."

Zaverza motioned for Sabine to follow her. Wrapping the drying cloth tighter around herself, Sabine headed into the adjacent room. It was similar to the first room, with lounging cushions scattered around the floor. Colorful lanterns cast their firelight upon the walls, giving the room a warm and welcoming appearance.

Rika was standing near a low table, her knuckles white as she gripped the handle of the jug she held. Her eyes were wide as her gaze darted back and forth between her grandmother and Sabine.

"All is well, granddaughter," Zaverza said, gesturing for Rika to put down the jug. She turned back toward Sabine. "Your belongings are on the table. No one will disturb us in here. Please, dress and relax. Would you care for more wine?"

"That won't be necessary," Sabine said, walking to her bag and the clothing Malek had purchased. Her weapons had been laid out beside them.

"M-may I help you dress?" Rika approached hesitantly as though fearful of being rebuked.

Sabine paused, studying the young girl she was about to accept as her charge. After a long moment, she nodded. Rika picked up the blue dress and approached her, showing her how to fasten the silvered metal rings of the belt to keep the lightweight material in place.

"The color becomes you, mistress," Rika said softly as she finished fastening the last buckle.

Sabine took Rika's hand and gently pulled her around to stand in front of her. "Your grandmother told me you've inherited her gift. Is this true?"

Rika swallowed and nodded.

"Can you *see* me as I truly am?"

Rika's expression became fearful. In a voice barely above a whisper, she said, "Not yet. I caught a glimpse when you approached from outside, but when I tried to focus on you, I couldn't see you again."

Zaverza adjusted the shawl over her shoulders and said, "It will be some time before she can pierce the illusions of your people at will. I had warned her you would be arriving today, and she was outside keeping watch for you."

Sabine nodded, accepting the explanation. "Is it your desire to travel with me, Rika?"

Rika hesitated and lowered her gaze to stare at the floor. Sabine's heart went out to this young woman, on the cusp of womanhood and about to embark on an unknown future. Gods. It was like looking at herself when she'd been forced to leave Faerie.

Softening her tone, Sabine said, "There is no wrong answer, Rika. I'm not sure what you've been told about the Fae, but I won't steal you away from your home if you don't wish to leave."

Rika raised her head to meet Sabine's gaze. "I don't want to leave my friends and family, but I know I must." Her lower lip trembled, and her eyes glistened with unshed tears. "Grandmother won't survive the next burning festival. If you don't take me with you, they'll kill me too. I... I'm afraid to go, but I don't want to die."

Her heart broke at Rika's words. Sabine sighed and said, "All right. Have a seat. We need to discuss a few more things and make some plans. I want you to understand exactly what you may face if you choose this path."

Rika nodded and helped her grandmother to one of the cushions before sitting beside her. Using the opportunity to gather her thoughts, Sabine equipped her weapons underneath the dress. The skirt portion had a long slit up each side, which allowed not only a great deal of movement but would also allow her to easily draw the throwing knives attached to her thigh. Her normal dagger was easily affixed to the chained silver belt around her waist.

Once she finished, she walked to the cushions and sat down. Sabine withdrew her dagger and rested it on her lap. Rika paled a little, but Zaverza snapped, "None of that, girl. If she wanted to harm you, she wouldn't need weapons to do it."

Sabine arched her brow at Zaverza but didn't argue. In truth, Sabine wasn't sure how much Fae magic a seer could deflect.

Focusing again on Rika, Sabine said, "Your grandmother is right. This knife is to make a blood oath, not to cause anyone harm. My magic doesn't always affect seers the way it does other humans, but a blood oath is tied to *your* power. This is a way for both of us to protect ourselves. Why don't you hold on to the knife while we're speaking?"

Sabine offered her weapon to the girl hilt first, and Rika tentatively accepted it. She hesitated but then placed it on her lap the way Sabine had been holding it. From the way Rika handled the blade, Sabine guessed she had very little experience with weapons.

"How old are you, Rika?"

Rika lowered her gaze. "Fifteen, mistress."

Gods. She was even younger than Sabine had been when

she'd had to leave her home. At least the children she'd helped in Akros hadn't been forced to leave everything they knew. This was going to be more difficult than she'd thought.

Determined to set Rika at ease, Sabine gave the girl a small smile. "Call me Sabine. If we're going to be traveling together, we should probably get to know each other a bit better. I'm willing to answer any questions you might have, but you'll need to swear not to reveal anything I share with you. Are you willing to do that?"

Rika nodded.

"Good," Sabine said and gestured to the knife. "Go ahead and make a tiny cut on your palm, just enough to draw blood. Your grandmother will also do the same. Then you both must repeat my words."

Rika picked up the knife. She pricked her hand and winced before passing the blade to her grandmother. Zaverza repeated the gesture before handing it back to Sabine.

"Repeat after me," Sabine said and slid the knife back into its sheath. "I swear not to reveal any secrets that divulge the identity of Sabin'theoria or any of her companions. Anything seen, heard, or learned while in her company or under her protection is sacrosanct and shall never be revealed except by her leave."

Sabine waited until they finished repeating her words and then continued, "I further swear to protect the secrets of the Fae and Sabin'theoria's companions. No harm shall be done by my hand or by my leave, either to Sabin'theoria or any of her sworn allies."

After they uttered the last words, Sabine held out both her hands. The two women exchanged a look and then placed their injured hands onto hers.

Sabine leaned over their hands and blew gently over them, infusing her breath with the magic of her ancestors to seal their bargain and heal their wounds. Closing her eyes, she whispered in the language of Faerie, "By blood and moonlight, I accept and bind your oaths."

The weight of their agreement settled over Sabine like a heavy mantle. For better or worse, their fates were now intertwined. Sabine wasn't sure what this meant when it came time for her to be reunited with her people, but Rika would remain under her protection. Even the fiercest of the Fae would hesitate to raise a hand against Rika for fear of reprisal.

She opened her eyes to regard them and said, "It is finished. When my business in Karga is concluded, Rika will travel with me and my companions. It's unlikely we'll ever return to Karga, so you should say your good-byes before we depart. Do you have a small piece of wood or a piece of metal?"

Rika nodded and jumped up. She picked up a piece of wood from a pile, which appeared to have been gathered for a fire. Holding it out, she offered it to Sabine. "Is this okay?"

"That will work," Sabine said and snapped off a small piece. Using a small amount of magic, she traced the first letter of her name on the wood and then handed it back to Rika. "Hold on to that and do not let it out of your possession."

The girl's eyes widened in surprise as she studied the altered wood.

Turning back toward Zaverza, Sabine said, "Our ship was damaged en route to Karga. My companion is in the process of hiring workers to repair the damage. If you believe Rika's life is in immediate danger, send her north with the workers. One of my sworn allies, Bane, has remained with the ship to oversee the work. If she gives him that marker, he will honor our agreement and protect her while I'm absent."

Zaverza's eyes watered, and she patted Rika's hand. "I told you she would help you, child. You will be safe."

Sabine watched the exchange, hoping the girl wouldn't panic when she learned Bane was a demon. She wasn't sure how many of the city's superstitions Rika had inherited, but that would be something to be dealt with later. With any luck, she'd be there to make the introductions the first time Rika met Bane. "Did you have any questions for me, Rika?"

Rika hesitated and then gave her a shy smile. "You're really Fae?"

Sabine smiled. "I am. I was born in Faerie, although I haven't been back in almost ten years."

"Why not?"

Sabine sighed. "That's a long and rather unpleasant story. Like you, I needed to leave my home to stay safe. I'll return one day, but not for a long time yet."

"Can… can I see you without your illusion?"

"Ah," Sabine murmured, glancing around to make sure no one else was around. "Just for a moment."

Sabine carefully lowered the magical illusion hiding her true appearance. Her skin began to glow with power, and the silver vines etched on her skin began to pulse.

Rika's eyes widened, and she said through a heavy breath, "You're beautiful."

Sabine smiled and reapplied her illusion. "It's not safe for me to walk around as I truly am, so my glamour is designed to give me more of a human appearance. I don't remove it often. Only my close friends and allies have seen me without it. You're now counted among those select few."

Rika's smile deepened, and she sat up a little straighter. She might still have some misgivings, but at least Sabine had put the worst of them to rest. Shining a little light on the shadows always made things less frightening.

Zaverza patted Rika's hand again. "See, child? I told you all would be well."

Sabine nodded. "Now that you've sworn to keep my secrets, you can ask me questions any time. I may not always be able to answer them, but I will always be honest with you. From now until your last days, as long as you stay true to your oath, you have nothing to fear from me."

"I understand," Rika said, folding her hands in her lap.

Turning back to Zaverza, Sabine asked, "Now as to the matter of the information you promised?"

"Of course," Zaverza said and held out her hand. "Place your hand in mine, and I shall aid you however I can. What do you wish to know?"

Sabine placed her hand in Zaverza's, understanding some magic required touch to be effective. "A woman came to the city not long ago to trade for supplies. She is one of the Merfolk, a shapeshifter in human form. She never returned home. How can I find her?"

Zaverza's eyes lost their focus, and she gripped Sabine's hand tightly. "The woman you seek is no longer in Karga. The Pearl of the Sea has been stolen away and taken deep into the desert. She will not be easy to locate. You need to find her to reunite those who were once separated." She paused, then swayed as though hearing music. "There is a grave danger. Something hunts you. You have thwarted them not once, but twice. They are more determined than ever to find you. Desperation makes them bold. You only have a handful of days before they are strong enough to hunt you once again."

Sabine forced her body to stay relaxed even though her heart pounded in her chest. This woman must be referring to the Wild Hunt or her family. Sabine waited, sensing the woman wasn't finished.

"I sense great power within you," Zaverza murmured, her

brow furrowing. "You have been touched by the gods, but their gift carries a great price."

Sabine swallowed and pulled away her hand, unwilling to allow this woman to continue. Some things were too dangerous to speak aloud, especially among strangers. "We have all been touched by the gods in some manner."

Zaverza's eyes were wide with fear as she urged, "You must find Pearl quickly and fulfill your agreement to the sea folk. If you fail to locate her by the deadline, our world shall be engulfed in flames and all those under your protection shall perish. She holds one of the keys!"

Sabine's brow furrowed, and she tried to ignore the cold chill that had taken root inside her. "What did you see?"

"The portal is failing," Zaverza whispered, wringing her gnarled hands together. "I saw the destruction of our world should that end come to pass. All will be lost if you don't find Pearl."

Icy tendrils of fear crept up Sabine's spine. If Malek hadn't expended most of his magic to fly the ship here, they might have missed their window to locate Pearl. Zaverza's words had offered some hope in stopping such a calamity from happening, but their recovery mission couldn't wait. They *needed* to find Pearl right away. It was no longer simply a matter of saving Esmelle and the others. More than her friend's life was at stake.

Sabine frowned. "Did you see where she was in the desert?"

Zaverza shook her head, her gray braids swinging from the movement. She reached over to touch Sabine's hand again and closed her eyes. "You must go to the inn to meet your companion. You will remain there only for tonight. Dance, sing, and make merry. Someone will approach you with an offer. Listen well and carefully. When they quit the city, you must travel with them. Only then might you find the one you seek."

When Zaverza opened her eyes, her shoulders were hunched and she appeared even older. The foretelling had taken a toll on her.

Sabine managed a weak smile, wishing she could ease the woman's pain. Healing had never been one of her gifts, or she'd be inclined to offer it now. "You have honored our bargain well, Zaverza. I will do as you have instructed."

"Good," Zaverza said and gestured toward her grand-daughter. "Help me up, child."

Rika jumped to her feet and helped her grandmother stand.

Zaverza patted her shoulder affectionately and said, "Have your uncle escort her to the inn. I must rest and then we shall prepare you for your travels. Time grows short, and we have much to do."

Without waiting for a response, Zaverza ambled out of the room, seeming to carry the weight of the world upon her hunched shoulders.

Sabine rubbed her arms to ward against the cold chill that had taken residence inside her. If the fate of their world truly rested upon locating Pearl, it was more vital than ever that she fulfill the Merfolk's request. Sabine hoped she was up to the task.

Chapter Nine

"And that's when I told him to get the hell off my docks!"

Malek chuckled at the dockmaster's story. Shorin was an older man, probably in his sixties, with graying hair and a long beard. He'd retired some years earlier from being a ship captain and had been running a successful business in Karga for the past ten years. Malek wasn't sure where Shorin was from originally, but he suspected it was one of the northern cities, maybe even Akros.

"I'm surprised you didn't push him off the docks for trying to cheat you," Malek said and leaned against the counter. "A swallow of seawater would have shut him up right quick."

"Thought about it," Shorin admitted aloud with a booming laugh. "But yer not here to listen to an old sailor's ramblings. What can I do for ye? I didn't see yer ship in the harbor."

"Right." Malek dropped a pouch onto the counter separating them. "I ran into a bit of bad luck myself. My ship was attacked, and we were forced to make landfall a few hours north. My crew's still with the ship, and they're fixing the damage as best they can. But we're going to need additional workers, treated lumber, and other supplies to make her seaworthy again."

Shorin opened the bag and dumped its contents onto the counter. Precious gems of all different sizes and colors spilled out. Shorin's eyes widened. He lifted one of them to the light and assessed it with a critical eye. "Aye, these'll do. I can send a few boys up to take a look. You'll need to pay extra for supplies."

"Of course," Malek agreed and pulled out a second pouch. "This should cover it, including pulling off a few more of your 'boys' from other jobs. We've got to be underway in a few days if we're going to beat the weather."

Shorin arched his brow. "Then yer sailin' south again for Razadon?"

Malek nodded. "The Merfolk hit us hard. I lost quite a bit of my cargo. If I'm going to recover from these losses, we need to make landfall there before the summer storms hit."

"I've often said the Merfolk are bad for business." Shorin picked up the second bag and looked inside. He let out a low whistle. "Bit more and you could buy a second ship. Shouldn't be a problem to have you outfitted and underway in a hurry. You've always paid your bills, boy. Hate to lose you if the 'Folk have it out for you."

Malek chuckled. "I'm not that generous, Shorin. One of my companions hails from the northern cities, and his features may give your boys a start. Make sure you send workers who won't balk at a bit of mixed magical blood.

Shorin snorted. "Aye. I've got a few who won't mind earning coin no matter what bilge rats you've got scampering below deck. You willing to take some advice from an old man?"

Malek paused, surprised by the offer. He didn't know

Shorin well, but the old sailor had taken a shine to him. "Of course. I'll gladly listen."

"Once yer done with repairs, turn your ship north. There's a strange wind shifting in the south. The crews that have docked here over the past few weeks have told some strange tales."

Malek froze, barely managing to keep his expression neutral. The portal was supposedly located in the lands to the south. He wasn't sure exactly where it was, but it shouldn't be too hard to find if the magic trickling out was gaining strength. "What sort of tales have you heard?"

Shorin stroked his gray beard. "Strange storms that turn the skies green. Lightning flashes without thunder. Animals suddenly moving north when they should be heading south. I expect they have the right of things." He tapped his finger against his nose. "Sailors always know when the winds are about to change."

Malek frowned. This wasn't good. If things were already deteriorating that much, they needed to hurry and locate the remaining artifacts. His research had indicated at least five relics had been used to seal the portal. They only had one of them in their possession, and Razadon was their only lead in discovering the location of the others.

Shorin leaned over the counter and whispered, "That's not all either. We're moving our burning festival up ahead of schedule. Sacrifices are due to keep the spirits calm."

Malek tried to ignore the sense of foreboding that filled him at the dockmaster's words. "It's that bad?"

"Aye. You'd best be gone before then. You know how Karga feels about outsiders. Took years before the Kiervan stopped followin' me around." The dockmaster spit on the ground. "I expect we'll have a larger number of sacrifices this year than we have in decades. Damn devils at work."

Malek nodded. "As soon as the ship is repaired, we'll be

departing. I appreciate your time and the warning. I wish you and your family good fortune, Shorin."

Shorin nodded and scooped the gems off the counter. While the former sailor locked them in a chest behind him, Malek headed out of the dockmaster's office.

He'd known Shorin for several years, but the fact the dockmaster had felt the need to offer warning was worrisome. Things must be dire if the city was moving up their festival. He'd always made pains to avoid Karga during that time of year. According to his schedule, they should have had at least another two months before they sealed the city. Keeping his pace even to avoid any suspicion, Malek headed back toward the inn to find Sabine.

Karga was intolerant to magic users, and Sabine could raise some eyebrows with her pointed ears and silver hair. Even though he found her glamoured appearance incredibly alluring, someone might decide her features could be a sign of the devil's magic. Here in the south, they were too close to the volcanic home of the demons. The residents had learned to be wary.

It had been more than a century since the demons had last attacked Karga and imprisoned some of their people, but their memories were long. The residents still sought out and destroyed anyone suspected of having magical ties. It didn't matter if their beliefs were founded. In their minds, any traits marking someone as different was a sign of demonic possession or some unholy pact with the demons.

Malek adjusted the bag over his shoulder, which contained a few other items he'd purchased in the marketplace. He'd hoped to do a bit more shopping to replenish his supplies, but they'd need to leave sooner than he'd anticipated. Hopefully, he'd be able to trade for additional items once they arrived in the dwarven city.

"Swears he saw a dragon flying near the city."

The conversation of several men caught Malek's attention, and he slowed his pace to listen.

"Tovi's been drinking again, eh?"

"No. He swears he saw a dragon. He's already told the Kiervan about it. If those damned demons don't destroy the city, then the cursed dragons will. We need to seal the city now and start the purge. These outsiders are a blight that will bring madness down upon all of us. It needs to be ripped out, stem and root."

One of them noticed Malek and nudged the man beside him. The group fell silent, and they turned their suspicious gazes upon Malek. He continued walking and avoided making direct eye contact, pretending he hadn't heard their conversation. Nothing good would come from a confrontation. If they were determined to place blame somewhere, a stranger walking through their city would suffice. It didn't matter they were right about a dragon flying overhead. Their fears and comments only incited him to quit the city sooner. It would destroy part of him to leave Levin behind, but he couldn't risk their mission by remaining too long. He and Levin had both understood some sacrifices might be necessary and they might lose their lives, but it didn't make the reality any easier.

Malek approached the inn and entered the courtyard in front of the building. Night had fallen, and the air had cooled quite a bit. A few people were lounging on cushions in the small outdoor area, sipping from large mugs of spiced wine or ale while they warmed themselves by the firepits. They were busy drinking and talking with their companions and paid him no attention. His shoulders relaxed a bit. These people were mostly outsiders like himself, but that didn't mean they'd be any friendlier than Karga's residents. By nature, sailors were a superstitious lot. They might not capture and torture him like the Kiervan would, but they'd cheerfully share a drink with him and then cut his throat while they robbed him blind. It was a cleaner death, but Malek had every intention of surviving this night.

The inn was different from many of the other buildings in the dock area. The sprawling structure stood two floors in height, with the second floor predominately for guests. It wasn't a large inn, but it was clean and inexpensive. No one would blink twice at a few more strangers who were staying there.

He stepped into the entry room and took a few moments for his eyes to adjust. Several lanterns were placed throughout the room, casting the glow from the firelight along the walls. Perfumed smoke rose from incense burners scattered around, which created a hazy effect. The room was already packed, which wasn't altogether surprising. Karga was a major port city, and most ship crews eventually made their way to the dockside inn. The drinks were inexpensive and potent, and the proprietor usually had the sort of entertainment that appealed to sailors who had been at sea and without companionship for far too long.

One of the entertainers currently performing was a buxom dark-haired woman who was gyrating her hips as she danced. Patrons called out encouragement and tossed coins on the raised floor at her feet. She worked the room like a master, occasionally stopping to wink or flirt with a particular customer, much to the amusement and appreciation of the rest of the inn.

Malek swept his gaze through the room, but he didn't see any sign of Sabine. It wasn't the sort of place he was thrilled with having her stay, but she'd proven to be more than adept at handling herself. If she could hold her own against a couple demons, these sailors didn't stand a chance.

After making his way through the crowded room, he approached the bartender, who was pouring a drink.

Leaning against the counter, Malek asked, "Did the woman I told you about arrive yet?"

"I sent her up already." The man jerked his head toward the stairs and waggled his eyebrows. "Nice woman you have there—exotic. You should see if she'll come down and dance. She'll make a nice bit of coin from this lot. Hell, you convince her to dance and I'll discount your room for the night."

"I'll keep that in mind," Malek said with a chuckle and headed toward the stairs. It was an intriguing thought, but he couldn't imagine Sabine performing for this drunken crew. The wooden stairs creaked under his feet, and he stepped aside to allow another guest to pass him who was headed in the opposite direction. The hallway smelled like stale smoke and sweat, and he debated whether he should have chosen a different place for the night. Even in Dax's tavern, Sabine's room had been better than this.

He located the door to the room he'd purchased for the night and tapped lightly. The door opened a moment later, and Malek froze. Sabine was standing in the doorway, the lantern light shining behind her and illuminating her figure through the thin material of her dress. Her silver hair was loose, tumbling over her shoulders in careless waves that he briefly imagined spilling over the bed. The blue color of her dress made her eyes even more striking, highlighting the lavender tones of her irises. In a word, she was exquisite. And he was well and truly screwed. He had no idea how he was going to keep his hands off her tonight when all he wanted was to take her to bed.

He scanned her up and down, his mouth suddenly dry. "I should have paid that merchant double. You're stunning."

Sabine laughed, her eyes dancing with amusement as she moved aside to allow him to enter. She closed the door behind him and moved toward the bed. Her dress clung to her curves more than he'd initially thought, and he nearly groaned at the sight. This was going to be impossible. He might need to sleep in the stables with the thontin. He doubted even Blossom's presence would deter his thoughts.

"Were you able to arrange for the ship repairs?"

Malek cleared his throat, needing a moment to comprehend her question. He dropped his bags onto the bed. "I did. The dockmaster's going to start working before dawn. I told him about our time restrictions and paid him handsomely for it. Unfortunately, I have some bad news."

Sabine frowned and sat on the edge of the bed. "What happened?"

"It looks like we're going to need to leave the city sooner than I'd planned," he said, catching sight of the open window. Blossom apparently hadn't returned yet. They'd need to keep their conversation quiet to avoid being overheard. Although, from the sounds of revelry coming from below, it was unlikely anyone would pay them much attention. "I overheard some people talking on my way here. Someone spotted a dragon outside the city. Not only that, but they've also moved up their burning festival sooner. I don't know exactly when, but we need to be gone before it happens."

Sabine nodded, trailing her fingers over the blankets. "I gathered as much."

"Oh?" He arched his brow, and she gave him a slight smile.

"Not about the dragon, although I can imagine he's quite fearsome," she teased and winked at him. "But Zaverza, the woman who runs the bathhouse, told me about the burning festival. Bane's suggestion about remaining behind with the ship was for the best." Her smile faded, and her expression became more serious. "I have some information about Pearl."

Malek regarded her with surprise. "I'm impressed. I wasn't expecting you to find anything out so quickly. What did you learn?"

Sabine stood and crossed the room to close the window. Once it had been fastened shut, she said, "Zaverza's a seer, one with the gift of foresight. In exchange for us taking her granddaughter away from the city, she agreed to tell me what she knew about Pearl. She claimed Pearl's been taken farther into the desert by raiders."

Malek frowned. "You agreed to take her granddaughter?"

Sabine nodded. "Yes. It was the only way. Rika's inherited her gifts, and Zaverza's worried she'll be executed by the Kiervan. Both of them swore a blood oath to me."

Malek rubbed the back of his neck. A blood oath was no small thing, and it was even rarer someone from Karga would ask for help from a stranger. It gave additional weight to the dockmaster's warning. Things in Karga must be reaching a crescendo if they were confiding in outsiders. "You trust this woman?"

"I do. Zaverza claims someone will find us at the inn tonight. She told me to 'dance, sing, and make merry.'" Sabine frowned and stared at the closed window. "I decided to wait for you before venturing downstairs."

"I'm not sure who we can expect to meet downstairs. Most of the patrons are dockside workers or sailors, but I suppose it's the only lead we have for now. I made a few discreet inquiries about meeting with a smuggler, but it may take a few days."

Sabine crossed the room toward him. "We can't afford to stay that long. I know we need supplies, but something strange is going on in this city. I'd feel better once we leave it behind."

"I agree. From what rumors the dockmaster's been over-hearing, the portal is failing even faster than I thought. If it comes down to it, I'll fly you and Bane down to the dwarven city and we'll retrieve my ship later."

Sabine paled. "You want to fly with us again?"

Malek winced. Her concern for his wellbeing and the way she'd touched him when he was in dragon form had made him hope she'd warmed up to the idea. "It's not ideal, but we might not have a choice. I'm not willing to risk anything happening to you. Everyone in this city is on edge. It's only going to get worse."

Sabine frowned and didn't answer. Deciding to change the subject, Malek opened the bag he'd brought. He'd spent more coin than he'd intended, but they'd hopefully recover most of it once they arrived in the dwarven city. He pulled out some toiletry items for Sabine and handed them to her. "After I left you at the bathhouse, I stopped by a few more stalls. I figured you'd need a brush, and I found some tea you might like. It's not the same as Esme's, but—"

Sabine's gaze softened. Closing the distance between them, she stood on her toes and kissed his cheek. "You've already done a great deal for me, Malek. This is a wonderful and extremely thoughtful gift. It means a great deal to me that you would do this."

He paused, his eyes roaming over her features. There was no doubt; he was falling for her, hard and fast. "I'd like to do a lot more for you if you'll allow it."

Malek reached up and tucked her loose hair behind her ear and trailed his fingers downward along her soft skin. "I like your hair loose like this."

"Hmm. I'll have to keep that in mind," Sabine said with a small smile. Clutching the items in her hand, she moved to the bedside table and then placed the items on top of it. The firelight once more danced along her skin and illuminated her figure, making it impossible for Malek to tear his eyes away from her. Her attire was more than a little distracting. It left very little to the imagination, and he was having a difficult time thinking about much else.

He cleared his throat and said, "I'm afraid we're going to

need to share the room. The inn doesn't have much space, but you can have the bed. I usually sleep on the ship when I come here, but we don't have a lot of options at the moment."

Sabine turned around, and her lips twitched in a smile. "I don't bite, Malek. We can share the bed. There's plenty of room."

He hesitated. If he didn't need Sabine's help to secure the remaining artifacts, he wouldn't give it a second thought. "I'm not sure that's a good idea. I don't quite trust myself around you."

She smiled, her eyes twinkling with amusement. "I'd say the feeling is mutual."

He arched his brow, wondering if he'd heard her correctly. She walked toward him, pressed her hand against his chest, and lightly kissed his lips. Unwilling to let the opportunity pass, he wrapped his arm around her waist and pulled her closer. He tasted a hint of spiced wine, but more potent and even more enticing was the taste of Sabine that lay underneath. She softened against him and he groaned, threading his fingers through the softness of her hair. This woman was going to drive him to the edge of all reason.

Sabine broke their kiss, and her hands curled into his shirt as she gazed up at him with passion-filled eyes. In a soft voice, she said, "If we don't go downstairs now, we won't make it down there."

"If Levin and Esme weren't depending on us, nothing could convince me to leave this room," he murmured, cupping her face. "I don't think I've ever wanted someone the way I want you."

"I'm starting to believe what's happening between us is inevitable," she murmured, still looking up at him. "I don't know if it's a good idea or not, but I want you too, Malek. Only... I'm not sure how safe we are here." She paused, and her eyes filled with regret. "These people are actively trying to destroy anyone who's not human. I'm very good at hiding who I am, but I'm not sure I'll be able to keep my magic suppressed when we're intimate. Something about you calls to my power. I can try, but I can't make any promises."

He grimaced and forced himself to release her. Running a hand over his head in agitation, he said, "You're right. I wish you weren't, but the only thing that's kept me from responding to your power is this warding medallion. You have no idea how tempting you are."

"The same could be said for you, Captain." Sabine walked back to the window and unlatched it. Pushing it open, she sighed and said, "I suppose it's time to sing, dance, and make merry. Shall we?"

He nodded and offered her his arm. "I just hope I don't have to kill anyone once we go down there. None of their usual entertainment holds a candle to you, my dear. Your presence is going to create quite a stir."

She smiled mischievously. "Oh, you have no idea. Have you ever seen a Fae dance, Malek?"

He paused, suddenly wary. "No, why?"

She laughed and slipped her arm through his. "Come along, Captain. You're about to find out."

SABINE SAT at an empty table while Malek went to order some drinks. Her nerves were a tangled mess, and it was unlikely even a strong drink would help settle them. Bane's words kept replaying in her head, and she knew the demon was right. The smart thing to do would be to use Malek's emotions and attraction as a catalyst to bind him to her.

But she had no intention of being smart, especially not where Malek was concerned. She admired and respected him far too much to use him in such a manner. No. Whatever was happening between them was something else entirely, and she wouldn't sully it by misusing him. In Malek, she'd found a glimmer of hope she might find some happiness away from Faerie. Life wasn't just about duty and survival. She wasn't willing to give up on the possibility of something more just to secure a throne.

Malek leaned against the counter, chatting to the bartender while he poured the drinks. Her eyes drank in his powerful physique and the way his dark hair accentuated his golden skin. She had to force herself to take a steadying breath and remember their purpose. Gods. She was a mess. It was only a matter of time before they ended up in bed together, and she still wasn't sure about the consequences of that decision.

Normally, the Fae didn't think twice about such intimacy. She'd never given much thought to her relationship with Dax. He hadn't either. It had started as a training exercise, one designed to ensure her magic wouldn't falter unless she allowed it. Dax had been good in that regard, always challenging her beyond what she believed was possible. He'd forced her to become more disciplined, but he'd never fostered any of the softer emotions Malek evoked.

She didn't trust herself with Malek. The few times they'd come close to being intimate or she'd felt his power trailing along her skin, it had threatened her tight control. She worried that once they crossed the line, she'd never be able to keep her heart separate. As it was, she was already losing the battle.

Sabine sighed and tried to push away these distracting thoughts. She needed to focus on their purpose instead of her attraction to the charming and enigmatic dragon.

A few women were dancing, and Sabine studied them to gauge the customers' reactions and the skill level of the musicians. Even with her magic locked down, a Fae dancing could be extremely provocative. There was power in movement and song, especially when combined by a Fae. She'd need to be careful not to betray herself. Even someone of mixed heritage would be regarded with suspicion in Karga.

"You look like you could use some company," a man said in a slur, bumping into her table. "Lemme buy you a drink."

Sabine arched her eyebrow and mentally kicked herself for being so distracted. It had been a long time since someone, even a drunk, had thought to proposition her. Back in Akros, Dax had always made it clear she was off limits. Even if he hadn't, she'd never been shy about discouraging unwanted advances.

Before she could send him away, Malek placed two glasses and a bowl of food on the table and said, "Keep walking, stranger. The lady's taken."

The man wavered, looking Malek up and down as though taking his measure. Sabine bit back a smile, watching as Malek's eyes narrowed on the drunk who hadn't moved.

Taking a threatening step toward the man, Malek slapped his hand against his weapon and said in a low voice, "Do you need me to make it clearer? Move along and leave the lady alone. Now."

"Imma goin'." The man held up his hands in defeat. Without waiting for a response, he belched loudly and moved away in the direction of another woman.

Resting her head on her hands, Sabine asked, "What made you think I wasn't interested in his offer?"

Malek looked so bewildered by the possibility, she couldn't help but laugh. Patting the seat next to her, she said, "I suppose you'll have to entertain me instead."

Malek slid into the seat beside her. "Far be it for me to stand in the way of true love. I can always call him back."

Sabine wrinkled her nose. "That's all right. I'm just glad I couldn't smell him over the incense. I'd much prefer your company over his."

"That's a relief." Malek passed her one of the glasses. Draping his arm across the back of her chair, he said, "I ordered you some spiced wine. The bartender says it's popular. If it's not to your taste, they also have dwarven ale." He pointed at the bowl filled with flat bread pieces topped with small balls of meat. "Those are kavastya. I've had them before, and you won't find their equal."

Sabine smiled and took a bite. They were spicier than she'd expected, but the breading helped offset the burn. She took a sip of her drink and settled back in her chair. "They're both very good. I think this wine is even better than the glass I had earlier at the bathhouse."

"Good. I'm glad you like it." Malek's thumb absently trailed over her shoulder, but she noticed he was paying more attention to the room.

"You look worried," she said and swirled the wine in her glass.

"Sailors tend to be a rough lot, and we're trying to keep a low profile. You're attracting quite a bit of attention just sitting here." Malek glanced at her and picked up his glass to take a drink. "I spoke with the bartender. He says he'll discount the room if you're going to dance. The man was practically tripping over himself when I mentioned you were interested. Are you sure you want to do this?"

Sabine nodded. "Yes. Zaverza wouldn't have suggested it if it wasn't necessary, but I'll need you to warn me if I'm betraying myself. It's easy to get lost in the moment."

He frowned and swiped his thumb over his chin. "Is that gesture too subtle?"

"No. It's perfect," she said and took another drink. "I have no idea how long it'll take for the person we're waiting for to make contact, but I'll only be able to dance for one or two songs. Any more than that, and we may run into a problem."

"You have me intrigued," he murmured.

Sabine leaned closer to him and whispered, "Our emotions and desires are closer to the surface when we dance. That's why I need a warning, especially if I'm going to be keeping my eyes on you. One day soon and when we're away from here, I'll give you a private dance. Then you'll understand... everything."

Malek put down his glass. "That tears it. We're leaving at dawn. Hell, we could even leave tonight."

Sabine laughed and finished off her wine. The musicians were finishing their song, and it would be her turn next. She stood and made her way toward the musicians, adding a little extra swing to her hips. She could feel the eyes of more than a few people on her, but Malek was the only one she was going to be dancing for.

Two musicians were seated near a stage area at the front of the room. One of them was tuning a small handheld stringed instrument that resembled a lyre, while the other had a drum sitting at his feet.

Sabine smiled at them and asked, "Do you take requests?"

"Aye, if yer the one asking," the man with the lyre agreed. "What did ya have in mind?"

"Know anything northern? Maybe a ballad?"

The man grinned. "Not sure this lot will appreciate them, but we know a few. How about 'Memories of a Dream'?"

Sabine smiled at the irony, remembering the cup of magical wine she'd shared with Malek. "Perfect. Afterward, can you switch to something a bit livelier?"

"No problem, pretty lady. I'm Ryley, by the way. The drummer there is Kobin."

"A pleasure," she said, nodding at them both in greeting. "I'm Sabine."

"Pleasure meeting you," Ryley said and tipped his hat. "Good luck, not that you'll need it. Half these boys are already in their cups. You'll either wake them up or drown them. Not sure which will be more of an improvement."

Sabine grinned. The woman who had just finished dancing climbed off the stage and asked, "That your man in the corner?"

Sabine glanced at where Malek was sitting. "Not yet, but he will be soon."

"Lucky girl," the woman muttered and headed to the bar.

Sabine took her place in the center of the raised floor area and turned around to face the audience. In some ways, the inn reminded her of Dax's tavern. There was a camaraderie here which immediately set her at ease. These sailors and other individuals might be rough around the edges but no more so than anyone in Dax's crew.

She locked eyes with Malek. He lifted his cup in a silent salute, and she winked at him. He chuckled and took a long drink. Sabine glanced at Ryley and gave him a nod. He immediately started into a rendition of the ballad made famous after the portal had been sealed.

She lowered her head and closed her eyes, allowing the music to fill her and caress her soul. Focusing on the confusing emotions she felt whenever she was around Malek, she enfolded each note with her magic, keeping it contained within her glamour. Lifting her arms, she opened her eyes and held Malek's gaze.

The musician sang of a time long past, of love and betrayal, and of secrets and mysteries. She moved effortlessly, using her body to enhance the emotions of the song. Her eyes always went back toward Malek, whose hungry gaze hadn't wavered. The thin material of her dress nearly shimmered in the firelight, emphasizing her movements even more. As she danced, she threaded her desire for Malek into each of her gestures, telling him without words how much she wanted him.

When the musician came to the chorus, she raised her voice to join him.

"'Twas but a memory of a dream.
Of life and love, I nearly lost.
But for you, my love, I shall always remain,
A dream within a memory."

A hushed stillness fell over the audience when the musician played his last note. As one, the customers began pounding their mugs on the tables. Coins were thrown on the stage at Sabine's feet. Shouts filled the air as they demanded more.

Sabine tossed her hair back when the musicians began playing a fast-paced song she wasn't familiar with. Based on the audience's cheers and awkward accompaniment, they knew this song well. It was easy to see why it appealed to them. It was a catchy tune, and she smiled as she raised her arms and swung her hips.

A few of the patrons whistled loudly, and she gave them a teasing smile as she danced upon the stage. By the time the song finished, most of the audience was on their feet. Out of breath and oddly exhilarated, Sabine stepped off the stage and was swept up in Malek's arms.

He crushed his lips against hers and thrust his hand in her hair. Undeniable need filled her, and she curled her hands into his shirt. Returning his kiss with equal fervor, her magic surged to the surface. He abruptly broke their kiss, and she blinked up at him. Pressing his forehead against hers, he gripped her hips tightly and didn't release her.

Out of breath, her heart pounded as she gazed up at him. "Malek?"

"Give me a moment," he whispered, his voice ragged as though speaking had cost him a great deal. Sabine pressed her hands against his chest, feeling the warmth of his skin under the thin material of his shirt and his heart beating as fast as hers. In truth, she needed a moment too. She'd nearly revealed herself with just that kiss.

Dimly, she became aware they were standing in front of the musicians. Malek released her, but he wrapped his arm around her waist in a gesture that was far more intimate than their actual relationship. He'd made his point. No one was approaching her, even though more than a few were watching her with frank appraisal.

Oddly touched, she smiled up at him. "Claiming me, are you?"

"Not yet, but I intend to."

A small thrill rushed through her at his words, but it also left her disconcerted. She'd meant her comment innocently, but the predatory look in his eyes made her wonder if she'd pushed him too far. He was a dragon, and she couldn't afford to forget their nature was to hoard valuable items and treasures. He couldn't claim her, not in the manner he was speaking. No matter what transpired between them, she would never belong to him.

"The gods must have been smiling down on me the day you decided to come to this inn," Ryley said, putting his instrument to the side and getting to his feet.

The mark of the goddess on her wrist warmed, and she pressed it against her leg in a silent entreaty to calm. The warmth faded a moment later, but it had effectively cleared her head of Malek's confusing presence.

Sabine smiled at Ryley and gestured at the coins littering the stage. "Without your talents, my dance never would have been so rewarded. It's only fair to share the profits. Will you divide up the portions among the three of us?"

Ryley's smile widened, and he exchanged a glance with the other musician. When the drummer jumped up and began collecting the coins, Ryley turned back to her. "You honor us with your generosity. Most people wouldn't have even considered it. You've got a rare talent, but I expect you come by it honestly." He gestured at her pointed ears. "Last person I met with features similar to yours was also gifted but not nearly as skilled. Have you ever considered performing with a troupe?"

Sabine paused and considered Ryley thoughtfully. This conversation must be the reason Zaverza had encouraged her to sing and dance. Most of the other patrons were sailors or dockside workers. If Pearl had headed to the desert, perhaps this troupe could lead her there.

Deciding to play along, she said, "You're very kind. I can't say I've ever thought about it. Are you part of such a group?"

Ryley glanced around to make sure no was close enough to hear them. Leaning in, he said, "Kobin and I have been part of a traveling troupe for the past few years. The rest of our group is camped outside the city walls. Like yourself, many of them also come from mixed heritages. Karga's changing, and in a bad way. It's been getting even worse over the past few years. It's not safe for someone like you."

Malek frowned, his arm tightening around her waist. "This is Sabine's first time here, but I've been docking in Karga for a couple years. I've also noticed a change, more so during our current visit."

"Aye," Ryley said in agreement, rubbing his chin. "I don't say what I'm about to lightly. Normally we all have to vote on this sort of thing, but I'm not willing to let a talent like yours slip through my fingers. My group's leaving in the morning. If you're looking to earn a bit of coin, you have a spot with us. We can also offer you a bit of protection if you're planning on doing any traveling."

Sabine hesitated. She wasn't sure about traveling with a

group of unknown people into unfamiliar territory, but she was desperate to find Pearl. "Where are you heading?"

"Thought we might head south or east." Ryley shrugged as though to say it didn't matter. "Some of the desert tribes pay in meals for our performances, but the biggest profit is from the cities. There are a few larger cities between here and Razadon where you can earn quite a bit."

Sabine frowned. "Your offer is generous. I'm assuming you have room for both of us?"

Ryley assessed Malek, his eyes lingering on Malek's weapons. "You know how to use those?"

"I do."

"Good." Ryley gave him a curt nod. "We can always use another guard on the road. It helps discourage bandits. Besides, you may need them to keep people in line if she keeps performing like that."

Kobin brought over the coins he'd collected. He divided them up and gave both her and Ryley a portion.

Ryley slipped his coins into his belt pouch and dipped his hat to her. "We're leaving from the south gate at sunrise. If you're there, I'll assume you're interested in joining us. Otherwise, good fortune to you both."

Sabine smiled. "To you both as well."

Malek said good-bye and led her back toward the stairs. In a quiet voice, he said, "Well, in addition to getting a free room for the night, at least we now have a plan."

Gripping the aged railing, she began climbing the stairs. "Then we're both in agreement? We leave in the morning to travel with this troupe?"

"It's our best lead, and it'll get both of us out of this city. There's no guarantee the smugglers will even stick around once word gets out that they're moving up the festival." Malek put his hand against her lower back as they headed down the hallway to their room. He unlocked it with a heavy metal key and stepped aside so she could enter. "If we're going to be up before the sun, we should probably get some rest."

Sabine nodded and scanned the room, but Blossom hadn't yet returned. They still had some time before the pixie was scheduled to come back. After walking to the nightstand, she adjusted the crystalline lantern to give them a little extra light. She picked up the small container of tea Malek had purchased for her and inhaled the dried herbal blend. It was such a thoughtful gift, made even more precious because it had been given without any expectations. Dax had usually only given her gifts when he had wanted her forgiveness for some transgression.

She picked up the tea and toiletry items and placed them in her bag. She glanced over at Malek, but he was focused on organizing the contents of his bags. While they'd been on his ship, she'd had the opportunity to observe him unaware quite a bit, but never in such an intimate setting. Malek always moved with a quiet competency, confident in his abilities and his strength. It was apparent even now as he systematically sorted through the items and repacked them.

His dark hair was tied back at the nape of his neck, but a few loose strands had escaped. She longed to brush them back, exploring the strong lines of his jaw and then the rest of his body. From the brief glimpse she'd already had, the full package promised to be every bit as delicious as the rest. Gods. She wanted him more than she'd ever wanted anyone.

As though sensing her silent observation, Malek lifted his head. Something in her face must have given him an insight into the direction of her thoughts because he said, "If you keep looking at me like that, I can't be held responsible for my actions. We won't leave this room again before morning."

She tilted her head and gave him a teasing smile. "Did you have some place else you'd rather be?"

His mouth curved upward, and he crossed the room toward her. Without waiting for a response, he wrapped his arm around her and yanked her against him. His head lowered, and he claimed her with his mouth. Running her hands down his chest and then up under his shirt to touch his heated bare skin, she showed him with her kiss how much she wanted him.

This brief taste of him wasn't going to be enough. She'd held back for too long, and the emotions she'd channeled with her dance downstairs had only flamed her desire even hotter. She gripped the edge of his shirt, then pushed it upward in a silent demand. He yanked it over his head, tossed it aside, and eased her back onto the bed. His heavier weight pressed her to the mattress, and he ran his hand up her leg under the hem of her dress.

His hand was hot against her cooler skin, and he accompanied it with a teasing brush of his magic. She trembled, and her skin pebbled as goose bumps broke out on her skin. The thought of having him touch her everywhere was more erotic than anything she'd ever imagined.

Undeterred and desperate for more, she hooked her leg over his and rolled over so she was straddling him. He gripped her hips, staring up at her with a predatory gaze. She smiled down at him and pressed her hands against his chest. For now, she intended to be the predator, and he was her prey.

She leaned down to nip at his lower lip and asked, "Does this count as riding a dragon?"

He chuckled, his hands tightening on her hips. "I'd say it does."

She kissed him again, tasting a hint of the spiced wine on his lips. The light and alluring smoky scent she'd begun to attribute with Malek filled her nose, and she breathed him in, wanting to memorize this moment. His hands moved up to her waist, and he unhooked the metallic rings of her belt. He started to change their positions, but she sat up and pressed her hands against his chest to keep him down.

Running her hands over his bare chest, she sent a brush of her magic along his skin. "On my terms, or I'll lose control."

"Sweetheart, if you aren't losing control, I'm not doing this right."

Sabine laughed. "You enjoy playing dangerously, don't you?"

"With you? Absolutely," he murmured, unlacing the front of her dress before she'd even had a chance to register his words. If he had his way, he'd distract her completely, and she wasn't willing to relinquish her advantageous position.

"You're wearing too many clothes," she said, deftly unfastening his pants so she could see all of him. Moving down his body, she explored the hard ridges and lean contours of his physique with her hands and mouth. He tasted and smelled incredible, like spicy wood smoke or some other exotic spice she couldn't name. And as she suspected, he was magnificent all over.

Malek sat up abruptly, then hauled her up his body and kissed her like she was the air he needed to survive. She clung to him as he deepened their kiss, wanting everything he offered.

He rolled over with her and pressed her against the bed. Gazing down at her, he asked, "I want to see you—the real you. Will you remove your glamour?"

Unable to refuse, she nodded and slowly released the illusion hiding her identity. Her magic started to surge to the surface, but she forced it back down. Malek's gaze roamed over her as he drank in her image. "You're so beautiful, Sabine. I can't tell you how long I've imagined seeing you like this."

"Malek," she whispered, feeling uncertain for the first time. Without the pain of her glamour in place, this intimacy was even more dangerous. She wasn't sure she could do this without losing control.

He cupped her face, trailing his thumb over her cheek, and kissed her lightly. "Will you trust me?"

She hesitated and then nodded. "Yes, but I'm not sure I trust myself."

His mouth curved upward, and he kissed her again. "I can hide your magic if necessary, but I've been wanting you for far too long not to touch you. We'll go slowly and stop if the magic between us builds too much."

She relaxed slightly. Malek removed the warding medallion and pulled her closer. Lowering the neckline of her dress past her shoulders, he kissed her collarbone and then traced the pattern of the magical etchings on her skin. He treated every inch of her like she was something precious, kissing and nibbling along her skin as he explored her body with expert hands.

He lowered his head and took her breast in his mouth, and she gasped at the erotic rush of heat that strummed through her body. She threaded her fingers through his hair and squeezed her eyes shut, unable to do anything but ride the waves of pleasure he sent through her. Her hands clenched the bedding and she thrashed, blinded with ecstasy as he continued to send surges of pleasure through her with his draconic power.

Sabine responded in kind with her magic, wanting to bring him to the same heights he was taking her. It worked. The rest of their clothing and weapons disappeared, and she ran her hands over the hard lines of his body, wanting to touch every inch of him. When he finally slid inside her, she whimpered and threw her head back, needing more. He was everywhere all at once, inside and outside. Her heart pounded in time with his as the passion between them became explosive.

He grabbed her hands and held them over her head as he brought her to heights she'd never imagined were possible. Needing more, she incited him, using her magic to touch him as intimately as he was touching her.

"Please, Malek!" she cried, unable to think beyond the sensations. Her skin glowed as he pushed her to even greater heights, and he enfolded her in his power. The pace he set was consuming. She couldn't stop. Her magic was fused to him, and his to her. She couldn't tell anymore where he began and where she ended. They were one: one body, one heart, one purpose. The mark on his wrist pulsed in time with their racing hearts and her marks of power, one more indicator they were irrevocably entwined.

"Sabine, with me!" he shouted, continuing to drive into her at a relentless pace.

She screamed his name as he destroyed the last of her barriers, fracturing her thoughts and overwhelming her senses. His head dropped onto her shoulder, and he held her tightly against him. Struggling to catch her breath, she couldn't even form a coherent thought, much less speak. He'd completely destroyed her.

He rolled over, taking her with him. She sprawled across his chest, too shattered to protest even if she'd wanted to. They lay like that for a long time, neither able to speak.

Normally, intimacy was a way for the Fae to renew or gift their magic, but Malek hadn't used her for her power. The idea left her strangely disconcerted. Dax had always siphoned off her magic when it surged to the surface, but Malek offered her a balance of mutually sharing power. For the first time in her life, she had a glimmer of what had been missing in her life.

Malek trailed his hand down her naked back and

murmured, "I don't think I ever want to let you leave this bed."

Sabine made a noise of agreement. She kissed his chest and lifted her head to gaze down at him. "Why didn't you take any of my magic?"

Malek arched his brow and frowned. He reached up to tuck her hair behind her ear and asked, "You thought I would?"

Sabine hesitated and then nodded. "I've never done this without gifting power."

His brow furrowed. "I would never take your magic, Sabine. You need it."

Her heart melted at his words. Pressing her hand against his chest, she kissed him deeply, putting everything she was feeling into the gesture.

When she eased back, he cupped her face and murmured, "If you kiss me again like that, we'll miss joining that troupe in the morning."

She smiled and trailed her fingers along his well-defined chest. Part of her was in complete agreement; she never wanted to leave this bed. She couldn't remember the last time she'd felt so safe and treasured. It was strange to think a dragon had been responsible for this new awakening.

"Oops!"

Sabine turned to see Blossom had flown inside the room. The pixie was grinning widely, not the least bit troubled by what she'd walked—or rather flown—into. Blossom clapped her hands in delight and exclaimed, "I knew it! I knew you were going to take him as your lover!"

Malek grimaced. "So much for knocking before entering. I suppose we should have closed the window."

Sabine laughed, reapplied her glamour, and kissed Malek lightly. "Her timing could have been worse. Next time, we'll lock the doors *and* windows."

"As long as there's a next time." Malek chuckled and continued to trail his hand up and down her back, completely unabashed by their nudity. She'd been around humans for too long, and his nonchalance was refreshing.

Blossom landed on the edge of the bed, her gaze darting back and forth between them. "I saw you dance and sing, Sabine. I've never seen you dance before!"

"I should have known your timing wasn't a coincidence," Sabine said and climbed out of bed. She walked to the window and latched it. The night air was cooling considerably.

Turning back toward Blossom, Sabine picked up her discarded dress and asked, "I didn't notice your presence downstairs. Is your glamour getting better?"

Blossom grinned. "Nah. It's only because you were too busy watching Malek."

"I was watching him so he could warn me about my magic," Sabine said with a laugh. "I'm glad you're back. I was starting to get concerned."

Blossom's smile faded, and her expression became worried. "I think we should leave right away. This is a bad place. They'll try to hurt you if they find you."

Sabine's hands tightened on her dress, and she sat on the edge of the bed. "What did you learn?"

"I listened in on the Kiervan. They're getting ready to start the burning festival. It's bad, Sabine. Really bad. You can't be here for it."

"We heard they were moving the festival sooner," Malek said, picking up his discarded clothing and then walking to the window to peer outside. "We're planning on leaving before they seal the city."

Blossom shook her head. "You can't wait. You have to leave now. Tonight."

Sabine frowned and started to dress. Blossom had a

tendency to overdramatize certain things, but her dust was tinged with red, a sign of stress. "What exactly did you hear?"

Blossom flew to the nightstand where Sabine had placed the decorative box. She'd packed the rest of her belongings, but she'd decided to leave the box for Blossom to sleep in that night. It was still lined with the flowers Sabine had cut from the desert.

Blossom picked up one of the flowers and buried her nose in the petals. Sabine waited, knowing the pixie needed a few moments to collect her thoughts. Whenever pixies were stressed, they always retreated to nature. There might be some plant life in Karga and the desert, but it was all foreign and lacked the same reassuring qualities of their homeland.

After taking the opportunity to finish equipping her weapons and Ilwan's necklace, Sabine glanced up to see that Malek had done the same. He nodded toward Blossom with a question in his eyes. She held up her hand and shook her head in a silent request for him to wait. Some things couldn't be rushed. Pixies were resilient, but this entire journey had been taxing on Blossom. Malek nodded in understanding and turned back toward the window.

"They burn people alive, Sabine. Young, old, babies... It doesn't matter to them. They were laughing and cheering about it." Her wings drooped. "They have a special dwarven crystal that can detect magic users. They're going to use it for the first time this year."

Sabine's eyes narrowed. "*That* is why they refer to it as a burning festival? They're burning them alive?"

Blossom clasped her hands together. "The Kiervan are going to kill a bunch of people. They were testing it out on a few people tonight. I had to leave because I didn't know if it would detect pixies."

Furious, Sabine paced the room. "This is outrageous. Magic has always been present in our world. If they think to destroy it, they'll further weaken the balance. I'll destroy the Kiervan outright before I allow this to come to pass."

"Hey," Malek interrupted, grasping her shoulders to stop her. "What they're doing is wrong, but we run the risk of getting caught up in their politics if we intervene. I don't want to see anyone die either, but how many more will die if that portal opens again? We need to find those artifacts."

"I will *not* sit by and allow them to murder innocents."

Malek studied her for a long time and then nodded. "All right, but we'll need to be covert in our efforts." Turning back toward Blossom, he asked, "How many crystals are there?"

Blossom's eyes widened, her gaze darting back and forth between them. "Just the one, but it's bigger than me. Are you really going to stop them?"

Malek nodded. "At the very least, we'll destroy the crystal so they can't use it against these people. Do you know where it's located?"

Sabine paused, staring at Malek in surprise. "You're willing to help me destroy the crystal?"

Malek's gaze softened. He reached and tucked her hair behind her ear. "Your desire to protect people is one of the things I admire most about you, Sabine. You're loyal and fierce, with a passion that's inspiring. I saw it the first time we met when you offered that kid a chance for a better future."

Her heart melted at his words. She wound her arms around his neck and kissed him. All the emotion she poured into her dance downstairs surged within her. Malek wrapped his arms around her, drawing her close as he returned her kiss.

Gratitude and desire rushed through her in equal measure. Bane and Dax had never understood her determination to protect the innocents in Akros. They would have agreed to help with the crystal, but only because they'd likely find it entertaining to cause mayhem. Yet here was a man who was willing to stand by her side, not because it might benefit him in some way but because he had a good heart.

Running her hands down his chest, she continued kissing him, telling him without words everything she was feeling. Malek's kiss became more demanding, and she responded with equal passion. She needed this dragon and everything he offered. He was her balance in so many ways. She'd been blind to it before, clouded by the terrifying stories of her youth.

Blossom giggled, interrupting the moment.

Sabine ended their kiss and smiled up at Malek. "It's been a long time since I trusted someone to stand by my side simply because it's the right thing to do. I can't tell you how much it means to me."

He cupped her face and kissed her again, this time a light pressure against her lips. "You can always trust me."

Sabine turned back toward Blossom and asked, "You know where they're keeping the crystal?"

Blossom perked up and nodded. "Yep. It's in the Kiervan's headquarters. It's going to be hard getting close to it. You can't use the shadows to hide. It will probably detect you. Dwarven magic is tricky like that."

"What color is the crystal?" Malek released Sabine and walked to one of the bags he'd brought containing additional weapons.

"It's purple."

Sabine frowned, trying to remember everything she'd learned about the dwarves and their magic. "Their crystals are naturally clear when they're dormant, but they infuse magic into each of them. Each color denotes a different characteristic."

Malek nodded. "They use the red ones for offense. It's what we use on our lances on the ship."

Sabine sat back down on the bed. "Have you seen purple ones before?"

"Yes. In Razadon. They act as a warning system or alarm. They're attached to the entrance of the city and also over the gates to the different quarters. They glow purple and also make a strange wailing noise when magic users get too close."

Sabine considered him for a long time and then stood. "Did you ever set them off?"

Malek shook his head and gestured at the medallion around his neck. "No, but I was always wearing this. The rest of my abilities are a physical manifestation of my nature."

She reached up and ran her fingertips over his metal necklace. It was cool to the touch, but it had likely been calibrated specifically to Malek's type of magic. "I don't think either one of us could get close enough to destroy the crystal without being detected. Together, we might have a chance. It won't stop this burning festival, but it may help protect some innocents."

Malek nodded. "Let's pack up the rest of our belongings first. They'll seal the city once they discover it's been destroyed, and we need to escape without raising any suspicion."

Chapter Ten

Sabine walked beside Malek down the darkened streets of Karga. At this late hour, they were mostly deserted. An oppressive weight fell over the city as though even the buildings held their breath against the future threat of violence. Sabine shivered, both from the chill in the air and from the sense of foreboding that filled her.

"You're cold?" Malek asked with a frown.

"I'll warm up soon enough," she said quietly, recognizing the street they were on. "We need to make a stop."

Without waiting for a response, she walked up to the door of the bathhouse and knocked loudly. Blossom hugged her neck and said, "This is where you came earlier, right?"

Sabine nodded, dimly hearing movement from the other side. She took a step back just as the door opened.

Zaverza held up a lantern and frowned, glancing back and forth between her and Malek. "You're back already? Did you not meet up with the person who would take you to your friend?"

Sabine shook her head. She didn't want to alarm the elderly woman, but there wasn't any good way to share her news. "You were true to your word, Zaverza. We've made arrangements to leave in the morning. I need to speak with you about a related matter, and I'm afraid this won't wait. May we come in?"

Zaverza's frowned deepened, and she stepped aside to allow them to enter. "Men are not permitted into the bathhouse by Karga law, but we may talk in this chamber or I can take you to our living quarters."

"That's not necessary. We won't be staying long. Is your son here, or is there a place we can speak privately?"

"My son is out for the evening. He will not return until the morning. You may speak freely."

"Grandmother? Is everything okay?" a girl's voice asked from another doorway.

Sabine smiled at the young girl she'd agreed to take on as her charge. "Rika, this concerns you too. Please come in here for a moment."

Rika moved closer into the firelight, and Sabine gestured toward Malek. "This is Malek, the captain of the ship I was telling you about. You can trust him just like you'd trust me."

Rika gave him a shy smile. "Well met, Captain Malek."

"You as well," Malek said gently. "I'm looking forward to having you travel on our ship."

Rika blushed, obviously charmed by Malek.

Sabine glanced at him and asked, "Do you have a coin or other piece of metal you won't miss?"

His brow furrowed, but he nodded and withdrew a pouch. He pulled out a coin and handed it to her. Using a trace of her magic, she quickly transmuted the metal into wood and then traced her initial into it. When she was finished, she handed it to Rika.

The girl's eyes widened. "You changed it. It was silver, but now it's not. I didn't know you could do that."

Sabine nodded. "Yes. I have an affinity for nature, but we

can discuss more of that later. I need you both to do something very important for me."

Zaverza's face turned ashen, and she wrapped her arm around her granddaughter's shoulders. "What's brought you here to do magic in the middle of the night? The Kiervan have been watching everyone closely."

"I know, and it's why I've come. You both need to leave the city immediately. We learned they're planning to use a dwarven talisman to seek out magic for this next burning festival."

Zaverza inhaled sharply. "What are the fools thinking? The Kiervan are sworn to destroy any source of magic, yet they are willing to employ the same? This is a blatant disregard for our oldest laws."

Rika looked up at her grandmother. "They'll discover both of us."

"Hush, child," Zaverza said sternly. "Sabine wouldn't have come here to warn us if there wasn't any hope."

Sabine nodded. "Your grandmother's right. There's a way out, but you both must act quickly."

"What would you have us do?"

Gesturing at the coin, Sabine said, "Take that and the stick I gave you to Malek's ship. It's a few hours north of the city. There's a demon overseeing the crew and repairs. You need to give him both of those items and relay a message for me."

Zaverza inhaled sharply and made the sign to ward against evil. Rika's eyes widened in fear, and she clung to her grandmother.

Sabine straightened, and she snapped, "Enough. Both of you. If you want to survive, you'll put aside the foolish superstition that's plaguing your city. You more than anyone know how destructive such practices can be."

Zaverza's eyes narrowed, but she didn't argue.

Sabine sighed. Rubbing her temples to stave off her headache, she said, "The night grows short, and we have much to do. You need to give that coin to Bane so he'll know you're acting on my behalf. You have my sworn oath he won't harm you."

Rika's hand closed over the coin. "Truly? A demon that won't hurt me?"

Sabine nodded. "Bane has been my protector and friend for many years. Demons aren't inherently evil. They're just different. But I need you to give him an important message for me."

Rika bit her lip. "What—what do you want me to tell him?"

"Let him know Malek and I found a lead on Pearl. We're leaving the city at first light and heading out the south gate. If he needs to find me, tell him to avoid the city at all costs."

"The badlands are to the south," Zaverza said, clutching her shawl around her tighter. "You will not survive the desert without a guide."

"We have one," Sabine said, dismissing her concerns. Even if they didn't have a guide, she'd still risk traversing the badlands in the hopes of locating Pearl. "It's very important you show him the stick and the coin. With the stick I gave you earlier, he'll protect you. With the coin, he'll know you carry an important message. Will you do this for me?"

"I swear it," Rika said, straightening her shoulders. "Should I leave tomorrow too?"

Sabine hesitated and turned her head. "Blossom, do you know when they're going to start the purge?"

Blossom peeked out from her hair. "Tomorrow or the next day."

Zaverza gasped. "A fairy!"

Rika's eyes widened, and she said, "She's so pretty. She almost looks like a miniature version of you."

Blossom grinned and tugged on Sabine's hair. "Did you hear, Sabine? She said I'm pretty! And they think I'm like you!"

Sabine smiled and said, "Zaverza and Rika, I'd like you to meet my dear friend Blossom. She's actually a pixie, and one of the most loyal and treasured companions you could ever hope to have."

Blossom trilled happily at Sabine's words. Rika took a step closer, staring at Blossom with wonder. All her earlier fear was gone, and Sabine was tempted to send Blossom with the girl for her first meeting with Bane. She'd forgotten how easily humans were charmed by pixies. Unfortunately, she'd need to keep Blossom with her. The pixie had talents Sabine couldn't hope to duplicate.

Blossom fluttered off Sabine's shoulder. Sabine reached out and took Rika's hand, then opened it so Blossom could land on the girl's palm.

Rika grinned and said, "I thought pixies were just stories."

"There's always some truth in every story. Once we're back on the ship, you two can have a chance to get to know each other better."

Blossom beamed a smile at Rika. "You're going to like meeting Esme too. She's a dryad witch, and she loves flowers. Oh, and there's Levin who's a wyvern. And Malek—"

Malek cleared his throat. "I think that's enough, Blossom. You can share more later, after we're back on the ship. We have a more urgent focus right now."

Sabine nodded, but she was secretly pleased by how quickly Rika had accepted Blossom. It would make introducing Rika and Zaverza to the rest of her companions a little easier. "Malek's right. We came here tonight to give you a warning. After we leave you, we're going to destroy the crystal they're planning to use to detect magic. Once we do, it'll be too risky for you to remain here. I expect they'll seal the city immediately. How quickly can you both finish packing?"

Zaverza frowned. "I won't be going."

Sabine's gaze flew to the elderly woman. Before she could argue, Zaverza shook her head and said, "No. I must remain here. I foresaw my death during the burning festival." Her eyes took on a faraway cast. "No one cheats death forever, and this is my time. I go willingly, to pacify the demands of our city. Even if I were to leave with you, my illness will take my life in a few months' time. In truth, I have fought to remain this long only to ensure Rika would be taken to safety."

Malek frowned. "The wisdom of seers is legendary, but your granddaughter still needs you. Even a few months would make a difference."

Zaverza's eyes crinkled as she grinned, revealing her gapped and discolored teeth. "I think not. Rika is prepared as much as possible. I can do no more. Rika will be safe, especially with strangers who are willing to take grave risk to help protect our city. You will save a number of innocents tonight. For that, you have my gratitude."

"You shall be remembered, and your wishes honored." Sabine lowered her gaze and pressed her closed fist over her heart in a gesture of respect. Among her people, once Elders made the decision when it was time to fade from this world, it was up to the rest of the Fae to ensure their wishes were followed.

Malek's brow furrowed, and he sighed. "All right. If you refuse to leave, allow me to offer a suggestion."

Zaverza's gnarled hands adjusted her shawl. "I'm listening."

"I retained the services of the dockmaster earlier today. He's sending a crew north in the morning to begin making repairs to my ship." Malek reached into a pouch and withdrew a few more coins. He handed them to Zaverza. "Shorin's a decent man. Pay him with this, and he'll make sure your granddaughter arrives at my ship safely."

"Bless you both," Zaverza whispered, her eyes crinkling with a smile. "I know Shorin and his wife well. I'll call upon him tonight and make the arrangements. Even if the city is sealed, we can ensure Rika gets out."

Sabine smiled warmly at both women. "Good. With a little luck, I'll see you at the ship in a few days, Rika." Turning to Zaverza, she added, "I understand destiny more than most, but sometimes a foretelling is only a prediction of possibilities. The future is yet unwritten. If you change your mind, you will be welcome with us."

"I appreciate the offer," Zaverza said with a bow. She removed her dark shawl and offered it to Sabine. "You should cover your hair when you leave. You are too recognizable for what you are about to attempt."

Sabine smiled and shook her head. "Keep it to ward against the chill. With your permission, I will perform additional magic and alter my appearance. It's minor enough that it won't be detected, but I'd rather not leave the same way we came in. Do you have another way out of here?"

Zaverza nodded. "Through our living quarters. We're the only ones here, so no one will witness anything."

Sabine nodded. Closing her eyes, she allowed her glamour to fall away. Her magic rose to the surface, and the marks on her skin pulsed with power. Reining her power in, she focused on using the marks as anchor points to bind her new illusion to her skin.

Using her impressions of Karga's residents as a guide, she darkened her hair and skin, even making her eyes a soft brown. Her ears were a bit trickier. Adding or reducing physical traits required more magic, but her ears were too distinctive. Forcing herself to breathe through the pain, she gently shortened and then rounded them, giving herself the illusion of having earlobes.

The trick with glamour was keeping as close to the original appearance as possible. Subtle changes were easier to maintain and required far less power. When she finished crafting the illusion, she affixed it against her skin with hundreds of pinpricks. Only the Fae possessed such mastery of illusions. Even if someone touched her, they wouldn't be able to differentiate the illusion with reality.

She opened her eyes and found everyone staring at her. Zaverza shook her head and said, "I would not have believed such a thing was possible if I hadn't seen it for myself. Your companion already has our same coloring, but you could easily pass for a native now."

Sabine smiled. "That was my hope."

Malek's gaze roamed over her features. "I still prefer your true appearance, but it's a very effective disguise." After turning back toward the two other women, he nodded at them. "I wish you both good fortunes. It may be a few days before we're able to return to the ship. If we don't arrive within a week, then we likely won't have survived."

At Rika's worried expression, Sabine said, "If something happens to us, Bane will know. He'll take you to safety."

Zaverza nodded. "Let us show you through our living quarters. You have a long night ahead of you. The watch will be changing at dawn, and you'll need to be well away before that happens."

Both Sabine and Malek exchanged glances and then followed the two women into their home. Sabine felt a twinge of regret. A wave of destruction was following in her path. First Akros, then Malek's ship, and now Karga. She only hoped she might save some innocent lives before it was all over and done.

Chapter Eleven

alek walked through the streets with Sabine at his side. He still couldn't get over the marked difference in her appearance. If he hadn't seen her change, he never would have recognized her. More troubling, however, were the implications of such an ability.

Sabine frowned up at him. "What's wrong?"

Malek adjusted the bag over his shoulder. "I still can't get over how easily you can alter your appearance. For almost seven years, I've been searching for someone with enough Fae magic to locate the portal artifacts. Now I'm wondering if I've encountered more of your people in my travels and never knew."

Sabine hesitated and then shook her head. "It's unlikely. You would have had more of a chance closing your eyes and catching a butterfly. There may be some Fae living in parts of the world, but I only remember one other person leaving Faerie while I was living there. Before that, it had been almost a century."

"Nobody could catch me," Blossom protested from beneath Sabine's hair. "I'm faster than any butterfly."

Malek bit back a grin. It had been a stroke of luck meeting Sabine, and he thanked his good fortune he'd docked in Akros. "The person who left Faerie, what made them leave?"

She shrugged. "It was a punishment of sorts. Whatever he had done was considered unforgiveable by our Elders. He was given a choice to either surrender his magic to his heirs or leave Faerie." Sabine darted a glance at him. "He chose exile."

Malek frowned and stepped over some broken crockery littering the alley. The route they were traveling was circumspect and not easy to navigate with their sandals. "What would have happened if he had surrendered his magic?"

Sabine lifted the hem of her dress to step over another broken pot. "He would have been treated as less than a human. Forgoing our magic is one of our oldest and most dire punishments, second only to having the Wild Hunt called upon us. Those Fae who surrender their magic typically choose to fade in less than a year's time."

He did a double take, floored by the possibility. Among his people, dragons who were no longer able to fly would never have gone gracefully into the Beyond. His magic might manifest differently than Fae power, but he couldn't imagine wanting to die if he couldn't change forms. He hadn't realized how dependent the Fae were when it came to their magic. "Seriously? They would choose death over living without their power?"

Sabine's mouth formed a thin line, and she gave him a curt nod. "My people are proud, almost to a fault. They have a hard time imagining a different life."

Malek paused and took her arm, then pulled her around to face him. The more he learned, the more extraordinary he found her. She'd not only dared enough to embrace a different life for herself, but she'd also found the courage to thrive. "Is that why you thought you'd be safe in Akros?"

"It was actually my Beastman protector who decided for me," she replied, lowering her gaze. "Balkin knew it would never dawn on my family to look for me in a human city. Before I left my home, I wouldn't have considered it either."

Malek blew out a breath. Needing to continue touching her, he pressed his hand against her lower back and continued leading her down the alley. "It was brave of you to leave everything you knew to try a new way of living."

She darted a glance at him and smiled. "Not exactly. I was foolish and arrogant in my thinking, like most of the Fae. It's taken me a long time to realize there's a great deal I don't know about this world and its inhabitants."

"You're not like the rest of the Fae," Blossom said and patted Sabine's hair. "That's why we follow you, Sabine. You're different."

Malek glanced at the pixie sitting on Sabine's shoulder. "What do you mean? Do all the pixies follow Sabine?"

"Not yet, but they will soon," Blossom said with a grin and winked at him. "Barley went to rally the troops. It's why he went back to Faerie with the rest of my family."

Sabine stopped in her tracks and said, "Blossom, why don't you scout ahead? We need to know how many people are guarding the crystal so we can make a plan."

Malek arched his eyebrow but didn't dispute Sabine's suggestion. He was curious about the pixies and what they were planning, but he wouldn't push, especially not right now. They were close to one of the main thoroughfares, and they couldn't risk anyone overhearing anything.

Blossom's appearance shimmered slightly, and she turned back into a dark moth. Against the dark brown of Sabine's hair, the pixie was nearly impossible to see. Blossom fluttered her wings and took flight, disappearing into the darkness.

Sabine turned back to him and asked, "Do you know which building is our target?"

Malek gestured toward the intersection ahead of them. "At the next street, we're going to turn left. The Kiervan's headquarters is a large building at the end. It's not far from the southern gate."

Sabine nodded. "What's the range of the crystal?"

"Not sure. I wasn't eager to test it out," Malek said with a frown. "The dwarves have them embedded into the gates of their city. In order to enter, you have to walk underneath them. I believe the larger the crystal, the greater the distance it can detect anything."

"Can they be shattered with our current weapons?"

A small group passed the adjacent intersection, laughing and talking among themselves. Lowering his voice to a whisper, he said, "Possibly, but we may need to use arcane means. If this crystal is similar to the lances on my ship, it'll be designed to withstand mundane weapons."

Sabine frowned and tapped her weapons, as she did when she was considering solutions to a troublesome problem. Malek was beginning to recognize some of her mannerisms, and most of them he found endearing. From everything he'd seen since they'd met, Sabine had a tendency to put the welfare of others above herself. It was going to be up to him to make sure she stayed alive and unhurt. He just didn't want to alienate her in the process.

She looked up at him and asked, "What about dragonfire? Can you use it without removing your necklace?"

Malek shook his head. "No. It'll shatter the warding. I'm not sure I have enough strength to shift into dragon form either. Flying with the ship took too much out of me."

He fell silent as he weighed the possibilities. With both of them being unfamiliar with the city and its residents, they were at a disadvantage. A plan began to form in his mind, but he suspected Sabine wasn't going to like it. Unfortunately, any other option would put her at risk. He wasn't willing to allow anything to happen to her.

"Do you remember when we broke into the councilman's home?"

Sabine tilted her head, causing her dark hair to partially cover her eyes. She absently brushed it away and regarded him with curiosity. "Yes. Why? What are you thinking?

"You obscured visibility that night, making it darker and harder to see. Can you do it again? Here?"

She frowned. "Yes, but it requires major magic to shift an entire town into darkness. There's also a proximity issue. We need to maintain our distance to prevent anyone from seeing through the shadows, and the crystal will still recognize us if we get too close."

"All right. I think I might know how we can accomplish our goal." Malek reached up and tucked her hair behind her ear, momentarily taken aback by the lack of their pointed tips. He'd be grateful once she could return to her normal appearance. It was strange looking at Sabine but not truly seeing her.

Blossom reappeared suddenly, shedding her illusion as she landed on Sabine's shoulder. "I looked all around. There are three Kiervan in the room next to the crystal."

Sabine nodded and glanced in the direction of the intersection. "Good. That's at least a manageable number. How many outside the building?"

"Just one guarding," Blossom said, her wings twitching fast enough to lift her off Sabine's shoulder again. "The ones inside are sleepy. I think they're going to bed soon. They said their shift is almost over."

Sabine frowned and turned back toward Malek. "We need

to do this soon before the shift change. They won't be as alert."

Malek nodded. "I can shield your magic if you can hide me from sight. I'll sneak in, take care of the guards, and destroy the crystal. We just need to get rid of the guard in the front without having him raise the alarm."

Sabine arched her brow and gave him a teasing smile. "Distracting him won't be difficult, especially if he's outside the crystal's range. I'll take care of him if you can handle the rest."

He hesitated, flexing his hands into fists, and then forced himself to release them. The idea of putting Sabine in danger was anathema to him. Unfortunately, they didn't have any other options. She'd proven to be capable of taking care of herself, but it was hard to reconcile the truth with his instincts. The urge to whisk her away and keep her safe from harm was overriding all sense of logic. It was becoming more difficult to suppress his tendencies where she was concerned.

He reached out and took her hand in his to draw her closer. She came to him willingly, her eyes revealing nothing but trust. He paused, staring down at Sabine. She was quickly becoming one of the most important things in his life. At a time he could least afford complications, he was falling in love with the woman who held the key to either saving his people or damning them to oblivion.

She placed her hand against his chest and searched his expression. "What's wrong?"

He shook his head and wrapped his arms around her, needing to hold her. Now that he had her in his arms, his need to steal her away was beginning to ease. "I don't like the idea of putting you in danger, sweetheart."

Her gaze softened. Standing on her toes, she brushed a light kiss against his lips. "I'll be fine. You're the one with the most difficult task, but Blossom can help you."

"Oooh! Can I?" Blossom asked, fluttering her wings in excitement. "We'll be the dynamic flying duo. A pixie and a dragon! We'll be unstoppable."

Malek frowned, unsure how Blossom could help but not wanting to offend the pixie. For such a tiny person, Blossom had a rather large and forceful personality.

Sabine smiled at him, leaned in close, and whispered, "I know she's small, but don't discount her effectiveness. Blossom has numerous abilities she doesn't usually share."

Malek hesitated, glancing at Blossom, whose eyes were filled with hope and enthusiasm. Sheesh. He never thought he'd be concerned about disappointing a pixie. "I don't want Blossom to get hurt. If I'm taking out the guards, I won't be able to keep an eye on her."

"You don't need to worry. She's pretty tough, and I think she'll be more helpful than you might expect." Turning toward Blossom, Sabine held out her hand and said, "I need some of your dust."

Blossom landed and fluttered her wings furiously, sending a smattering of pixie dust onto Sabine's palm. Sabine held her other hand over Blossom, not quite touching the pixie. The air between her hands shimmered from Sabine's power, and Blossom trilled happily. The pixie flopped onto her palm and wriggled around in the dust as Sabine's magic flowed through her.

Sabine smiled. "That's enough, Blossom. You can play later. It's time to go to work."

Blossom jumped up and flew off her palm. Sabine dipped her finger into the dust and spread some of it across her lips. She closed her eyes a moment, a look of intense concentration on her face. Malek's gaze lingered on her lips, which shimmered in the moonlight. He wasn't sure what sort of magic she'd enabled.

Blossom grinned and said, "My turn!"

Sabine nodded and blew the remaining dust back over the pixie before turning back toward Malek. "As long as the guards aren't too close to the crystal, Blossom can send some of them to sleep with her modified pixie dust. Nothing will wake them for at least an hour."

Malek's eyes narrowed, understanding the implications. "That's how you intend to distract the guard? You're going to send him to sleep by *kissing* him?"

Sabine paused and frowned. She closed the distance between them, her shoulders tense and unyielding. "We all have different strengths, Malek. I'm decent with weapons, but I have other skills more suited to my nature. As do you. This is the easiest way to disable the outside guard without killing him. I'd rather not take more lives unless it's necessary. After your reaction with the desert hunters being slaughtered, I assumed you felt the same way."

Well, damn. She had a neat little way of cutting to the heart of the matter and making him out to be a complete ass if he objected. Sending a guard to sleep with a kiss would be better. He just didn't like the idea of Sabine being the one to do it.

He could try to see if he had enough magic left to shift into a dragon and burn the crystal to the ground. If he'd had more time to fully recover, he might insist upon it. But even if he could, shifting into a dragon would garner too much attention. Not only would it jeopardize their efforts to save Esmelle and Levin, but it would most likely drive a wedge between him and Sabine if he suggested it.

He was becoming far too possessive of her, and she'd likely object once she fully understood his true nature. It grated on him, but he'd have to defer to her decision. He had no idea how he was going to handle things once she was reunited with Bane. He supposed that would be something to consider later, if they managed to survive the next few days.

"Very well. I trust your judgment." With a sigh, he removed the warding medallion around his neck. Once he dropped it into his pocket, he rested his hand against the back of her neck. His heated draconic power rose up, wrapping around Sabine. Her skin prickled in awareness, and he idly stroked his thumb across her neck.

Sabine withdrew her knife and pricked her finger. Her magic rose to meet his, and he had to focus on not responding further. The more time they spent together, the stronger his need became to merge their powers. He'd nearly lost control back in that inn with having her in his arms and pressed against him. Damn. He was falling—and fast.

Sabine uttered the ritualist words he was beginning to recognize. Squeezing her finger, she allowed two drops of blood to fall to the ground. He looked up and saw the clear sky from earlier was gone. Clouds streaked across the sky, stealing the light of the moon and throwing the street into near total darkness. Unlike Akros, the streets of Karga were mostly quiet and empty during the night. Oil lamps hung from posts at most intersections and in front of public houses, but all other businesses were closed.

Sabine turned and held out her finger toward him to offer the third drop. He wrapped his hand gently around her wrist and kissed her finger, accepting the blood offering. Power, deceptively sweet and impossibly potent, filled him and strummed through his veins. His skin tingled as the deepening shadows clung to him. His own magic rushed to the surface, and he closed his eyes as he sought control.

Sabine slipped her knife back in its sheath. "It's done. The magic will obscure you from sight unless you touch them, but try to stay at least an arm's length away from anyone. Their gazes should pass right over you, but it won't prevent them from hearing you if you're too loud."

Malek released her and put the medallion back around

his neck to hide his powers. It was no wonder why Dax had managed to lead such a successful criminal enterprise with Sabine at his side. "Good. I'll leave the bags in the alley here. Can you hide them from view too?"

Sabine nodded and gestured at a spot farther away from the intersection. Malek placed the bags on the ground, careful not to damage any of their contents. Sabine put her bag beside his and then knelt, running her hand over top of them. Their appearance shimmered, reforming in the guise of broken crockery.

"That could come in handy," he murmured, remembering an occasion or two where he'd nearly gotten caught smuggling items.

Sabine smiled up at him. "Indeed, but it'll only last an hour or two."

"We won't need it longer than that. If we're not back to retrieve our belongings by then, we probably won't have any further need for them."

Sabine stood. "Give me a few minutes to lead the guard away before you try to slip into the building. You'll need to keep your distance, since the shadows are only designed to hide you from view. I'll leave the guard in this alley and cover his presence with another illusion."

Blossom fluttered to his shoulder and said, "I'll tell you if you're getting too close to anyone. I can see through the shadows."

Malek nodded, watching as Sabine turned toward the main street and then headed around the corner. The streets were still deserted, which would make their plan a bit easier. He only hoped it remained that way. Following slowly behind her, Malek made sure to keep almost an entire building's length between them.

Sabine's pace was unhurried as though simply out for an evening stroll. As they approached the building where the

Kiervan were headquartered, Sabine tripped and fell to the ground with a pained cry.

Alarmed, Malek started to go to her. Blossom patted his neck and whispered, "It's a trick. She needs him to come to her so she doesn't set off the crystal."

Malek halted, watching as the guard left his post outside the building. He knelt beside Sabine and helped her to her feet. She tossed her dark hair back and said something too low for Malek to hear. The guard grinned. He glanced back at the building behind him and then wrapped his arm around Sabine's waist. Limping slightly, Sabine leaned against the guard as he brought her back in the direction of the alley they'd just abandoned.

Malek moved to the opposite side of the street, but the guard never even glanced in his direction. He was too busy staring at Sabine in a way that set Malek's teeth on edge. If he didn't know Sabine could handle herself, he might be inclined to go back to make sure the guard didn't try anything. Instead, he forced himself to head toward the building where the crystal waited.

Blossom whispered, "I'll scout ahead. Sabine gave me enough of her magic to send five of them to sleep."

Malek nodded, watching as the pixie shifted her appearance again and took off. Keeping to the shadows, Malek moved along the wall of the building toward the front entrance. He waited outside for several minutes, but he couldn't hear anything from within.

Blossom reappeared in the form of a large black moth and perched on his shoulder. "The front room is clear."

Malek slipped around the corner and into the main entrance area of the Kiervan's headquarters. Several low tables were set up with lanterns and weapons scattered over top of them. Three guards snored loudly, their bodies resting on top of cushions scattered around each of the tables. Two of them appeared to have been cleaning their curved swords when Blossom had dusted them. The other had been eating a meal, and his head was resting not so comfortably on his plate.

Blossom pointed at a doorway where a curtain had been strung up to separate the two areas. "The crystal's in there, but I hear someone moving around. I'm sorry, Malek. He wasn't there earlier."

Malek nodded, his hand immediately going to the knife at his side. In tight quarters, a shorter weapon would prove more advantageous. He shifted the curtain slightly and caught sight of a man turned away from him. He was staring at something on the far side of the room. Motioning for Blossom to stay back, Malek crept into the room, prepared to take the guard unaware.

A high-pitched keening noise filled the air, and a purple light shone against the walls. The guard spun around, shouting a warning, and drew his weapon in one fluid movement. Damn. Sabine's shadow magic coating his skin must have tripped the crystal alarm. Abandoning his knife, Malek grabbed his sword and blocked the guard's attack. Metal rung against metal as he continued to block and parry.

Blossom flew into the room, fluttering her wings furiously over the guard. Pixie dust cascaded and the man sneezed, upsetting his footwork. Malek shifted his weight, angling his weapon downward, but the man sneezed again. The guard staggered, and his weapon clattered to the ground. He followed a moment later and crashed onto the ground, sound asleep.

Malek jumped over his body and rushed toward the shrieking crystal. With both hands, he brought his sword down against the purple stone. Nothing happened. A slight mark was the only indication he'd hit his mark.

"Hurry, Malek," Blossom urged, yelling over the sound of the crystal. "More people are coming!"

Malek's jaw clenched. He gripped the warding medallion around his neck and yanked it off. Infusing his breath with dragonfire, he breathed over the crystal. The purple surface began to bubble at the intense heat, but it still wasn't enough.

"Get out of here, Blossom!" Malek shouted, grabbing the sleeping guard and dragging him out of the room. What he was about to attempt would likely kill anyone in the immediate vicinity.

Running back to the crystal, he focused on summoning the full strength of his power. He inhaled deeply, the staggering heat in his blood pulsing through his temples. His human form hadn't been designed to contain the raw power of what he was attempting. His vision blurred and sweat poured off him as the molten lava in his veins prepared to erupt. Unable to contain it any longer, he flung his power outward. Blue fire erupted from his body, consuming the crystal in a blast of heat.

The last vestiges of his strength fled, and Malek dropped to his knees. The sharp smell of burnt clay and smoke filled Malek's nose, but he barely noticed. He swayed, pressing his hands against his knees to stay upright. Blinking through the smoky haze, he tried to focus on the crystal. The table was gone, and the crystal was nothing more than a pile of purple dust. Most of the floor in front of him was gone, including part of the wall.

Relief flooded through him. He tried to stand, but he couldn't make it to his feet. His strength fled, and he fell sideways onto the hard ground. Even if he didn't make it out of Karga alive, at least he'd saved some innocents. Sometimes, that had to be enough.

SOMETHING WASN'T RIGHT. Sabine wiped the rest of the pixie dust from her lips and peered out of the alley at the building where Malek had disappeared. It was taking longer than she'd thought for him to destroy the crystal. She hesitated a moment and slowly started making her way back to him.

If the Kiervan had caught Malek, there was no way of knowing what they might do to him. Flying with the ship had taken a great deal from him, and he'd likely have difficulty defending himself. Sex and the magical spring water had helped restore her power, but Malek still wasn't at full strength.

"Sabine! Come quick! Malek's going to—" Blossom's words were interrupted as an explosion rocked the Kiervan's headquarters. The ground trembled under her feet, and smoke poured upward from the roof.

"Malek!" Sabine screamed, running toward the building. Gods. If anything had happened to him because she'd pushed him to do this, she'd never forgive herself. She couldn't lose him, not when she'd just found him.

She staggered inside the building, the smoke making her eyes tear up. It was nearly impossible to breathe. "Where is he? Blossom, where is he?!"

Blossom coughed and pointed at another room. "In there, Sabine. Hurry!"

Sabine scrambled over the sleeping bodies of the guards, intent on finding Malek. Grasping the edge of the doorframe that was falling down, she stepped into a secondary room. The smoke was even worse in here. She coughed and crouched low, spotting Malek on the far side of the room. His clothing was burnt, and he was lying facedown on the ground. Her heart fell into her stomach as fear gripped her.

"Malek," she whispered, rushing to him and dropping to her knees beside him. Rolling him over, she searched for any injuries, but it was impossible to tell. His skin was darkened from soot as though it had been burned. "No. Please, no."

Blossom landed on Sabine's shoulder. "It's okay. He's not dead, Sabine. Look! His chest is moving."

Tears streaked down her face, both from the harsh acrid smell of burnt building materials and from her tumultuous emotions. She focused on Malek's chest and saw what Blossom had meant. His breathing was labored, but his chest rhythmically moved up and down.

"Malek, please talk to me," she whispered as she reached toward him and then stopped. She wasn't sure if touching him would make things worse. She leaned over him, trying to figure out how she could get him out of here. People would be arriving any minute to investigate.

He opened his eyes and managed a weak smile. "It's destroyed. They're… they're all safe."

A hysterical laugh bubbled out of her, and she wiped away her tears. "You wonderful, foolish dragon. What have you done to yourself? You never should have taken such a risk."

"Had to," he whispered and reach up to cup her face.

Leaning into his touch, she held his hand against her skin. For a moment, she'd feared she'd lost him. "We need to get you out of here. Can you stand?"

"Need sleep," he whispered, his eyes closing.

"You can't sleep right now," she urged, reaching toward him. If he hadn't objected to her touching his hand, he was probably mostly unharmed. She tried to pull him up, but he wouldn't budge. Sabine frowned, panic growing as she searched the room for anything she could use to lift him. There was nothing. Everything in the room had been destroyed.

Blossom squeaked. "Sabine, I think someone's coming."

Sabine frowned, leaning over Malek and using her

glamour to disguise them as rubble. She pressed her fingers against Malek's lips in a silent gesture for quiet as footsteps rushed toward them.

"What the hell happened?" a man shouted from the other room.

"No idea. I can't wake any of them."

Malek opened his eyes, and Sabine shook her head in warning. His eyes closed again, and he drifted back out of consciousness. If she couldn't get him out of here, these people would kill him. He was too weak to defend himself. They'd never believe he created this much destruction without the use of magic.

"Go find Captain Kaveil and wake him up. One of those damn cursed demons is responsible for this. We need to search the city. Now."

Sabine swallowed at the guard's words, knowing they needed to hurry. They'd do a full search of the building once the smoke cleared, and their presence would be discovered. Sabine stared at Malek and brushed his dark hair away from his face. She wouldn't lose him. There was a way to help him —but it would bind her even tighter to Malek. The alternative, though, would be to watch the Kiervan kill him—and she'd *never* allow that to happen. But first, she needed to get him out of the building.

Leaning over Malek, she pressed a light kiss against his lips. He blinked open his eyes, and she smiled at him. Using the mark connecting them, she sent some of her strength to him. Their connection was still in its infancy, and she couldn't share much with him until the level of trust between them deepened.

Malek sat up and cupped her face, searching her expression. She gave him a small smile and leaned forward, kissing him again softly. Keeping her movements silent, she rose to her feet and then helped Malek up. He was a little unsteady, but at least he was able to stay awake. She'd need to give him more of her power once they were outside, but it would likely deplete her remaining strength. She had some magical water left, but once it was gone, they'd need to return to the spring to recover more. Otherwise, she'd be without magic until they came to another forest.

From the sound of footsteps and approaching voices, more people had arrived to investigate the disturbance. Blossom had shifted back into the guise of a moth and fluttered over near one of the walls that had melted. Understanding the pixie's silent direction, Sabine gathered the shadows around her and Malek. He leaned heavily on her as she led him toward the burnt and crumbling wall of the building, which had partially collapsed.

She climbed over the low wall and helped Malek do the same. For a large man, she'd always been impressed with how well he moved, but now his movements were clumsy and awkward, as though even lifting his feet was difficult.

She wrapped her arm around his waist and indicated with gestures for him to lean on her. Struggling under his weight, she managed to guide them toward the alley, narrowly avoiding more guards as they converged around the Kiervan's headquarters. Once they finished in the building, they'd expand their search to the surrounding areas. She needed to hurry.

As soon as they were back in the alley, she eased Malek to the ground and knelt beside him. Soot streaked his face, his cheeks were gaunt, and the patches of skin she could see were far too pale. Pressing her hand against his forehead, she frowned at the marked drop in his temperature.

Blossom landed on Malek's knee and shed her moth illusion. "He doesn't look too good, Sabine."

"I'll be fine," he said quietly, slumping against the wall and closing his eyes. "Just need a few minutes to rest."

Sabine glanced toward the street where people were trickling out of their homes. "We don't have that long. They'll likely seal the city soon, and we need to be outside these walls when it happens."

"Go. I'll catch up. You need to join up with that troupe if you're going to find Pearl."

"I'm *not* leaving you," she said firmly, not willing to even consider such a thing. "You didn't leave me back in Akros, and I won't leave you now. Our fates are now intertwined."

She reached toward the bags they'd left behind and located the Faerie water. After pouring a tiny amount of water into her hand, she offered it to Blossom. It wasn't enough to get her drunk again, but it would give her a boost. The pixie had used up a great deal of her magic this evening, and there weren't enough accessible plants in Karga to easily replenish Blossom's power.

Once Blossom had drunk her fill, the pixie yawned and curled up in Malek's lap. Sabine lifted the flask to her lips and drank a large swallow. The power helped fortify her, but she wasn't back to full strength. Using magic to surround the city in shadows had cost her dearly.

She drained the rest of her flask. The magic in the water was still potent, but not as strong as it had been when they'd drunk directly from the spring. The small amount she'd taken was barely enough for what she intended. Malek still had a bit left in his flask, but they'd need to conserve it for their journey into the desert.

"Malek," she whispered, scooting close to him. "Can you wake up? I need to share my magic with you."

He murmured something intelligible but didn't awaken. Sabine frowned and tried to shake him. He didn't stir. She blew out a breath. It looked like she was going to have to do this the hard way.

Withdrawing her knife, she cut her palm and winced at

the sharp pain. Pressing her bleeding hand against his mouth, she stroked his throat and urged, "Drink, Malek. You'll feel better soon."

He swallowed, and she sighed in relief. Closing her eyes to focus on the magic, she whispered in the language of Faerie, "By blood and magic, and by my rights to both, I share my power and my destiny—both to be shaped by our wills. Drink and accept this gift, freely offered and freely given, that we might merge our futures as one until the last of the magic fades."

She opened her eyes and looked into his striking blue ones. He held her gaze and wrapped his hand around her wrist to pull her closer. Her blood flowed through his body as her power surrounded and fueled him from within. She was now part of him, just as he'd taken up residence in her heart almost from the moment they met.

The wound in her hand closed as the magic sealed them together, both in purpose and intent. Somewhat shaken by what she'd done, she pulled away her hand.

He sat up and frowned, studying her with no small measure of scrutiny. "What did you do?"

"I shared my strength with you," she said quietly and started to stand. He grabbed her hand and pulled her back toward him. She nearly fell onto his lap, but he caught her and held her close, careful not to disturb Blossom who was still lying on him.

"What did you do, Sabine?"

Sabine pressed her finger against his lips and said, "Please, Malek. We don't have time for this. You have my word no harm will come to you from what just transpired, but we need to leave."

He gripped her wrist gently, still holding onto her. "That was never my concern. I felt something in the mark shift when you did... whatever you did. Did it hurt *you*?"

Touched by his concern, she gave him a small smile and shook her head. "No. It didn't hurt me. If you were anyone else, I wouldn't have offered this."

His brow furrowed, and he looked like he was about to object.

She leaned forward, brushed a soft kiss against his lips, and whispered, "We'll talk later. I promise."

Pulling away from Malek, she carefully lifted Blossom and cradled the pixie as she rose to her feet. Malek stood and asked, "Is she drunk again?"

"Just sleeping. I gave her a small amount of water, but it wasn't enough to get her drunk. She's just tired from performing so much magic. Pixies tend to burn out quickly, but she'll wake up in a few minutes."

Malek opened one of the bags and located the box containing the flowers Blossom had slept in earlier. He held it out, and Sabine placed the pixie inside.

Malek looked down at his charred clothing and frowned. "I need to find a place to get cleaned up unless you have enough magic to hide me with glamour. I have some clothing I can change into once I get rid of the smokiness, but we should hurry. We need to join the troupe before they close the gates."

Sabine frowned and picked up one of the bags. "To be safe, I should conserve as much magic as possible. I can keep your appearance hidden from view for only a short time without endangering myself. We could try to go back to the bathhouse. I know men aren't allowed, but I don't think we have a choice."

"All right," Malek said in agreement, adjusting the two remaining bags over his shoulder. He walked beside her as they headed back toward Zaverza's home. Fortunately, it wasn't far to go. They tapped lightly on the door to their residence. It opened a moment later, and Rika waved them in.

"Grandmother had another vision and said you'd be back. She's preparing everything for you so you can both clean up. You can go ahead into the scrubbing room, but you need to hurry. You won't have time to use the springs, and you need to be careful so they don't know a man was in here."

Sabine nodded. "I understand. Can you leave the city tonight?"

Rika nodded and lowered her gaze. "Grandmother's taking me to Shorin's place in a few minutes. She wants me to leave the city right away, even if I have to go by myself. If I wait any longer, I won't be able to get out."

Sabine reached out and took Rika's hand. "It takes a very strong person to leave what's familiar and set off for the unknown. I did the same several years ago, and I see that same strength in you."

Rika's eyes widened as she gazed up at Sabine with a shred of hope in her eyes. "Truly?"

Sabine smiled and nodded. "Yes. I'll tell you more about it once we're all together on the ship. Having good friends at your side will help you, just as it helped me. You won't be alone, Rika."

"Thank—"

Sabine pressed her fingers against the girl's mouth to stop her. "No. Don't ever try to thank a Fae," she warned sternly. "Bargains and debts are our currency, and any acknowledgment of such could lead you into peril. I won't harm you, but someone else might try to take advantage of you."

Rika's mouth formed a thin line, and she nodded. "My grandmother warned me, but it's going to take some getting used to."

Sabine lowered her hand and smiled. "We'll work on it.

I'll let you finish packing so you can be on your way. Malek and I can let ourselves out when we're finished."

Malek nodded. "Shorin's a good man. He'll get you out. But if he doesn't have people leaving immediately, Sabine and I left two thontins outside the north gate. They have matching blue-and-purple saddle ribbons. Take one of them and head north. You should see the masts of my ship from the road."

"I will," Rika replied. She gave them both a shy smile and darted out of the room.

Sabine rubbed her temples, exhausted from the events over the past few days. "I didn't think to tell her about the thontins. I'm glad you said something. I almost suggested Blossom accompany her, but we'll need her with us to keep an eye on the people we're traveling with."

Malek took a step toward her, his nearness making the mark on his skin flare to life and sending a frisson of awareness through her. "You're too hard on yourself, Sabine. You've done a great deal. Rika's lucky to have met you. Someone else would have taken advantage of her or her grandmother."

"I don't want to let her down or put her in more danger by taking her with us," Sabine admitted, staring at the door where Rika had disappeared.

"That's exactly why she's lucky. Someone else wouldn't care as much about a girl she'd met only a few hours ago." Closing the distance between them, he said, "She's not the only one who's lucky, Sabine. I've thought the same thing since the moment we met. My life is already far richer having you in it."

Both his words and the intense look in his eyes were enough to make her magic falter. The illusion masking his appearance flickered slightly, but it was enough to bring her back to awareness. She frowned at his burnt, charred clothing and the streaks of soot on his skin. "We should get cleaned up. If Zaverza had another vision, the danger might be greater than we anticipated."

Malek nodded and gestured for her to lead the way. She headed back into the main room and then into the area where she'd scrubbed her skin. Zaverza was already there. She clucked her tongue when she saw them and motioned for them to hurry.

The elderly woman placed a brush beside a large bowl and said, "There is no time to soak. You must cleanse yourselves, change your clothing, and leave this place. Leave any ruined clothing in the fire pit. I will ensure they are destroyed and no trace of you remains behind."

Sabine gestured for Malek to use one of the bowls situated behind a small panel designed to offer a trace of privacy in the open room. She stepped behind the other, and Zaverza asked, "I trust you have other clothing?"

"We do," Malek said from behind his screen.

"Good. I'm taking Rika now to the docks so Shorin can get her out of the city. We likely won't meet again."

Sabine lowered her head and pressed her closed fist over her heart in a gesture of respect. It likely wouldn't do any good to ask her to join them again. Zaverza had chosen her path, and Sabine needed to respect her decision. "I wish you the best, Zaverza."

"You as well," Zaverza murmured and left the room.

Sabine placed Blossom's box on the low table beside the bowl and began removing her clothing. Hers wasn't as damaged, but trace amounts of soot had transferred onto the material. In case anyone had spotted her, it would be better to change anyway. She couldn't maintain multiple illusions for prolonged periods without draining a significant amount of magic.

Blossom yawned and stretched in her box. "Are we there yet?"

"Not yet. We're leaving Karga as soon as we change," she said, scrubbing the soot off her body and face. She quickly dressed in the red dress and affixed the metal rings of the belt over the lightweight material.

Blossom hopped over and sniffed the water. "They added lavender oil to it. It smells like one of the northern varieties. Think they have any plants?"

Sabine smiled and reattached her weapons. "It's unlikely. They probably have it shipped here."

Blossom wrinkled her nose and flew away, probably to investigate the rest of the room. Pixies had short attention spans, but Blossom would stay nearby. Sabine looked down at the blue dress smudged with a few soot streaks. It might be silly, but she wasn't willing to part with the gift Malek had bought her. Instead, she folded it and placed it inside the bag to be cleaned later.

Reemerging from behind the screen, she smoothed out her dress and released the modified illusion she'd crafted. Her normal human appearance wasn't any less painful, but she'd grown accustomed to it. Even if the guard she'd lured away had awakened, he wouldn't recognize her.

"We may have a problem," Malek said from behind his privacy screen.

Sabine approached the screen and asked, "What's wrong?"

Malek came out from behind his screen and gestured at his neck. "The medallion's gone. I had to remove it to destroy the crystal. It either melted or fell somewhere in the building. Either way, we need to leave without it."

Sabine froze. "We can't enter the dwarven city without it."

He ran a hand over his damp hair. "We'll have to figure something out. But if we don't get out of Karga right away, it won't matter."

She nodded, knowing he was right. She picked up her bag and slung it over her shoulder. Blossom flew toward Malek and sniffed at him. "Yep. That medallion was pretty powerful. It even hid your scent. You smell like burnt leaves again."

"I'm not sure if that's an insult or a compliment," Malek said dryly. Blossom grinned and landed on his shoulder.

Curious, Sabine approached him and inhaled deeply. Blossom was right. He did have a slight smoky smell to him. She'd noticed it back when they'd been in their room at the inn, and it had attracted her more than she'd expected. She gave him a warm smile. "It reminds me of roasted chestnuts or a campfire. I like it."

He arched his brow and picked up his bags. "Well, then. I'll definitely take *that* as a compliment."

Sabine laughed and headed toward the front entrance. At least they were exiting the same way they'd first arrived. If anyone had noticed their arrival, she hoped they'd believe she and Malek were simply visiting Zaverza. She just hoped it didn't cause more problems for the older woman.

Malek held open the door for her as she stepped out into the street. Even though it was the middle of the night, Karga's residents were emerging from their homes and speaking in frightened voices. The commotion and cries of alarm from the destruction of the Kiervan's headquarters had obviously awakened them. Malek placed his hand against her back, leading her toward the dock area.

"I thought we were leaving," she whispered, apprehensive by the sheer number of people in the street. Most of the residents were eyeing them with suspicion and even fear, which didn't bode well.

In a voice barely loud enough to be heard, Malek said, "We're going toward the docks and then cutting across to the southern gate. I don't want to risk walking by the Kiervan headquarters."

She nodded, glancing over at Malek's shoulder. Blossom had disappeared again, likely hiding herself from sight and scouting ahead. Both she and Malek fell silent, trying to walk as quickly as possible without raising any alarms. When they approached the large gates, Sabine had to force herself to maintain a calm she didn't feel. The gates were already locked and barred, the giant wooden slats making any possible escape a dim reality.

"Damn," Malek muttered, slowing his footsteps and looking around as though checking for an alternative route.

Sabine glanced at him. "How do you want to handle this?"

"We can try a bribe," Malek suggested, pulling one of his bags off his shoulder and rifling through it. He withdrew a small pouch and attached it to his belt. "They'll likely be more receptive to us if we play up the performance troupe angle."

Sabine frowned, not completely convinced. "I suppose it's our best chance."

Blossom appeared a moment later, slipping under Sabine's hair in the guise of a moth. "There are two guards at the gate. They're turning away most people, but a few are getting through. They're searching them first. Want me to put one of them to sleep so you can sneak through?"

"You have enough magic left?"

Blossom leaned against her neck. "Only for one. You'll have to get rid of the other one or magic your way out of here."

Sabine shook her head. "Too risky, and I'm running low on power. We'll try it Malek's way first. If we can't make it through, we'll figure out something else. I need you to stay back and keep watch. We can't risk them finding you."

"Got it," she replied and disappeared into the night.

Sabine adjusted her hair to cover the tips of her ears. Trying to hide them with glamour would take a little too much out of her. Besides, if these people had seen her already, changing such a small thing would only cause them to be more suspicious.

Malek put the bag back on his shoulder and led Sabine forward. Feigning an almost bored expression, Malek approached the guards stationed at the gate. Both of them narrowed their eyes at Malek, but they didn't make any other threatening gestures.

"The city is now sealed," the taller guard snapped, gesturing at the closed gate. "If you are visitors to Karga, you need to return to your ship or to the inn. Someone will come to assess you for contraband shortly. After the city is purged of all undesirables, you'll be free to leave."

Malek arched his brow. "You're sealing it already? We were told the burning festival wouldn't be happening for several more days. We're supposed to meet up with our troupe outside the city."

"Plans change," the shorter guard sneered. "We're not allowing anyone through."

Malek gestured toward Sabine and said, "I suppose you weren't in the inn tonight. You didn't see her perform?"

Sabine tilted her head and gave them a small smile. "I don't think they were there. I would have remembered two such memorable and important people in the audience."

The taller one scanned Sabine up and down, his eyes flickering with interest. "You're a dancer, eh?"

Sabine's smile deepened and she approached him, putting an extra swing in her hips. "That's one of my talents, yes." Placing her hand against the guard's chest, she sent a slight trace of her magic over him to soften his resistance. Leaning close, she whispered, "We could always discuss a private performance when I'm next in Karga."

The guard grinned and turned back toward Malek. "What's your business with the troupe?"

Malek gestured at the weapons on his waist. "Security. The customers can get a little too friendly when Sabine performs. Ryley suggested I stay close to protect her."

The short guard frowned. "How do we know you're telling the truth, eh?"

Sabine blinked at him. Something about this one made her wary, and she wasn't willing to risk using her magic on him. If he had some dormant magical ability, her own might cause his to flare to life. "If you speak with the innkeeper at the dockside tavern, he'll confirm everything we've shared. Ryley told us to meet him at the camp before dawn. He should have already passed this way with another man and their instruments."

The shorter guard rubbed his chin in thought, pretending to consider it. The gesture was enough to encourage her.

"My friends are waiting for me, and I really must rejoin them before they depart. If I lose my place with them, I'm afraid they may never allow me back." She lowered her gaze, pretending to be dismayed by the prospect. "I'd like to return to your city, and staying with the troupe is the best way to make that happen."

The taller guard frowned. "Come on, Xuthin. They're all right. Let them through."

"I suppose we might make an exception, but it'll create more work for us," Xuthin replied and looked expectantly at Malek.

Malek pulled out the pouch containing her portion of the earning from the performance. He offered it to Xuthin. "For your trouble."

Xuthin grinned and snatched the bag out of Malek's hand. Walking back to the gatehouse, he called over his shoulder, "Toma, take a look at their belongings and let them through."

The taller guard, the one named Toma, winked at Sabine

and reached for her bag. He glanced through it, and she had a moment of panic remembering the clothing she should have discarded. It had been a sentimental decision to keep it, and it might come back to bite her.

Determined to distract Toma, she angled closer to him and gave him a flirtatious smile. "I wouldn't mind seeing you again. Do you always work the gate?"

"Nah. Usually I'm patrolling the streets, but there was a bit of an incident earlier. Next time you're in town, stop by our headquarters and ask for me. I'll show you a good time."

Sabine placed her hand on his arm and said, "That sounds promising and a good reason to return to Karga soon. I'll keep your offer in mind."

She took her bag back from Toma, and the guard turned toward Malek. After unceremoniously dropping Malek's bags on the ground, he searched through them, taking longer to inspect each item. "What is all this stuff?"

"Trade items to sell," Malek said with a shrug. "As we move from city to city, I'm able to turn a bit of a profit with what I find. You'd be surprised what people want. If there's something you're hoping to get, let me know and I'll keep an eye out."

The guard grunted and handed the bags back to Malek. "I wouldn't say no to a bottle of dwarven ale. You come across any of that?"

Malek hefted the bags over his shoulder and grinned. "Aye. We should find some when we head south. I'll see if I can find a bottle for you."

"Good man," Toma said and gestured at the gate. "Good fortune to you both."

"To you as well," Malek said and walked to the closed gate. Toma motioned to the other guard, and a loud groaning noise of mechanical wheels turning accompanied the slow movement of the gate sliding open. When it was wide enough for them to pass, both Malek and Sabine slipped through.

Forcing herself to keep her footsteps unhurried, she headed down the road with Malek beside her. It was only an hour or two past midnight, but Sabine was exhausted and barely able to keep one foot in front of the other. Through their shared mark, she could sense Malek was in a similar state.

They'd walked only a short distance when Blossom landed on her shoulder and said, "That was close. You guys got out just in time. Right after they closed the gate, someone else came up and told them not to allow anyone else in or out under any circumstances."

Sabine frowned and glanced behind them at the sealed gate. "Do you think Rika made it out?"

Malek's expression turned grim. "Zaverza seems like a resourceful person. I suspect she'll find a way to get her granddaughter out. The dockmaster, Shorin, also has some smuggler contacts. If he can't get his workers out through the main gate, he'll take them out by ship or some other way. He won't want to return the price I paid for ship repairs. Sailors talk, and he won't risk his reputation."

Sabine nodded and turned back toward the rolling desert that lay before them like an endless beach. The moon was high overhead, casting its silver light over the desolate landscape. "Then it looks like we need to meet up with Ryley and hope they lead us to Pearl. If we don't find her soon, Esme and Levin will be lost to us forever."

Chapter Twelve

Sabine shivered and rubbed her arms. The thin material of her dress hadn't been too bad within the confines of the city. Without the city walls to shield the night wind, however, it was colder than she'd expected. Blossom was equally uncomfortable, and the pixie had decided to huddle against Sabine's neck to stay warm.

Malek stopped and opened his bag. He pulled out one of his shirts and said, "This should help. Once we locate Ryley, we can get out of this wind."

Sabine nodded and slipped the shirt over her dress. It was far too large for her, but it helped alleviate the worst of the chill. "How far away do you think they camped?"

"Not sure," Malek replied, scanning the horizon. Unfortunately, the rolling sand dunes made it difficult to tell what was over the next rise. "I'm reluctant to travel too far from the city. Zaverza was right about the Badlands being an unforgiving place. We're on the main road right now, but it's always safer to travel with an escort."

He hefted his bags back over his shoulder, and they continued walking. The stars shone brightly overhead, which prevented the need for any lanterns. Other than the chill, it was a pleasant night. Even though they were potentially walking into danger and both of their magic was running low, she was surprisingly content having Malek at her side.

Trying to envision one of Malek's maps in her head, she asked, "If we had to travel across land to get to the dwarven city, how long would it take?"

Malek frowned. "By sea and with the weather holding, we could be in Razadon in another week. By land? If I had to guess, I'd say it could take three times that long. That's assuming we had mounts. It would be much longer on foot."

Sabine winced. They'd already spent a week at sea, and she wasn't looking forward to another week. If he hadn't been able to acquire additional supplies in Karga, they'd run into problems while they were waiting for Malek's ship to be repaired. "Do you think Ryley and his group regularly travel that far?"

"Anything's possible. I've seen a few traveling troupes in some port cities I've visited. Some stick to a small area, but others go much farther. It depends on the city, but some troupes are highly regarded and offered generous incentives to perform for several weeks."

Sabine frowned. "What's the nearest city to us?"

Malek adjusted the bag over his shoulder. "I believe Gorvin. It's a smaller port city, with more of a focus on fishing and maritime wares. I've only stopped there once. It's about a day south by ship."

From the top of a hill, Sabine spotted almost two dozen colorful tents and wagons painted with whimsical designs. Some of the designs were more abstract swirls and lines, but Sabine noticed several stars and even the phases of the moon were represented. One of them even had what appeared to be a forest painted on the side of it.

A few fires were burning low, with one large one in the

middle of the tents and wagons. A few figures were sitting around the central fire, but they were angled toward it, which masked their faces. She couldn't tell if they were men or women, or if the musicians they'd met were part of the group.

"Looks like we found them," Malek said with a frown. "Not quite what I was expecting, but there's no one else out here."

"It's charming," Sabine said, admiring the designs they'd painted.

Blossom wriggled against her neck and poked her head out. "Oooh! I see a flower painted on that wagon. Think they have any real flowers inside?"

Sabine smiled. "I wouldn't count on it unless they're desert flowers. Perhaps they have some other plants you'll like. It may be different from home, but the desert has quite a bit of plant life. We'll find you something."

Sabine and Malek headed down the hill toward the small camp. Before they could even call out a greeting, a small furred creature lifted its head and howled a warning. Almost as one, the people around the fire stood and turned in their direction. A few of them had already drawn weapons, and the light from the fire reflected on the metal.

Malek raised his hands in a peaceable gesture and called, "Is Ryley here? I'm Malek, and this is Sabine. He invited us to the camp."

One of the men said something too low to be overhead and then stepped forward. "Come closer so we know you are who you say."

In a voice too low for the group to overhear, Malek said, "That's not Ryley."

Sabine frowned. "No, it's not. Still, I don't think we have many options. We can't go back to Karga."

"No, we can't," Malek muttered and rubbed his chin. "I

suppose we'll have to take the chance. Keep your weapons handy until we find out if they're friendly."

Sabine studied the four people who were still waiting and watching them. Malek started to take a step forward, but Sabine grabbed his arm to stop him. "Wait a moment. Let me check something."

She'd had to force herself to rely less on her magic over the years, but it was still an essential part of her. With a little luck, she should be able to discern something. Relaxing her vision, she focused on the energies surrounding the people. She might not be able to see them well from this distance, but magic worked differently.

Three of them were men while the fourth was a woman. At the core, each of their energies was more blue or turquoise than any other color. Right now, a thin sliver of orangish red streaked through the colors, a sign of caution and even fear. It was enough to make Sabine relax. If they'd intended any harm, the colors would be switched and red would be the predominant focus.

The animal howled again and raced toward them. Malek immediately drew the sword at his side, but Sabine tightened her hand on his arm. "No, don't."

A small foxlike animal with large pointed ears and a bushy tail approached, wagging its tail happily. Sabine laughed and knelt down, holding out her hands in greeting. The creature immediately bounded toward her and nuzzled against her hands. She dug her fingers into its coarse fur, rubbing behind its ears.

"Oh, you're beautiful and you know it, don't you?" Sabine crooned, continuing to scratch the hard-to-reach places.

Malek shook his head, his expression bewildered. "What in the name of the underworld is that animal? It looks like a small dog or something."

"Not even close. She's a kumili," Sabine said with a laugh

as the animal licked her cheek. "I haven't seen one in years. They're shapeshifters, but this one is only a baby. It'll be a few years yet before she can shift. When she does, she'll freely be able to change back and forth from this form to human."

"Not many people know about us, especially this far south," a woman said from a short distance away. "You can read energies?"

Sabine glanced up to find the woman from the fire had approached, along with the three men. Her use of that particular talent was likely what had prompted the kumili to run toward her. Kumili could also read energy and detect when the ability was being used, as could most other shapeshifters. "Yes. It's a common talent for anyone who is part Fae."

The kumili yipped and danced around Sabine. The woman frowned at the animal and said, "Enough, Nallia. You shouldn't have left the camp. You're lucky this woman was able to recognize you, but you won't always be so fortunate. These people could have harmed you."

Sabine stood and assessed the group in front of them. Like most kumili in human form, the woman was striking, with curly dark hair and eyes that were the palest of gray. The men, on the other hand, varied in physical appearance. One of them towered over Sabine and was completely hairless, a sign he possessed quite a bit of ogre blood in him. The other two were harder to differentiate and appeared more human. The taller one likely had a trace amount of Fae from his light hair and pointed ears.

The one who was part Fae stepped forward, scanning her up and down. "You must be Sabine. Ryley described you, but I must say, he didn't do you justice."

Malek's eyes narrowed. "Who are you?"

"I'm called Tathaln." The man grinned, revealing a toothy smile. He gestured at the woman and his other companions.

"This is Gina. You've already met her daughter, Nallia. The tall, ugly fellow there is Eruk, and the little guy is Zoty."

Eruk grunted at them and scratched his bald head. Zoty clapped his hands together and bowed, turning his hands so his palms were outstretched. Sabine's eyes widened in surprise at the sight of the webbing between his fingers. He was one of the lizardmen, and few of them were capable of normal speech patterns. They preferred mind contact, like the Beastpeople.

Sabine smiled at him and mirrored his gesture of greeting. Zoty's eyes crinkled as he smiled, and he nodded happily.

"Well met," Malek said, nodding at each of them in greeting.

Tathaln gestured at the fire and said, "Feel free to join us and know you are welcome in our camp. I apologize for not welcoming you properly. Ryley has already retired for the night, but I could have sworn he said you'd be joining us in the morning."

Malek nodded. "That was the plan, but they sealed the city a short while ago. We barely made it out."

Gina's eyes narrowed. "You mean for their famed festival? It is nothing more than an excuse to celebrate the death and destruction of countless innocents." She spat upon the desert sand in disgust. "They are the invaders here. My people were here for centuries before Karga even existed."

"Enough, Gina," Tathaln said, the pinched expression on his face broking no argument. "We have heard your complaints countless times. We might agree with you, but for tonight and tomorrow, we have cause to celebrate. These two lives have been saved by escaping from that accursed city, and we have gained two new family members."

Gina tossed back her dark hair and shrugged. "Very well. I will have to celebrate with you tomorrow. It is past the hour when little ones should be in bed. Come, Nallia. Bad dreams or not, you need to go back to sleep. We also need to have another talk about running away from me and greeting strangers."

Nallia whined but obediently followed behind her mother. Tathaln motioned for Sabine and Malek to follow him down the hill toward the camp. Blossom wriggled against her neck, but she didn't poke her head out. Until Blossom was sure it was safe, the pixie would probably remain out of sight and snoop around using her glamoured form. Pixies were extraordinarily curious, and she had to be itching to get a good look at these people. Unfortunately, it was too cold to explore.

"So you're a performer, eh?" Tathaln asked, leading them toward the fire.

"I suppose we've all been performers at some point in our lives," Sabine replied, studying the intricate designs on the wagons they passed. Blossom had been right; decorative flower blossoms in all sorts of colors had been painted on the side of one of the wagons.

Eruk, the large ogre, glanced at her and arched his hairless brow. "You like?"

Sabine nodded. "Very much. They're beautiful."

Tathaln grinned and gestured at Zoty. "He's our resident painter and artist, among other things."

"You're very talented. I'm looking forward to seeing more of your work when it's daylight." Sabine smiled warmly at Zoty, who blushed furiously and shuffled his feet.

Malek dropped his bags in front of the fire, and Sabine did the same. The heat from the fire helped ward against the worst of the night's chill. She unbuttoned her shirt and handed it back to Malek. He tucked it back inside one of his bags.

Sitting down on one of the large rocks beside the fire, she asked, "What do you do, Eruk?"

The ogre flexed his muscles. "Games of skill and strength."

Tathaln picked up a stick and poked at the fire, sending a burst of flames upward. "You'll find most of us have different talents. Like yourself, I'm more of a performer. Theater is my preference, but I also have a fair hand as a musician. Gina also occasionally dances, but she prefers telling fortunes and reading cards. We change our acts to suit our audiences."

Zoty brought over a large flask and hesitantly offered it to Sabine. Malek sat beside her, close enough that she was extremely aware of his presence. Without the dragon medallion around his neck, her magic was responding to him every time he was within touching distance. It was requiring more effort on her part to keep her power suppressed.

She accepted the flask and took a sip, mildly surprised by the subtle herbal mixture. "This is very good. Did you make it?"

Zoty nodded. Sabine passed it to Malek to try and then smiled at Zoty.

"I have a close friend who also makes teas. She'd love to exchange recipes with you."

Zoty grinned and crouched near the fire, his posture reminding her of the Beastman who had been her sworn protector since she was a baby. She needed to be careful not to let the familiarity affect her too much. It had been a long time since she'd been around so many magical people, but it wouldn't be smart to completely let down her guard.

Tathaln studied both her and Malek. "What brought you to Karga? I'm surprised you'd risk going there this close to their burning festival." He gestured at Sabine's ears. "Your features are more Faelike than mine, but your companion could easily pass for a human."

Malek frowned. "It was supposed to be a quick stop. Our ship was attacked by the Merfolk and took significant damage. We went to Karga on foot to arrange for repairs."

Tathaln arched his brow. "The Merfolk attacked your ship without provocation?"

Sabine hesitated, trying to decide how much truth to share with them. If these people were the key to saving Esmelle, she needed to tell them something. "Not exactly. I believe they objected to some passengers we had on board with us."

Zoty nodded and pointed at himself.

Sabine frowned and asked, "They don't like your people, Zoty?"

Zoty's shoulders slumped, and he shook his head.

Eruk scowled. "Don't like mine either. Don't think they like anyone."

Tathaln leaned back and said, "That's why we travel by land. The Merfolk seem to attack more ships every year, especially those with magic users on board. I'm surprised you managed to make it to shore."

"It was a near thing, and the situation in Karga wasn't much better," Malek replied, glancing around the camp. "I'm anxious to put some distance between us and that city. What time do you normally head out in the morning?"

Tathaln rubbed his chin. "Shortly after daylight. Normally, we'd stay a bit longer into the day, but not if they're starting the burning festival early. There won't be any profit in the city until they reopen the gates and their need for vengeance is pacified. None of us were happy Ryley wanted to try his luck in Karga again."

Zoty made several hand gestures, and Tathaln nodded. "Right. We usually have a few people assigned to keep watch throughout the night for safety. Ryley mentioned you knew your way around weapons?"

Malek nodded. "I do."

"Good," Tathaln said and stood. "You'll help with the watch tomorrow night. In the meantime, you two can get some rest in my wagon. We'll figure out the rest of the sleeping arrangements when Ryley gets up in the morning. Come along, and I'll show you where you're bunking."

Sabine and Malek picked up their bags and followed Tathaln to a dark-blue wagon painted with a smattering of stars. Images of trees lined the bottom, as though the wagon represented the night's sky over the Silver Forest. Sabine ran her hand over the painted surface. "Extraordinary. Zoty is incredibly talented."

Tathaln nodded and opened the door to the wagon. "He is, and we're lucky to have him with us. He seems to like you, as does Nallia. Both of them are normally more suspicious of outsiders."

Sabine smiled. "Both the kumili and lizardmen are shrewd judges of character. They likely sense we're not a threat."

"Perhaps," Tathaln said, studying her thoughtfully. "Make yourself at home. We'll wake you at first light so we can get underway. Breakfast will be served by Eruk, who also doubles as our cook. We'll need your help to break down the camp."

Malek nodded. "We'll see you in the morning."

Sabine walked up the small ramp into the wagon and ducked inside. It was fairly tight quarters with Tathaln's belongings piled everywhere. With the addition of two people, a pixie, and their three bags, sharing the space with Malek would require a bit of creativity. But at least it was warmer within the confines of the wagon. There were two windows on each side, but they were latched shut to keep out the cold night air.

After placing her bag on the floor, she scooted to the far

side of the wagon and pulled off her sandals. She removed most of her weapons and placed them near the bedding where they were easily accessible.

Malek did the same and sidled up next to her. "I was starting to wonder if we'd get any sleep tonight."

Sabine smiled and took his hand. "Me too. I'm glad you're here with me."

Blossom wriggled out of Sabine's dress and fluttered her wings. "Oh! I like this."

The pixie hopped down and started investigating Tathaln's belongings. Several chests and musical instruments had been lined against the far wall and reached all the way to the ceiling. Blankets and a stuffed mattress took up the other side of the wagon, forming a makeshift bed with enough room to fit two people. It was cozy and far preferable to staying in Karga, where fear permeated the air like a bitter perfume.

Sabine retrieved Blossom's box and opened the lid so the pixie could sleep in comfort, surrounded by flowers. With a yawn, Sabine crawled to the bedding. If they were lucky, they might manage to get a few hours of sleep before they had to be up. Malek joined her and lay beside her.

The silence in the enclosed wagon was heavy, and Sabine knew Malek was as much aware of her presence as she was of his. This setting was even more intimate than their room in the inn, but no less fraught with danger. Sabine bit her lip and stared up at the wooden slats forming the wagon's ceiling. "I'm not sure why, but I feel as though we can trust these people."

Malek put his hands behind his head. "Maybe. More than some people in Karga anyway."

"I like them," Blossom said, peeking inside a carved flute. "I can snoop around the camp tomorrow when it's warm.

What sort of desert bug could I turn into? Do they have butterflies here?"

Sabine turned and propped herself up on an elbow. "I'm not sure, but be careful. Most of these people have more than a small amount of magical ability. They've probably encountered pixies before."

Blossom grinned. "I know how to be sneaky."

"Yes, you do," Sabine said in agreement and winked at the pixie.

Malek reached up and tucked some of Sabine's hair behind her ear. "If they spot Blossom, will they know who you are?"

Sabine smiled at his concern and lay back down. "I don't believe so. Pixies gravitate toward anyone with Fae magic. The stronger the source of magic, the larger the colony they can sustain. Since Blossom's the only one here, they shouldn't think too much of it."

"At least that's one less worry," Malek said quietly, wrapping his arm around her. Sabine lay her head against his chest, enjoying having him this close.

"I'm sleepy," Blossom said with a yawn and crawled to her box. She moved around the flowers, patting them affectionately and whispering too quietly for Sabine to hear. She was either trying to communicate with her family or with the essence of the flowers to keep them alive.

Sabine was exhausted but too worried to sleep. If Zaverza's vision was wrong, they could be wandering around the desert well past the Merfolk's deadline. It was too dangerous to ask the goddess to intervene again. Lachlina had proven unreliable and with too little regard for human lives. If Sabine didn't have to worry about the burning festival, she could have asked around Karga a bit more for any information about Pearl.

The thought of the burning festival made her more

cognizant of her surroundings, as well as the dragon beside her. Without his medallion hiding his identity, she could pick up a trace of the faint smoky scent that belonged to Malek. It was strange knowing she felt safer in here cuddled against a dragon than outside in a city full of humans.

"Sabine," Malek said in a voice barely above a whisper. "Will you tell me what you did back in that alley?"

She hesitated and then sighed. "I suppose I owe you an explanation."

He didn't respond. Instead, he simply waited.

Sabine sat up again, needing a moment to collect her thoughts. She stared at the grains of wood on the wagon's walls in front of her and wrapped her arms around her knees. If he'd been Fae, he would have understood immediately what she'd gifted him. This was just another reminder of their differences.

"I mentioned before about marks having different purposes. The first time I marked you when we met, it was simply to acknowledge a debt. That's the most common type of mark and can be done by almost anyone with shared Fae heritage."

"I was surprised when you suggested it. Was that the only reason you did it?"

She shook her head. "No. It was also to ensure Dax would hesitate before deciding to harm you. He's always been fairly unpredictable, and I was… curious about you. I would have been annoyed if he tried to kill you before I got to know you better."

"As would I," he replied with a chuckle. "The second change was to deepen our connection so we could share energy without blood?"

"Yes," Sabine said quietly and then paused. "There are other types of bonds too, but they're less common. Most of them can only be forged by a member of the royal family or by members of specific bloodlines."

He frowned. "You mentioned other marks earlier. What do they do?"

She shrugged. "It depends on the need. Sometimes they can be used to indicate fealty. Other times, they can be used between bonded mates to share power or even communicate telepathically. Both Balkin and Bane have marks indicating a deeper connection or blood debt to me, but the purpose of their marks is different from yours."

"I feel more connected to you than I did earlier," Malek said, studying her thoughtfully. "It's an awareness of sorts. I believe I could pick you out of a room even if I were deaf and blind."

"That's not too far from the truth," she said and lowered her gaze, somewhat ashamed she'd changed the mark without asking his permission.

Her people used to do such a thing and far worse to unsuspecting strangers, but Sabine had never counted herself among them until now. She'd always prided herself on maintaining balance and not subjecting her will onto others. It didn't matter that her reasons for changing Malek's mark were altruistic. The result was the same. It was a gift, but she'd stolen his choice on whether to accept it.

With a sigh, she continued, "Our previous mark required both of us to have the same intent to use the connection between us. You weren't in a position to help me share my strength with you, so I had to change the mark to force you into accepting my magic."

Malek's frown deepened, and he traced the mark on his wrist. "If that's all it was, that's not so bad. It's strange though. I swear I can even feel your heart beating when I touch it."

She swallowed and met his gaze. "It's because I'm tied to

you now, Malek. You have the ability to pull power from me as you need it. You could even strip away my glamour and negate my magic if you chose to do so. I won't be able to pull power from you the same way."

His eyes widened, and he sat up. "What? Why would you do this?"

Sabine turned to face him completely, needing him to understand. She hadn't made this sacrifice lightly, and she never would have considered it if he were anyone else. "Because I trust you with my life. Back in Akros, you protected me when I was powerless and too weak to even stand. You showed me with your actions who you are, Malek. I wasn't about to leave you defenseless and surrounded by enemies when I could protect you."

"It's *not* the same, Sabine," he replied, his eyes blazing. "You shouldn't have done this. What happens if I'm not aware of what I'm doing and pull power from you when you need it? What if I accidentally strip your glamour and expose you?"

Sabine paused, taken aback by his response. Of all the reactions she'd expected, anger wasn't one of them. "I did what was necessary, Malek, nor do I regret it. What kind of person do you take me for? Do you think I should have allowed you to be harmed after you went to such lengths to protect me back in Akros? You stayed with me then and put yourself in harm's way to keep me safe."

"I was *never* in danger in Akros," he said with a low growl. "After you used up your magic to break the chalice's hold on Dax, I had a choice. I *chose* to do as you instructed and take you to your friends because you trusted them. At the time, we barely knew each other. You never would have forgiven me if I had taken you away from the city until you'd recovered. I could have shifted and flown away at any time."

Sabine arched her brow, not wanting to think about that

possibility too closely. Gods. She'd have lost her mind if he'd done such a thing. "That may be, but what about when you decided to lead the Wild Hunt away from me? When you put yourself in harm's way to protect those children?"

"Dammit, Sabine," he muttered, running a hand over his head. "I admit I don't know nearly enough about the Fae, but I know the value your people place on maintaining balance. That's why even words of gratitude can be an acknowledgment of a debt. By doing this, you've upset the balance between us, haven't you?"

Sabine squeezed her eyes shut. She should have known he'd cut to the heart of the matter to expose the true source of her concern. Even now, the imbalance weighed upon her soul. "Yes."

Malek reached over and took her hand in his. "Can you change it back?"

She shook her head. "If there's a way, I don't know how. My magic is still evolving, and there are nuances to it I don't understand." She paused, frustrated with her limitations and lack of knowledge.

"What do you mean?"

Sabine bit her lip, trying to figure out how to explain. "In Faerie, young Fae are trained by tutors and Elders until they reach at least a century in age. Afterward, our magic becomes more specialized. By that point, we're able to explore the depths of our power and its limitations without guidance."

He nodded. "My grandmother told me the same."

She looked away, staring at the wall of the wagon without really seeing it. "How old do you think I am, Malek?"

Malek paused, studying her for a long time. "From what I've seen, your power is substantial. I assumed you were close to the century mark. That's not the case, is it?"

Sabine lowered her gaze. "No. I'm only twenty-seven."

"What?" Malek whispered, his hand tightening over hers.

"How could that be? You're telling me you were only seventeen when you left Faerie? You barely understood your magic. How the hell did you manage to survive without a guide?"

Sabine lifted her head to meet his gaze. "Dax and Bane. When Balkin left me with them, I resented it—and them. It wasn't easy for any of us, but we eventually managed to find a way. I owe them a great deal. I wouldn't have survived without them."

Malek rubbed his thumb over the back of her hand. "Demons aren't altruistic, Sabine. They wouldn't have helped you if they didn't get something out of it."

"I know," she replied, staring down at their clasped hands. "I was always stronger with my Unseelie magic, and they helped teach me to temper it. When I couldn't control my power, they siphoned off the excess to keep me hidden. They may have received some benefits, but I did too. It was Balkin's hope I'd learn enough out in the world to stand a chance against my father one day."

Malek frowned. "So that's why you're so close to Dax and Bane? I know you and Dax were lovers, but I also thought you were intimate with Bane. The rumors in Dax's crew suggested that was the reason for their falling out."

Sabine shook her head. "It wasn't like that. After I left Faerie, I had to relearn new ways of doing things. My first impulse was always to use magic, but I couldn't do that if I was to stay hidden. Dax and Bane both taught me how to protect myself using non-magical means. Once I became proficient in fighting with mundane weapons, Dax began to challenge me in other ways."

"What do you mean?"

She hesitated. "For a Fae, magic and intimacy go hand in hand. I needed to control my power under any circumstances, not just in matters of life and death. Dax and I became lovers, not because of any real affection we had for each other, but simply as a way for me to gain more control over my magic. I needed to know I could be physically intimate with someone without betraying myself. Later on, it was more about companionship and exchanging power. It was exhausting trying to hide my identity all the time, and I didn't have to pretend with him."

Malek stared at her, his expression one of stunned disbelief. "And Bane?"

Sabine gave him a small smile. "Never. It wasn't necessary because of the type of mark we share, and it would have caused problems with Dax. We've slept together in the same bed, but it was always done as an exchange of power and magic. It was never anything more, nor will it be. Other than Esme, Dax and Bane were the only two people outside of Faerie who knew some of my secrets. That was the basis of our relationship."

His brow furrowed. "I had no idea. I've seen the way you two look at each other. I thought..."

Sabine shook her head. "No. Don't get me wrong; I care for both of them a great deal. They helped me through some very difficult times. In their own way, they care for me too."

Malek regarded her with skepticism, and she laughed.

"Really," she insisted with a smile, darting a glance at Blossom to make sure the pixie was still asleep. "Bane and Dax do care, but it's different for them. Sometimes, it's hard for them to understand me or my motivations. Demons are more focused on physical needs and will manipulate any situation to achieve their goals. They don't always understand the softer emotions and even view such things as a weakness. They wouldn't have considered protecting the children in Akros like you did by trying to lead the Wild Hunt away."

Malek gave her a dry look. "That explains why the children were frightened when you summoned Bane to their hideout."

Sabine nodded. "Bane is more even-tempered than his brother, but he's still a demon. He wouldn't have harmed them since it would have been a violation of our agreement, but the children didn't know that. I always warned them to stay away from demons, especially when they weren't with me."

"I'll have to take your word for it," Malek said with a sigh and looked down at the mark she'd given him. "Well, I suppose we're both swimming in uncharted waters. Tell me more about the change you made back in Karga. Maybe we can figure out a possible solution."

Sabine frowned, trying to decide on a suitable analogy to help clarify things. "Instead of sharing a bucket, I suppose you could say I forced open a one-way valve. It allows a significant amount of magic to flow from me to you. Once such a valve has been opened, it's difficult to close it again. Over time and if it's not used, the bond between us may lessen. I can't guarantee it though."

He blew out a breath. "Can we change it further so you can do the same to me? Take my power whenever it suits you?"

Sabine stared at him in surprise. "There's no need, Malek. I don't regret my decision. I knew what I was doing when I offered my power to you."

"I want things to be equal between us, Sabine. Do whatever is necessary to restore the balance between us," he stated, his shoulders tense and unyielding.

She tilted her head and studied him. The look of determination in his eyes softened her resistance, but she didn't want him making this offer out of obligation. "We're allies, Malek—and now we're also lovers. Whether you offer me your power won't change that."

"Forget our alliance for a moment." He reached over and took both her hands in his again. "I want a deeper connection with you, Sabine, but not because of what you can offer me with your magic. This is about who you are as a person. After what you just told me, I have even more respect and admiration for you. I'm not willing to risk anything interfering with what's developing between us."

Her heart melted at his words. May the gods help her. She was falling in love with a dragon, and it was both equally thrilling and terrifying. "Are you sure about this, Malek? You're willing to give me the ability to use your power as I see fit?"

He lifted her hand and kissed her knuckles. "I'm sure. I don't want any distance between us, and any imbalance will likely lead to such. If things between us continue to progress like I hope, I don't want you to have any doubts about me."

Sabine leaned forward and kissed him. He pulled her closer to deepen their kiss. His power wrapped around her, and she responded in kind. This is what she'd wanted from him. It wasn't about using him to achieve her goals but about something deeper and far more precious.

He cupped her face and murmured, "If I keep kissing you, I'll forget everything else. As it is, I'm going to have a hard time keeping my hands off you tonight. Before I get distracted completely, how do we make this happen?"

Sabine smiled and sat back. "A small cut will be sufficient. There's power in blood, and a gift of such will seal the binding. As long as the intent is there, the magic will take care of the rest."

Malek picked up her knife. When she nodded, he cut his finger the same way she'd done and held out his hand. She held his gaze and cradled his hand, trying to quell the butterflies in her stomach. Once they did this, they'd be irrevocably entwined until they departed this world. She took a steadying breath and lowered her head, accepting the blood offering.

The sharp metallic taste of his heated blood touched her tongue. She swallowed, and his power slammed into her, threatening to burn her alive from within. The scent of burnt leaves filled her nose, and she cried out, struggling to wrest control of the magic. Her skin was on fire, the pain nearly unbearable. It was everywhere, even shooting down her arms and legs. She couldn't think beyond the fire racing through her body.

"Shit. No. Not like this," Malek said in a frantic voice. He wrapped his arm around her and pulled her onto his lap. "I will *not* allow my magic to harm you. I know it hurts, but you should be protected from the worst of it. Please, sweetheart. Breathe."

She tried to focus on his words and rise above the excruciating agony. His power wrapped around her, cocooning her with his strength and easing the worst of the burning sensation. She blinked open her eyes to stare up at him. His worried eyes met hers.

"Let her go!" Blossom shouted, zipping around them wildly.

"Ow, what the—" Malek jerked, slapping a hand against his neck. "Blossom, what are you—"

"You're burning her! Let her go!"

"Ouch! I can't—Stop, dammit. What are you doing? That hurts."

"Blossom, no," Sabine whispered, gesturing for the pixie to stop her attack.

Blossom's eyes were wide with panic. "He hurt you! He promised me he wouldn't ever hurt you."

Sabine shook her head and slumped against Malek. "It—it wasn't intentional."

Malek rubbed the back of his neck and grimaced. "Shit.

Blossom, that really hurt. You got my back too. Did you bite me?"

"Pixie dust," Sabine managed to say, still shaking from the pain. It was starting to subside, but she should have known better. Her magic was strongest in the forests, and fire was their greatest threat. She hadn't expected to be nearly boiled alive by accepting his offering.

"You deserved it," Blossom said, crossing her arms over her chest and glaring at Malek. "I hope you keep itching for a week."

Malek scratched his neck, shifting Sabine slightly so he could reach his upper back. "Blossom's right about deserving it. I'm sorry, Sabine. I wouldn't have suggested this if I thought it might hurt you."

Sabine curled her hand into Malek's shirt, not wanting him to blame himself. "I didn't know either, Malek."

Blossom picked up one of her flowers and brought it to Sabine. She lifted it to her nose and breathed in the light floral scent, using her memories of Faerie to ease the remainder of the effects. When it had subsided, she returned the flower to Blossom.

Malek reached over and picked up his flask containing the last of the enchanted water. "I know you wanted to save this, but you should drink some of it. Otherwise, I'm tempted to fly you to the nearest forest until you're fully recovered."

Sabine nodded and took a small sip. The magic in the water helped steady her even more. With a sigh, she closed her eyes and leaned against Malek again. She wasn't sure she had the strength to move yet. "It's getting better. I just wasn't expecting that."

Malek took the flask from her and kissed her hair. "Try to get some rest, sweetheart. I think we should hold off on anything else magical for a while. If nothing else, at least you have enough resistance to dragonfire now to keep you safe from it."

Sabine nodded and closed her eyes, too tired to even consider arguing. Safe and secure in a dragon's arms, she surrendered to oblivion.

Chapter Thirteen

A thin shaft of light awakened Malek. Sabine was still lying in his arms, her silvery hair tumbling in waves across his chest. He breathed in her alluring scent, remembering his panic at the realization his blood had harmed her. He turned his head toward the door of the wagon and the source of the light.

A tiny head peeked inside, with wide blue eyes blinking at him. Malek's mouth quirked in a small smile at the curious young boy. The boy gasped, and the door shut tightly.

Sabine shifted in his arms, and she murmured, "Is it morning already?"

Malek kissed her hair, not eager to release her. They'd only been asleep for a few hours, but he couldn't remember the last time he'd slept so well. He reached over and adjusted the small curtain covering the window to allow some light into the wagon. "We had a visitor just a moment ago."

Sabine sat up, brushing her hair away from her face. "Ryley?"

"Someone much younger," Malek said and sat up, nearly hitting his head on the low ceiling of the wagon.

"Time to wake up," Sabine said and lightly tapped on Blossom's box.

Blossom rolled over and flung out her arm. "Five more minutes, Mom. Go wake up Barley."

"Okay, but Barley will probably eat the last honey cake."

Blossom jumped up, fluttering her wings wildly as she looked around the cabin. "Aww. No honey cakes?"

Malek chuckled and grabbed his boots. He pulled them on as Sabine dug around in her bag. She broke off a small piece of a sweetened cake he'd purchased in Karga and handed it to Blossom.

"It's not like the ones back home, but it's very good."

Blossom's eyes widened, and she shoved the entire piece of cake in her mouth. Her cheeks bulged as she chewed. She held out her hand in a silent gesture for more.

Sabine sighed and finished equipping her weapons. "I suppose there's no use in telling you to pace yourself."

Blossom shook her head and held out both hands, her eyes pleading. Malek chuckled. He'd seen his little sister make that face often enough over the years when she wanted something.

Sabine sighed and broke off another piece of cake. "That's the last one for now. Don't you dare get crumbs everywhere. We're just borrowing this wagon."

Blossom nodded and shoved the second piece in her mouth. She was barely able to close her mouth, but she somehow managed to chew.

Malek frowned at the pixie, wondering where she kept all of it. "Is she going to choke?"

"Doubtful," Sabine said and crawled to the door. "I've seen her eat much larger pieces. She usually makes a mess, but she always manages to eat more than her weight in honey cakes."

Malek grabbed the scabbard for his sword. "I thought pixies preferred fruit or sipping nectar from flowers."

"They do, but it won't be easy for her to forage in the desert," Sabine replied, gesturing for him to hand her the bags. He reached over and handed her the one containing her belongings.

Sabine opened the door, allowing the sunlight to filter in. The sun was just beginning to emerge, painting the sky in a kaleidoscope of warm colors. For some reason, the sunrises and sunsets in the desert were among the most beautiful he'd seen anywhere in his travels.

"Oh," Sabine murmured, halting right outside the wagon as she stared up at the sky.

He smiled and put his arm around her waist. "It's beautiful, isn't it?"

"Is it always like this?" she whispered and leaned against him.

"Most days. The first time I saw it, I had a similar reaction. Although, it never seems to get old."

She smiled up at him, and his heart skipped a beat. In this light, she was absolutely breathtaking. He tucked her loose hair behind her ear and murmured, "I'm trying to decide which is more beautiful, you or the sunrise."

Her smile deepened, and she kissed him lightly. "Flatterer."

"Ah, good. You're up," a man called, heading toward them.

Malek turned, automatically angling himself in front of Sabine. She placed her hand on his arm and whispered, "He's a kumili."

Malek didn't know much about them, except they were shapeshifters of some type. The man walking toward them had the same dark hair and golden skin of the woman they'd met the previous night. While she'd been delicate and feminine, this man was taller than Malek and barrel-chested. He had a long scar on the side of his face, which disappeared into his hairline.

"I'm Bruin. You must be Malek." He scanned Sabine up and down. He grinned, revealing very white teeth. "You must be the infamous Sabine."

She tilted her head, studying him thoughtfully. "You're Nallia's father."

Bruin laughed, a rich sound that exuded warmth. "That I am. I heard Nallia was rather taken with you. Gina wasn't terribly pleased she ran off into the night."

"She's a beautiful child," Sabine said, returning his smile. "The gods have favored you both."

"Aye," he said in agreement and gestured at the central campfire. "We're sitting down to break our night's fast before we get moving. Join us and be welcome. No harm will come to you here."

Malek had some misgivings, but Sabine was oddly trusting of these people. It was surprising, given her history. She'd been more reserved back in Akros, but something about these people set her at ease. He wished he'd asked her more about the kumili when he'd had the chance, but he'd been too focused on how she'd changed the mark on his wrist.

Sabine poked her head back into the wagon and said something too low to overhear. Blossom zipped outside a moment later, her eyes wide with excitement. "Really? You think it's safe?"

"It should be," Sabine said and picked up her bag. "Just stay close to me until I get a feel for all of them."

Malek picked up the other two bags, wanting to keep them close until he was sure they were going to remain with these people. "How did you know he was a kumili?"

She smiled at him and walked toward the fire. "His energy signature. His daughter's magic was similar, although I would have recognized him either way. They're kin to the Beastpeople, but they left Faerie centuries ago and have remained independent. They aren't beholden to any particular family. They're something of an anomaly."

Malek frowned but didn't dispute her words. From what he'd seen, Sabine didn't trust easily. Something about these people had set her ease, but he wasn't sure why. If anything, she seemed almost excited about traveling with them.

Hefting the bags over his shoulder, he swept his gaze over the camp as he followed Sabine. A few people were outside their wagons, packing up their belongings. The setting had the feel of a small community or extended family. He caught sight of the foxlike creature again, or another kumili with similar markings. It darted underneath one of the wagons before he could get a good look.

Ryley, the musician they'd met in Karga, smiled at them in greeting. "Good morning to both of you. Tathaln mentioned you'd arrived last night. Bit of trouble in the city, eh?"

"You could say that," Malek said and dropped his bags on the ground. "Looks like they're starting the burning festival early. Your warning came just in time."

Tathaln, the part-Fae from the night before, handed Sabine a plate. "Here you go. Most everyone else already ate, but we figured you'd want to sleep as late as possible. You can get to know everyone once we're underway. Nothing much else to do once we're on the road."

Sabine smiled and sat beside the fire. Malek accepted the plate he was offered and sat beside her. The food consisted mostly of roasted meat and something that resembled flattened bread. His stomach grumbled in appreciation, and he took a bite of the meat. It was a little tough and chewy but flavored well with the smoke and some herbs he couldn't quite place. He suspected Sabine would know which ones they'd used, but she was nibbling on a piece of the flatbread.

"This is very good. It reminds me of the biscuits they served in Karga. What is it?"

Tathaln sat next to her, a little too close in Malek's opinion. "We just call it travelbread. If you know where to look, you can find these trees in the desert with little bean-shaped pods. We dry the pods, grind them down, and mix them with water to form a dough. Then we add a bit of salt, some other seasonings, and roast them over an open fire."

A young boy came running out from behind one of the wagons, with Nallia at his heels. Malek froze, staring in shock at the young boy who was almost an exact miniature version of his closest friend. He was the same boy who had peeked into the wagon and awakened him.

Sabine must have noticed his surprise. She followed his gaze, and he heard her inhale sharply. "He looks almost exactly like Levin."

"He does," Malek said quietly, still staring at the boy. He couldn't have been more than five or six, with dark hair and blue eyes, but the long-scaled tail was a giveaway into his mixed heritage. This boy was at least part-wyvern, but he appeared somehow caught in between shifts. That wasn't completely unusual, since most wyverns didn't gain control over their ability to shift until they were a bit older.

Nallia yipped at him, and he said something to her before racing over to where the adults were sitting. He grinned and skidded to a halt beside the fire. "Hi!"

"Hello," Malek managed to say, unable to tear his gaze away from the boy.

The boy blinked at Malek and scratched his head. "You mad at me?"

"Of course he's not mad at you." Sabine scooted over and patted the ground beside her. "Will you come talk to me? I'm new here, and I could use a friend who knows all about living with the troupe."

The boy grinned and puffed out his chest with pride. He flopped onto the ground in front of them. "Sorry 'bout waking you. Nallia got to meet you last night. I wanted to say hi too."

Sabine smiled at the boy. She broke the rest of her travel-bread in two pieces. Handing one of them to the boy, she offered the second to Nallia. "That's all right. I'm Sabine, and this is Malek. What's your name?"

"I'm Tobbin," he said and rubbed his nose. "You've got magic too, huh? Ryley said you're Fae."

Sabine lifted her hair to show him her pointed ears. "Good guess."

His eyes widened. "You have ears like Tathaln!"

Tathaln snorted and stood. "Aye, but she's much prettier."

Ryley chuckled and handed both of them steaming cups. "She's a better dancer and singer too."

"Are you all performers?" Malek took a sip of the tea, his eyes nearly watering at the bitter taste. He put it aside and took another bite of his breakfast.

"We are. Even the young ones are learning," Ryley said and gestured toward Tobbin. The boy was picking up small stones with his tail and putting them in a towering pile. "We try to keep to our strengths as much as possible, but at the end of the day, we all do whatever's necessary for the good of the troupe."

Sabine wrapped her hands around her mug and sipped her tea. "How far do you usually travel?"

"As far as the winds take us," Ryley said, gesturing toward the great expanse of desert. "The world holds no boundaries for us, except by our own design. We're not beholden to anyone, and we like it that way. I sense you both have traveled quite a distance already. Where are you two from?"

Malek glanced at Sabine, who gave him an encouraging nod. For some reason, she wanted him to share some of the truth with these people. "We met in Akros. I docked my ship there and invited Sabine to join me. We were heading to the dwarven city when my ship was attacked by the Merfolk."

Ryley frowned. "Tathaln mentioned something to that effect, but the Merfolk usually leave those of Fae descent unhindered. Who were you traveling with?"

Sabine took another sip of tea. "My demon friend was with us, and they took offense to his passage."

Tathaln froze. He and Ryley exchanged a worried look. Almost as one, their hands went to their weapons and they narrowed their eyes at Malek, regarding him with suspicion. Ryley motioned for Tobbin to get back. "Go find Bruin. Now."

The boy raced off with Nallia at his heels.

Sabine put her plate aside and said, "We mean you no harm, and Malek's not a demon. My friend is still with the ship, helping to oversee the repairs. When we were attacked, some of our companions were taken hostage. One of them is a part-dryad witch and a very dear friend of mine. We're trying to save them."

"If your friends are lost at sea, why are you here?" Ryley gestured toward the desert in the distance. "There are no Merfolk in the Badlands."

Malek put his plate aside too, no longer interested in eating. Whatever happened in the next few minutes would dictate whether they would be allowed safe passage with this group. He stood, angling himself beside Sabine in a protective stance which would allow him easy access to draw his weapon. His movement caused both men to tense, but he wasn't willing to remain passive in this situation.

Sabine stood and put her hand on Malek's arm in a silent gesture to hold. "We have reason to believe you're the key to saving our friends."

Both Ryley and Tathaln exchanged another look. Ryley nodded and said, "I'm not sure how, but go on."

"I made a bargain with the Merfolk. In exchange for them releasing my friends, I agreed to locate a woman from their clan who went missing. A seer in Karga suggested you could lead us to her."

Tathaln's shoulders relaxed slightly, but his hand still hadn't left his weapon. "I'm afraid you've been misinformed. We have no Merfolk woman living among us."

Malek shook his head. "We don't believe she's with you either. We were told she was taken farther into the desert. Wherever your path takes you, we need to follow."

Ryley frowned. "I still don't see the connection. As I mentioned to you back in the inn, we don't know where we're heading yet. We usually decide once we're underway."

Sabine smiled, the gesture softening her features even more. "I understand your doubts. We share them too, but you're our best chance at saving our friends. The seer said someone would approach us if I performed at the inn. That person was *you*."

Ryley shook his head. "I wasn't the only one who approached you, Sabine. People who claim to be seers frequently mislead people for their own purposes. How do you know she's not leading you on a foolish errand to rid their city of another magic user?"

Sabine hesitated and then sighed. "Because she swore a blood oath to me. In exchange for information leading to us locating the missing Merfolk woman, I agreed to protect and shelter her granddaughter."

Ryley's entire body went ramrod straight, and his eyes narrowed. "I knew you had a significant source of magic after I heard you sing last night, but what you're suggesting shouldn't be possible. How much Fae blood do you possess that you can bind someone with a blood oath?"

Malek tensed, his hand going to the weapon at his side again. It was impossible to know how these people might react to Sabine. He didn't know why she'd decided to reveal herself, but Sabine rarely did anything without good reason. He could try to shift into his dragon form if necessary, but he wasn't sure he could change back easily. He'd been using too much of his power lately without giving himself enough time to recover.

Sabine stood and held out her hand. "Blossom, show yourself."

Blossom zipped out from wherever she'd been hiding and landed on Sabine's palm. The pixie waved at everyone and said, "Hiya!"

"A pixie," Tathaln whispered, staring at Blossom in wonder. "I've heard stories about them but never met one. My grandfather was Fae, but I don't possess enough magic to sustain one." He turned back toward Sabine, his eyes filling with avarice. "My lady, you are full of surprises."

"That's what Nallia sensed from you last night," Bruin said, approaching from a nearby wagon. His face was anything but friendly, and his curved sword was already in his hands. "You have enough magic to call the kumili to your side as well. Gina couldn't figure out why our daughter would abandon safety to seek out a stranger." His eyes narrowed. "Would you try to enslave us again, little Fae?"

Malek had to give her credit; Sabine didn't even flinch. She tossed back her hair and said, "I have no intention of trying to enslave anyone, Bruin. The kumili are a free people, and I respect that. I simply seek a… temporary alliance, if you will. In exchange, I will help you however I can while we travel with you."

Ryley studied Sabine for a long time and didn't answer right away. Tathaln was still regarding Sabine with no small amount of desire, which set Malek's teeth on edge. Bruin, however, didn't appear pleased at the prospect of having them join the group.

Malek released his weapon and held up his hands in a peaceable gesture. "I know you have no real reason to trust us, but everything Sabine has told you is the truth. She is, without doubt, one of the most loyal individuals I've ever met. You could not ask for a better ally at your side."

Ryley frowned. "You misled me from the first, and now you ask for our trust?"

"You guys are stupid," Blossom said, crossing her arms over her chest.

Tathaln's mouth twitched. "How so, little pixie?"

"First of all, my name's Blossom," she said and flew to the part-Fae man. "Sabine didn't want to trick you. She couldn't tell you the truth back in Karga. There are bad people there who might try to hurt her."

Ryley arched his brow. "I suppose you have a point."

Blossom nodded and fluttered her wings. "I used to live in Esme's garden behind her shop. She's good people too. If you help us, you'll be helping her."

Tathaln chuckled and held out his hand so Blossom could land on it. "They have my vote, especially if we can keep the pixie with us."

Bruin scowled. "I say no. I won't have my wife and child put in danger by someone with close ties to the Fae. Give me one good reason why I should believe anything you say."

Sabine clasped her hands together and took a step toward Bruin. He tensed but made no other move toward her. She held his gaze and asked, "You wish to know the truth?"

Bruin hesitated and then gave her a curt nod.

Sabine released her glamour, revealing her true appearance. Even now, Malek couldn't tear his gaze away from her. The sunlight caressed her hair, causing the strands of silver to shimmer brilliantly. The marks on her skin pulsed with the full scope of her remarkable power. All three men gasped. She immediately reapplied her glamour, leaving them with nothing more than a memory of her true appearance.

Tathaln dropped to his knees, lowering his head in deference. "I apologize if I offended you."

"You didn't, and obeisance isn't necessary," Sabine said and knelt beside Tathaln. She took his arm, brought him back to his feet, and gave him a sad smile. "I'm not here to force any of you to my will. You aren't my subjects, but I would like to name you friends."

Bruin stared at her, the large man clearly shaken. It was apparent he was battling the urge to also fall to his knees. "Your markings. How is this possible? Your kind never leave Faerie."

Malek tensed and kept his hand on his weapon, prepared to defend himself and Sabine if these people decided to view her as a threat.

"Not usually," Sabine admitted quietly. "I was born in Faerie but fled my home more than ten years ago. Some of the Fae want me dead because I possess the magic of both the Seelie and Unseelie. They fear what they don't understand. Like you, I'm simply trying to survive. None of you have anything to fear from me."

Ryley swallowed, clearly uneasy by her admission. "Why are you telling us this? We could have easily continued to believe you were only part-Fae."

Sabine straightened, her bearing regal. After seeing her like this, it was a wonder he'd ever believed her to be a member of Dax's crew. She didn't belong in this desert wasteland either. She was both of the light and dark, and as multi-faceted as the flicker of a flame.

"You're right," she replied with a sigh. "The kumili have always been skilled at discovering the truth. I could have continued the charade at great sacrifice to myself, but I chose to reveal myself because I would like to have you as allies."

"The Fae have been overlords to the kumili, never allies," Bruin argued, but his tone lacked its earlier threatening cadence.

Sabine tilted her head in acknowledgement of his words. "I wish it was otherwise, but all I can give you is my word. You know the Fae cannot lie." She took another step toward Bruin, and Malek had to force himself to stop from yanking her back to safety. "I swear to you here and now: I will not make any demands upon you which are not freely given. As long as I travel with you, I will protect your daughter's life as if she were my own."

Bruin inhaled sharply. "You would place an equal value on a kumili's life?"

Sabine nodded. "Yes. With your permission, I can even help ease Nallia's transition into a human. There is no need for her to hold on to her animal form."

"If you don't agree to keep the Fae woman with us, you'll be sleeping outside our wagon for the next lunar cycle," Gina said, approaching Bruin from behind. She gave Sabine a wide smile and nodded in appreciation. "Nallia is several years away yet from being able to shift for the first time. We've had too many close calls with hunters who want to mount her pelt on their walls. If you are willing to help my daughter, I will call you ally."

Bruin frowned and darted a quick glance at Gina. "She could force all of us permanently into our animal form."

Gina shook her head and gripped her husband's arm. "She won't. Look at her, Bruin. Use your sight and *look*."

Bruin turned back toward Sabine, and his eyelids drooped as he studied her. Malek wasn't sure what Bruin was doing, but Sabine simply held the kumili's gaze and waited. After a moment, Bruin bowed to Sabine. He thumped his fist against his chest and said, "You are welcome in our camp, Your Highness. I would be honored to travel with you."

Ryley's brow furrowed, and he snapped, "Will someone tell me what in the name of the underworld is going on?"

Bruin grinned and gestured toward Sabine. "Not only is this Fae a member of the royal line, she's been touched by the gods themselves. If she had a mind to it, she could decimate all of us with only a thought. She comes to us in a gesture of friendship, and her energy shows no trace of malice or deceit. If she's here and willing to name us friends, we'd be fools not to accept her offer."

Malek lowered his hand from his weapon, sensing the danger had passed.

Ryley glanced around at the others who had gathered, but everyone seemed almost excited at the prospect of Malek and Sabine traveling with them. The camp leader shrugged and stepped forward, offering his hand in welcome. "Well, I suppose it's decided. Welcome to the troupe. We have a lot of ground to cover today, and I'm sure you're anxious to find this missing woman."

Sabine smiled and shook his hand. "I'm looking forward to it."

SABINE WOUND her braided hair and pinned it on top of her head. The midday heat was stifling, and not even the shade of the wagon offered any salvation.

Blossom sprawled out on the wagon floor. Her translucent wings drooped as she begged, "Make a forest, Sabine. Pretty please?"

"No forests, Blossom," Sabine said and leaned back against the wall of the open wagon. Only a thin hide covering the top offered them a reprieve from the sun.

They'd stopped traveling for the time being and were waiting out the hottest part of the day. The thontin used by the troupe to pull their wagons were accustomed to navigating the desert, but they refused to budge during these hours. Instead, they'd unhooked the creatures and allowed them to dig large holes in the sand where they were curled up and napping.

"What about a tree? Just a little itty-bitty tree?"

Sabine's mouth twitched in a smile, and she shook her head. "No. If you're not feeling well, I can give you a bit of magic. But I'm *not* making a forest."

Blossom flung out her hand and panted. "So hot. I'm melting. My wings are now stuck to the floor. It's all over for me. You'll have to go on without me."

Malek chuckled. "She's got a flair for the dramatic, doesn't she?"

Sabine made a noise of agreement and looked up at the cloudless sky. It was too risky to make a forest, but she might be able to do something about the sun. Blossom might be exaggerating a bit, but pixies couldn't tolerate extreme temperatures. She needed to conserve her strength, but she wasn't sure Blossom could handle another several hours wandering the desert. Turning toward Malek, she asked, "Can you shield me?"

He arched his brow. "You're not seriously considering making a forest?"

She shook her head. "No. But I can give us some cloud cover. It should cool things off enough so we can travel the rest of the way. Ryley said we'd probably arrive at one of the desert camps by morning. Maybe we can speed things up a bit and give everyone a bit of relief?"

"It's worth a try," Malek said, scooting closer to her. He wrapped his hand around her neck, enveloping her with his magic. She paused, mildly surprised the additional heat wasn't bothering her. Malek's blood offering must have given her a substantial immunity to hot temperatures.

Holding out her hands, she summoned her Seelie magic. It surged to the surface, demanding to be used. Staring up at the sky, she spiraled it outward, shooting it toward the sky in a wide array of power. The blue sky almost seemed to shimmer, and clouds formed where none had been present a moment earlier. The ground rumbled slightly, and a light sprinkle fell across the area.

"Rain! You made it rain! Yippee!" Blossom hopped up and flew out of the wagon.

Sabine laughed and climbed out the back of the wagon. A few of the other people traveling with the troupe joined them, exclaiming in wonder at the sight of a desert rain. Sabine lifted her head to the sky, allowing the light rainfall to coat her face. With the cloud cover and light rainfall, the temperature was already dropping.

"You're something of a miracle, you know that?" Malek said quietly from behind her, staring at the sky in wonder. "Seeing you do this kind of thing will never got old."

Sabine laughed and held out her hand, enjoying the feel of the raindrops. "It won't last long. Ryley was telling me flash floods are always a danger out here, and I won't risk putting anyone in peril. But it does feel nice."

Malek wrapped his arms around her, and she leaned back against him, enjoying the closeness. No one had ever touched her like this simply for the sake of holding her.

The rain continued to fall, and even the two children were scampering around, laughing gleefully. Ryley approached them and grinned. "I'm assuming we have you to thank for this?"

Sabine winced and shook her head. "Don't ever thank a Fae."

He frowned. "Huh?"

Tathaln approached from behind and slapped his hand on Ryley's shoulder. "You'll find yourself owing a life's debt if you thank them for every little thing. I've warned you about it before."

Ryley scratched his head. "I thought you were kidding."

Tathaln chuckled. "Nope. You're lucky you haven't met any other Fae until now. Every time someone thanks me, it feels like an itch in the middle of my back. And I don't have a fraction of Sabine's magic."

"Strange customs," Ryley said and shrugged. "Come on, Tathaln. Let's go wake up the thontin and get underway. At this rate, we should make it to the desert camp before nightfall."

The two of them headed to where the thontin were slumbering. Malek's hand caressed her midsection, sending a delicious shiver through her.

"How did you deal with people thanking you when you lived in Akros?"

Sabine shrugged. "It wasn't an issue. Bane and Dax offset much of it. Most of their crews were too intimidated to even speak to me. I warned Edvar and the other children about such practices, and they made it a point never to say such things."

Tobbin and Nallia ran toward them and skidded to a halt. "Where'd the pixie go?"

Sabine glanced around, but she didn't see any sign of Blossom. "I'm not sure. She should be back in a minute."

"Aww. We wanted to play hide-and-seek with her," Tobbin muttered and kicked at the sand under his feet. Nallia yipped and danced around the boy.

Sabine knelt beside Nallia and scratched her behind the ears. The young kumili stretched her paws out and purred from the attention. Sabine smiled and said, "I'm not sure you're going to have time to play. Ryley and Tathaln just went to hook the thontin back up to the wagons. Now that it's cooled off, we're going to head out again."

Malek crouched beside the boy and said, "You know, my best friend has a tail just like yours."

Tobbin's eyes widened. "Really?"

Malek nodded. "Yep. He's a wyvern named Levin."

Tobbin's mouth dropped open. "That's what Tathaln said I am!"

"It appears you two have even more mysteries surrounding you," Gina said as she approached. The dark-haired woman was carrying a small bag over her shoulder, and she didn't seem the slightest bit fazed by the rainwater coming down.

Malek tousled the boy's hair and stood. "Nah. It's not that mysterious. I've been friends with Levin for most of my life. When I met him, he wasn't much older than Tobbin."

Gina put her hand on Tobbin's shoulder and said, "Why don't you ride up front with Bruin while he drives the wagon? I need to sit back here with Nallia and our new friends."

Tobbin's lower lip jutted out in a pout. "But I want to hear more about the wyvern!"

"Later, my sweet boy. We'll have plenty of time for that tonight," Gina said and gestured for him to go to the front of the caravan. "Bruin should be waking up the thontin. You can help him with the harnesses. Perhaps he will even let you drive."

Tobbin's eyes lit up but then he hesitated, glancing back and forth between Malek and the thontin. Sabine bit back a smile at the boy's reluctance. His parents might not live in the camp, but it was obvious every adult here cared deeply for him. They all seemed to take equal measures in raising both Tobbin and Nallia.

Malek chuckled and nodded in the direction Gina indicated. "We'll talk later, and I'll answer whatever questions you have."

"Promise?"

Malek nodded. "Promise."

The boy's hands shot up in the air in victory, and with a loud yell, he ran toward the front of the caravan. Gina brushed her wet curls away from her face and picked up her furred daughter. She placed Nallia in the wagon and then gracefully leaped over the side.

Sabine climbed in behind her, and Malek joined them. A minute later, Blossom flew into the wagon and landed on Sabine's shoulder.

"Can we keep the clouds for the rest of the trip?"

"The sun needs time to shine too, Blossom," Sabine reminded her and sat cross-legged in front of Gina. Nallia scooted closer to Sabine and rested her chin on her lap, twitching her ears in Sabine's direction.

"She likes you," Gina said with a trace of a smile.

"I like her too," Sabine replied and rubbed Nallia's ears. "I'm guessing you wanted to join us so we can try shifting her?"

Gina nodded. "I'd feel better if she was in human form before we arrive at the next desert camp. We usually try to keep our distance until we can ascertain whether they intend us harm, but Nallia's always at risk." Her nose wrinkled in distaste. "People either confuse her with a dog or try hunting her. We've had quite a few close calls."

"It's better to do it now and in private anyway." Sabine motioned toward her bag. "Malek, would you mind getting out my water? There's not much left, but I'll likely need it afterward."

He nodded and started rummaging for it.

Gina bit her lip. "Will you tell me what's involved? Both Bruin and I had to learn to shift naturally. It was a painful and messy process the first time. He wanted to be a part of this, but I didn't think it would be a good idea. I'm not sure he can handle seeing Nallia suffering during her first change."

Sabine smiled. "I understand, but she won't experience any pain. I can spare her from it. I've heard it can be a little uncomfortable, like wearing a shirt that doesn't fit quite right. Once the first shift happens, it'll get easier and she should be able to change back and forth at will."

Gina's shoulders relaxed, and she nodded. "Good. It's difficult after the first shift. The pain makes you reluctant to return to your animal form. If we stay as a human for too long…" Gina's voice trailed off, and she shuddered.

Malek frowned. "What happens if you don't shift back?"

Gina hesitated, darting a quick glance at her daughter who was regarding her with a measure of fear. Using a trace of her magic to accompany her touch, Sabine rubbed Nallia's ears again in a soothing motion. The kumili relaxed immediately and sighed in contentment.

Gina gave Sabine a grateful smile before turning back to Malek. "It starts off innocently. We simply become irritable and short-tempered. If we continue to delay changing, the shift comes upon us violently." She paused, darting another worried glance at her daughter. "We risk losing ourselves to the animal when that happens. Some of us aren't ever able to return to human form."

Nallia's body shook again, and Sabine wrapped her arms around the kumili. In a soft voice, she infused her words with power to set Nallia at ease and said, "That won't happen to you, Nallia. My magic will help you transition. This is how it was meant to be centuries ago when your people first embraced their other form."

Blossom landed in front of Nallia and patted her nose. "It's okay, Nallia. Sabine will take care of you. She took care of my little sister when the main vein of her wing snapped. We didn't think she'd ever be able to fly again, but Sabine's magic fixed it. She'll help you too."

Nallia looked up at Sabine, a question in her brown eyes.

Sabine nodded at the kumili and said, "She's right, Nallia. You have my word."

Malek leaned back against the wall of the wagon. "Forgive me for asking, but I'm unfamiliar with the kumili. I've known several other shapeshifters, and their abilities are innate. How can Sabine help with the transition?"

Gina tossed back her dark hair. "We are a relatively new people, created by the Fae just as they were created by the gods. We were here before the Beastpeople. While we are true shapeshifters, the Beastpeople remain trapped between animal and human forms. They still remain as slaves to the Fae."

Sabine bristled at the comparison. "They don't consider themselves slaves, Gina. Servants, perhaps, but never slaves. Balkin Lioneyes, of the Lion Clan, is my sworn and bonded protector. He has always been the father of my heart, and I would never consider him a slave. Neither would he."

Gina arched her brow. "Then you are rare for a Fae. Many of your people use and abuse the Beastpeople as their divine right. That's why my people rebelled against yours centuries ago."

Unwilling to argue, Sabine fell silent. Nallia was listening very closely, and Sabine didn't want to upset the child before she attempted to shift for the first time.

Gina turned back toward Malek and continued. "The Fae wanted creatures who could blend in with the humans and do their bidding. Using the magic of the gods, the Fae evolved the animals of their forests and gifted them with a variation of their glamour ability. That's how the first kumili were born."

Malek let out a low whistle. "I had no idea the Fae had created an entire race of shapeshifters. Why did your people rebel and leave Faerie?"

"To protect our young," Gina said, the love in her eyes staggering as she gazed at her daughter. "When our children were born, they would be claimed by a particular family. That family would aid in transitioning the kumili into their human form at a very young age. Many times, the parents of the child were excluded from the same family's service and my people were never allowed to see their children, except at a distance." Gina's jaw hardened, and her tone took on a sharp edge. "They began taking our children younger and younger. Oftentimes, they were stolen away from their mother's arms when they were little more than nursing pups."

Malek gaped at her. "They would take your children away from you?"

Gina nodded, her hands tightening into fists. "That was why our people rebelled. We had the unique ability to blend in with the humans, so it was easier for us to escape. After we left Faerie, the Fae created the Beastpeople and corrected their mistakes. They will never be accepted into human society."

Sabine sighed as the weight of her people's failings fell heavily upon her shoulders. "It's impossible for me to make amends for everything my people did to yours, but I *will* help Nallia."

Nallia whined, and Sabine ran her fingers over her head. "All will be well, Nallia. I can help you transition without binding you to me. I would never take you away from your parents."

Gina nodded, but there was a trace of worry in her eyes. "It will be all right, baby girl. Just do as Sabine says. You saw her energy. She doesn't mean you any harm."

Blossom patted her nose again, distracting the kumili. Sabine took the opportunity to withdraw her knife. Nallia tensed again, but Sabine said gently, "This is for me, not for you. I will accept the pain of your transition so you might enjoy your true nature without any suffering."

Using the tip of her blade, Sabine pricked her finger until her blood welled to the surface. She lowered her hand enough to hold it in front of Nallia's nose. The kumili whined and cocked her head in a silent request for permission.

Sabine gave her an encouraging nod. "It's all right. Go ahead."

Nallia leaned forward and licked the blood off Sabine's finger. With her other hand, Sabine dug her fingers into Nallia's thick pelt until she could feel her magic taking effect within the kumili. Nallia trembled slightly and Sabine pulled her hand away, not wanting to risk interfering with the shift. Sabine took a steadying breath and drew upon her power to mentally will the kumili to find her human form.

A nearly blinding silver light filled the wagon, and Sabine looked away from the brilliance. When it was gone, she turned back and saw a young girl no older than eight or nine crouched on the floor of the wagon. Long, dark, curly hair fell around the girl's shoulders, and she blinked up at Gina with wide brown eyes.

"Mama!" she cried and leaped into her mother's arms.

"Nallia! You're even more beautiful than I imagined," Gina whispered, wrapping her arms around the naked girl and holding her tightly. Tears streaked down her cheeks, and she squeezed her eyes shut as she rocked the child.

Nallia clung to her mother and then leaned back. With a grin, she wriggled her fingers. "Look! I have fingers!" She stuck out her feet and repeated the gesture. "Toes too!"

Gina laughed and kissed Nallia's fingertips. "Yes, you do, my baby girl. Ten of each."

"It didn't hurt at all, Mama."

Blossom sniffled. "She's so pretty. You did it, Sabine! You made her human!"

"No, she could always shift. I only helped her transition sooner." Sabine's eyes teared up as she watched them. "She looks just like you, Gina."

"She does," Malek said, staring at the mother and daughter in wonder. "I've never seen such a beautiful sight."

Gina's face filled with joy, and she smiled at Sabine. "How can I ever thank you for helping us? I've never seen such an easy and fast shift, not even for an adult. It takes me almost ten minutes to change."

"Allowing us to share this precious moment is payment enough," Sabine said gently, not wanting to accept such a debt. "Consider it a fair exchange for allowing me to travel with you. I hope this may help ease some of the pain my people have caused yours."

"I would like to count you as a friend, Sabine. I thought the gods had abandoned all of us when the portal closed, but perhaps they still look upon us favorably if they decided to send you to help."

Sabine gave Gina a small smile, but she knew the gods didn't have anything to do with it. The Beastpeople were close cousins to the kumili, and Balkin had saved her life countless times over the years. In some small way, she hoped it would help balance the scales. At least it was a beginning.

Gina reached for her bag and pulled out some clothing. "Darling girl, we'll have to get you some clothing that fits better. I thought we were years away from needing it. Try this on, and I'll make a few alterations while we travel."

"Aww." Nallia pouted, still touching her skin. "But I want to see myself!"

"Remember, you have to pretend to be human when we're around the desert tribes. It's too dangerous for them to know you're a shapeshifter."

Nallia's expression became serious, and she nodded. "Can I show Tobbin?"

"You can show him your new form as soon as we stop," Gina said and kissed her daughter's hair. "Now let's get you dressed so I can start altering this outfit."

While Gina helped her daughter change, Sabine sidled up closer to Malek. He draped his arm around her shoulders, and she leaned against him. He leaned in close and whispered, "You did an amazing thing just now."

Her heart welled with pride. "It's not enough to make up for what my people did to theirs, but it's a start."

Gina shook her head. "No, Sabine. You proved what I knew the minute I *saw* you. You're not like the other Fae. You're something far more, and I'll be grateful for your arrival every day for the rest of my life."

Chapter Fourteen

Sabine climbed out the wagon along with the others. They'd made better time than she'd expected. Gina had explained the troupe usually traveled until they located one of the desert tribes. They were never sure of how their arrival would be treated, so they would remain close to their wagons until Ryley confirmed their presence would be welcomed. Sometimes, they'd visit three or four camps before they found one that might allow them to perform.

Sabine wasn't sure what she'd been expecting, but this particular camp was closer to a small village than a temporary location. A palisade had been built around the encampment within a short distance's walk from a small oasis. It made sense, she supposed, for them to establish a place near a water source. Although, she wasn't quite sure why these desert tribes would choose to remain so isolated.

She looked up at Malek and asked, "How do they survive out here? There are no forests to forage, no farms, crops, or even stores."

"They're accustomed to the hardships of the desert," Malek whispered in a voice low enough not to be overheard.

"The desert tribes are skilled at finding food and water where most people believe none exist. They send out hunting parties to gather food and such. If we'd stayed with the hunting group we'd first encountered, they would have brought us to a place like this."

Sabine frowned, thinking of some others who had distinctive features marking them as not being human. "Is it dangerous for Tobbin and the others to be here?"

"Possibly," Malek replied as he scanned their surroundings. His hand hadn't left his weapon since he climbed out of the wagon. "When you were helping Nallia shift, I was thinking about Tobbin. The boy's tail is the biggest feature marking him as a wyvern. I might be able to help him hide it."

Sabine's eyes widened. "You can do that?"

Malek shrugged. "Not sure. The magic is similar to mine but not identical. Levin or another wyvern would be better suited to teach the boy, but I might have some success."

"I wonder what happened to his parents," Sabine mused aloud, glancing around at the others in the troupe who had gotten out to stretch their legs while they waited for Ryley and the others to return.

"No one knows," Blossom said and perched on Sabine's shoulder. "I asked Tathaln. He said a desert woman left Tobbin out in the desert to die when he was a baby. They said his tail was the mark of a demon. Ryley refused to abandon him, so they adopted Tobbin."

Sabine frowned, her heart breaking at the pixie's words. "So he's likely part wyvern?"

Malek rubbed his chin. "Sounds like it. The wyverns rarely travel this far south, but anything's possible. Not sure if he has enough wyvern in him for a full shift, but we should be able to at least hide his tail. We won't know whether he can fly until he reaches puberty."

Gina approached them and asked, "I was going to head over to the oasis with Nallia and some of the other women to get cleaned up. We can't go into their village until Ryley lets us know if we're allowed to stay, but the oasis is open to all travelers. Would you like to join us, Sabine?"

Sabine nodded. The brief rain shower had helped cool things off for a while, but she was once again hot and sticky. The lighter-weight clothing she was wearing helped, but she wasn't used to these temperatures.

Malek placed his hand against her back and said, "I'll find you in a bit. I'm going to see if I can work with Tobbin."

"Even if you can't help him hide his tail, I'm sure learning more about his heritage will be invaluable." Sabine stood on her toes and kissed Malek's cheek before picking up her bag and following Gina away from the wagons.

Gina arched her brow. "He seems quite taken with you."

"Sabine's quite taken with him too," Blossom said with a wide grin.

Sabine frowned at Blossom, but Gina laughed. Her eyes danced with amusement as she teased, "So I've gathered, from the way they look at each other. He's not Fae, is he?"

"No, he's not," Sabine said before Blossom could volunteer any information. She wasn't willing to divulge Malek's secrets without his permission. It was one thing to share her identity with these people, but it was up to Malek if he wanted to do the same. If Nallia hadn't recognized her by her energy signature, she probably wouldn't have revealed herself. She'd known it was only a matter of time before the other kumili identified her.

Nallia came running up and leaped over a rock to land at her mother's feet. The girl had managed to adapt to her human form faster than Sabine had expected. Gina said it was normal for their kind, but it was still surprising.

"Kalli and Vervaina are already at the oasis," Nallia said in a rush, bouncing up and down. "Some desert people are there, but they said it's okay for us to come too."

Gina took Nallia's hand and smiled at her daughter. "That's because you're no longer in your animal form. Come on. Let's go see how you handle swimming."

"Let's race!" Nallia tugged on her mother's hand, trying to get her to run faster. Gina laughed and ran toward the oasis with her daughter. Sabine slowly walked behind them, not bothering to hide her smile.

Blossom pressed her hand against Sabine's cheek. "Should I hide?"

Sabine nodded. "It's probably a good idea until we're away from these people. I'll share my magic with you later if you're running low. There may be plants near the oasis where you can feed. You might want to choose a form to better blend in."

Blossom nodded, and her image shimmered into a beige moth. It was a good choice, being similar to some desert moths they'd spotted while they traveled.

As she walked, Sabine took note of some characteristics of the desert area. She'd always thought of this place as being lifeless, but that wasn't accurate. A few spiny plants poked through the sand, and orange colored rocks littered the ground. As they approached the oasis where a number of people were gathered, she saw even more unfamiliar plants.

She knelt beside one of them and ran her fingers along the leaves. It was a deep green, with veins of silver running through it. Several small purplish fruits clustered together at the top, protected by sharp thorns. Something about the plant bothered her, but she wasn't sure why.

"We call it a Lifegiver Brittlebush."

Sabine lifted her head to see an older man had approached. She hadn't sensed anyone's presence, which immediately set her on guard. He was probably one of the oldest humans she'd ever seen, but he moved with an undeniable grace, even with his large walking stick. His tunic was extraordinary, made from some sort of fibrous material that had been dyed in the soft oranges and reds of a sunset. Beaded necklaces in equally captivating shades of color draped almost to his waist.

"My apologies for startling you. I saw your interest in the plant and thought I should make my introductions. We rarely have such lovely strangers visiting our desert." He grinned, revealing extremely white teeth not affected by age or decay. "My name is Aberforth, and you are?"

"You may call me Sabine," she said, tilting her head in greeting.

"Ah, Sabine. Lovely name," he murmured, closing the distance between them until only the plant separated them. "The leaves of this plant can be boiled down and the fibers extracted for all different purposes. The desert tribes use them to make rope or even clothing. The fruit, on the other hand, is quite tasty. If you find yourself wandering the desert, they can be a good source of food and even water."

She frowned, noting he didn't include himself as a desert tribesman. She had the suspicion it wasn't an accidental omission. "My companions told me some desert plants contain water. Is this one of them?"

"Yes, but not like you might expect," the man said and knelt to deftly pluck one of the purple fruits from its thorny cage. He tore it open, bit off half, and swallowed. He offered the other half of the fruit to Sabine.

She accepted and turned it around to study the purplish fruit. The inside was a bright pink, while the center of it was a deep, almost red color. Raising it her nose, she inhaled and was mildly surprised at the sweet floral scent. She might be wary of this stranger, but she knew the fruit was safe to eat.

Sabine took a bite, and her eyes widened. It was far more

refreshing and juicier than she'd expected. She felt her magic surge to the surface, the moisture helping to replenish her dwindling supply. The fruit contained power.

The man grinned and finished off his piece. "Good, eh?"

Sabine wiped the juice from her chin. "Very. I can understand why you call it a Lifegiver Brittlebush. It's mostly water."

The man nodded and held up a finger as though giving her a lesson. "Indeed, but the plant does far more. Sometimes you will find it near an oasis. Other times, it grows in areas where water is hidden. Either way, you will find water nearby anytime you discover a Lifegiver."

Sabine arched her brow and studied the plant's leaves again, remembering the magical Faerie water they'd discovered. The silver veins threading through the plant could be a sign it had ties to her people. She wouldn't know unless she accessed her dormant memories, and it was too risky around a stranger. There might be another source of Faerie magic around here, which was why the fruit had helped replenish her power. "When you mentioned hidden water, are you referring to something like an underground spring?"

His gaze sharpened on her. "Yes. Have you found an underground spring?"

"Far north of here and rather by accident," she replied, once again feeling uneasy by this man's scrutiny. She glanced over and saw Gina and Nallia were already at the oasis. "I should probably join my companions."

"Indulge an old man for another moment if you will," Aberforth said, edging closer to her.

Sabine froze, aware he was intently studying her ears. She mentally kicked herself for not hiding them when they had arrived. She hadn't planned on encountering anyone other than the troupe until Ryley indicated whether they'd be staying.

"You're not human."

Sabine straightened and inclined her head. The Fae might not be able to lie, but she could skirt the truth. "Only a rare few can claim to be purely human anymore."

"Very true," Aberforth said in agreement and gestured at a large rock formation a short distance away. "Before you rejoin your friends, will you take a short walk to those rocks with me? I wish to show you something."

He gripped his walking stick tightly and headed toward the rock formation without waiting for a response or checking to see if she was following him. She glanced toward the oasis, but no one was paying them any attention. With a frown, she turned to follow behind the unusual man. If necessary, she could handle herself. But if this man could lead her to information about the missing Merfolk woman, she needed to find out.

Aberforth walked to a large orangish rock formation jutting out of the ground. It was an imposing landmark that offered a bit of shade. On the side of the rock surface, different pictures had been carved out and then darkened with some material, possibly charcoal.

Aberforth turned to face her. "Tell me what you see."

Sabine frowned and moved closer to study the carvings. On the surface, most of the lines appeared to be abstract squiggles, but as she approached, she realized that wasn't the case. The patterns appeared to tell a story, one with people and fish.

She cocked her head and pointed to three curved lines in an up and down slant. "Do these lines represent the ocean? They remind me of waves."

"Very good." Aberforth nodded. "What else?"

Her frown deepened as she tried to follow the story depicted by the images. "I see fish in the water and people on land. The people are catching the fish, perhaps to eat?" She moved to study the next set of images. These appeared to be mostly land images, while the earlier ones represented the sea. One of them showed the fish and the people with waves over top of them. Underneath were more squiggles in a spiral pattern she couldn't identify. They were vaguely familiar.

She reached out and brushed her fingers over them. "I don't know what these symbols represent."

"The purification of fire," Aberforth said, and she jumped. The elderly man's ability to move silently was unnerving. She'd never known humans to possess such a trait.

She took a step away from him, wanting to keep some distance between them. "Purification of fire? You mean like the burning festival in Karga?"

"A corrupted and stolen ritual," Aberforth said with no small measure of disgust. He brought his walking stick down hard on the ground. Without another word, he headed around the outcropping.

Sabine frowned and followed him. "What do you mean about it being a stolen ritual?"

Aberforth didn't answer. He gestured toward the next set of images and leaned against his walking stick. Sabine narrowed her eyes at him, but he merely arched his brow and continued to wait. This man reminded her of the Faerie Elders with his cryptic words and lack of cooperation. He wanted her to know something, but she'd have to figure it out on her own.

Frustrated, she scowled and tried to focus on the carvings. The fire symbol he'd pointed out was in the center of this side. The people were standing on land on one side of the fire while the water and fish were on the opposite side. Underneath the fire was a person holding a fish, but they were lying on their side rather than standing upright like the others. It almost appeared like they were sleeping.

"The people are on land, and the fish are back in the water." Her eyes widened, and she straightened. "This describes a ritual. You're saying Karga stole this fire ritual from the desert tribes?"

"There is one more thing you need to see," Aberforth said and walked to the far side of the rock formation. Sabine blew out a breath, but she was too caught up in the mystery to abandon it now.

Aberforth halted beside part of the rock formation that was jagged compared to the smooth surfaces where the carvings were located. It almost looked like something had split open the rock, allowing her to see what was hidden within.

She gasped at the sight of large bones sticking out from the sand where the rock had broken. Kneeling beside the bones, she reached out to touch one of them. A frisson of excitement flowed through her, and she knew without asking that this creature had never stepped foot on land. "These are from the sea. How is this possible?"

"Your ears mark you as Fae," Aberforth said, his penetrating gaze scanning her up and down. "Yet you would ask this?"

Sabine slowly rose, wary of his accusation. It wasn't the first time she'd been questioned about her origins. "Many people have pointed ears. It only indicates Fae heritage, no matter how distant."

Aberforth smirked. "Do you deny you're Fae?"

"Who can say what is the truth or a lie?" Sabine shrugged, pretending the question didn't bother her. She was getting a little too close to revealing herself. "I've never met anyone who could name the origins of every person in their family tree."

"Very well. You may keep your secrets for now." Aberforth chuckled and gestured toward the expanse of desert around them. "Our world was once very different, including this place. It wasn't only the Fae who abandoned their lands during the Dragon Wars. What do you think was once here, child?"

Sabine frowned. "Are you suggesting this land was once part of the ocean?"

Aberforth shrugged. "I make no suggestions. I simply encourage you to observe and draw your own conclusions."

Sabine turned back toward the bones. The only logical conclusion was this area once belonged to the sea. It explained the sand, which reminded her of the nearby beaches. The bones couldn't belong to anything other than a sea creature. Even the images carved on the face of the rock formation indicated a relationship between the land and the sea.

"What do you know of the Merfolk, Aberforth?"

"Ah," Aberforth murmured and gave her an approving nod. "Did you know they refer to themselves as the True Folk? What makes them True, I wonder? Who started calling them Merfolk?"

Sabine's brow furrowed. "I don't know."

"A wise answer." Aberforth grinned and gestured again at the desert. "The Lifegiver plant you saw earlier is one of the treasured secrets of the desert. It's one of the few things still remaining from the time before the desert tribes settled here. There are many other such secrets hidden, waiting to be unlocked. Perhaps you should take a walk and see what you can discover."

She frowned, guessing she wouldn't get any other infor-mation out of him. The Faerie Elders used to do the same thing. They would talk in riddles until she managed to find her own answers. She'd grown up being reminded the journey was the most important part of the lesson. "All right. Can you at least tell me which way I should go?"

Aberforth inclined his head and pointed toward the west. "Do you see that rock formation?"

Sabine looked in the direction he indicated and could barely make out the rocky outcropping. It was at least a twenty- or thirty-minute walk away. "Are there more carvings there?"

"Indeed, and beyond too. You may want to take a look. Perhaps you'll find the answers you seek. Now, if you'll excuse me, I should return to the oasis while the day is still warm. The sun is rather unforgiving to these old bones."

Sabine nodded and watched him depart. When he was gone, she walked back around the rocky outcropping to view the carvings again. Aberforth hadn't blinked when she'd asked about the Merfolk, and few people knew they referred to themselves as the True Folk. Sabine ran her fingertips along the carved images, debating the possible meanings.

"I don't know if I like him. He's not fully human, but I can't tell what he is," Blossom said as she landed on Sabine's shoulder. "Why do you think he wanted to show this to you?"

Sabine bit her lip and traced the image of the fish. "I'm not sure, but I'm wondering if there's some connection between the Merfolk and this area. Aberforth said the burning festival was a stolen and corrupted ritual. What if it's tied to the Merfolk?"

"Want me to ask the goddess?"

Sabine hesitated. "I'm not sure we should ask her for any favors. I don't feel her right now, and I'd rather not encourage more interference."

Blossom nodded and flew over to look at the images. "These look like dead people and fish."

Sabine walked closer to view the carving where the person and fish were lying on their side under the fire. "That was my thought too. Everyone else is upright, except for them. Perhaps they were burned alive? Like in the burning festival?"

Blossom wrinkled her nose. "Ewwww."

"I agree," Sabine said and pointed at the other outcropping Aberforth had pointed out. "There are some more carvings over there. I'd like to check them out before it gets dark. It might explain a few more things or give us some insight about the Merfolk."

"Should we tell Malek so he can come too?"

Sabine hesitated and then shook her head. The sun would be setting in the next hour or so. She wasn't inclined to go far without letting Malek know, but he'd be able to sense her location with their modified mark. "No. It's not far, and he's busy helping Tobbin. We have some time before Gina and the others are finished at the oasis. We can take a quick peek at the next rock formation and then head back. If we discover anything, we can fill him in when we return. If we lose too much daylight, we might miss something."

Blossom flew back onto her shoulder. "It'll be an adventure!"

"Not much of one," Sabine said with a smile. "We're only going to look at the next set of rocks. I'm not inclined to go exploring the desert without more supplies, but I have enough water with us for a short walk, and we can always find more."

Sabine adjusted the bag over her shoulder and walked in the direction of the outcropping. Glancing at Blossom, she asked, "What made you think Aberforth wasn't fully human? He reminded me of the Faerie Elders, but he's not Fae."

"He smelled weird." Blossom wrinkled her nose. "It was like he was wearing glamour, but it's not as good as yours."

Sabine frowned. "Could he be lesser Fae, maybe?"

"Maybe, or something else I've never met." Blossom shrugged.

Sabine fell silent for a while, considering other possibilities. "What if he's one of the Merfolk? Only in human form? He spoke of the desert tribes as though he wasn't one of them."

Blossom rubbed her nose. "He didn't smell fishy. The other guy smelled like fish."

Sabine laughed. "True, but maybe he didn't smell the same because he was in human form. Ilwan never changed forms in front of us."

"You always smell like flowers and the forest," Blossom replied. "It doesn't matter if you look like a human."

Sabine arched her brow. She hadn't been aware she smelled like flowers to the pixies. Interesting. Maybe it was part of the reason why they were drawn to the Fae. "How many of the Merfolk have you met? Could you say with certainty he wasn't one?"

"I guess not. I only met the one," Blossom muttered and then perked up. "If you don't want to ask the goddess, I could try contacting my clan. Think we can find more flowers?"

Sabine frowned, glancing around at the expanse of sand and rocks around them. "I didn't think you could contact them with desert flowers."

"If we find more Faerie flowers, I can!"

Sabine smiled. "We'll keep an eye out, but I wouldn't count on it. When we get back to the oasis, maybe we can talk to Aberforth again. He might drop a few more clues about his identity."

"Oh, look! Plants!" Blossom flew off Sabine's shoulder and zipped down the hill. Sabine followed her, making her way a bit more carefully. Tripping and twisting an ankle wouldn't be ideal, especially not this far away from the encampment.

"That's another one of the Lifegiver plants," Sabine said, glancing around the area, but she didn't see any water.

"Aberforth said they grew around sources of water. There may be an underground spring nearby or even the same one fueling the oasis. I'm not sure how far away they can grow."

After crouching beside the plant, she ran her fingers along the spiny leaves. This one had more fruit than the last one, and she used her knife to carefully remove one of them without damaging the stalk. Cutting it open, she said, "You should try this, Blossom. I don't know if you'll be able to contact your family with it, but you'll like the taste. There's magic in the fruit."

Blossom landed on her hand and sniffed at it. "Nope. Can't contact them." She took a small bite, and her eyes widened. "Yum! I like it. It packs a bit of a punch."

"Good. I'll bring a few more with me for us to eat later." Sabine placed part of the fruit on the ground so Blossom could finish it off. Using her knife, she cut off a couple more fruits from the stalks and placed them carefully in her bag so they wouldn't get crushed. Blossom didn't require much sustenance, but she always fared better with a variety of different food choices.

When she finished, Sabine picked up her bag again and continued walking. The rocky outcropping was much closer now, but she was still too far away to see if it contained the same type of images. The sun was beginning to slip past the horizon, an indication she needed to hurry. She could always generate a light source with her magic, but it was too risky out here with the desert tribes.

"Oh! I see more of those plants," Blossom said and pointed toward their destination.

"You're right," Sabine said in surprise. Dozens of the spiny Lifegiver plants surrounded the rock formation, their distinctive purple fruits acting as beacons. She walked a little faster, anxious to reach the rocks before the sun disappeared.

By the time she arrived, she was slightly out of breath. It had been farther than she'd thought.

Blossom flew off her shoulder to investigate the nearby plants. In addition to the Lifegiver, there were several others Sabine didn't recognize. Some of them had flowers, their blossoms both exotic and appealing as they filled the air with their sweet perfumes.

Sabine put down her bag and approached the stone formation. She could make out a few marks, but they hadn't been darkened like the previous ones. She squinted, but they were barely visible. "I don't think these are pictures. It almost looks like letters have been carved onto the surface."

"Can you read them?"

Sabine frowned. "Not sure. Maybe."

Using her hands, she tried to brush away the sand obscuring the carvings. It helped a bit, but a bit of charcoal or dye would work better. Sabine moved closer, trying to make out the words. One of them was vaguely familiar…

Sabine gasped. "This isn't written in the common tongue. It's in the ancient language of the gods. I've only seen it in the Faerie libraries and never carved in stone."

"What?" Blossom flew to where Sabine was standing. "Are you sure? Can you read it?"

"Some of it," she replied, brushing away more of the sand. Part of the words were worn away by time and erosion, but she could make out a few of them. "This part says something about blood and the sea."

"Blood magic? Like when you cut your hand?" Blossom questioned, hovering in front of the stone.

Sabine shook her head. "No. It's not the same. I think…"

Her voice trailed off as she caught sight of several more lines of text. Moving farther down the face of the rock, she managed to decipher a few more words. "This is talking about a sacrifice, Blossom. It ties into the pictures on the last set of rocks, like the dead people and fish underneath the smoke. But that was a visual interpretation of these same instructions. If I'm reading this correctly, a sacrifice is needed for the Merfolk to change forms."

"They're killing people?"

Sabine sat on the ground and stared at the inscription, trying to piece it all together. "I don't know. All magic demands a sacrifice of sorts, but it varies depending on the magic. Fae magic doesn't require taking a life, which is what those other images suggested. The Merfolk are most closely related to the Fae, so I find it difficult to imagine they'd need to sacrifice their people."

Blossom frowned. "Do you know how Merfolk magic works?"

"Not really. I assumed it was similar to Fae magic." She studied the words again, debating possible meanings. "Aberforth said the burning festival had become corrupted. What if someone misinterpreted the gods' intent when they read about a sacrifice being necessary? With the portal closed and the gods disappearing from our world, there's no way to commune with them."

"Oh no," Blossom murmured, her wings fluttering in agitation. "Pixies can't survive in the desert or ocean. If they don't have anyone who can still listen to the gods, they won't know the truth! We aren't there to warn them!"

"Exactly," Sabine said in agreement and frowned as she considered another possibility. "When Gina was talking about the kumili and their origins, her side of the story was far different from what I'd heard growing up."

"What do you mean?" Blossom asked, perching on her leg.

Sabine absently trailed her hand over top of Blossom and sent a small wave of fortifying magic over her. "When the portal was first created, humans were among the first who came through. My people wanted to learn more about them and whether they were a threat to our world. The humans were too much like the dragons with their attraction to fire. We feared the destruction of our forests. The kumili were created originally as spies to study them."

Blossom's eyes widened. "That's why they can shapeshift?"

Sabine nodded. "They needed to able to blend in with the humans."

Blossom frowned. "But Gina said your people took away their babies."

"Unfortunately, that part was true," Sabine said with a sigh. "We managed to repel the invaders for the most part. Then, the humans promised the kumili riches and their independence if they'd allow them entry into the Silver Forests. When we realized what was happening, we stole away their children to try to force them into submission. It was a terrible and evil thing, and it only incited the kumili to hate us."

Blossom patted her leg. "It wasn't your fault, Sabine. You weren't there."

"No, but it makes me wonder if the truth is somewhere in the middle." Sabine frowned and continued to stare at the words. "The person who holds the quill always controls the message. If someone was able to decipher part of these instructions, they could have interpreted it incorrectly. Many humans confuse the word 'sacrifice' with death, instead of just giving something up."

"What do you mean?"

Sabine looked down at Blossom. "They don't understand our concept of balance. In Faerie, we have libraries containing the records of our people detailing our understanding of magical principles. The dwarves use their crystals to contain their knowledge, but this entire area was once underwater. Those bones we found were proof of that. What if this rock formation was carved by the Merfolk and based on instructions given to them by the gods?"

Blossom's mouth dropped open, and she flew into the air. "And the desert tribes thought it was a way to stop the magic users?"

Sabine nodded. "It makes sense. Aberforth *must* be one of the Merfolk. That's why he called them the True Folk. Maybe he's also here trying to find Pearl. Either way, we need to ask him about this."

Sabine started to get to her feet and then gasped. "Ow!"

A razor-sharp pain shot through her hand, pulsing with its intensity. A strange chitinous creature slithered away and buried itself under the sand. Her hand burned like it was on fire, and she studied the red mark it had made. "I don't know if it bit me or stung me. What was that thing?"

"You're hurt?" Blossom asked and flew back to her.

Sabine frowned. The burning was getting worse, not lessening. Her fingers were beginning to tingle too. She tried shaking it off with a brush of power, but nothing happened. "I think we need to get back to the oasis. Water might help alleviate the burning. At the very least, I can rinse it off."

With her good hand, Sabine picked up the bag and headed in the direction of the oasis. Her vision began to blur, and the landscape shimmered. She blinked, trying to clear her focus. Her legs seemed to be getting heavier too. "Blossom?"

"Are you okay? You don't look too good. Your glamour is flickering."

"Something's wrong," she whispered, turning around to survey their surroundings. Instead of endless sand dunes and rocky outcroppings, she was standing in the middle of a forest. The trees were bleeding. Thick silver sap streaked down their trunks, and a wailing noise filled the air.

A blonde woman stood beyond the ring of trees, wearing

a loose green cloak. Her silvery white hair cascaded around her shoulders, almost a mirrored image of Sabine. Her lips quirked in a smirk, and she threw back her head and laughed. A man stood opposite her, his dark hair contrasting sharply with the woman's fairer features. Sabine recognized him. She'd seen her father often enough in her nightmares.

He shouted something, but Sabine was too far away to hear his words. It didn't matter. Sabine knew what was coming.

"No! It's a trap!" Sabine screamed and dropped the bag, running in their direction. If she could get to her mother in time, she might be able to save her. Sabine tried to fling her magic outward to stop her father, but nothing happened. She tried to move, but her legs wouldn't work. She was paralyzed and unable to do anything but watch.

Dozens of others emerged from the ring of trees to surround the woman. The woman's expression became haughty, and she gestured widely toward the people. The man flung his hand outward, flinging sparkling energy in the woman's direction. She deflected it easily, but Sabine knew what was coming. She'd relived this memory thousands of times, but never with this degree of clarity.

The group raised their hands, encasing her mother in a bubble. Tears streaked down Sabine's cheeks as she watched her mother struggle to fight against the Fae who were determined to destroy her. Over and over, her mother flung magic outward, sending a cascade of magic over the forest. Sabine's father brushed aside her mother's power as though she were nothing more than a bothersome insect.

Oh, gods. She couldn't fail again. She'd never survive it. Summoning her remaining magic, she prepared to destroy the paralytic effects and fight against the man who had spent most of her life trying to kill her.

Chapter Fifteen

 alek frowned and said, "Harder."

The boy tugged, groaning as he strained against Eruk's strength. "I can't. He's too strong."

"I thought you wanted to go to the oasis to swim tomorrow," Malek prodded, not wanting the boy to give up so easily. Some of the others had indicated Tobbin would have to remain inside the wagon while they were here. It was too dangerous to allow a young wyvern to be spotted by the desert tribes.

Tobbin's jaw clenched and he squared his shoulders, pulling again on the ogre's hands. The boy was stronger than Malek had expected, but the lesson was working. His tail was retracting.

"You've almost got it," Malek said to encourage him, absently rubbing his hand again. It had been bothering him for a while and was getting worse. He'd had to enlist Eruk's help with training the boy because his arm had started to go numb. "A little more effort and you'll be able to hide your tail until you're ready to shift."

Tobbin panted from the exertion and turned to check his tail. His eyes lit up in victory, and he beamed a smile at Malek. "Will you teach me how to shift?"

Thunder rumbled, and the ground shook from the force. Malek frowned and looked up at the darkening sky now strewn with clouds. Flash floods were always a concern in the desert, but the approaching storm had moved in faster than he'd expected. Sabine and the others would likely be back from the oasis any minute. It was starting to get late, and they'd been gone for a while. They wouldn't risk getting caught in the storm.

Turning back toward Tobbin, he said, "You're a few years away yet from shifting. Levin was around twelve when he had his first full shift."

Tobbin blinked up at him. "Will you take me to meet him?"

Eruk frowned. "You want to leave us, little man?"

Tobbin hesitated and then shook his head. "No, but I want to meet the wyvern."

"I'll make you a deal," Malek said, not wanting to disappoint the boy but also not willing to take him away from the only family he knew. "Stay here for now with your family. When you're an adult, and only if Ryley agrees, then you can seek your own kind. If you travel north to the Sky Cities, you'll meet the wyverns."

Tobbin's eyes widened. "How many are there?"

"Too many to count," Malek said with a smile. Another rumble of thunder interrupted him, and a strange misgiving began to fill him. Something wasn't quite right, but he didn't know what. If he didn't know better, he'd think Sabine was manipulating the weather again. He knelt in front of Tobbin. "There are dragons in the Sky Cities too. They're like wyverns but bigger."

Tobbin's mouth dropped opened. "Eruk, do you think Ryley will take the troupe to the Sky Cities? So I can meet the wyverns?"

Eruk scratched his head. "Not sure about that, little man."

Malek chuckled and shook his head. "Sadly, Eruk's right. You have to be able to fly to visit the Sky Cities. They're large floating islands far above the ground."

Tobbin grinned. "I'm going to fly there one day."

"Is that so? The Sky Cities?" Ryley asked as he ducked underneath the canopy they'd strung up to offer a modicum of shade. He tousled Tobbin's hair and arched his brow. "Well, I'll be damned. That tail of yours is almost gone."

Tobbin grinned and nodded. "Malek's teaching me all about being a wyvern."

"Is he now?" Ryley asked, darting a questioning look in Malek's direction. "Well, it looks like we'll be staying for a few days and performing for this group. We need to start getting our camp set up before the storm hits, but I'd like to see this training really quick."

"Okay, let's try one more time." Malek gestured for Tobbin to resume the position. "Remember to take a deep breath, plant your feet firmly on the ground, suck in your belly, and then pull. The motion will retract your tail."

Tobbin nodded, his eyes once again taking on a determined glint. He grasped Eruk's hands and growled as he pulled against the half-ogre.

"Malek!" Blossom screamed and darted in between the wagons. Her normally translucent wings were tinged with red, and pixie dust was scattering everywhere. "You have to help her!"

Malek looked behind the pixie, but he didn't see any sign of Sabine. "What's wrong? Where's Sabine? Is she okay?"

"Come quick, come quick!" Tears streaked down Blossom's cheeks, and her eyes were wide with panic. "An angry bug stung her, and now she's saying weird things. Her glamour went away too. She thinks she's back in Faerie! You have to help her. You promised! You promised to protect her!"

"Show me where she is," Malek demanded, starting to follow the pixie when Ryley grabbed his arm.

"Wait. What did this bug look like?"

Blossom took a shaky breath and said, "I only saw it for a second before it went under the sand. It was black with a red head. The tail had a really sharp point."

Tobbin's eyes widened. "That's a red entangler. Those are really bad!"

"Is—is Sabine going to die?" Blossom sniffled and wiped her nose. "She wouldn't listen to me. She was talking to someone I couldn't see!"

Ryley frowned. "The entanglers cause you to hallucinate. There's no telling what she'll see, but it explains why she was talking to someone that wasn't there. The venom works quickly and disorients the person so they're unaware of what's happening. It also paralyzes them. Once they collapse, the rest of the colony feeds on them."

"If it's a venom, is there an antidote?" Malek demanded and rubbed his hand. Dammit. That's why it was bothering him. The insect must have stung Sabine in the same spot.

Ryley nodded. "It's easy to overlook, but ironically enough, the plants are usually found near the entangler colonies. It's a short wide bush about this tall." Ryley held his hand off the ground to indicate the size. "It's similar to a cactus with red and yellow flowers. You need to find one with yellow flowers. The red ones are toxic."

Blossom sniffed and nodded. "I can find it. I can find any flower."

"What do we do with the flower once we locate it?" Malek

asked. He was anxious to get to Sabine, but he needed as much information as possible if he was going to save her.

"Peel back the petals," Ryley instructed. "There should be a small seedpod inside. You need to find one that's white or yellow. If it's black, it's rotten and it won't work. Have her eat the pod. It won't take long to work, and it's the only chance you have to save her. If she's too far gone, you won't be able to pull her out of her hallucinations."

Malek nodded. "Yellow flower. White or yellow pod. Go, Blossom. Find the flower and then track down Sabine."

Blossom nodded and took off.

Ryley frowned and asked, "How will you find her? She could be anywhere by now."

Malek rubbed the mark Sabine had given him. "I can find her. I only hope you'll forgive me for what I'm about to do."

Without waiting for a response, he darted out from underneath the canopy. He ran as fast and as far as possible away from the wagons. Summoning his magic, he shifted into his dragon form in a flash of light. He pushed up from the ground, dimly aware of cries and exclamations from the people in the troupe. He hoped the distance he'd managed to put between them and the encroaching darkness of night would camouflage his appearance from the desert tribe. If not, well… he couldn't think about it right now. He needed to find the woman who had captured his heart.

Malek flapped his wings, finding a low but powerful upstream of wind to soar upon. Using his enhanced sight, he scanned the ground, searching for any sign of Sabine. Darkness had already fallen, and the cloud cover hid the light from the moon. Rain would fall any minute, and he needed to find her before visibility got any worse.

He passed near the oasis Sabine had planned on visiting, but the few remaining people screamed in terror and ran toward the encampment. Turning away, Malek flew over the nearby areas and continued to search.

Lightning flashed, narrowly missing his head, and he dove sideways to avoid it. Clenching his claws tightly against his belly, he continued to search for any sign of Sabine. Now more than ever, he was convinced this storm was her doing. If she was employing her magic, it was without the benefit of any shielding. He needed to find her before her family or the Wild Hunt began its pursuit.

Bellowing out a stream of fire, he lit up the night. It was enough to give him a brief view of the sand and rocks below, but Sabine was nowhere to be seen. A sharp crack of thunder filled the air, and several lightning strikes struck the ground near him. He was getting closer.

In the distance, he caught sight of a figure standing upon a large sand dune. The wind whipped her silver hair away from her face, and her skin glowed with an ethereal light. Malek angled his body and descended sharply, just as a bolt of lightning struck his wing. He screamed in pain and dove toward the ground, aiming for Sabine. At the last second, he pulled his dive and shifted forms. He landed badly on the ground, clutching his injured arm.

"I won't allow you to kill her," Sabine shouted in the language of the Fae. She flung out her hand, shooting red magic in his direction. He dove to the side, recognizing the color as belonging to a death curse.

"Sabine, stop! It's me!" He scrambled to his feet, but she didn't even seem aware of his words. Now that he was closer, he could see she'd been crying. Whatever hallucination was trapping her, it was a terrible one. She lifted her hand again to attack him, and he shouted, "Please, sweetheart! It's not real. None of this is real. It's me—Malek!"

She hesitated, and her brow furrowed. "Malek?"

"You're hallucinating," he urged and approached her. "An insect stung you. Its venom is causing you to imagine things."

"Another trick," she whispered and shot more magic in his direction. He dove again to the side, but she continued her assault. He couldn't get near her without taking a hit. Supposedly, the bond they shared would prevent her magic from harming him, but he wasn't sure it was wise to test that theory.

"Sabine, stop!" he shouted, scrambling back to his feet. "Dammit. It's me. We're allies! You have to stop attacking me. I'm trying to help you find the Merfolk woman, remember?"

Sabine paused again and blinked at him. "Malek? Merfolk? How are you in the Silver Forest? Where's Blossom?"

He held up his hands and cautiously approached her, aware any second she might succumb again to her hallucinations. "Blossom will be here any minute. She's trying to find the antidote flower to help you. We're not in the Silver Forest. Look around. It's the desert. There are no trees around here. Do you remember your hand hurting? An insect stinging you?"

"My hand?" Sabine frowned, and she looked down at her hands. One of them was red and swollen, a sign of the venom at work. She swayed. Falling to her knees, she held out her hands and whispered, "So much blood. Why is there so much blood? I couldn't save her."

"Shhh." Malek knelt beside her. Grasping her hand gently, he searched, but there was no sign of any blood. He wrapped his arms around her, and she buried her head against his chest. "There's no blood, sweetheart. Who couldn't you save?"

"My mother," she whispered, curling her fingers into his shirt. He ran his hand down her back, mentally willing Blossom to hurry.

Stroking her hair, he murmured, "Your mother isn't here, Sabine. It's not real. You're safe."

"Do you hear that? He knows I'm here." Sabine tensed in his arms, and she lifted her head. Her eyes widened in fear as she stared at something only she could see. Pushing Malek away, she urged, "He's almost here! Go! I can't protect you from him."

Malek frowned and gripped her arms. "Sabine, stop. It's not real. No one is here but us. I won't let anything happen to you."

She clutched her head and winced. In a strained voice, she whispered, "What's happening to me?"

"You have to fight it," he urged, still holding on to her. "Look at me, Sabine."

Sabine lifted her head to meet his gaze, but she kept blinking as though she was having trouble focusing on him. She pressed her hand against his chest and asked, "You're real? Not an illusion?"

He nodded. "No illusions. Just keep looking at me."

"I found it!" Blossom shrieked, carrying what appeared to be a small white stone.

"No!" Sabine yelled and lifted her hand as though preparing to attack. Malek tackled Sabine, knocking her to the ground. Silver sparks cascaded into the air from her thwarted attack.

"Dammit, Sabine," he growled, holding her down as she fought against him. Her magic pulsed up his arms like thousands of tiny pinpricks. If he hadn't been bound to her with a connection of her own making, the pain would have been excruciating. "It's Blossom. You don't want to hurt her."

"Sabine, it's really me. I'm your friend," Blossom said, landing beside Malek and dropping the pod beside him.

"It's a trick," Sabine managed to say, still fighting with him. He winced as she managed to land a particularly brutal blow. "Where's Blossom? What have you done to her? I'll kill you if you hurt her!"

"She's confused and thinks you're someone else," he said to the pixie, still struggling with Sabine. She was stronger than she looked and didn't mind playing dirty. Now that she realized her magic wasn't affecting him, she was trying to reach for her weapons. Without sparing the pixie a glance, he yelled, "Get out of here, Blossom. Leave the pod and stay back."

"Malek, you can't trust him. That's not Blossom," Sabine whispered and grabbed one of her knives. "That's how he fooled my mother. He's the master of illusions."

"It's not a trick. Blossom's safe. I swear it." Malek snatched the weapon out of her hands and tossed it safely out of reach. With Blossom hiding, Sabine had stopped fighting him so much. He suspected the pixie was still hovering nearby and shrouded in her glamour. "Sabine, listen to me. We have the antidote. If I let you go, will you help me?"

"We have to kill him, Malek," she pleaded, her lavender eyes shimmering with tears. "He'll destroy everyone I care about if we don't. I can't lose you. I can't lose Blossom. Please, help me find her."

His heart broke at her words, but he needed to be careful or she might confuse him too. Her awareness seemed to flicker back and forth. One moment he was her ally, and the next, her enemy. He reached over and grabbed the pod Blossom had dropped onto the ground.

Deciding it would be best to play along, he replied, "I know. We'll find Blossom together. But first, you need to eat this. It'll make everything better."

"Are you trying to trick me?" Sabine frowned and her eyes narrowed. "How do I know you're really Malek?"

He hesitated, trying to figure out a way to prove himself

to her. Shifting forms again that quickly would be too dangerous. Not only that, but he couldn't communicate with her in dragon form. There was one way to convince her, but he wasn't sure it would work.

Holding her down, he lowered his head and kissed her. She started to struggle, but he refused to release her. Finally, her body relaxed against his and she kissed him back. He released her hands, and she immediately wound her arms around his neck. At least he'd found a way to fracture her hallucination.

He broke their kiss and pressed his forehead against hers. "I swear this isn't a trick, Sabine. It's me, but I need you to take the antidote. Everything will make sense once you do. Will you trust me? Please?"

Sabine stared at him and slowly nodded. He sighed in relief and handed her the pod. She hesitated, so he gripped the wrist holding the antidote and said, "It's safe. I swear it."

She nodded and put it in her mouth. Her nose wrinkled as though it tasted bad, but she swallowed it down. He sat back, watching for any indication the hallucination was taking hold again.

Sabine blinked several times and then sat up. Malek waited, prepared to tackle her again if necessary.

Sabine frowned and looked around them. She rubbed her temples and whispered, "I don't understand. We're still in the desert. It was so real. I could have sworn..." She shook her head and studied her hands. "There's no blood. My hands were covered in it."

He took the hand which had been red from the insect sting and turned it over. Her skin was once again smooth and unblemished. Whatever was contained in that pod acted faster than he'd expected. "How do you feel?"

She frowned and looked across the desert landscape. "Strange, like I'm still not completely here. I thought I was back in the Silver Forest. I saw my father kill my mother again. I tried to save her just like I did then, but…" Her voice trailed off, and a tear slid down her cheek.

"Will you tell me what happened?" He sat beside her and put his arm around her shoulders. The moon was rising overhead, and the temperature was already cooling. The thin material of her dress wouldn't offer much as far as warmth was concerned.

Sabine leaned against him. "I told you before about my parents not being a love match. It was simply a way to further their family lines."

Malek nodded. "Yes, you mentioned the Elders had pushed them into it."

Sabine was quiet for so long, he thought she might have changed her mind about confiding in him. He was reluctant to push her too much, but if anything like this ever happened again, it might make a difference. If he'd taken a little longer to get to her, he might have lost her. That possibility was unfathomable.

His arms tightened around her, and he said, "Sabine, I need you to talk to me. What happened with your father?"

She pulled away from him and frowned. "He killed her and blamed me for it."

He turned her to face him and gripped her shoulders firmly. "No. There's something more you're not telling me. Why were your hands covered in blood? Why were you convinced it was a trick?"

Sabine pushed him away and stood. "Enough, Malek."

"Dammit, Sabine," he snapped and rose to his feet, aware his fear for her was overshadowing his judgment. "If something like this happens again, knowing the truth might be the only way to reach you! I almost lost you just now. You could have killed Blossom. What more has to happen for you to open up to me?"

"Knowing the truth wouldn't have changed anything," she retorted, her hands curling into fists. The silvery marks on her skin pulsed with her power, a sign of her temper taking hold.

"Then tell me and let me be the judge! You've trusted Bane and Dax with your secrets. What else do I need to do for you to trust me?"

She squeezed her eyes shut. "Dax doesn't know either. Bane only knows a small part of it."

He froze, his anger and frustration dissipating and leaving him bemused. "What?"

Sabine lifted her head to meet his gaze, the pain in her eyes wounding him almost as much as her tears. "I don't know everything that happened that night, Malek. What I do know, I wish I didn't."

He frowned and closed the distance between them. "Tell me, sweetheart. Help me to understand."

She hung her head. "My mother could be… cruel. When it came to the Unseelie, no one could match her in the shadow magics. Maybe she was different at one time, but not in her later years. She had no qualms about using people to suit her purposes. She was arrogant in her power, and many of the Fae resented her. My father was one of them."

Malek's brow furrowed. Sabine was more unlike that description than anyone he'd ever met. "Go on."

"When my mother realized I possessed both the magic of the Unseelie *and* Seelie, she began plotting. She believed she could force the two courts into one and then rule all of Faerie by acting as regent until I came of age."

His eyes widened. "Your mother wanted you to rule all of Faerie?"

"No." Sabine stared out at the desolate landscape and wrapped her arms around herself. "Balkin overheard something that made him believe my mother planned to kill me.

She had to wait until after she began ruling Faerie on my behalf, but the plans were already in place."

"Wait," Malek said, trying to get his head around what she was suggesting. The politics in Faerie were even more convoluted than he'd realized. He hadn't thought anything could be more twisted and diabolical than his people's machinations and scheming, but he'd been wrong. They were more similar than he'd realized. "I thought your father wanted you dead. You're saying your mother did too?"

Sabine looked up at him and nodded. "Balkin was sworn to protect my mother's line, but it went beyond that; he loves me like a daughter. When he realized what my mother was planning, he left Faerie for almost a year under the guise of brokering a trade agreement with the humans. It was during that time he forged the blood debt with Dax and installed him in Akros. Balkin knew I'd eventually need to leave Faerie and go into hiding."

Malek blew out a breath. "I'm guessing you were forced to leave earlier than you thought?"

Sabine nodded again. "I wasn't aware of these plans at the time. Balkin thought we would have years before I'd need to leave, so he sought to protect me by keeping me ignorant. Should his plans be discovered, I would remain innocent of any wrongdoing. He kept waiting and watching, but Faerie plots can sometimes take decades to come to fruition. All we know is my mother was lured out of our home in the middle of the night by my father."

"Do you know why he wanted to meet with her?"

Sabine shook her head. "No. By that point, they hated each other. My mother's magic was always stronger at night, when the shadows are deepest. It must have been why she felt confident enough to meet with him."

Malek rubbed the back of his neck, trying to figure out what would entice Sabine to meet with one of her enemies.

"Maybe he lured her out by claiming he wanted to talk about you or your brother. If he knew she was strongest at night and wanted to get her alone, he could have intentionally chosen that time to take advantage of her confidence."

"Possibly, but I don't think we'll ever know the truth. I'm not sure it even matters anymore." Sabine rubbed her arms as though to ward away the chill. He was tempted to reach out to her again, but she'd already pulled away from him twice. It pained him to do it, but he needed to give her some space.

He nodded. "All right. Tell me the rest."

"Something woke me in the night," she said softly, her eyes taking on a faraway cast as though she were reliving the nightmare. "I thought it was a friend of mine, Averia. She was also Unseelie, and it wasn't unusual for us to sneak out into the forest after dark. But when I looked outside, I saw my mother disappear into the forest. Balkin believes it was actually my father projecting an illusion to trick me."

His brow furrowed. "What do you mean?"

She turned back toward him. "Among other things, my father is referred to as the King of Illusions. No one is his equal when it comes to glamour. He can even project illusions at a great distance or manipulate large groups of people at once. It's possible my mother was already dead by the time I was awakened."

"You're saying your father lured you out of the house after he killed your mother?"

"I wish I knew," she whispered and lowered her head. "I can't seem to sort out the reality from the illusions. I went into my brother's room to see if he'd seen or heard anything. By that point, Rhys didn't stay with us often. He usually stayed with my father in his court, but he hadn't yet denounced his ties to my mother's line. He was asleep when I went into his room."

"You didn't wake him?"

Sabine shook her head. "Maybe things would have been different if I had, but I decided to let him sleep. Rhys and I were already divided by that point, with him following my father and me following my mother. In my mind, I was Mother's heir. I believed I had a right to know what she was doing. So I decided to leave him and follow my mother into the forest."

Malek let out a low whistle. "Okay. Gutsy move, but I probably would have done the same."

"Perhaps. But looking back, I'd say I was more foolish than gutsy." Sabine gave him a small smile. "Since my mother was already out of the house, I didn't bother staying quiet. Rhys always slept soundly. One of my tutors saw me leaving, which was the only reason I survived that night. It wasn't the first time I'd snuck out, and she thought I was planning on meeting Averia. She probably planned on catching and punishing us both."

Malek's lips twitched in a smile, trying to imagine Sabine as a young and headstrong teenager. He would have loved to have known her back then, before all the horrors had touched her life. "What happened when you followed your mother into the forest?"

Her smile faded. "I couldn't catch her. I kept seeing flashes of her cloak through the trees, and I went deeper and deeper into the forest. Finally, I came to a place where I'd never been. There was something on the ground in the clearing, but it looked like a wounded animal. I started to go in to check on it, but my tutor stopped me."

"How?"

Sabine frowned. "This is where everything gets confusing. Giannia, my tutor, grabbed my arm. She did something to me to make me unable to move or talk. She cut my hand, smeared my blood over her face and then changed her image to look like me."

Malek stared at Sabine uncomprehending. "She did *what?*"

Sabine sighed and shook her head. "My mother had sworn Giannia to blood service when I was born. It's not unusual for those who serve any of the royal families. Giannia used my magic against me, just like Balkin did back in Akros. Using my blood, she sent out a telepathic call to Balkin, summoning him to my side. I was forced to stand there, unable to move, and she changed my image to hide me from sight. Then she went out into the clearing. I couldn't stop her."

"What happened then?"

Sabine's eyes filled with tears, and her voice was ragged as she whispered, "I don't know. I only remember bits and pieces, and I can't be sure what was real or not. I saw flashes of light. I heard my father's voice and several others I didn't recognize. It could have just been my father or dozens of people. They kept changing appearance so I couldn't focus on any of them. I'm not sure if they were even Fae."

Sabine took a shaky breath and continued, "The wounded animal in the clearing was really my mother. The images kept flickering until I was certain of it. They'd bound her with cold iron and she'd been cut into pieces, bleeding on the ground."

"No," he whispered, shocked and horrified by her father's actions. Cold iron was incredibly rare on this world. During the war, his people had brought over large quantities through the portal while it was still open. It was one of the things that could kill a Fae, and they'd forged thousands of weapons to weaken the gods' hold on this world.

Sabine nodded, her expression pained. "When Gianna entered the clearing, they attacked her too. They bound her, stripped her, and then started torturing her. They laughed, Malek. They laughed as she lay there bleeding and helpless. She screamed so much. I never thought it would end, but I couldn't move or do anything to save her." She took a steadying breath and said, "It felt like forever until Balkin found me and released me from the binding."

"Sabine," he whispered, pulling her into her arms. "I'm so sorry, sweetheart. You don't need to say anything more."

She buried her head against his chest, and he stroked her hair, trying to get ahold of his tumultuous emotions. It took everything in him not to fly to Faerie and burn those damned silver trees to the ground to get his hands on Sabine's father. It was astonishing she wasn't more jaded, given her history. Instead, the woman in his arms had a remarkable resiliency. Her warm, giving nature and compassion was inspiring.

Sabine wiped away her tears and managed a half-hearted smile. "I'm sorry. I'm a mess. It was more than a decade ago, but—"

He arched his brow. "What the hell are you talking about? Anyone else who had gone through what you did would be curled up in a ball right now. I'm so damned sorry you had to live through that, and I'm sorry for making you relive it."

"You didn't," she whispered and then her eyes widened. "Oh, gods. I attacked you. When I was hallucinating, I attacked both you and Blossom. Where is she? Are you both okay?"

She ran her hands down his chest, searching him up and down. He grasped her hands and kissed her fingertips. "I'm fine. We're both okay. We were both worried about you, but we know you weren't in the right frame of mind. Blossom managed to find the antidote in time."

"Sabine?" Blossom asked, appearing suddenly beside them. "I heard what you said. Your father's a really bad man. Want me to send Barley to dust him?"

Malek grimaced. "That's a pretty nasty punishment, but if anyone deserves it…"

Sabine laughed and wiped away her tears. She held out her hand so Blossom could land on it. "You're very sweet, but I wouldn't want anything to happen to Barley."

"Okay. But if you change your mind, let me know."

Sabine smiled. "I'm sorry for trying to hurt you, Blossom. Can you ever forgive me?"

Blossom hugged Sabine's thumb. "I heard what you said. You didn't know it was me." She bit her lip and cocked her head. "Would you really have attacked someone for hurting me? Even though I'm just a pixie?"

"You're one of my most treasured friends, Blossom. Fae or lesser Fae, it doesn't matter. I will *always* try to protect you, just like you do for me."

Blossom gave her a shy smile. "You were only a little scary."

Sabine laughed and gave the pixie a warm smile. "It would seem I owe you a debt for finding the antidote. How can I repay you?"

"Make me big!"

Sabine's smile deepened, and she nodded. "Very well. Do you want to be big now? Or wait until we're back on the ship when you can show Bane?"

Blossom's eyes widened. "On the ship! On the ship!"

She laughed again. "All right. We'll make it happen."

"I'm going to go find more of the antidote in case we run into any more of those bugs," Blossom announced and flew into the darkness.

Malek arched his brow. "Should we worry about her?"

Sabine shook her head. "No. She's resourceful. She can meet us back at the camp when she's finished."

Malek grimaced. "Uh, about that… We may not be welcome there anymore."

Sabine paused. "Oh?"

Malek sighed and scrubbed his hands over his face. "I panicked when Blossom said you were in trouble. I shifted into a dragon not far from the troupe. I was trying to get to you as quickly as possible."

Sabine bit her lip and then her shoulders started shaking.

Malek frowned and leaned back to study her, worried she might be crying again. His eyes narrowed as suspicion filled him. "Are… are you laughing at me?"

Sabine burst into laughter and didn't answer. Malek arched his brow, watching as she covered her mouth with her hand. She was still giggling hysterically. Despite himself, he chuckled and shook his head. "If I were a lesser dragon, I might take offense to you laughing at me."

Her eyes danced with amusement. "I was just imagining everyone's reactions when you shifted. I almost fell off the roof the first time I saw you, and that was *after* I knew what you were."

"I suppose it'll give them something to talk about," he replied with a grin. "I saw the wagons starting to pull away while I was searching for you. At least the belongings I left there will compensate the troupe for any inconvenience. I doubt the villagers would have welcomed them after that."

"Mmhmm," Sabine agreed and reached up to cup his face. "How can I ever repay you for saving me again? Blossom wants to be big, but what do *you* want?"

He swallowed as he gazed down at her. "You. Like this. Right now. Just having you look at me like you are and trusting me is payment enough."

Her eyes softened, and she smiled. "If I didn't know any better, I'd think you were trying to make me fall in love with you."

"It would be nice if I wasn't the only one," he said, tucking a lock of her silvery hair behind her ear.

Sabine stilled, and her eyes filled with panic. "Don't say that. Don't ever say that again."

Without waiting for a response, she turned and headed toward the troupe's wagons. Malek frowned. If she thought he'd allow her to simply walk away after everything they'd shared, he intended to prove her wrong.

Chapter Sixteen

Sabine wrapped her arms around herself, needing to put some distance between them. Gods. She'd known this conversation was inevitable, but she still wasn't prepared to deal with her emotions for him. This could ruin everything.

He took her arm and turned her around to face him. "I think you owe me an explanation. Why does the idea scare you?"

She swallowed, her throat going dry at the intensity in his gaze. Trying to navigate these waters and keep her feelings in check was going to be impossible. "Don't do this right now, Malek."

He frowned. "I've tried not to push you, but I won't allow you to put distance between us. Not now. Not after everything we've been through together. Talk to me, Sabine. Why are you so scared?"

She squeezed her eyes shut and started to turn away, but he took her chin in his hand and tilted her head back. She looked up into his blue eyes, taken aback by the tenderness in his gaze.

He smiled at her and said, "Sabine, I've been falling in love with you since almost the first moment we met. Give me one good reason why I shouldn't."

She inhaled sharply, her resistance melting at his words. Pressing her hand against his chest, she could feel his heart pounding under her fingertips. She took a steadying breath and whispered, "Nothing can come of it, Malek. You're a dragon, and I'm Fae. One day, I have to return to Faerie. My people need me."

He arched his brow. "Do they? They abandoned you, Sabine. They chased you out of Faerie and forced you into hiding simply to survive. They don't deserve you or your loyalty."

Sabine pulled away from him, needing some space. When he was that close, it only made things even more confusing. What he was suggesting wasn't simply a physical relationship like she'd been expecting. It sounded like he was proposing something more long term. This was what she and Bane had feared might happen. It would break her heart to walk away from Malek, but she didn't have another choice. The Wild Hunt had only granted her a brief reprieve.

Even now, her family probably knew she was still alive. It would take a bit more time before they could make another sacrifice large enough to call the Wild Hunt, but it was inevitable. She wasn't sure the Huntsman would be able to exploit another loophole to save her life. No one was lucky enough to dodge the Wild Hunt forever.

Malek's arms wrapped around her, and she tensed. He drew her against his chest and murmured, "Don't push me away, sweetheart. I know you feel it too."

"It's not that," she said, turning back around to face him. "I do feel it. Too much. Gods, I can't even think when you're this close. But I have a duty to my people and an obligation to take my rightful place as the queen of the Unseelie. I can't be with you in that way, Malek."

"Is that truly what you want?" he asked, placing his hands on her hips. The thin material of her dress made his touch even more intimate. "Forget duty. Forget obligation. Tell me what you really want, Sabine."

She squeezed her eyes shut. For the first time in her life, she wished she could lie. If she could only form the words and tell him she didn't want him, he would walk out of her life and find his happiness elsewhere. It was the safest course of action, but the thought of sending him away broke something inside her.

She opened her eyes and whispered the painful truth. "You, Malek. I'll likely damn us both for this, but I want you."

His eyes filled with a victorious light and he lowered his head, claiming her with his kiss. She melted against him and wound her arms around his neck, needing and wanting everything he offered. For so long, everything she'd done was to further her efforts at claiming her throne. But just this once, she wanted something for purely selfish reasons. Malek had a way of touching her that transcended everything and reached the most intimate places within her. He might be Faerie's most fearsome enemy, but only she was in danger of losing her heart to this dragon.

"Sabine! Come quick!"

Sabine broke their kiss and turned to see Blossom flying toward them. "What is it?"

"Aberforth is over at the second set of rocks where you dropped your bag. He saw through my glamour, Sabine!" Blossom scowled and crossed her arms over her chest. "He told me to fetch you, like I'm a servant or something."

Sabine narrowed her eyes, a suspicion creeping into her mind. "What were you doing when he saw you?"

Blossom frowned. "I was putting another pod by your bag in case more bugs bit you."

Malek looked down at her. "What are you thinking?"

"I'm thinking Aberforth is not only one of the Merfolk, but he also arranged for that insect to bite me," Sabine said, her hands curling into fists. "He specifically sent me to that rock formation, and no one has the ability to see through pixie glamour unless they're Fae and have a blood bond with their clan."

Blossom's wings fluttered furiously, the tips tinged with red. "He must have stolen your blood when his insect bit you! He's not Fae. He used a spell, Sabine!"

Malek's jaw clenched. "I'll kill him for putting you in harm's way. Where is this rock formation?"

She put her hand against Malek's arm. "Wait, Malek. I'm of the same mind as you, but I think we need to find out exactly what game he's playing before we do anything. If he knows something about Pearl, this could be our one chance to save Esme and Levin."

Malek hesitated and then gave her a curt nod. "Very well, but the minute we find out what he knows, he's mine."

Sabine's mouth curved upward. "Then let's go find out what he knows."

They walked together toward the rock formation. She'd run farther than she'd thought before the paralytic effects of the venom had taken effect.

Blossom landed on her shoulder and pouted. "I should dust him for trying to steal me. I'm yours, Sabine. Not his."

"I don't think he was trying to steal you, but we *will* deal with him," she said quietly as they reached the top of a sand dune. Aberforth was leaning against the rock formation, his image illuminated by the moonlight. He was still gripping his walking stick, but Sabine didn't buy the old-man routine for a second.

Straightening her shoulders, she walked down the hill toward him. Any sign of weakness could be used against her, and she needed to ensure he was kept off guard. Dammit. She still had quite a bit of magic, but she'd feel better about dealing with Aberforth if she was at full power. The minute she had the opportunity, she planned on eating another of the fruits to help restore her strength.

When she was a short distance away, she stopped and said, "Explain yourself. Now."

Aberforth gave her a mock bow and grinned as though enjoying a good joke. "A Faerie Royal. Not quite what I was expecting when I brought you to these stones, *Your Highness*." The last was said almost mockingly.

Sabine narrowed her eyes. It was tempting to lash out with her power to remind him who he was dealing with, but it would only escalate the situation. She needed him cooperative if she was going to learn anything about Pearl. Calling upon her earliest training exercises, she sought out a calm oasis in her mind and embraced it.

Blossom patted her neck and whispered, "Let me know if you want me to dust him. I'll make sure it gets everywhere, especially all the places you don't want itching."

Sabine forced her expression to remain neutral, deciding it would be best to bury her appreciation for Blossom's suggestion. It wouldn't be wise to encourage the pixie, but it was tempting.

Aberforth turned toward Malek, and his grin deepened. "A dragon, eh? My, my. What interesting company the Fae are keeping these days." When Malek didn't reply either, Aberforth arched his brow and chuckled. "Nothing to say, dragon? Are you a Fae pet then?"

Malek crossed his arms over his chest and looked bored. "I'm waiting until you're done talking so I can tear your head off your body. Or I could always burn you alive where you're standing." Malek shrugged. "Your choice."

Aberforth's eyes widened slightly, and his knuckles whitened from how hard he was gripping his walking stick. They were the only indication he was actually frightened of them. Sabine considered him for a long time, speculating his performance was simply false bravado. It was time to force him to talk.

"Enough with the games," Sabine demanded, infusing her voice with enough power to reinforce her words. "Not only did you send your minion to attack me, but then you try to provoke me and my allies? Are the True Folk so secure in their position they are willing to challenge the Fae? You are on land, not the sea. This is *my* dominion."

Aberforth blanched. "I—I did not know who you were. I suspected you were part Fae, but I never dreamed you were one of the first of their line."

"You'd better start explaining yourself," Malek replied and gestured at Sabine. "She just knocked a dragon out of the sky. What do you think she'll do to you if you keep dancing around?"

Sabine stilled. It appeared Malek was going to play up her power level. She suspected his magic was low, which was why he was leaving this in her hands. It was a good gamble. If he pretended to defer to her, Aberforth would hesitate before challenging her. She just hoped the ruse worked and they could obtain some information.

"My apologies if I have offended," Aberforth said, his gaze darting back and forth between them. "Unlike the humans who encroach on our territory, you were never in any danger from the entangler. It was simply a mechanism to try to remove your glamour. I needed to know what you were hiding and whether you were a threat to our home. Like your

Beastpeople and pixies, the entanglers are one of our defenses and able to adapt to both land and sea."

Sabine didn't reply right away. If he was one of the True Folk, he wouldn't have the ability to lie. There was no way he could have known how he'd endangered her with his actions. Her use of magic without being shielded had announced to her family she was still alive. She still didn't trust Aberforth, but she'd hold off on killing him until she learned more.

Aberforth cleared his throat. "With your permission, I will take you to our city as a guest of honor. It's our hope you might be of some help with a rather… delicate situation."

Sabine arched her brow. "You insult me and then ask for my help?"

Aberforth winced. "A grievous mistake. I will do what I can to make amends. My city is a short walk from here. Will you allow me to offer you safe passage?"

Malek placed his hand against her lower back and murmured, "We have no way of knowing what we'll face if we go with him or even if our magic will work. I should still be able to shift, but we'll be taking a risk. Are you sure you want to do this?"

She wasn't, but if Pearl was in their city, they needed to find her. As long as they remained on land, she'd have access to her magic. With the troupe departing the area, traveling with Aberforth was their best option in finding her. She found it hard to believe Pearl could have been waylaid by the human desert tribes.

She nodded at Malek and then turned toward Aberforth. "Very well. We'll accompany you, provided you assure us of safe passage both to and from your city. I assume the True Folk still acknowledge guesting rites?"

Aberforth inclined his head. "You have my word. No harm will come to you, provided you also adhere to guesting rites."

"Then lead the way," she said, picking up the bag containing the fruit she'd collected.

Aberforth gripped his walking stick and headed away from the desert tribe's encampment and the oasis. Blossom huddled against Sabine's neck and whispered, "How can I snoop if he can see through my glamour?"

"He can't," Sabine murmured in a voice too low for Aberforth to overhear. "You were carrying the pod, right?"

"Yeah."

"It's not a native land plant. If it's the antidote to the entangler venom, it's one of the True Folk's creations. By carrying it, you weren't able to mask it with your glamour. He probably didn't see you, but he saw the pod."

"That sneaky so-and-so," Blossom muttered, vibrating against her neck. "I'm definitely going to dust him."

Sabine smiled, knowing Blossom hated the idea of anyone seeing through her glamour. Pixies were among the lesser Fae, so they didn't have the same magical ability as the true Fae. Discreetly, Sabine pricked her finger and held it up to Blossom. "Drink."

Malek arched his brow. "What are you doing?"

"Giving Blossom's magic a boost," Sabine whispered as Blossom accepted her offering. "Aberforth can't break my glamour without trickery, and this will allow Blossom to move throughout their city undetected. She'll be able to give us a warning if anything untoward is happening."

Blossom hiccupped and patted her neck. "I bet I could glamour the whole world now."

"Conserve your strength. I may not be able to fortify you again for a while," Sabine reminded her.

"What are guesting rites?" Malek asked quietly as they continued to walk.

"As long as we don't break any of their laws or endanger any of their people, Aberforth is assuring our safety."

Malek frowned. "So we just need to be on our best behavior and wait for some form of trickery."

Sabine nodded. "You have the right of things. Safety doesn't necessarily mean they won't try coercion or deceit. Don't eat or drink anything while we're there unless I can verify it's safe. Aberforth wants something from me very badly. Otherwise, he wouldn't have invited us."

Aberforth stopped walking and turned around to face them. Sabine frowned and looked around, but there was no sign of any city. They were surrounded by nothing more than the desert.

"Behold," Aberforth said, bringing his walking stick down hard on the sand. The air in front of them shimmered, and a nearly transparent doorway appeared. She inhaled sharply, recognizing the magic.

Aberforth and his people were manipulating the in-between to hide their city from view. The gods had created these magical doorways, and only the Fae should have the keys to open the locks. She'd used them back in Akros to give the human children a place of refuge, but this was something completely different.

The mark of the goddess on her wrist began to warm, but she wasn't sure whether it was a warning or something else. Unfortunately, she couldn't risk asking Blossom about it. She didn't want Aberforth to know about the goddess unless it was necessary.

Aberforth gestured for them to enter the doorway. Sabine walked toward it, taking note of his walking stick as she passed. As she'd thought, it was a branch from one of Faerie's silver trees and allowed him to unlock the doorway. The royal families didn't need such trappings since their magic was closest to the gods, but sometimes objects of power were given to loyal servants to better perform their tasks. That walking stick should never have left the possession of her people, unless Aberforth's party had somehow stolen it. But magic couldn't be used if it hadn't been gifted. Something wasn't right about this.

She took Malek's hand and led him through the doorway, using their connection to cement his reality with hers. It was impossible to know whether a dragon could navigate the in-between, but she wasn't going to risk losing him. Blossom was still touching her, but she pressed up even closer against Sabine's neck as they crossed over.

The tingle of magic coated her skin, and for a brief moment in time, she was suspended in silver nothingness. This was the in-between, the space between worlds where magic was born. It was deadly for most people to pass through without a guide, but Sabine had grown up learning how to walk in the footsteps of the gods.

The walking stick may have opened the door, but there was no way to know where it led. Sabine wasn't sure if this was another trick. Summoning her power to guide them, she reached outward to determine whether the doorway was safe. Impressions of greenery, light, and the smells of forest flitted through her mind, and Sabine frowned. Wherever this place was, it wasn't part of the desert.

Sabine emerged on the other side of the doorway, her eyes widening at the sight in front of her. Trees never seen outside the Silver Forests stood straight and tall, their leaves swaying gently in the breeze. Flowering plants of all sizes and colors surrounded them and she inhaled deeply, breathing in the sweet and intoxicating perfume. Magic unfurled inside her, replenishing her dwindling supply. She released Malek's hand, too shocked to even form a coherent thought. This shouldn't be possible.

"I thought their city would be underwater," Malek murmured, moving to stand beside her and looking up at the blue sky overhead. "What is this place?"

"Faerie flowers!" Blossom cried, darting off Sabine's shoulder to investigate.

Sabine reached out and pressed her hand against one of the trees, marveling at the silver webbing interwoven through the bark. The tree responded to her, sending a sliver of awareness through her in greeting. She returned its power, connecting with the magic of this place.

Something wasn't quite right with the tree, but she'd need to see more of this place to know what was wrong. It could simply be a different flavor to the magic since they were so far south, but her instincts warned her the trees were ill. She needed to be careful not to take too much from them.

One of the branches reached down and caressed her with its leaves, making her laugh in delight. With a grin, she said, "Welcome to Faerie, Malek. I believe you're the first dragon to visit here."

"Faerie? How is this possible?" Malek stepped toward her, staring up at the tree that still hadn't released her. "They're similar to the trees you showed me in your memories."

"Mmhmm," she agreed, running her hand along the rough bark. "This must be an independent pocket of Faerie. I'd heard many such places like this still exist throughout the world."

"That tree appears to like you," Aberforth said from behind her. "I've never seen it respond to anyone like that."

Sabine turned and found Aberforth had removed his glamour. As Sabine had suspected, he was much younger than the human persona he'd adopted. If she had to guess, she'd say he was a few hundred years old and in his prime.

He was similar in appearance to Ilwan, the Merman they'd met on Malek's ship. His blue-green hair was long, falling almost to his waist. His skin shimmered from what appeared to be scales, and his ears sloped upward into a point. The only difference was he'd traded his tail for a pair of legs and very large feet.

Out of courtesy, Sabine lowered her own glamour. There was no point in hiding her identity here. Once they met more of Aberforth's people, they'd learn who she was anyway. Besides, the tree liked her silver markings. The branch was still rubbing against her, wanting her attention.

She glanced at Aberforth. "How did you come to occupy a place in Faerie?"

Aberforth sealed the doorway behind them. "We claimed this lost city for ourselves when the Fae retreated from this region centuries ago. It's been our home ever since."

The silver tree wrapped a branch around her, easing her closer in a protective gesture. The wind rustled its leaves, and Sabine idly ran her hand along the branch, understanding what it was trying to tell her.

"Shh, it's all right," she murmured, leaning against the tree trunk and sending a wave of reassuring magic over it. "I know he's a dragon, but he won't harm you."

Malek did a double take. "The tree is speaking to you?"

Sabine smiled and continued to listen. Her magic was rapidly spreading through the root structure. Other trees were paying attention and investigating her magic simultaneously. Even the wind had changed directions to announce her presence to the other plants. The flowers were turning toward her, eager for the touch of her power. In return, they were offering theirs.

"It's more of an awareness based on impressions," she replied, looking up at the tree with affection. It had been too long since she'd been able to listen to their song. "They don't really speak the way we do, but they understand words and intentions."

Malek took a step toward her. "What is it saying?"

"They remember the dragons and were preparing to

defend me. I was reassuring them you don't mean them any harm. They're spreading the word now."

Sabine patted the trunk, and it released her. "I hadn't thought I'd see any of the silver trees again until I returned home."

Aberforth frowned and said, "We have tried to tend to them as best as we can, but we've never been able to communicate with them. They've never reached out to any of us the way that one did."

Sabine turned toward him. "You've never sent an emissary to Faerie. Why?"

Aberforth hesitated. "I'm afraid I can't answer all of your questions. When you awakened the underground spring, we sensed your arrival. But we weren't sure how much power you had readily available. If you'll follow me, I'll take you to our Elder. He will want to discuss these issues with you."

Sabine nodded and followed him down the forest path. Malek walked beside her, his hand lingering close to his weapon and scanning the surrounding area. It was tempting to do the same, but she didn't want Aberforth to know how unsettled she felt. It wasn't the pocket of Faerie that had her concerned but rather the people who had claimed the city for themselves. With every footstep she took, she knew something very wrong had happened here.

The plants reached out and brushed against her, and she held out her hand to caress them as she passed. She'd never seen so many trees and plants all starving for magic. Like humans needed plants to breathe, they needed the Fae to sustain themselves. Something had kept them alive for so long, but there was a sickness she couldn't identify that became more apparent the farther they walked.

One of the plants reached out and wrapped its vined tendrils around her ankle. Sabine nearly tripped and muttered a curse at the insistent vine.

Malek's mouth twitched in a smile. "They don't want you to leave."

"No, but it needs to remember its manners," she chided gently, but she didn't put any real heat into her words. She couldn't bring herself to get angry with the plant since it had been so long since they'd last seen another Fae. Sending another pulse of her magic over the plant, she mentally instructed it to share her power with the others. It caressed her skin one last time before retreating.

"The city's just up ahead," Aberforth said, gesturing at the path in front of them. Sabine nodded and continued to walk. None of the other plants tried to stop her again, but she could sense their eagerness at her arrival.

They cleared the ring of trees, and Sabine's eyes widened in shock. Tall crystal spires in a rainbow of colors swirled upward, touching almost to the sky. Trees, as large as any near her home, were scattered around the crystal structures, but they were withering or possibly even dying. One of the branches reached down to touch her, and she stared at the leaves in shock and horror. Instead of the deep green she'd expected, these had turned nearly yellow. The silver veins were more gray and spidery than strong and pulsing with life.

Sabine sent a trace of her magic over the tree, and it shuddered. The leaves changed to a normal healthy color, but it wasn't enough. The sickness was still there. She needed to locate the heart of the forest to see what was going on. This was the wrongness she'd felt since the moment they'd stepped through the doorway. The goddess must have sensed it too.

"This is incredible," Malek said, staring up at the crystal spires that towered overhead. "These crystals remind me of the ones in the dwarven city."

Aberforth arched his brow. "I take it you haven't seen

Faerie before? I've heard the Fae have similar buildings in their city up north."

Sabine frowned and put her hand on Malek's arm before he could respond. Something warned her it was better not to let Aberforth know Malek had never been to Faerie. She'd been surprised at his willingness to allow a dragon here. "Your city has some similarities to my home, but the dwarven influence is much stronger here. I expect it's due in part to your proximity to Razadon. Don't you think so, Malek?"

Malek glanced over at her and nodded. "That must be it."

Sabine relaxed, grateful he'd understood her silent warning. "How many of your people live here, Aberforth?"

"Only a couple hundred," Aberforth replied, turning down a path leading to one of the largest spires. Sabine frowned. A city of this size could easily support several thousand. The True Folk weren't prolific, but even the Fae who had been slaughtered during the Dragon War had thousands living in their cities.

Several of the True Folk were going about their tasks, and they all stopped in their tracks at their approach. They stared at Malek and Sabine with a combination of fear and apprehension, but no one challenged their presence. It was a little surreal to be in one of her people's cities and not see any Fae.

A heavily armed Merfolk woman was standing at the bottom of a crystalline staircase. She wore clothing in a similar style to the desert hunters, but her long blue hair was threaded with a combination of seashells and pieces of crystals. Like Aberforth, she also had exceedingly large feet. Sabine studied them thoughtfully, wondering if it was connected to their ability to swim.

The woman gaped at Sabine and said, "She's Fae! She's the one Marsious sensed?"

Aberforth nodded. "Yes. She goes by Sabine. Is Marsious upstairs?"

The woman nodded and straightened her shoulders. "Yes. He's been waiting for you. He sent me down here once we received word the doorway had been opened and you'd brought someone here."

Aberforth turned toward Sabine and said, "This is Lausianne, and Marsious is our Elder. After you finish speaking with him, Lausianne will show you to some rooms so you can refresh yourselves. She'll also arrange to have a meal brought to you."

Sabine nodded and walked toward the crystal lift situated beside the spire entrance. It was one of the largest structures in the city, an indication it was used to house guests and also as a central meeting hall.

"We're going to need to take the stairs," Lausianne said, gesturing at the spiral staircase that led upward to a nearly dizzying height. "Unfortunately, we've never been able to figure out how the lifts work."

Sabine frowned. The stairs were usually only there in the event repairs were needed in areas the trees couldn't easily reach. The idea these people had been walking up and down them for centuries was surprising. It would have made more sense to occupy some of the ground level structures. "I should be able to make it work. Would you like a ride to the top?"

Lausianne hesitated, a trace of fear in her eyes. It was quickly gone, and she shook her head. "No. I can't attest to how safe it is. As our guest, your safety is paramount."

Sabine hesitated and then shook her head. This would at least give her a chance to get a better look at the city and to speak with Malek privately. "I'll take my chances. I release you from your guesting rites and assurances to our safety only insofar as riding on the lift."

Lausianne and Aberforth exchanged a look. Sabine kept her expression neutral and lifted her hand. The nearby tree grasped the top of the crystal rings with one of its branches. With a creak and groan from disuse, it moved the platform to rest beside her. Both Lausianne and Aberforth gasped, stepping away from her.

Sabine ignored them and opened the door to the lift. Malek chuckled and joined her on the platform.

"Quite a show," he whispered, his eyes dancing with amusement.

She bit back a smile and checked the floor for any sign of damage. Only a bit of dirt and fallen leaves marred the pristine crystal flooring. The domed top was made from the same crystal material, and it appeared a little weathered, but it was in remarkably good shape considering it hadn't been used for ages. Vined ropes were threaded through the interlocking crystal rings on the top of the dome and fastened to a nearby tree.

Sabine closed the door, placed her hand on the railing, and sent a trace amount of her magic through the lift. It slowly raised them into the air.

Sabine waved her hand, encasing both her and Malek in a soundproof bubble. Turning to Malek, she said, "We don't have long to talk. I've ensured they can't hear anything we say for now, but I'll need to lower it at the top so they don't get suspicious. I've asked the tree to take us up slowly to give us a bit more time."

Malek frowned, studying the people on the ground who were pointing up at them. "Did you notice these people are afraid of you?"

She nodded. "I don't know why. I thought they'd be more afraid of you."

Malek rubbed his chin and nodded. "I was a bit surprised too. Although, pretending to be your dragon pet is setting them off guard. I don't have any experience with the Merfolk or Faerie, so I'm thinking it would be best to follow your lead."

Sabine bit her lip. "Something's wrong in this city, Malek. I'm not sure my limited experience is going to help much. That's why I wanted to get a better look at everything from up here. I think the entire city may be dying."

His head whipped toward her. "What? Why do you think that?"

Sabine scanned the surrounding city, trying to get a better idea of the condition of the land. She pointed at the yellowed leaves on the trees. "There. I wanted to see how far the sickness has spread. It's strongest near the northern part of the city. That's where the royal families would have lived and where they would have nurtured the heart of the city. Whatever they're doing to keep this place running is corrupting the balance."

"Shit," Malek muttered, pointing at the piles of crystal rubble sparkling in the moonlight. "The entire north section of the city is nothing but ruins. Is that a symptom or the cause?"

Sabine blew out a breath. "I'm not sure. As a normal routine matter, the Fae living here would offer up their excess power to the crystals to store. It's similar to what we do with our silver markings on our skin. When those crystals shattered, the magic would have seeped into the soil. It would have been enough to allow the forests to survive for centuries without us, but it's not renewable."

"Can the city be saved?"

"Not without a Fae here to tend it," she replied, wondering if this was why they'd wanted to know how much power she possessed. When the trees died, the city would die with them. They had to be seeing the signs. "It might be possible to reconnect this city with the rest of Faerie. Then the Fae could care for the trees and plants."

He arched his brow. "Can you reconnect it?"

She hesitated. "I'm not sure. In theory, yes. But I've never done anything on such a large scale without a more experienced tutor to guide my magic."

"If you were to reconnect it, how would it work?"

Sabine bit her lip, trying to figure out how to explain. "This isn't common knowledge, but all of Faerie is connected through the in-between. It has different names, but it's essentially a sticky web connecting different areas of our reality. The gods gifted us with the ability to use doorways to the in-between to travel over large distances, but when the Dragon Portal closed and the gods left us, the doorways became more difficult to locate and use."

Malek rubbed his chin. "So they're like smaller portals to different areas within this world?"

Sabine nodded. "Yes, but unlike the Dragon Portal, these doorways can usually only be opened by a Fae or someone gifted with the knowledge. I'm thinking it would be best to send word to Faerie to let them know this city still exists. They could send one of the Elders to reconnect it to their realm. I'm just not sure these people can wait that long if the city is already dying. I think that's why they tested my magical strength back in the desert."

Malek's eyes narrowed. "You believe that's why Aberforth had the entangler bite you? To see if you were strong enough to tend their plants?"

She hesitated and then shrugged. It sounded absurd when he put it that way, but she couldn't imagine any other reason why they'd need a Fae. "It's possible. If I'm right, I'm not sure how insistent they'll be in trying to keep me here—especially if they know the city is dying. I might be able to use my connection with Bane to force open the doorway again, but it depends on how much magic he has left. If we need to leave in a hurry, can you shift into dragon form and fly us out?"

He frowned and placed his hand over hers. "Yes, but I can feel wards within this place that will make it more difficult. My magic is somehow being suppressed. I won't be able to do an instantaneous shift, and I can't travel extended distances without more rest. I'll get you out of here one way or another."

Her home had similar wards in place to prevent dragons or outsiders from using foreign magic. Lifting them would be difficult, especially since she didn't know how the original denizens of this city had formulated them. She'd never had a chance to learn about the wards before she'd been forced to flee Faerie.

They were approaching the top of the spire. She'd need to remove the bubble surrounding them to prevent any suspicion. "How long will it take you to shift?"

"Ten minutes, maybe less. If we run into trouble, I won't be able to do anything while I'm in between forms."

She nodded. It wasn't ideal, but at least they had an exit plan. "I have a really bad feeling about what they've done to keep the trees alive. There's a sickness in them that's beyond simply shattering the crystals. I'm hoping Blossom might learn something after she snoops around a bit. In the meantime, we need to be very careful with these people."

"I'm curious why they're so frightened of you," Malek said, studying the city below them. "You haven't made any overt threats against them."

"They're unwelcome squatters, and only a Fae can evict them," Sabine said, pressing both hands against the crystal railing. It pulsed under her touch, responding to her magic. "The city doesn't want them here, but they're the closest thing to Fae this city has seen in more than a thousand years.

That's the only reason it's tolerated their presence. I'm more concerned the city will try to keep me here."

Malek cocked his head and frowned. "You talk about the city as though it were alive."

"It is," Sabine replied, running her hand over the crystal. A rainbow of color accompanied the gesture, a sign the city was pleased she was here. The lift stopped at the top, and Sabine lowered the soundproof shield around them.

The door to the lift opened to a large balcony, offering an expansive view of the entire city and surrounding forest. Sabine walked across the balcony to the doorway of the central chamber. It was familiar enough that she recognized this building had been used as a meeting hall for the ruling family who'd controlled the city.

As soon as she crossed the threshold, the colors in the chamber shimmered and changed. Instead of the clear crystals surrounding them, the walls had shifted to deep blues and silvers, the colors of her family's line. The dancing fairy lights overhead twinkled like thousands of stars in the night sky. A crystal throne formed in front of them, beckoning her forward.

A loud gong echoed throughout the city, and Sabine blew out a breath. Faerie had just declared her the ruler of this city and announced the queen of the Unseelie was in residence.

She swallowed. "This is very bad. All of Faerie now knows I've returned—including my family."

Chapter Seventeen

"Is this why you've come? To try to claim our city for yourself?"

Sabine spun around to face one of the True Folk Elders. His face was weathered and creased from the passage of time, and his mostly silver hair was tinged blue at the ends. He wore his power like a weighty mantle, and judging by the amount of silver on his skin and in his hair, he had a substantial amount of magic at his disposal.

Lausianne ran into the room, breathing heavily as though she'd run the entire way to the top of the spire. Several other guards trailed behind her with their weapons drawn, and they fanned out into the chamber hall, trying to surround them. Sabine tensed, but she forced herself not to react outright. If they were wary of her and Malek before, they were now viewing them with outright hostility.

Malek frowned and moved to stand in front of her in a protective stance. His hand slapped against his sword, and he demanded, "You're Marsious?"

"Impertinent dragon," the Elder sneered, narrowing his eyes on Malek. "Your kind should have been purged from this world centuries ago. It speaks to how far the Fae have fallen if they've decided to make alliances with your kind."

"Enough," Sabine snapped, bristling at the insult. She moved to stand beside Malek, placing her hand on his arm in a gesture of solidarity. Malek didn't tear his gaze away from the Elder and the other True Folk, but his hand tightened on the hilt of his sword.

"I will decide when it's enough," the Elder retorted, narrowing his eyes on her. "You're the one who has come here and claimed this place as yours. This is *our* home, and you are only here because we will it."

Sabine had to force herself not to react. Instead, she studied the Elder carefully, suspecting his threat was originating from a place of fear. She'd hoped to ask about the sickness affecting the trees, but that was before the city had claimed her as its ruler.

No matter how much she might wish it otherwise, she wasn't sure she could extricate themselves from this mess peacefully. If these people feared losing their home, they might try to kill her and Malek to prevent that from happening.

Keeping the True Folk off balance might be the only way to get through the next few minutes. She might be able to use the city's magic to her advantage, especially if these people couldn't tap into it. After so many years of hiding her identity, embracing her heritage now might be the only way to save them all.

Sabine straightened, determined not to show them any sign of weakness. Focusing on the Elder, she said, "None may hold a piece of Faerie without its acquiescence. Whether I step aside as the city's ruler is yet to be seen. Be very careful of your next words or they may be your last. As of this moment, you stand within *my* city and it obeys my commands."

The Elder scowled. After a moment, he inclined his head in acknowledgement of her words. "The city may have agreed you are its rightful ruler, but who can know whether it's simply because you happen to be Fae? We have resided here for centuries, holding this city as our own." He took a threatening step toward them. "Who are you, other than a would-be child usurper, to claim otherwise?"

Malek's entire body tensed, and she gently squeezed his arm in reassurance. His presence gave her a hefty dose of confidence, and she intended to use it. Turning away from the Elder as though he were of little consequence, she moved to stand upon the dais where the throne was located.

Turning her back on him was a profound insult, and she normally never would have done it, but she needed to establish her dominance now that Faerie had acknowledged her as queen. If she deferred to the True Folk in any way, all the Unseelie would be forced to bend to their will—and that could *never* happen.

She seated herself, and a tingle of magic surrounded her. The weight of the Unseelie crown settled on her head, a gift from Faerie itself. It took everything within her to keep her expression neutral and even bored. Faerie wanted to keep her here, and she needed to not only pacify the magic contained within the city but also the True Folk.

"I am Sabin'theoria, daughter and heir of Queen Mali'theoria, and great-great-granddaughter of Theoria, first of the Fae and child of the goddess Lachlina and the god Vestior. I have been acknowledged by the Wild Hunt as the rightful ruler of the Unseelie and crowned by Faerie herself." Infusing her voice with power, she leaned forward and demanded, "Who are *you* to stand within a city of Faerie and dare call *me* a usurper?"

The Elder blanched. Even Lausianne and the other guards appeared shaken by her announcement. He bowed low and said, "My name is Marsious, Your Highness. No disrespect was intended; however, it has been more than a thousand years since one of the Fae has entered this city."

Malek moved to stand beside her throne in a position that would afford him a tactical advantage if necessary. The Elder had backed down somewhat, but they were playing a dangerous game. If these people viewed her as a threat, they had the numbers to strike both of them down.

It grated that she didn't have enough magical knowledge to fight against people who dwarfed her not only in years but also in experience. Malek might be skilled with a sword, but she was uncertain how much he could help if it came down to a battle. His magic was still being suppressed by Faerie. Only their changed bond was allowing him to move throughout the city unharmed. It was imperative she find a peaceful way to turn this situation around to her advantage.

Leaning back, she drummed her fingers upon the crystal armchair. The throne was uncomfortable, and she wished it wasn't necessary to sit in it to make her point. Almost as soon as she had the thought, a pillow formed underneath her. She bit back a smile. She'd forgotten how Faerie magic could change to suit the whims of its rulers.

"Marsious," she began, deciding it would be best to soften her approach, "I haven't come here to evict your people or even to rule over you. However, I need to understand a few things to make a determination on how to proceed. As one of the True Folk Elders, your wisdom and insight will be invaluable."

Marsious hesitated and then inclined his head. "Very well. What do you wish to know?"

Sabine waved her hand, and another chair appeared. It was a small thing, but Marsious and the other True Folk stared at it in surprise. She had a moment to wonder how they'd managed to function in a magical city without the ability to tap into its power. Even the humans had resources at their disposal in the form of advancing technology, which made their existence easier. Without access to Faerie's magic, these people would have had to cart in all sort of furniture, food, and even basic supplies from the outside world. The city wouldn't have provided for them.

She gestured for Marsious to have a seat and asked, "Will you tell me how your people came to this place?"

Marsious sighed and settled in the chair. "How much do you know about the True Folk, Your Highness?"

She frowned. "Sadly, very little."

He nodded as though unsurprised by her admission. "Most of our spellcasters are shapeshifters, able to live on both land and sea. During the Dragon War, we fought alongside your people, trying to push back the dragons' advances. Not only did the dragons burn your precious forests to ash, but they also used their wings to beat back the waves, cutting us off from the sea and turning the entire area outside this city into a desert wasteland."

Sabine glanced at Malek. From the tight rigidity in his shoulders, she guessed he hadn't heard this story. She hadn't either, but her tutors had told her equally horrific tales of the destruction during the war.

Marsious's eyes took on a faraway cast, as though reliving the events once again. The thought gave her pause. If he'd been there during the war, he was among the most ancient of Elders. Even if Marsious didn't intend any harm to her, Malek was in a great deal of danger. She couldn't hope to protect Malek against an Elder who had centuries of knowledge and experience at his fingertips.

"For more than a month, our people wandered in search of a haven. They were injured, starving, and the dragons still continued to rain fire from the skies. One of the Fae who had fought alongside us brought us here to wait out the siege, but he perished shortly afterward from his wounds. Since your people had already abandoned this city, we claimed this one for ourselves and have resided here ever since."

Sabine studied him carefully. On the surface, he appeared sincere. The True Folk couldn't lie, but something warned her Marsious was hiding something. His words almost seemed rehearsed, and they lacked the depth of emotion she'd heard from Faerie Elders recounting their experiences during the war. It didn't matter how long ago tragedy had occurred, the scars always remained.

Malek frowned. "I can't imagine what you or your people endured, but why didn't you eventually try to return to the sea? It's less than a few day's walk from here."

Marsious glared at Malek. "I do not answer questions issued by a dragon. You are the reason we were forced from the sea."

Sabine's hands tightened on the arms of her throne. Her heart went out to these people and what had occurred, but Malek wasn't responsible. "The old ways are no more, Marsious. Malek is my ally, and he speaks on my behalf. Anything he wants to know should be treated as though I'm the one asking the question."

Malek regarded her with surprise, but she continued to focus on the Elder. They needed to present a united front, or these people would try to divide them. Other than Blossom, Malek was the only other person in this city she trusted implicitly.

"Very well," Marsious grumbled, eyeing Malek with distaste. "We are only able to retain our secondary form for a limited amount of time. If we do not return to the sea within one cycle of the moon, we lose the ability to shift forever. Our true home has been forever denied to us. Many of those living here have never known the sea's embrace."

Sabine frowned. That must be why Ilwan had only given

them until the next full moon to locate their missing Merfolk woman. If Pearl was here, she'd lose the ability to shift forever if she wasn't returned to the ocean.

"Marsious, let us speak frankly," she said, deciding to try a different approach. "This city is dying. The trees are losing their leaves, and the magic within this pocket of Faerie is dwindling. It's only a matter of time before it fails completely."

Marsious's mouth formed a thin line. "I'm aware of the dissipating magic. It's why I had Aberforth seek out and test anyone of Fae descent."

Aha. Sabine leaned back, not surprised her suspicion had been confirmed. Marsious had to know no one other than a true Fae could hope to revitalize the city. She was still missing something, and he wasn't going to volunteer the information willingly.

There were some benefits to living among the jaded and manipulative Faerie Elders for years. She'd learned to search beneath the surface of their words for the truth.

"I'm afraid any Fae won't be enough anymore," she said, studying Marsious's body language carefully for some insight into his true purpose. "The city is too far gone. Once the magic of this place has been depleted, you will no longer be able to travel back and forth using the doorways you've discovered. Your people will be trapped."

A few of the guards whispered among themselves. All of them seemed to defer to Marsious, but it was interesting that none of them, save Marsious, had any inkling something was wrong. She might be able to use that to her advantage later. She just wished she could read him better.

"The doorway has been more difficult to open lately," Marsious replied, glancing at his entourage with a frown. "Do you have a solution? Other than banishing us from the only home many of us have known?"

Most of the guards had stiffened at this pronouncement. Sabine suspected Marsious was trying to paint her as a villain in this scenario. Perhaps he didn't have as much authority here as he wanted. She wished she understood the dynamics within the city better. More than anything, she needed information. She hoped Blossom might discover something while she was snooping around the city.

No matter what the pixie might learn, Sabine was running out of time. If her instincts were correct, she had maybe a couple of days before the Wild Hunt could be summoned again. She needed to be far away from this pocket of Faerie before that happened. They couldn't afford to spend any more time catering to the Elder and his entourage.

Determined to extricate themselves from this situation as quickly as possible, Sabine shook her head and said, "I may not have a solution yet, but I have no wish to endanger your people by banishing them from this place. Give me this evening to commune with the land to determine the best course of action. We can reconvene in the morning to discuss our options."

Marsious studied her and then nodded. "Very well. I will leave Lausianne and these guards in your care to ensure your needs are met. I will see you tomorrow."

He rose from his chair and swept out of the room, stopping only to speak softly to Lausianne before he disappeared. Once he was gone, Lausianne approached and bowed low. "May I show you to your quarters, Your Highness?"

Sabine didn't answer right away. Since Faerie had already proclaimed her as queen, the city probably had its own ideas about the location of her quarters. But these people were already worried about what her presence might mean for their future. Until she could figure out a solution to save the city, they would continue to view her as a threat. Right now, they were backed into a corner and far more dangerous than she'd anticipated.

She didn't want to hurt anyone, but forcing them out of the city might be the best thing for the land. She couldn't shake the impression these people had done something to corrupt the natural order of things.

Deciding to play along for now, Sabine stood and said, "That will be fine."

Malek fell into step beside her, his hand still lingering on his weapon. Sabine could relate. She had to force herself not to reach for her knives as the group of guards trailed behind them.

Sabine and Malek followed Lausianne out of the main chamber room and down a long hallway. They turned down several corridors until Lausianne stopped outside an ornate doorway. Crystals infused with Fae magic had been carved into the walls, and the sight was enough to make her relax. With the city as her unconventional ally, they should be able to escape from the room if necessary.

Lausianne opened the door and said, "I trust these quarters will be sufficient for your purposes. For your safety and since our people are wary of outsiders, it would be best if you remain here. A guard will remain outside in the event you need anything. In the interim, Marsious has instructed me to have a meal prepared for both of you. It will be brought up shortly."

Sabine tilted her head in acknowledgement of Lausianne's words and waited until the woman had withdrawn from the room. As soon as the door was closed, Sabine let out a sigh of relief. She removed the crown and placed it on a side table, then trailed her fingers over it thoughtfully. It was crafted with delicate silver webbing and inlaid with several diamonds that glittered in the light like stars in the night sky. The crown was a replica of the one her mother had worn. It might even be the same one. No one knew exactly how Faerie's magic worked.

"I don't know much about these guesting rites, but they're going to try to kill us the first chance they get." Malek swept his gaze over the room. "We need to find Pearl and get out of here as soon as possible."

Sabine frowned, knowing he was right. Their safety had been guaranteed when they were simply guests, but the moment Faerie claimed her as its ruler, she could no longer claim she was simply a visitor. The stakes had risen dramatically. "Blossom may have learned something. She'll find us soon now that we're alone."

Malek nodded and prowled around the room, checking under the antique furnishings, which were remarkably well preserved given their age. "Do you have the ability to check for magical traps? I can look for physical ones, but I'm not as sensitive to magic."

Sabine hesitated and then nodded. It wasn't her strength, but she should be able to pick out magic that didn't belong here. Holding out her hands, Sabine scanned the floors, walls, and furnishings for any trace of foreign magic. She hadn't considered the possibility of magical traps, but it made sense. Marsious, at least, wanted her out of the way.

Their quarters consisted of several rooms, a combination of bedrooms, a study, dining area, and lounging areas. Each was lavishly decorated in an extremely outdated and almost garish style. It made sense given this place had been isolated for so long, but it was a strange glimpse into what her people's cities must have been like centuries ago.

The rooms were nicer than anything they'd stayed in up to this point, but it was bittersweet. Regardless of whether Faerie had crowned her as the ruler of the city, Sabine was under no illusions; they were little more than prisoners.

Malek prowled through each of the rooms, investigating

the furnishings and taking inventory of all entrances and exits. Sabine did the same, but she didn't detect anything. Part of her wondered if these people had crippled themselves magically by abandoning the ocean. Her own power needed the magic of the forests to renew itself.

After walking to the balcony, she leaned against the railing and looked out over the city. It wasn't nearly as large as the one where she'd been born, but this was the closest she'd been to home in more than ten years. She'd missed it more than she wanted to admit. Sometimes she wondered if she'd ever make it back there.

Malek joined her a few minutes later and stood beside her. "For what it's worth, I thought you handled yourself well."

"I managed to buy us a few hours of time, but that's all," she replied, frustrated by her shortcomings. "Malek, we're in trouble here and I don't know how to get us out of it."

He turned to face her and reached up to tuck a lock of hair behind her ear. "I may not be accustomed to navigating the political and magical intricacies of the Merfolk and your people, but I'm willing to help you however I can. You're not alone, sweetheart."

Sabine looked up into his eyes, taken aback by how quickly she'd come to depend upon him. Bane might be sworn to protect her, but he didn't always grasp the subtle nuances of politics. Malek had kept a cool head, understanding intuitively what she needed to extricate themselves from a potentially disastrous situation.

Pressing her hand against Malek's chest, she stood on her toes and kissed him lightly. "I'm glad you're with me. I don't think I would have been able to handle that situation without you."

He chuckled. "You didn't seem to have a problem. Every time you waved your hand or the city's magic responded to you, they practically fell over themselves trying to accommodate you. The crown was a nice touch."

She smiled, but her worry over the situation didn't decrease. "They made sure to place us on the opposite side of the spire away from the lift. I won't be able to summon it to this balcony like I'd hoped."

"Damn. Well, we're not without resources. Between the two of us, we'll figure something out." He studied the balcony and frowned. "I don't think this area is big enough for me to shift. I can try it, but my size will likely take out the railing."

She rested her elbows against the crystal railing and leaned over the side. From this location, she could see most of the city. "You should conserve your power. Shifting is a last resort, and it may come to that. Even once we're back on the ground level, they're not going to allow us to move freely throughout their city. We're not strong enough to handle a confrontation."

Malek arched his brow. "Not strong enough? Even if you only had a fraction of your power readily available, these people don't know that. You put on a good show, Queen Sabine."

She managed a halfhearted smile. What she'd done was as close to a lie as the Fae could manage. "I got lucky they didn't call me on it. By most of these people's standards, I'm little more than a child, and the Elder knew it. I may have more raw power than a great number of them, but I'm lacking training and experience. There are hundreds of True Folk living in the city. If they're united against us, we don't stand a chance. I need them to believe I want an alliance with them until I can figure out what they're doing here."

Malek rubbed his chin. "I'd expected you to ask about Pearl, until we met that Elder of theirs. Something about him is a little off."

"I agree. It was too risky to divulge our true purpose,"

Sabine said and sighed. "Once Blossom gets back and we figure out what she's learned, I want to take a trip to the heart of the city so I can figure out what's making the trees sick."

Malek leaned over the balcony. "Can she fly all the way up here?"

"Yes, assuming she hasn't passed out from drinking Faerie nectar," she said, but a knock on the door interrupted them from continuing.

Malek's hand immediately went to his weapon, and he motioned for her to stay back. "These people think I'm subservient to you. For now, let's continue to reinforce their belief. It'll keep them unsettled. Can you put on another performance like you did in the throne room?"

Sabine didn't bother to hide her smile. "Of course."

Using the memories of her mother to help inspire her performance, she waved her hand and used the magic of Faerie to change the furnishings and colors of the room. They now reflected a similar appearance to the throne room. Picking up her discarded crown, she placed it on her head again. She straightened her shoulders and nodded at Malek to indicate she was ready.

"That'll do it," Malek said with a chuckle and headed for the door. He opened it, and Lausianne entered with two other guards.

The woman faltered, her eyes widening at the changes in the room. She recovered quickly and motioned for the people accompanying her to bring in the trays they were carrying. They entered and made it a point not to meet Sabine's eyes as they placed the food on a center table.

"We weren't sure what you would like, so we brought a few different items," Lausianne said, motioning for the other two guards to depart. "I trust you have everything you need?"

"This will be fine," Sabine said, walking toward the table

to inspect what they'd brought. Most of the items appeared to be different roasted meats she couldn't identify. It was rather telling they'd chosen not to provide any fruit or vegetables, even though the bounty of the forest would be overflowing with such items.

Lausianne smiled, but it didn't meet her eyes. "If you need anything, just let the guard outside know. Good night to you both." Without waiting for a response, she turned and walked out of the room.

Malek closed the door behind her and frowned. "How much do you want to bet it's poisoned or drugged?"

"No bet," Sabine said, turning away from the food they'd brought. "They wouldn't have risked bringing anything I could tell had been altered. Each of those meats is from an animal either native to the desert or the sea, not from the forests."

"A shame," Malek muttered, looking over the trays. "I'm a bit hungry."

"Me too. I have a few fruits I collected in the desert, but Aberforth was the one who pointed them out to me. I don't trust anything they're willing to provide us." Sabine walked to the crystal control panel on the wall and placed her hand on it. Closing her eyes, she sent a wave of her magic outward along with a mental image of what she desired. A moment later, the trays of meat had disappeared and a large bowl had reappeared in their place. It was filled with the finest quality fruits and vegetables.

Malek let out a low whistle. "Impressive, but is it safe?"

Sabine picked up a handful of the berries and sniffed them. No trace of the sickness infecting the forest was present. She replaced it and then checked the rest of the produce. "Yes. It's all safe. I know dragons tend to eat meat, but I can't risk it here. We need to find out what's affecting the city first."

"This is fine, Sabine," he said, popping one of the berries into his mouth. "I wouldn't be able to survive solely on it, but it's enough to offset the hunger."

Sabine smiled and picked up a small round fruit. She absently nibbled at it as she walked through the rooms. Their quarters were laid out like the ones where visiting dignitaries usually stayed. The location was fairly central, but it also limited the movement of the visitors. Other than the balcony, there was only one entrance and exit.

Turning toward Malek, she said, "I think I know how we can get out of here without them knowing."

He finished off one of the vegetables and arched his brow. "How?"

She smiled and placed her hand on the crystal panel again. Infusing her touch with a strong burst of magic, she said, "These quarters are designed for foreign dignitaries. My companion and I will need access to my personal quarters."

The panel shimmered, elongated, and then darkened as it reformed into a doorway. Malek approached her, staring at the door in surprise. "Can they tell you've done this?"

"I don't think so, but I can't swear to it. We won't be traveling through the in-between, so it's a bit safer. We're simply moving to another location within the city." Motioning for Malek to follow, they stepped through the doorway and emerged in an even larger and more spacious set of rooms.

An enormous circular bed was situated in the center of the room, while low tables and plush seating were scattered throughout. Crystal lanterns chased away the deepest shadows, playing their light against the walls and making the atmosphere warm and inviting. She caught a glimpse of additional seating areas in the next room, while a large table conducive to entertaining was in another. Even though it had been abandoned for centuries, there wasn't a trace of dust or dirt anywhere. The magic of Faerie had kept everything immaculate.

Malek chuckled. "Wow. I'm surprised the Elder didn't claim these rooms for himself."

"He can't," Sabine said with a smile, crossing the room toward the balcony. She opened the set of double doors and stepped outside. They'd been transported to another building, closer to the northern part of the city where the broken spires were located.

"What do you mean? The Merfolk can't come here?"

Sabine glanced at Malek. "This entire spire is only accessible through arcane means. No one who isn't a blood relative or sworn to the royal family's line can enter without permission. We're safe enough for now."

"Impressive," Malek murmured, scanning the balcony. "I can easily shift here. I'm still not sure about my weight on this crystal floor, but there's enough room if we want to fly out of here. We may need to worry about the light when I change forms. Can you mask it?"

"Yes, but I have a less flashy way to get down." Sabine leaned over the side, checking to make sure the lift was visible from their location. "Aha. A little bit of glamour and some help from the trees, and we'll be the invisible flying Fae and dragon, whenever Blossom joins us and we're ready to depart."

Malek chuckled. "All right. But one of these days, I intend to take you for a ride."

"Oh? I thought I'd already taken you for a ride," Sabine said teasingly and waved her hand to motion for the tree to bring the lift to them.

Malek paused for a heartbeat. The next second he was in motion, crossing the balcony toward her in a handful of steps. Without a word, he yanked her against him and pressed his lips against hers. Malek's hands caressed her through the thin material of her dress, sending his heated power over her skin.

She whimpered and wound her arms around his neck, returning his magic with her own. Here, in Faerie, her power was stronger than it ever had been, and she used it to send spiraling waves of pleasure crashing over him.

Malek picked her up, and she wrapped her legs around him as he deepened their kiss. Gods. She wanted him. Her hands clung to his shoulders, needing more. He carried her to the bed and laid her on it, then trailed his lips along her skin in an intimate caress.

"We shouldn't do this," he whispered, running his hand up her thigh while he kissed her neck. "I know we need to find Pearl, but you have no idea how irresistible you are."

She tilted her head to give him better access to her neck as she tried to remember how to breathe. Her fingers ran through his hair, imagining all the other places she wanted him to touch her. Their timing was terrible. "No, we shouldn't. But gods, Malek. I want you too."

He paused and then shifted so he could look down at her. "One day soon, I'm locking you in a room like this where we won't be disturbed." He kissed her deeply and pressed his forehead against hers. "And I'm not letting you leave for a long time."

She nipped at his lower lip and ran her hands up his chest. "Maybe I'll lock you up in a room like this instead. You can be my prisoner, and I can have my way with you whenever I want."

Malek chuckled and trailed his fingers down the side of her face. "I love seeing you like this. You're… different somehow. Playful. Happier. We're in the middle of a dangerous situation, but there's a light inside you." He ran his thumb across her cheek. "I've never met anyone like you, Sabin'theoria."

Her gaze softened. It was the first time he'd ever used her true name, and it touched something deep inside her. Sabine kissed him, putting everything she was feeling into the kiss. He responded the same way, telling her without words how deeply he was falling in love with her.

When they finally pulled apart, they were both breathing heavily. She saw the answer to every question she'd ever wanted to know in Malek's eyes. Here, in the last place she'd ever expected to find happiness, she'd found it in a dragon.

Cupping his face, she kissed him again and said, "You make me happy, Malek. If there's a light inside me, it's because of you."

"You're not making this any easier, sweetheart," he murmured, interlacing their hands.

"No, but you're going to need to hold that thought. We're about to be interrupted."

Malek's brow furrowed. "What?"

"Sabine! Malek!" Blossom shouted, darting into the room from the open balcony. "You couldn't have found a lower floor? Sheesh. My wings are tired from zipping all over the place."

"Yeah, I'm definitely locking us both in," Malek muttered in exasperation and shook his head. Rolling over, he looked at the balcony area and said, "Nice to see you, Blossom."

Blossom froze, her eyes as wide as saucers. "Oops. Did you want me to come back later?"

Sabine grinned and propped herself up on her elbows. "It's all right, Blossom. What did find out?"

Blossom landed beside them, her wings still fluttering with excitement. "I found Pearl! Well, I think it's Pearl. I couldn't get close enough to ask, but she's one of the Merfolk, and she's a prisoner. They have her chained up and everything!"

Sabine sat up. "Where is she?"

"There are some ruins in the north part of the city. She's being held there in one of the collapsed spires. Part of it is still standing."

Malek stood and held out his hand to help Sabine to her feet. "Do you know how many people are guarding her?"

"Three. Maybe four," Blossom said and rubbed her nose. "It's stinky there. The plants are all dying. The other pixies said it's a bad place and we should stay away."

Sabine straightened. "You found more pixies?"

Blossom grinned and nodded. "Yep. Several clans, but they don't come into the city anymore. One of them was helping me find Pearl."

Sabine glanced in the direction of the balcony area. "Well, perhaps you should invite your new friend inside so I can meet her."

"I told you she'd know you were watching, Lily," Blossom called. "Come meet her!"

A tiny pixie wearing a pale-purple dress peeked around the corner. "But the dragon's there."

Sabine smiled and said, "It's all right, Lily. This is Malek. He's a very dear friend of mine."

Lily bit her lip, her translucent wings twitching. "Are you sure he won't eat me?"

Malek angled his head to hide his smile.

"You have my word," Sabine said gently, noting the different details of Lily's dress. Her clothing was much more old-fashioned than the pixies who lived near her home.

Lily dove toward Sabine, hovering just out of touching distance of Malek. Sabine held out her hand so Lily could land. She was a pretty little thing with her yellow hair braided in an unfamiliar style, but she was much paler and smaller than Blossom.

Lily blinked up at Sabine, her wings still twitching in excitement. "Ohhh. Blossom was right! You sparkle!"

Sabine's mouth twitched in a smile. Blossom also landed on her hand, her weight more substantial than Lily's. It made her wonder if the pixies here had been suffering from some malady the same way the plants had been.

"Will you magic us?" Blossom asked, clasping her hands together in a pleading gesture.

Lily's eyes widened, and she mimicked Blossom's movements. "Like this?"

"Stick out your bottom lip more and try to look pathetic," Blossom whispered loudly.

Malek snorted. "Great. Blossom's teaching these pixies all her tricks. By the time we leave, the pixies are going to be taking over."

Sabine laughed. Even if Blossom hadn't asked, Sabine had intended to share magic the moment she'd gotten a good look at Lily. Holding out her other hand over the pixies, she sent a light rush of magic over them.

Lily's cheeks flushed, giving her a much healthier appearance. Even her eyes were brighter. She was still too thin, but it was a definite improvement.

The tiny pixie dropped to her knees, tears streaming down her face. "Please don't leave us, Your Highness. I'm sorry we failed you. We've tried to keep the forest alive, but it's not working. All the trees are sick, and it's spreading. We can't stop it."

Blossom wrapped her arms around Lily, holding her tightly while the pixie cried. She patted Lily's hair and said, "It's okay, Lily. Sabine will help the trees and your family. She saved my family too."

Sabine's heart broke at the sight. "I'll do what I can to help, but can you tell me what happened here? What's wrong with the trees?"

Lily sniffled and wiped away her tears. "The trees don't like the True Folk's stinky fish magic. We're too weak to keep the balance. Everyone's sick. Mama and Papa can't even fly anymore."

Blossom bit her lip. "Sabine, they've never met another Fae. They've been trapped here for centuries."

Sabine stared at Blossom in horror. Pixies couldn't survive without a strong source of Fae magic. If they'd been trying to subsist on trace amounts of the remaining magic here for centuries, it was no wonder Lily and her family were so weakened.

Malek sat on the bed. "What? How is that possible?"

Lily's lower lip trembled, and she lowered her head. "The True Folk won't let us use the doorway to the in-between. They don't want the Fae to take away their home. We begged them to let us go back and forth, but they call us bugs and try to squish us. Their Elder is the worst of them. He told the others to kill us."

Sabine blew out a breath. The True Folk were affecting the natural balance of everything here. They needed to be stopped. If they were controlling the doorway that tightly, her people probably didn't know this city still existed until Faerie had announced her arrival. Even if they tried to send an emissary here to investigate, it was unlikely they could find this place without help. "Lily, do you have the ability to share magic with your parents and the rest of your family?"

Lily nodded. "Yes. I'll go share your magic with them right now."

"Not yet." Sabine gently placed both pixies on the bed. She pulled out her knife and pricked her finger. Holding it out to Lily, she said, "Drink as much as you can. I know it's a little unusual, but drinking directly from a Fae is more potent than simply sharing magic. This gift should sustain you and your family for over a month. When you're finished, Blossom will help you get back home so you can share the magic with your family and the other clans."

While Lily drank, Sabine turned to Blossom. "Once you're sure her family's okay, come find us in the northern part of the city. I'm going to need your help."

Blossom stroked Lily's braided hair and said, "There are only a few hundred pixies still living here, Sabine. Most of them have already died out."

Sabine frowned. "Their sickness is tied to whatever's affecting the trees. If we can figure out how to stop it, they'll be safe. In the interim, tell the other pixies to elect one representative from each clan. I'll allow them to drink so they can share my magic with the rest of their families. They don't take much."

Lily finished drinking and swayed where she stood. She giggled and plopped face first onto the bed. Sabine sighed and gestured for Blossom to help her new friend. Blossom grinned and propped Lily up.

"Come on, Lily. Let's go fix your parents. Find your wings and start fluttering. I'll steer!"

Lily hiccupped, and the two pixies took off for the balcony.

Malek stared after them and frowned. "I had no idea the effects would be so widespread. Can you save them?"

Sabine nodded. "My magic will help with whatever's making them sick, but we need to restore access to the rest of Faerie, or it won't last. This city should be large enough to sustain tens of thousands of pixies, not just a few hundred. That's part of the reason the trees are dying. The Merfolk have upset the natural order of this place."

Malek's jaw hardened. "Then let's go save Pearl and heal the forest. I'm not about to allow another pixie to die."

Chapter Eighteen

Sabine held her illusion magic over the crystal lift while the tree carried them to the ground. To any curious onlookers, they wouldn't be able to tell anything was happening. Sabine knew some of the True Folk could track her by searching for sources of foreign magic. The Elder was probably one of those with such talent, especially if he was sensitive enough to detect when the doorways to the in-between were opened. Fortunately, the moon was high in the sky, and her magic had always been stronger at night. She just hoped they hadn't discovered they were missing yet.

The lift settled soundlessly on the ground, and Sabine withdrew her glamour from the tree. After motioning for Malek to follow, she surrounded them in shadows as they walked along the path to the northernmost part of the city.

Many of the crystal pathways were broken, and entire buildings had collapsed. Even the trees in this part of the city had either died or were struggling to survive. Sabine had to battle her instincts not to help them, knowing it would only make her presence known that much faster.

A few of the True Folk patrolled this area. Sabine and

Malek crouched off the path while these armed men and women moved past them. Once they were out of earshot, Sabine and Malek crept forward, trying to locate the building Blossom had described.

"Blossom said it was a partially collapsed spire," Sabine whispered to Malek after another patrol had disappeared into the darkness. "I didn't realize how many there were. We could spend all night searching and not locate the right one. We may need to wait on Blossom to show us the rest of the way."

"Are you sure the guards can't track her?"

Sabine shook her head. "I'm not sure of anything when it comes to these people. Lesser Fae magic is different and in some ways stronger than ours because it's harder to detect. I have to trust Blossom can handle herself."

Malek nodded and led her off the path. They walked in silence for several minutes, climbing over fallen rubble and fractured crystals. She'd never seen such widespread destruction. Placing her hand against one of the crystals, she wondered whether these buildings had been destroyed during the Dragon War.

Malek turned back to look at her. "What's wrong?"

She pulled her hand away and shook her head. There wasn't any point in discussing it. They both knew what had happened here.

"I was worried about this," Malek said quietly, taking her hand in his. "I had a feeling my people were responsible for this destruction as soon as we saw the rubble. When Marsious told us how he'd come to be here, I thought you'd pull away from me then."

Sabine looked away and murmured, "I didn't."

Malek sighed and ran his thumb over her hand. "No, but this can't be easy on you. It's not easy for me either. But please remember, you're not those Fae, and I'm not those dragons. What we're building together will make the world better for all of us. Don't allow the past to divide us."

She lowered her gaze, desperately wanting to believe he was right, but she couldn't forget the fear Lily had exhibited when she'd realized Malek was a dragon. Even the Elder had been scared of Malek. She knew her people would never accept a dragon at her side, no matter how much she'd grown to care for him.

Sabine swallowed and whispered, "Seeing what happened here makes it a little more real. I heard stories growing up, but it's different when you see it for yourself. All those lives and all their magic, gone forever. It's been ground into dust, just like these shattered crystals."

Malek lifted her hand and kissed it. "We're going to make sure nothing like this happens again, sweetheart."

Sabine managed a weak smile and moved forward, determined to focus on their task. He was right; it was in the past and they were working on building a better future. She needed to keep that in the forefront of her mind. This destruction needed to serve as a reminder of their purpose. And for that, they needed each other.

The lack of foliage in this area was nearly as shocking as the rubble. Every breath she took had an unfamiliar weight to it, slightly tangy and even metallic. It was *wrong*.

She lifted her head, detecting something else buried under the surface. "The treeheart should be up ahead, but it... I'm not sure." She shook her head. "It doesn't feel like it's complete."

Malek glanced at her. "That's the heart of the city, right? What does it look like?"

Sabine hesitated and then shrugged. "It could be anything. The previous ruler of the city would have chosen the vessel. Most of the time it's a tree, which is why it's usually referred to as the treeheart. It could be a crystal or maybe even a weapon of some kind. It depends on the focus and preference of the caretaker. If the city has claimed me as its ruler, I should be able to find it."

"You can sense it?"

She nodded. "Yes. The magic of the treeheart has been calling me since it proclaimed me as ruler of this city."

Blossom appeared suddenly beside them. "It worked! Lily went to go rally the other pixie clans so you can fix them too."

Sabine smiled. "I'm glad to hear it. Her parents are able to fly again?"

Blossom nodded. "Yep. They're all better."

"Good. Can you show us where to find Pearl?"

Blossom pointed straight ahead, almost in the exact direction of where the treeheart should be located. "Up there. The building's hidden behind that hill."

They crept forward, keeping off the road as much as possible. At the top of the rise, they crouched beside a partially collapsed crystal wall. Down below was the ruined spire Blossom had mentioned. A large tree was beside it, pulsing softly with strange colors. They kept shifting between blue and silver, the colors of Sabine's house. It could be a trick of the moonlight reflecting on the shattered crystals scattered around, but she didn't think so.

Sabine squinted, trying to get a better look. "Do you see that? What color is that tree?"

Malek's brow furrowed. "The leaves? They look green to me. A little lighter than the ones outside in the forest, but they're green."

"It looks like a tree," Blossom said, cocking her head to look at it. "Is it a tree? Want me to sniff it to find out?"

"That must be the treeheart, but something's wrong with it," Sabine said, angling her body so she could study it without revealing their location. The shifting colors must be a beacon only she could detect.

Malek pulled her back and motioned toward where a patrol was walking. Sabine inhaled sharply and pressed her back against the wall. They'd come from a different direction than she'd expected. If she wasn't more careful, they would be caught.

They waited until the footsteps had passed before Malek asked, "Can you tell what's wrong with it?"

She shook her head. "Not from here. I need to get closer."

Blossom scratched her head. "Uh, looks like they brought over more guards. I see more than twelve now. Think they know you're missing?"

"Shit," Malek muttered and leaned to the side so he could get a look from behind the outcropping. "They're moving around in some sort of formation. Maybe Blossom can get close enough to see what's gotten them all riled up."

Sabine shook her head. "No. If they know we've escaped, they'll be watching for her."

Blossom frowned. "I can be sneaky."

"I know," Sabine said, holding out her hand so Blossom could land on it. "We don't know what abilities these people have, and Lily said they don't treat the pixies kindly. I don't want anything to happen to you."

Blossom hugged her thumb. "What should we do? They're holding Pearl in that building. We need to rescue her to save Esme."

Another patrol came through, this one even closer than the last. They'd need to move soon or risk being discovered. Malek motioned for them to remain silent, but he drew his weapon. Sabine did the same, hoping they wouldn't need to use them. The Merfolk weren't enemies with the Fae. Once she crossed that line and killed one of them, there was no turning back. No matter what they wanted from her, they technically hadn't hurt either her or Malek yet.

Footsteps crunched on the broken pathway, and Sabine tensed, mentally willing them to keep walking. She couldn't even deepen the surrounding shadows without fear of being detected. Any trace of foreign magic could reveal their presence.

"I thought Aberforth wanted the woman alive," one of the men said to his companion. "Marsious said to kill them both?"

"No. Kill the dragon, but capture and subdue the Fae. Marsious says she's a threat and can turn the city against us. If we sacrifice her along with the Merfolk woman, we can infuse their combined magic into the city. We're so close to shifting back. This might finally be the turning point for us."

"It'll be war if the Fae find out we killed one of their Royals," the first man said in warning.

"And if we're forced out? War is nothing compared to…"

The voices trailed off as they moved farther away. The reality of what the Merfolk were intending made her stomach lurch, and Sabine squeezed her eyes shut. This was worse than she'd expected. It was no longer a simple matter of saving Esme and Levin. If they didn't save Pearl *and* the treeheart, thousands could die—including all of her people.

Malek blew out a breath and said, "I need to get you out of here. If you can open a doorway through the in-between, I can fly us out."

"I can't leave," she whispered, her heart clenching in pain. "I know how they're infecting this pocket of Faerie. I have to stop them before they destroy the city completely."

Malek grabbed her arms and held her tightly. "Have you lost your mind? Let the city die, Sabine. We can get the pixies out and escape together. They're going to kill you if they find you."

She shook her head. "You don't understand. They've poisoned the magic of the city. If we don't stop it here, it will gradually spread to the rest of Faerie. They're trying to turn this place into their city."

"Then let them," Malek argued, a trace of temper filling his eyes. "This city has been abandoned for centuries, and these people want you dead. You don't owe them any favors."

"No," she said, straightening her shoulders and pulling away from him. "Do you know what happens to a plant when it's nourished with saltwater?"

"It dies," Blossom whispered, horror filling her eyes. "They're going to kill all of Faerie if they change this place. The magic moves back and forth through the in-between. That's how I talk to my family."

Sabine nodded. "Exactly. That's why we have to save the treeheart *and* Pearl. Otherwise, it's not just the city that will suffer. All of my people will be wiped out—the pixies, the Beastpeople, and every living creature in Faerie. All parts of Faerie are connected through the in-between, even if this part has been mostly walled off."

Malek's brow furrowed. "You're saying there's a link between the missing Merfolk woman and the treeheart?"

"Yes. It's similar to the ritual described in the stone that Aberforth showed me. It's why they've brought Pearl to the treeheart. They're sacrificing captured Merfolk to change this place and themselves so they can return to the sea. They want to go home. They must think the city can absorb even more of Pearl's magic if they sacrifice me at the same time."

Malek glanced around to make sure no was approaching before leaning against the sloped crystal wall. "I need you to explain how the magic of the city works."

Sabine took a deep breath and nodded, hoping he might have some insight into how they could save everyone. "Unlike most of the other magical races, the Fae have to purge themselves of excess magic or it becomes too much to manage. We siphon it off and give it back to the land so it might blossom and grow."

He frowned. "You've mentioned something like that before. That's why you believe it'll be a while before your family can summon the Wild Hunt again, right?"

"Yes. They won't have enough strength yet. Rhys must have depleted most of his power to summon it before. My father wouldn't have risked giving up that much of his magic. We're safe enough for now, but we shouldn't stay in one place for too long or they'll send the Huntsman after me again."

Malek nodded. "Okay. How does the city store the excess magic then?"

Sabine paused, trying to figure out how to explain to someone who hadn't been born in Faerie. "The ruling family of the city is the caretaker of the treeheart since their magic is the purest and most powerful. It's the heartbeat of the city, fueling all the other parts with the ruling family's power."

Malek arched his brow. "I hadn't realized the ruling family is the source of all magic within the entire city."

"Pfft," Blossom said with a grin. "They're only part of the magic."

Sabine smiled down at Blossom. The pixies were often overlooked as being an important part of Faerie. "Blossom's right. The non-ruling families siphon off their excess magic to the crystals, plants, and trees. The pixies and other creatures help to distribute the magic to the outlying areas to keep everything running. Without them, the city couldn't survive."

Blossom beamed and puffed up at the recognition.

Malek glanced around the wall to check to make sure it was still clear. "All right. So you're saying the treeheart is like a pump of sorts, sending the magic outward?"

Sabine considered the analogy and nodded. "Yes. I thought the treeheart might have been damaged somehow, but the outlying areas are in better condition than the center of the city. Those should have been the first to fail if the pump wasn't working properly. I believe Lily and the other pixies have been able to help those areas, but they aren't allowed back in the city. The True Folk have made sure of that."

Blossom's wings drooped. "Then why are the pixies sick?"

"Because the True Folk are trying to change the purpose of the treeheart. It's the equivalent of taking us underwater and expecting us to breathe. You can't change someone's basic nature, nor can you change the function of the treeheart."

Malek rubbed his chin. "All right. I think I understand. If we believe the treeheart is the key to saving the city, is it possible to reverse what they've done?"

Sabine hesitated and then shrugged. "I won't know until I put my hands on it. I need to connect with the lifeblood of the city and infuse my essence with it. Only then will I be able to communicate with the treeheart. It should tell me how to correct the problem. If it's too far gone, we can try sealing it off from the rest of Faerie's magic. But then everything living here will die within days."

Malek frowned and took another look around the outcropping. "We're only going to get one shot at this, Sabine. If we free Pearl, they'll raise the alarm and you'll never be able to get to the treeheart. If we try to save the treeheart, we won't be able to get close to Pearl. I'm afraid we're going to need to decide between saving our friends and saving everyone living here."

Sabine shook her head as a plan began to form in her mind. "No. I think I know how we can save both. Blossom, go gather the pixie clans. We're going to need some help."

Chapter Nineteen

Sabine finished feeding the last of the pixies and sat back. Like Lily, they were all much smaller than Blossom or her family, an indication they'd been starved for magic for a long time. They'd listened attentively when she'd outlined her plans, and they were now buzzing with excitement and renewed power. Sometimes the most powerful warriors were those you least expected.

She'd been reluctant to ask for their help after seeing their condition, but they were eager to reclaim their portion of Faerie. Blossom had promised it was an important part of their healing, and Sabine had to agree with her assessment. With her offering to share magic, the pixies looked much better, but she wished they'd had more time to fully recover before asking them to help. If there were any other way to save the city, she'd do it.

"Blossom speaks with my voice, so you'll need to follow her direction," she reminded them, gesturing toward Blossom, who straightened at her announcement.

"That's right, soldiers," Blossom said, narrowing her eyes

at the pixies. "Fall in line and ready yourselves for inspection!"

The pixies' eyes widened and they all jumped up, more than a dozen tiny bodies all standing ramrod straight. Blossom marched in front of them, assessing them with a critical eye. She pointed at a few of them and snapped, "Suck in that gut. No drooping wings. You, over there, tuck in your shirt. We're not raiding honeypots here, boys and girls. This is serious. Get your dusters ready! On my mark, we attack and distract!"

Sabine had to bite back a smile as she watched their wings twitch in excitement. Even Lily had joined the ranks as the head of her clan, and her eyes were bright with eagerness. Sabine just hoped none of them would be hurt.

Blossom put her hands behind her back, continuing to march in front of them. "You all understand your mission?"

"Yes!" they all exclaimed, saluting their new commander.

"Then gather the rest of our forces and take your places! On my mark, we attack! We will show those stinky fish people what it means to try to steal our city!"

They squealed in excitement and took off into the night.

Blossom grinned and said, "That was fun!"

Sabine smiled. "Just do your best to keep them safe. When I connect to the treeheart, I'll ask it to send you a message so you can distract the guards. You just need to buy enough time to allow Malek to escape through the doorway with Pearl. If we fail for any reason, you need to get word to Balkin. Let him know what's happened here."

Blossom's face fell. "This is really dangerous, huh?"

Sabine nodded. "Yes, but I'm fortunate to have such fierce allies. With the pixies orchestrating the distraction, we have a chance to save everyone."

Blossom's wings drooped, and she whispered, "Don't let them hurt you, Sabine. We need you."

Sabine trailed a bit of magic over Blossom. Normally, such a thing delighted the pixie, but Blossom's fear overshadowed everything else. "Same goes to you, my friend. Take care of yourself and the other pixies for me."

Blossom flew up and kissed Sabine's cheek. Without another word, she disappeared into the darkness. Sabine took a steadying breath and looked at Malek, who had been watching everything in silence.

She frowned at him. "I don't see another way."

Malek looked in the direction of where they were holding Pearl and sighed. They'd moved away from the building so she could meet with the pixies without being detected, but more guards were moving into the area. "It's unnecessarily risky and dangerous, Sabine. I know it's not ideal, but choosing between the two would be the safest course of action. Although, if I'm honest, I'd rather just steal you away from here and say to hell with the whole thing."

Sabine tilted her head to study him, suspecting he was lying to himself. She'd seen the pain in his eyes when he'd met the part-wyvern boy who had reminded Malek so much of his friend.

Placing her hand on his arm, Sabine whispered, "I need to do this, Malek. I know you think we should choose between them, but I wouldn't be able to live with myself if I didn't try to save everyone. I don't think you could either. I know how much Levin means to you."

He sighed and placed his hand over hers, holding her to him. "You're right. I'll do what I can to stick to your plan, but I can't promise I'll be able to suppress my instincts. You've come to mean a great deal to me." His jaw hardened. "If they hurt you, I *will* kill them."

Sabine didn't know how to respond. She'd had years to understand Bane's and Dax's demonic instincts and how to work around them, but Malek was still a mystery in many ways. Their relationship may have begun because he needed her help to seal the portal, but the lines between them were now blurred.

Once emotions and intimacy had entered their arrangement, she'd noticed a subtle yet distinctive shift in his reactions. He was becoming more protective, and even possessive, where she was concerned. She wasn't yet sure how to handle it, but she needed to focus on living through the next few hours. If they survived, they'd need to figure out a way to manage the changing dynamics between them.

Sabine leaned forward and kissed him lightly. "You've come to mean a great deal to me too. Just make sure you get to Pearl while I'm keeping everyone focused on me. As soon as I connect with the treeheart, I can use the magic of the city to open a doorway."

"I hope you're right." Malek nodded toward the treeheart and said, "The patrol just finished making their rounds and won't pass this way again for a few minutes. If you're going to change your appearance, now's the time."

Taking a deep breath, she closed her eyes and focused on her impressions of Lausianne, the True Folk woman who had escorted them to their quarters. Once she ensured she had a fairly accurate image of Lausianne in her mind, Sabine attached the illusion to her skin with thousands of tiny pinpricks.

Gesturing toward herself, she asked, "Will it work?"

Malek frowned, scanning her up and down. "The eye color is off. Can you make them greener? I think her hair is a bit shorter too."

Sabine nodded and changed the glamour coating her skin. "How's that?"

"Better, but your voice isn't the same and your mannerisms are much more regal. I'm not sure the illusion will stand up to scrutiny, especially since they know about your abilities."

"I only need it to work long enough to get to the treeheart. Worst-case scenario, I distract them so you can rescue Pearl. If necessary, I believe I can convince them to take me to the treeheart. Then I can open a doorway for you to take Pearl back to the ocean."

Malek scowled. "You expect me to go through the doorway without you?"

Sabine nodded and touched the mark on his wrist. "You must, but I'll try to follow as soon as possible. My mark will keep you safe through the in-between since I'll be the one activating the doorway. You'll need to hold tightly to Pearl's hand to keep her from being harmed." Sabine removed Ilwan's necklace and offered it to Malek. "Take this. Your powers probably won't work to summon Ilwan for the prisoner exchange, but Pearl should be able to help you."

Malek gripped the necklace and studied it. He squared his shoulders and handed it back to her. "Keep it. I'm taking you with me, Sabine. When I leave this city, you're coming with me or we're not leaving at all."

"Malek," she replied, looking down at the necklace, "you need this to rescue Esme, Levin, and the rest of your crew. Otherwise, there's no point to this plan."

"You're putting a lot of weight on the conversation we overheard with those guards."

"Perhaps, but why would they sacrifice me if Pearl is gone? They need me. Marsious admitted he knows the city is dying. I'm the best hope they have."

He shook his head, and his jaw hardened. "No. I'm *not* leaving you here. I'll make every effort to get Pearl to safety, but I told you before—*you* are my priority. This is about something bigger than you, me, or even this city. If the portal opens and the war spills back into our world, how many millions will die?"

Sabine didn't respond. They didn't have time to argue about this. She wasn't the only Fae who would be willing to help him. If something happened to her, Blossom could find someone else who could locate the rest of the artifacts for Malek. She stared down at the necklace, wondering if his feelings for her were clouding his judgment.

Malek reached over to tuck her hair behind her ear. "Sweetheart, I understand you feel the need to do this. I'm not completely sold on the idea, but I won't try to stop you. I only ask you to understand I *need* to protect you."

She lifted her head and frowned. "Is this a dragon thing?"

His mouth curved upward. "You could say that."

She wrinkled her nose. "You're not going to budge, are you?"

He chuckled and shook his head.

"Stubborn dragon," she muttered with exasperation and fastened the necklace around her neck again.

He grabbed her and hauled her against him, then kissed her soundly. When he released her, he said, "And you're a very stubborn Fae."

Despite herself, she smiled. Without another word, she stood and began walking down the path. Using her memory of the True Folk woman she was impersonating, she tried to adopt the same swagger as Lausianne. It was impossible to get angry with Malek over his refusal to follow her orders. If she were in his position, she wouldn't have agreed to leave him either.

He might need to protect her, but she *needed* to protect this city, the forest, and all its inhabitants. This was why the Fae had been created, and it was hardwired into her psyche. Sabine couldn't change her nature any more than he could change his. It didn't matter what illusion she wore, she couldn't change who she was under the surface.

She approached the first patrol, but they were looking at something on the ground and barely spared her more than a passing glance. Sabine swallowed, forcing her body to stay relaxed while her heart pounded in her chest. More than a few of these True Folk would have the ability to detect foreign magic. If even one of them became suspicious too soon, her entire plan would fall apart. Everything depended on getting to the treeheart and buying enough time for Malek to rescue Pearl. Blossom and the pixies were a secondary distraction, designed to help Malek escape.

Sabine kept her footfalls even and unhurried, watching the treeheart pulsing with colors. The closer she came, the more the treeheart called to her, urging her to hurry. It could sense her approach, and its song was becoming more frenzied. On the surface, it appeared much like a centuries-old silver tree, but it was much more than that. Like her, it wore a type of glamour to hide its true self.

"What are you doing here?"

Sabine froze, turning to see three True Folk guards approaching her. Two of them were men and one was a woman. The man who had spoken carried himself as though accustomed to some form of command, while the other two remained a step behind him in a more submissive position. If her analysis was correct and the True Folk were structured similarly to the Fae hierarchy of power, he was the one she needed to distract and stall. The other two wouldn't make a move without his leave.

Feigning exasperation, Sabine asked, "What do you think I'm doing here?"

"Don't be flippant," the man said, his eyes narrowing on her. "You're supposed to be guarding Marsious. Who's with him if you're here?"

The treeheart's song became more urgent. Her palms grew damp, and she had to fight her instincts not to respond to the treeheart. It desperately needed her, but she couldn't even risk looking at it. She needed to buy Malek as much time as possible. The longer these patrols were busy with her, the more likely Malek could escape with Pearl. She wished he still had his warding medallion to hide his identity.

Tossing back her hair, she said, "If you have a problem with me being here, I suggest you take it up with Marsious."

The man hesitated and then shrugged. "Very well. Jaiva, stay with her. We're supposed to stay in groups while the Fae and dragon are loose. You know that."

The woman moved forward, scanning Sabine up and down. "You look different somehow. Are you feeling all right?"

Sabine arched her brow. "I think we're all out of sorts with the Fae and dragon here."

Jaiva frowned. "That's not Lausianne."

The man paused, narrowing his eyes slightly on Sabine. He took a step forward, his hand going to his weapon. "What's my name?"

Sabine resisted the urge to curse. Mentally willing Malek to hurry, she glared at the man and snapped, "What sort of game are you playing? We don't have time for this."

Jaiva shook her head and said, "It's the Fae, Zander! Grab her!"

The guards drew their weapons. Sabine's eyes widened. She'd thought it was a possibility, but the rest of the True Folk didn't get the message not to kill her. Abandoning the first part of their plan, Sabine took off running in the direction of the treeheart. Some foreign and metallic magic singed her shoulder, and she winced at the pain. It wasn't a severe blow, but it still hurt. Changing her trajectory to avoid their attacks, she zigzagged through the rubble and broken pathways trying to reach the treeheart.

"She's heading to the heart!"

"Cut her off!"

Sabine leaped over a wall as more shouts joined the chorus of alarm. She inwardly urged Malek to hurry, knowing she wouldn't be able to dodge the True Folk for long. Another magical bolt slammed into her arm, and she stumbled. She hit the ground, then looked up to see the treeheart was only a short distance away. After scrambling to her feet, she ran toward it but was tackled before she could make contact.

Shoving her magic outward, she blasted her assailant with her power. She pushed him off and tried to get back up, but Zander hit from the side. She was thrown to the ground again, struggling to take a breath under Zander's heavier weight. He hauled her upright, his grip hard enough to leave a bruise. Several other True Folk surrounded her, pointing their weapons in her direction.

Sabine swallowed and released the glamour. She'd need as much of her magic readily available as possible.

"Move or use any magic, and you'll die right here," Zander warned, still gripping her tightly.

"Isn't that your plan anyway?" she retorted, trying to stall for time. "I told Marsious I didn't want to force any of you out. The magic in this city is dying. Once it's gone, you'll all be trapped here. I'm the only chance you have to survive."

"You're wrong," Jaiva argued, still pointing her curved sword in Sabine's direction. "The magic here is already changing. We're all more powerful with each sacrifice."

Sabine shook her head. "You feel powerful because you're absorbing the magic from the treeheart. It's why the trees are dying. They can't sustain you. Faerie was designed to absorb power, not give it up."

"What do we care about a few trees?" Zander demanded.

Sabine had to force her temper down and not lash out at his callousness, but it grated. Making an effort to keep her tone even, she said, "If the magic of this city dies, you won't be able to leave Faerie. It's why my people abandoned it centuries ago. The ruling family died, and no one was able to sustain the treeheart. Without it, they knew it was only a matter of time before they died too."

Zander's grip loosened slightly. "How do you know this?"

Sabine nodded toward the large silver tree. "That's the treeheart. Aberforth holds one of the branches and uses it as a walking stick. It's how you've been opening the doorway to the in-between. I can try to fix it, but I need to commune with the treeheart. I'll also need the missing branch to be returned."

"It's a trick, Zander," Jaiva said, taking a step closer and continuing to point her weapon at Sabine. "If she takes our key to open the doorway, we *will* be trapped. We should kill her and be done with it."

Zander's jaw worked. He glanced at Jaiva and then back at Sabine. "Can you fix the magic of this place without the branch?"

Sabine hesitated. "I can try, but it won't be a complete healing."

Zander turned toward Jaiva and ordered, "Run back to the city. Grab Aberforth and Marsious. Have them bring the walking stick. If she can heal the heart, so be it. Otherwise, we'll do as Marsious instructed and sacrifice her and the Merfolk woman together. Their combined magic should be enough to bring our powers back."

"But Marsious wanted to wait until tomorrow," Jaiva replied, appearing unsure.

"Go now," Zander snapped.

Jaiva inhaled sharply and then ran in the direction of the

city. Zander dragged Sabine toward the treeheart and pushed her toward it. He pressed his knife against her neck and whispered, "Aberforth and I have some concerns about Marsious, but he's still our Elder. Heal the tree and prove you speak the truth. If I see anything out of the ordinary, you'll die before you take your next breath."

Sabine swallowed, her mouth going dry. It looked like Malek was out of time. If he hadn't gotten to Pearl by now, they were all lost. Taking a steadying breath, Sabine lifted her hands and pressed them against the tree containing the most concentrated magic within this pocket of Faerie. She only hoped she hadn't made a mistake.

Chapter Twenty

Malek wrapped his arm around the Merfolk woman, supporting most of her weight. She was in worse shape than they'd anticipated, and he wasn't sure what this meant for Sabine's bold plan. They'd been counting on Pearl being able to flee alongside them. The fools who had been keeping her captive had used some sort of magical restraints, which had weakened her significantly.

At least she hadn't screamed in fear at the sight of a dragon rescuing her. She might not trust him, but she was pragmatic enough to know her chances of surviving were better with him than remaining chained up by the Merfolk.

"Ilwan really sent you to rescue me?" Pearl asked in a hoarse whisper as they walked past the unconscious guards he'd had to knock out. They'd live, but they'd be smarting for a few days.

"He did. Sabine has his necklace to give you," Malek said, trying not to think about what was happening to Sabine. As far as distractions went, her plan was a good one. They wouldn't realize he'd freed Pearl until it was too late. Unfortunately, there was no way to know how the True Folk would react to Sabine once they caught her. He didn't like trusting in one overheard conversation that these people wanted Sabine alive.

Malek heard shouting from outside, and he had to force himself not to abandon Pearl. He'd hoped it would have taken longer for them to discover Sabine's identity. Sabine had proven to be capable of taking care of herself, but it didn't diminish his need to protect her.

He helped Pearl climb over a partially collapsed wall and then stepped over the rest of the way himself. She put her arm around his neck again, and he half-walked, half-carried her out of the prison where they'd been keeping her. The voices were even louder now, almost directly in front of them.

Crouching by another wall, he allowed Pearl a few minutes to catch her breath. He angled his head, trying to determine what was happening. From what he could see, they had Sabine surrounded. His fists clenched as his mind battled between the need to uphold his promise to her and his desire to save her. His magic surged to the surface, demanding he shift forms. He struggled to force it back down.

"They're not going to let us out of here," Pearl said, leaning back against the wall and closing her pale blue eyes. She might be one of the Merfolk, but with her blonde hair, light eyes, and pointed ears, she appeared more like a Fae in human form. "These rebels abandoned the old ways and are beyond redemption. If we'd known what they were doing, we would have killed them long ago."

Malek's mouth formed a thin line. "I'm not sure Sabine believes they're beyond redemption, but I can tell you this much: If they hurt her, I'll burn this city to the ground and them along with it."

"A dragon and a Fae," Pearl murmured with a trace of a smile. "Unusual times breed strange alliances."

"You're not including yourself in that alliance?" Malek asked, trying to catch a glimpse of Sabine. He could only make out the red color of her dress through the gaps of people surrounding her. She must have removed her glamour.

"Your kind have never treated fairly with my people. Why are you really saving me?"

Malek glanced down at Pearl. Her face was far too pale, and her cheeks were sunken and gaunt. "Your people attacked my ship on our way to Razadon. They captured some of our friends. We agreed to a prisoner exchange. You were part of that."

Her brow furrowed, and she absently brushed back her blonde hair. "Why was a dragon traveling by ship?"

"It wasn't just me. We had an entire crew with us of all different races," he replied, checking to make sure Sabine was still okay before turning back toward Pearl. "The portal is failing, and we need to locate the artifacts to seal it again. None of us want another war. This world barely survived the last one."

Pearl frowned. "We suspected the portal was failing. That was part of the reason I traveled to Karga for this last trading mission. We needed information from other parts of the world to determine how quickly it was happening. How many of the artifacts have you located?"

Malek froze. "You know about the artifacts?"

She nodded. "My father is one of the leaders of the True Folk. Our family was entrusted with the safekeeping of one of them."

Malek stared at her in shock. In his wildest dreams, he hadn't considered the Merfolk possessed one of the artifacts. It made sense, given they were one of the original races.

"That artifact is the key to saving everyone, including your people, Pearl. Sabine already has the one entrusted to the Fae. She's agreed to accompany me to help seal the portal. Will you help us too?"

Pearl shook her head. "I'd never survive it. If I don't return to the sea by tomorrow night, I'll die. It's not simply a matter of losing my ability to change forms. They've been siphoning off my magic little by little, weakening me so I couldn't fight back. They want to sacrifice me in some strange rite."

Malek frowned. It wasn't ideal, but he might be able to convince her to help once she'd recovered. But first, she needed to be returned to her people. "We'll get you back to the sea. As soon as Sabine connects with the treeheart, that's our signal to get you out of here. Just rest for now. I'll tell you when it's time."

Pearl nodded and closed her eyes. Malek looked out from the wall again, catching sight of one of the True Folk grabbing Sabine's arm and dragging her toward the treeheart. He tensed. It was time.

SABINE SLIPPED into the consciousness of the treeheart. When she opened her eyes, she was still standing within the city, but she recognized the hazy atmospheric quality which indicated it was an illusion. Instead of the ruins, the crystal spires still stood straight and tall, glimmering in the sunlight. The wind gently rustled the leaves, but there were no other noises. No animals, no people, nothing. It was empty... and far too lonely.

An old Fae woman was sitting on the ground smiling kindly at her. "You have the look of your mother, Sabin'theoria. I almost gave up hope we would be remembered."

Sabine paused and then hesitantly approached the Elder. This was the treeheart, adopting a form that was easiest for conversing. Since she'd chosen an Elder, Sabine decided it would be prudent to treat her as such. "Forgiveness, Wise One. I do not know what to call you."

The Elder gestured toward the grassy area in front of her. "Sit, child. You may call me Treeheart. As it always was, it shall always be. Names are not important, only purpose and intent. I am but simply a memory."

Sabine sat down across from the woman. "You need my help."

"Yes," Treeheart said in agreement, turning her face toward the sun. "We are dying. It will not be long now. Another day or two at most, and they will end my life."

Sabine frowned. The sun was a little too hot, which was strange. Something warned her this entire situation wasn't quite right. She'd never met with a treeheart before, so she wasn't quite sure what to expect. "I wanted to speak with you to find out how I can save you."

Treeheart studied her for a long time, her expression mildly curious. "Why?"

Sabine opened her mouth to answer and paused. A glimmer of understanding flashed through her. "You don't want to be saved, do you?"

"Look around, child," Treeheart said, gesturing at the surrounding area. "All my other children have already abandoned me. Your purpose will take you from here too. There is no one remaining to care for. Why should I fight to save this place when there is no one left to protect?"

Sabine shook her head, not understanding how the heart of the city could be so shortsighted. "There is still life here. The trees, the pixies, the birds, the butterflies, the animals... all of them need you."

"Ah," Treeheart murmured. "You wish me to live so I can

care for these creatures? They are not Fae."

Sabine folded her hands in her lap. "No, they're not, but that doesn't mean they're not important. The Fae are servants, just like all the rest. We're no better or worse than any of them."

Treeheart smiled, the lines around her eyes crinkling with pleasure. "You are correct, but few Fae would agree with you. I am glad you have finally come, child. There is much to discuss and little time to do it."

"Then you'll tell me how to save you?"

"I will, but I want two promises from you in return." Treeheart winced, holding her head as though it pained her.

Sabine tilted her head to regard the treeheart. She'd never realized they could experience pain. It was a little disconcerting. "What promises?"

"What? Why have you come?"

Sabine frowned, her unease growing. "I asked you what promises you want in return for information on how I can save you."

"Ah." Treeheart held up a finger and said, "You will install a Fae representative of your choosing to rule in your stead when you depart. I would not face an uncertain future again, holding onto hope you may return one day."

Sabine frowned. If Blossom could get word to Balkin, he could determine who was trustworthy enough to rule the city in her stead. The pixies still living here could act as message bearers, carrying instructions back and forth as necessary. There would be some challenges, but it was possible. In time, they could even bring this city back to its former glory.

Sabine nodded. "Very well. And the second?"

"Kill the dragon."

Sabine froze, unsure she'd heard correctly. "What?"

Treeheart smiled, but it was full of malice and hatred. A

cold chill wrapped around Sabine, and she swallowed. This wasn't the kindly Elder persona Treeheart had adopted but something far more insidious and evil. There was a madness in her eyes, which had previously been hidden.

"Malek hasn't hurt anyone," Sabine managed to say, shaken by Treeheart's demand. "He's saved my life repeatedly. He's not like the dragons from the old days."

"The dragons killed my children!" Treeheart screamed, her voice causing the trees and even the ground to tremble.

Sabine looked up as dark clouds filled the sky, covering the sun.

"Fire and death! They were all burned! I still hear their screams!"

Rain fell in the form of liquid fire, and Sabine cried out as the molten liquid splashed against her skin. "Stop, Treeheart! You're burning me!"

"No, no, no. Not my pretty Fae." Treeheart grimaced and clutched her head. The fiery rain eased, but the dark clouds still threatened overhead. "Kill the dragon. Must kill him. He will burn you. Promise me!"

"Malek's not that dragon," Sabine replied and stood, the urgency to flee this place growing by the second. She started to slowly back away from Treeheart, but the old woman cackled. Crystal bars shot up from the ground, enclosing around her. Sabine pushed against them, unable to escape the crystal prison the treeheart had forged.

"Release me," she demanded, but Treeheart continued to shriek with laughter. Strands of Treeheart's hair fell out, turning into crushed leaves the moment they touched the ground.

Sabine gripped the bars and stared at her in horror. Whatever the True Folk had done to her had broken something inside her. Either that, or this was a result of the Fae abandoning her for centuries. She'd never imagined a treeheart would dare try to imprison her. She hadn't thought such a thing was possible.

"Pretty little Fae," Treeheart sneered, rocking back and forth. Golden tears streaked down her cheeks, reminding Sabine of tree sap. "They left me. They all left me. The dragons killed my children, and all the pretty little Fae abandoned me. No more! You are mine! Mine! I won't let you leave!"

Gods. What had she done? Of all the possibilities, she'd never expected madness. And now she was trapped in the treeheart's fractured mind.

MALEK FROWNED. He could see Sabine better now, but she was just staring up at the tree and holding onto it. He knew the pixies were waiting for some signal to attack and distract, but nothing was happening. As far as he could tell, she was unhurt, but his instincts warned him she was in danger.

"Something's not right," he muttered, absently rubbing his wrist where Sabine's mark was located. He could feel her heartbeat, but the panic running through him wasn't completely his. Sabine was frightened. He knew it with every fiber of his being.

"What is it?"

Malek glanced down at Pearl. "I'm not sure. Sabine's in trouble, but I can't tell what's wrong."

"The rebels hurt her?"

Malek shook his head. "No. I think it's the tree."

Pearl brushed her pale-blonde hair away from her face. "How could a tree hurt a Fae? They are the caretakers of all forests. The trees must obey them."

Malek frowned. "Do you know anything about the treeheart?"

"Very little. It is Fae magic, and we are not privy to their secrets. All I know is the rebels possess a branch taken from the treeheart. They planned to sacrifice me using the branch so it might absorb the power from my blood."

Malek's eyes widened, and he crouched beside Pearl. "That's how they're changing the magic in this place? Sabine said something was making Faerie sick. Could that be how they're doing it?"

Pearl considered it and then nodded. "They have killed dozens of my people in this manner. I do not know if that is what is causing the sickness, but it is possible. Our magics are not compatible. These rebels are ignorant if they believe otherwise."

"This isn't good," he muttered, standing again. Sabine had said something similar about the magic not being compatible, but he hadn't realized they'd been using the treeheart itself to perform the sacrifice. He wasn't sure if Sabine was aware of it either or what it could mean.

"Pearl, I'm going to make every effort to save you, but we won't stand a chance in getting out of here without Sabine's help. We need her to open the doorway to get you back to the sea. I need to shift into my other form to eliminate the people surrounding her."

Pearl's eyes widened. "You intend to turn into a dragon? Now?"

He removed his knife and handed it to Pearl. "Yes. It'll take me a few minutes to change forms. Keep that to protect yourself in case anyone discovers you've escaped."

Her hand wrapped around the hilt of the blade. "Wait. The city will destroy you if you change forms. Your Fae may have shielded you from the hatred of the city, but it *will* attack you if she is not here, particularly if you change into your true form. I can distract the rebels so you can help her."

Malek frowned. "You're not in any state to fight them."

"No, but I am not without resources," Pearl said and slowly rose to her feet. "I may be weakened, but now that you removed my restraints, I am still more powerful than these rebels. My blood is made of seawater, and it still remains strong within me."

Malek hesitated, but the urgency of saving Sabine overshadowed everything else. "All right. We have several clans of pixies ready to distract them as soon as Sabine gives them the signal. I'm hoping I can reach her through the bond we share."

Pearl's eyes widened, and she stared at the mark on his wrist. "You are blood bonded?"

"We are connected," he admitted, not completely sure what a blood bond meant.

"Then you can enter her consciousness right here. Sit and I shall walk you through it."

Malek's brow furrowed, and he sat down. Pearl slid to the ground, her face far too pale. She looked better than when he'd first found her, but she was still in a weakened state.

"Close your eyes and think of your mate."

"She's not my—"

"Silence," Pearl ordered, her tone unyielding. "You must concentrate."

Amused by the fact that this injured Merfolk woman was ordering around a dragon, he closed his eyes. "All right. What do I do?"

"Think of your mate. Visualize her true appearance, the taste of her lips, the smell of her skin, the feel of her power. Surround yourself with her essence and relax. You will be using her magic to slip into her consciousness."

Malek recalled the evening he'd spent with Sabine in the inn. He'd been entranced when she'd danced for him and how she'd gazed at him with such adoring tenderness. She was beautiful both inside and out, with a heart purer than anyone he'd ever known. He concentrated on the smell of her skin and how it always reminded him of night-blooming flowers. Her magic was both alluring and addictive, and his own power surged to the surface when he remembered her passionate embrace.

"Malek?" Sabine whispered, closer than he'd expected.

He opened his eyes and saw Sabine staring up at him in horror. All around them were crystal bars, and they were standing in the middle of the city before it had been destroyed.

Sabine gripped his arm, her eyes wide with panic. "You can't be here. You have to leave!"

A woman cackled, and Malek spun around to see an old woman rocking back and forth on the ground surrounded by crushed leaves. "A pet! A pet! You've brought me a pet! I shall burn the dragon like he burned my city!"

"No!" Sabine shouted, moving in front of him. "He's mine, Treeheart."

"You're both mine! Mine! Mine!"

Malek stared at the old woman in shock. "That's the tree-heart? What's wrong with her?"

"Her mind's been affected," Sabine said quietly. "Malek, she doesn't want to hurt me, but she wants you dead. You need to leave here."

He put his arm around her shoulders, wanting to protect her from this strange creature. Sabine might think she wouldn't be harmed, but he wasn't going to take the chance. The creature had already locked her up. He glanced down and saw a burn mark on Sabine's arm.

"You're hurt," he managed to say, barely recognizing his own voice as his magic surged to the surface. His skin heated and began to glow, demanding he shift to enact vengeance upon this creature for daring to harm the woman he'd claimed as his.

Sabine grabbed his arm and urged, "Malek, no! You can't shift. She'll destroy both of us if you do. We're in her mind right now, and this world obeys her rules."

His skin prickled and he squeezed his eyes shut, struggling to combat his instincts.

Sabine reached up and cupped his face. In a soft voice, she whispered, "Look at me, Malek."

He opened his eyes and stared down into her lavender ones.

She smiled up at him and said, "Just focus on me. I'm right here with you. Do you remember when we shared Faerie wine together?"

"Yes," he whispered, struggling to form a coherent thought other than his desire to steal Sabine away. Staring into her eyes and listening to her voice helped, but the tree-heart's sobbing laughter in the background threatened his focus.

"When we shared Faerie wine back in Akros, you asked me if what happened in those memories also happened in the real world. Do you remember?"

"I do," Malek said, the need to shift beginning to fade the longer he stared into Sabine's eyes. "You said the intent needed to be there for it to happen."

"Memories," Treeheart wailed. "No more memories."

He started to turn toward the old woman, but Sabine grabbed his arm and whispered, "This place is part of Treeheart's memories. She's the one guiding us right now, but her thoughts are jumbled and confused. She was trying to tell me what happened here. That's when the burning rain began to fall, but she stopped when she realized it hurt me."

Malek nodded, remembering Pearl's warning about the city attacking if he were in dragon form. "All right. I won't shift, but I'm not leaving without you. She may not intend you harm, but if she's this confused, you're not safe. How do we get out?"

"Out, out." Treeheart rocked back and forth. "You want to steal my pretty little Fae? Like you stole the others? Burn her alive too?"

"He's not stealing or hurting anyone," Sabine said quickly, shaking her head in a gesture to indicate he needed to play along. "He was worried about me. I told you he's not like the others. Malek is my friend."

"Not sure you can reason with her," he said softly. "Even without shifting, I should be able to break these bars."

Sabine looked up at him and whispered, "Malek, I can't leave. She's trying to hold me captive because she doesn't want to be alone again. I can't break free without damaging her further. If I do, everyone and everything still in this pocket of Faerie will die immediately. Her mind is already fractured."

Malek turned back toward the old woman, who was babbling nonsense about fires and pretty little Fae. She was rocking back and forth, alternating between that strange cackle and sobbing uncontrollably. He grabbed Sabine's wrist where the image of the chalice had been etched onto her skin. "Then use the goddess. Use my power. Use Bane's. I don't give a damn. But I'm *not* going to lose you to some crazy tree."

Sabine's eyes widened. "I can't control the goddess if she emerges."

"Will the goddess hurt you?"

Sabine's brow furrowed. "I don't think so."

"Then do it, Sabine. We'll deal with whatever happens, but we can't stay in here. It's only a matter of time before the True Folk outside hurt you."

Sabine inhaled sharply and nodded. She closed her eyes, and a brilliant white light surrounded her. When she opened her eyes again, Sabine was gone. Her features had changed ever so slightly to be more alien, harsh and even cruel in their beauty. He gaped at her, knowing intuitively this wasn't the woman he'd grown to care about.

"You dare try to steal my child?" Sabine's voice intoned, but it had the same quality Blossom's had possessed when Lachlina had spoken through the pixie. Lightning struck the ground in front of Treeheart. *"You are a relic, a memory, a vessel designed to obey my children's will. Nothing more!"*

"No, no, no," Treeheart pleaded, rocking back and forth faster and faster. Branches sprouted through her patchy gray hair like antlers. "She's mine. Don't take my pretty little Fae away."

"She is mine! My creation and blood of my blood, just as you are her creation. Release her or I will destroy even your memory from this world!"

The crystal bars faded away, and Malek let out a sigh of relief. They still needed to escape the city, but at least Sabine was no longer in immediate danger.

Treeheart buried her face in her hands and sobbed. "No more mine. All alone. Alone. Alone. Always alone."

Lachlina ignored the distraught treeheart and turned toward Malek. *"Dragon, it was your idea to summon me. Have you grown to care so much for my granddaughter that you no longer fear for your life?"*

Malek paused. He wasn't sure he wanted to have this conversation with an angry goddess who was currently inhabiting Sabine's body. It was impossible to forget his people had warred against hers for generations or the callousness she'd displayed when slaughtering the hunters. Despite the fact Lachlina had been instrumental in sealing the portal, it wasn't from any fondness she had for dragons.

He studied the goddess, searching for any sign of Sabine, but it was a stranger standing before him. "I will do a great deal, even treat with someone who was once the enemy of my people if it will save Sabine's life. I care for her deeply."

Lachlina studied him for a long time. He had the impression she was weighing the truthfulness of his words. After a moment, she inclined her head. *"Then you may remain with her for now. I would have her... think kindly of me. In exchange, you will tell her I saved you both. She may negotiate with me at a later date to resolve her debt for my intervention."*

Malek frowned, uncertain what Lachlina would want in exchange for coming to Sabine's aid. "She can't hear us?"

Lachlina studied the sky and crystal spires towering over them. *"No. She has agreed to remain in my prison while I am here. There is much about this world I do not understand yet. Much has changed since I last walked this realm."*

The idea of Sabine being trapped in the goddess's prison sent a new surge of worry through him. "Will you release Sabine?"

Lachlina turned back toward him. *"Her imprisonment upsets you?"*

"Yes, dammit," he snapped, his hands curling into fists in frustration. He couldn't fight this goddess without harming the woman he loved in the process. Being powerless was a new concept for him, and he didn't care much for it.

Lachlina's mouth curved upward. *"Very well. Tell her the treeheart can be healed with a blood offering. All will be as it should be. Until we meet again, dragon."*

Sabine started to collapse, but Malek grabbed ahold of her and eased her to the ground. Her features softened, returning to their normal appearance. Sabine blinked open her eyes and murmured, "It was so dark. I could see you, but it was hazy and confusing."

"It was Lachlina," he whispered, holding her tightly. "She switched places with you to break whatever hold the tree had over you. Are you all right?"

Sabine sat up, holding her head as though it pained her. "I'll be fine. I'm just a little out of sorts. What—what happened?"

Malek frowned. "I'm not completely sure. Lachlina mentioned she wants you to think kindly of her, but I'm not sure of her reasons. She said you were in debt to her for saving us, but you could negotiate the terms later."

Sabine frowned. "That doesn't bode well. What did she do to Treeheart?"

Malek looked at the old woman, who was still rocking back and forth and crying. At least she wasn't doing the weird laughing thing anymore. "She said you can heal the treeheart with your blood."

Sabine's eyes widened. "It's that simple?"

Malek hesitated and then shrugged. "I don't see why not. Your magic is tied to your blood. If that's how the Merfolk have been corrupting the treeheart, by using that walking stick to murder the Merfolk, then it makes sense your blood would bring her back."

Sabine gaped at him. "They were sacrificing Merfolk with the treeheart itself? No wonder she's gone crazy. What were they thinking?"

"I don't think they were. Pearl said they're ignorant of the old ways."

Sabine stood and said, "You need to leave here, Malek. I'll take care of Treeheart, but I need that walking stick. Find Blossom and tell her we need to locate Aberforth."

"Will you be all right?"

Sabine nodded, turning her gaze back on Treeheart. "Yes. And she will be too. I'll make sure of it."

Chapter Twenty-One

*U*sing her dagger, Sabine cut her hand and offered it to Treeheart. The old woman gripped her tightly and drank deeply of her blood.

Infusing her voice with power, Sabine said, "By blood and magic, and by my rights to both, I command you to return to awareness and serve once again."

Treeheart released her hand, and her features softened. The wrinkles on her aged face faded away, and her thinning hair softened from stark gray to a brilliant silvery white. In less than a heartbeat, she'd changed to appear no older than Sabine. Treeheart's eyes sparkled liked the crystal spires, and she gave Sabine a beatific smile.

The sun shined brightly, gently warming the area. Nearby trees all shifted colors, turning to deep greens and silvers. The crystal spires caught the sunlight, casting a rainbow over the entire area. Everywhere Sabine looked was a glimpse of paradise. But there were still no animals or even birds. It was a little too quiet.

"It has been ages since I've been able to think and see

clearly. You have given me a great gift, Your Highness. I am forevermore your loyal servant."

"You're not completely healed yet," Sabine said, taking Treeheart's smooth and unlined hands in hers. "I need to locate your missing branch to make the rest of this place whole. Where is it?"

Treeheart frowned, and her grip tightened over Sabine's. "At my tree. The thief has brought it to me. The invaders wish to strike you down, but with your permission, I will repel them. Allow me to serve you, Your Highness."

Sabine shook her head. "I will handle the invaders. You will serve me best by restoring the forest and healing it with my power. I'll call upon you soon to make plans for the city and to install a representative to act on my behalf. You won't be alone again, Treeheart. I swear it."

"As you will it," Treeheart said, lowering her head in deference, but Sabine saw the glimmer of emotion in her eyes. "I shall await your command."

The world shimmered with light, and Sabine came back to awareness in the partially destroyed city. The Merfolk were still surrounding her, and Zander was holding the knife to her throat. She'd lost all sense of time, similar to how Faerie wine could affect perceptions.

"The tree is only partially healed. I'll need the branch to complete the process," she said to Zander, and he lowered the dagger slightly. She glanced around but noticed no sign of Malek. Her shoulders relaxed. At least he was out of harm's way.

Using her new mystical connection with Treeheart, the magic of the city beat steadily inside her like a second heart-beat. Through it, she knew the missing piece of the treeheart was close. It called to her, the same way the tree had called to her.

"I think not," Marsious said, stepping forward out of the

crowd to approach. He was carrying the walking stick, and Aberforth was a few steps behind him. From the way Aberforth was glaring at Marsious, his anger was directed toward the Elder and not her.

Sabine didn't respond right away. She studied Marsious a bit closer, catching a glimpse of the same madness in his eyes that had been plaguing Treeheart. If these people had been cut off from their home for this long, they must be feeling the effects just like Treeheart.

Sabine looked over the rest of the True Folk to see if she could detect any trace of madness, but they just seemed angry or frightened. Another realization struck her, and her eyes widened as she scanned the crowd.

Everyone here was much younger than Marsious. If she had to guess, none of these people except for him were over two hundred. Even when they'd been walking in the city, she hadn't seen anyone who could be considered an Elder. That must be why Marsious was the only one showing signs of madness; he'd been the one deprived of his magic for the longest.

Sabine frowned and asked Zander, "What happened to your Elders?"

"I *am* an Elder," Marsious said, his eyes narrowing on her.

"You're the only one I've seen. In Faerie, we have thousands of Fae of all different ages. Where are all your Elders?"

Aberforth stepped forward and crossed his arms over his chest. "Dead. Our longevity is one more thing we lost when our heritage was denied to us. Other than Marsious, all of us were born here in this city. We hear the call of the ocean, but we've never known its embrace."

"Because you have corrupted the balance," a woman's voice called.

The group surrounding Sabine turned to stare at the newcomer in shock. She was a striking woman with long, pale-blonde hair and light eyes. Her features were more refined than the other Merfolk, and she moved with undeniable grace. The necklace she wore could have been twin to the one Ilwan had given Sabine. That, and the very attractive and charming dragon walking beside her, made Sabine suspect this woman was the one they'd been seeking.

Sabine smiled at Malek before turning toward the woman. "Pearl, I presume?"

Malek winked at her and said, "Pearl, I'd like you to meet Sabine. Sabine, meet Pearl, our missing Merfolk woman."

Pearl inclined her head in greeting. Without another word, she flicked her wrist and the walking stick flew out of Marsious's hand and toward Sabine. She caught it, the wood warming under her fingertips. A feeling of completeness filled her, but the magic in the stick was still wrong.

Sabine quickly cut her hand and slapped her bleeding palm against the stick. It trembled in response before quieting down. Sabine smiled and threw it toward the tree, where it disappeared in a flash of light. The treeheart was now fully healed. Next time she reconnected with it, there would be birds in the sky.

Dozens of pixies were poking their heads out of the rubble and underbrush. Their wings all fluttered in excitement as they frolicked around the treeheart. Blossom landed on Sabine's shoulder and whispered, "I knew you could save the treeheart! Now we can rescue Esme too!"

Sabine nodded. The immediate danger had lessened, but they still needed to escape Marsious. The treeheart would need time to regain strength. Until then, they were on their own. "Soon. Go keep an eye on your friends and make sure they're ready to leave at a moment's notice. This could still go badly."

"You dare steal the key to the city." Marsious hissed at

Pearl in barely restrained fury. "I will destroy you all for this! This city is mine!"

Pearl narrowed her eyes. "I dare nothing more than a return of the balance. You are not my equal nor are you an Elder, Marsious. You were cast out of the sea for betraying our people. We have not forgotten your deception."

"I never betrayed them!" he shouted, the vein at his temple throbbing in anger. He slapped his fist against his chest. "I saved them. You left us all to die while you were safe in the sea. I brought them here and claimed this city as ours. Me!"

Malek walked toward Sabine and leaned down to whisper, "Our newly liberated Merwoman has more than a few secrets. There's a very interesting one she shared about the real pearl of the sea and how it was used to seal the portal."

Sabine arched her brow at him, but Malek didn't elaborate. She hadn't realized the Merfolk possessed one of the artifacts. But none of that would matter if she didn't concentrate on Marsious. The people living here still deferred to him, and the city was too weak to help evict them.

Pearl walked toward Marsious and said, "You thought to create and rule your own kingdom by using stolen magic to divide the ocean. The desert wasteland was your doing, Marsious! Your punishment was to wander the sand for eternity, never to feel the coolness of the waves again."

"The dragons created the badlands! Not me!"

"The dragons sought to cause havoc among our people to weaken the gods," Pearl retorted, glaring at him. "You know better than anyone the tides ebb and flow. You were the one who corrupted this place when you realized you were trapped in your current form. You are the reason the seas never reclaimed this land."

"You know nothing! While you've been trapped in the sea, I've found true power," Marsious shouted, lifting his hands into the air. A cold wind descended, and the strong scent of brine filled the air. Clouds streaked across the sky, and rain fell in torrents. The ground trembled underneath them.

"It's like the storm that nearly capsized our ship," Malek shouted over the wind. "How can he be doing this without the sea?"

Sabine shielded her eyes from the wind. Shattered crystals were spiraling through the air, hitting her skin with razor sharpness. "He must still have a hold on the city's magic. I need to get to the treeheart to sever it."

"Go! I'll try to distract him from noticing you."

"I protected all of you! You owe me your lives!" Marsious yelled into the storm. The wind whipped even more wildly, and Sabine could barely see in front of her.

"Stop this, Marsious! You'll kill us!" Aberforth managed to shout over the screams of people being struck with broken pieces of shattered crystals. Blue blood ran down their arms and legs, and several of them collapsed.

Sabine struggled to walk against the wind, trying to reach the treeheart. It was too weak to fight without help, but she might be able to cut off Marsious's access to the magic if she could figure out how he was tapping into it. She pressed her hands against the bark, searching for any ties Marsious might have to the magic of the city. There was nothing. Somehow, during the centuries of inhabiting this place, Marsious had managed to irrevocably entwine himself into the magic of Faerie itself.

This was why he'd gone mad, she realized with shocked horror. It wasn't because he'd been separated from the sea, but he'd gone mad because he'd tried to steal Fae magic and bend it to his will. He'd somehow corrupted his own power. This madness was of his own design, and the corruption of the treeheart had been a symptom of it.

"Betrayer! You would seek to harm your own people?"

Pearl demanded and lifted her hands, stealing the lightning from the storm and striking Marsious. But her efforts were clumsy, a sign the Merwoman was more weakened than she'd let on.

"You dare?" Blue lightning erupted from Marsious's palms, and Pearl screamed when it struck her. She collapsed a moment later and remained motionless.

"Pearl!" Malek shouted, rushing toward the fallen woman. His skin began to glow from an impending shift.

"Malek, no!" Sabine yelled, desperate for him not to change forms. She couldn't protect him from the magic of this place and also stop Marsious. She knew what needed to be done, and she needed Malek's help. He turned toward her, their eyes meeting in a moment of perfect understanding.

He gave her a curt nod. "Do it! Now, Sabine!"

Sabine took a steadying breath and yanked hard on Malek's magic through their shared bond. Wild heat filled her and pulsed through her blood, burning her from within. She gritted her teeth to fight through the pain. Her blood dripped onto the ground from where the crystals had sliced through her skin. The pain was a suitable sacrifice. It would have to be enough.

"This will not be!" Sabine shouted, lifting her hands and tapping into reserves of her power. Weaving Malek's magic with her Seelie power, she shot it upward and into the sky, breaking through the threatening storm clouds overhead.

The treeheart glowed, pulsing even more wildly with changing colors as the magic grew in its intensity. Sabine flung out her hand toward the tree, mentally willing it to obey her command. It groaned, shifting in the wind. After reaching down with one of its branches, it grasped Marsious tightly and yanked him high into the air. He thrashed wildly against the restraining branches, a scream ripping from his throat.

"By blood and magic, and by my rights to both," Sabine yelled, the wind whipping around her wildly as the elements obeyed her command. "You have been found guilty of destroying the balance and committing crimes against your brethren."

"I'll kill you all!" Marsious screeched, still trying to escape the treeheart.

"Faerie is under my protection, and you have violated her heart!" Sabine narrowed her eyes on the man responsible for so much corruption. With a flick of her wrist, she shot a crystal shard through the air and impaled the captive Elder through the chest. With a strangled cry, his face fell forward, his long silvered hair covering his chest as his blue blood dripped onto the ground.

The enormity of what she'd done crashed into her, and she took a shaky breath. She'd killed one of the True Folk Elders. It didn't matter she'd done what was necessary to protect Faerie, she'd taken a life the Fae were forbidden to take.

Dimly, she was aware of choked sobs coming from some of the injured people surrounding her. The pixies had retreated as soon as the storm had broken, hiding among the scarce foliage or in the branches of the treeheart. They creeped out from the underbrush, their eyes wide in fear and uncertainty.

Zander climbed to his feet, blood dripping from his cheek where a piece of crystal had struck him. He stumbled toward Sabine and said, "None here will hold you responsible for taking his life. We weren't strong enough to face him down on our own, or we would have done it years ago."

Sabine managed to nod, unsure how to respond. Malek was kneeling beside Pearl, who was sitting up, but the woman's face was far too pale. A burn mark was etched on her chest, and her clothing was blackened and charred. Aberforth crouched beside her, using some sort of foreign magic on Pearl's injuries.

Sabine walked toward them and asked, "Will she be all right?"

Aberforth nodded. "Yes. I have some skill with healing magic. I'll send a runner back to the city and have the rest of the healers meet us here to treat everyone."

Pearl winced when Aberforth's hand brushed over an area where her skin was angry and raw. "I'll recover faster once I return to the sea."

Sabine stared up at the tree still holding onto the body. She could feel the tree's aversion to having the Merfolk's blood so close to its roots, but it wasn't harming the heart.

"The True Folk owe you a great debt," Pearl said, following her gaze upward to Marsious's body. "You have no cause to worry about retaliation. He had been cast out of our ranks ages ago. With your permission, I will arrange to have our people cleanse the soil of Marsious's taint."

Sabine regarded Pearl with surprise. She inclined her head and said, "Your assistance would be welcome."

Zander stared up at Marsious's body and scowled. "I had no idea Marsious was the reason why we were forced into this hell and our families were unable to return to the sea. How could this have happened? Why did he lead our parents away from the ocean?"

Pearl brushed her hand against the injury on her chest, which still appeared to be causing her some pain. "Marsious was once one of our commanders. When the water dragons began attacking our cities, we sent a large group of our people with him to go into hiding. We had no intention of falling into the same trap as the Fae, so we divided our people rather than risk facing extinction. The Fae agreed to allow our people sanctuary within this city until they could establish another colony in a different part of the world.

When the city was attacked and the Fae received the call to retreat, Marsious must have claimed this place for himself."

Sabine swallowed and glanced at Malek. His jaw had clenched at the reminder of the dragons' influence, but he remained silent. Sabine slipped her hand in his, and he jerked his head toward her. She gave him a reassuring smile to let him know she didn't hold the past against him. Once again, he'd proven with his actions he was different from his predecessors. If it weren't for his magic, she wasn't sure she would have had the strength to stop Marsious's attack. As an experienced Elder who had stolen Faerie magic, she'd needed a dragon's power to destroy Marsious's ties to her land.

Aberforth stood and then helped Pearl to her feet. "If this is true, you know our families didn't have anything to do with Marsious's treachery. Can you give us back our true forms? So we can return to the sea?"

Pearl winced, and she shook her head. "I cannot. What you ask is beyond my power. We are all servants to the phases of the moon. As powerful as I might be, none may circumvent the gods' will."

Malek squeezed her hand and nodded toward her wrist. She bit her lip, understanding what he was suggesting. She just hoped Lachlina would feel the same way. The goddess was proving to be more than a little unpredictable.

Sabine cleared her throat. "I might have a solution."

Everyone turned to face her. Sabine whistled loudly, and Blossom appeared a moment later. "You're okay?"

Blossom nodded. "A couple of the pixies had their wings torn during the storm, but we're all okay. No main veins were broken, so they'll heal up pretty quick."

Sabine frowned. The pixies had gone through quite a bit, but hopefully they would be able to live in peace now. But first, she needed to resolve the Merfolk's situation.

In a low voice, Sabine whispered, "I need to speak with

Lachlina. Will you allow her to use your voice? It will mean revealing your ability to these people."

Blossom's eyes went round. She thought about it for a minute and then nodded. "Okay. I can do that if it'll keep the other pixies safe. One goddess coming right up."

Blossom's wings fluttered rapidly and she began to glow, growing more and more brilliant with every movement of her wings. The people surrounding her gasped, and many of them slowly backed away. Even Pearl appeared startled by the change in Blossom.

"You seek my help twice in one day, my little silver flower? Although, I have enjoyed watching the events unfold. Well done."

"Greetings again, Lachlina," Sabine said, still somewhat unnerved by the goddess's familiarity. Even though Lachlina had come to their aid with the treeheart, it would be a while before Sabine could forgive her for killing those innocent hunters. "Your assistance with the treeheart came at an opportune time; however, we could use your guidance again. Your people need you."

Lachlina sighed. *"My little silver flower, I know what you seek. But you do not reward those who try to kill you. Like a weed that is strangling the flower, you rip it out and crush it beneath your boots. They do not belong in your garden, Sabin'theoria. I thought you had learned better when you chose to punish that one."*

Sabine paused. The goddess had a point, but the other True Folk had been acting from a place of desperation. It didn't make it right, but she could understand their point of view.

She glanced around at the True Folk who had been forced into giving up their homes, just like she had. What they'd done wasn't much different from the thieving she'd done back in Akros. She couldn't begrudge these people for doing what was necessary to survive. They'd been cut off from their home and had chosen to make the best out of their situation.

"Even a weed has a place in nature," Sabine said, reminding the goddess that even stubborn plants have a purpose. "They are as much your children as I am. Their parents were betrayed by someone who should have protected them. Will you continue to punish them simply because they trusted the wrong person?"

A deafening silence greeted her at these words. Blossom continued to glow, her wings fluttering rapidly. Sabine waited, sensing Lachlina was trying to come to a decision.

"An exchange and a sacrifice," Blossom intoned, her voice sounding even farther away. *"The Pearl of the Sea shall be sacrificed to Sabin'theoria. In exchange, she will help forge a new path to the ocean. All those who are willing shall be returned to the sea's embrace."*

Blossom's glow quickly faded, and Sabine caught her before she could fall. The tiny pixie panted. "Ouchies. Rough landing. That one hurt."

Sabine frowned. Lachlina must have used up most of her remaining magic. The goddess still hadn't fully recovered, or something else was going on. Sabine placed Blossom on her shoulder, and the pixie grabbed her hair, scooting closer to her neck.

Turning toward Pearl, Sabine asked, "I'm assuming the Pearl of the Sea doesn't mean you?"

Pearl smiled and shook her head. "No. It is one of the artifacts your dragon mate has been seeking. It was entrusted to us by Lachlina to seal the portal. It shall be yours, once you have forged a path to the sea."

Sabine nodded. "Gather all of your people while I summon a doorway. Anyone who wishes to remain living in Faerie will be permitted to remain here. They will be subject to the laws of Faerie and become citizens of this city. If any of your people wish to be returned to the sea and embrace their true form, they will be allowed to do so."

The group gathered around them and talked excitedly among themselves. A few of them fell to the ground, crying in relief. Others didn't appear too sure what this meant, or they were in shock.

"Do we have to decide now?"

Sabine located the man who had asked the question. "Yes. This is the goddess's gift, and I can't promise it will be available later."

Pearl turned toward the man and said, "If you are unsure, I suggest you choose the sea. It is within our power to return you to your human form, but we cannot give you the gift of the ocean."

The man nodded, his shoulders relaxing. Several others appeared reassured by Pearl's words.

Another of the True Folk called, "What if some of our family wants to stay here? Will we be allowed to see them?"

Sabine nodded. "Yes. This city shall remain open to all True Folk while they retain their human forms. You and your people will be free to trade, visit, or even live within the confines of the city."

Pearl smiled. "Atlantia. This city was once called Atlantia, and that was its purpose centuries ago."

Sabine's eyes widened. She'd heard of Atlantia, but she hadn't realized this was the same place. The Fae had always thought it had been lost to the sea during the war. The rumors were true, but not as she'd imagined.

Pearl closed the distance between them and said, "You have done a great thing today. Our people were once allies, and I would see that relationship recognized once again. I would very much like to call you a friend, Sabine."

"As would I." Sabine held out her hand, and Pearl took it. "Both allies *and* friends."

Malek chuckled. "I don't suppose you'd consider a dragon in that description?"

Pearl smiled at him and held out her hand to him too. "Very strange alliances indeed."

~

SABINE WALKED through the magical doorway and emerged on the beach, along with Malek, Blossom, Pearl, and hundreds of True Folk. Even some of the pixies had joined them, wanting to see Fae magic at work.

The stars still twinkled in the night sky, but dawn would soon be approaching on the horizon. They were a short distance from Malek's ship, where Bane was waiting for her. It was tempting to reach out to her demon protector to let him know she was safe, but she needed to hurry while her magic was still strong.

Glancing at Malek, she asked, "Can you shield me?"

Malek nodded and placed his hand against her neck. Her family already knew she was still alive, but it wouldn't be wise to keep advertising their location. She intended to make this a permanent doorway to Atlantia, and it would be better if her family wasn't aware of its location. Once she'd entrusted the city to an Unseelie Fae of Balkin's choosing, they could safeguard it to prevent the rest of her family from accessing it. Only those who were aligned with the Unseelie could ever know about this place.

Pearl stood on the other side of her and asked, "Are you ready?"

Sabine nodded and withdrew her knife. She cut her hand and allowed the blood to fall onto the sand before passing the weapon to Pearl. The Merfolk woman repeated the gesture and held out her hand to Sabine. She accepted Pearl's hand, nearly staggering as the magic of both land and sea collided together in a tidal wave of power.

Sabine took a steadying breath. Kicking off her sandals, she focused on the connection she shared with the land. She was more than a part of this world. In addition to her power stemming directly from the land, she had also been appointed by the gods to forevermore serve as a caretaker for it. In exchange, the land offered her power beyond imagining. She was dimly aware of Pearl harnessing the power of the sea, and it cradled the Merfolk woman within its cool magical embrace.

They both simultaneously held out their hands, reaching toward the sea. The ground trembled, and Sabine cut a deep path directly to the sea from the doorway. Using her blood, she cemented the doorway into this reality. It would only be accessible to those who knew it was here. Once her Beastman protector installed a representative to act as her behalf, they would serve as its gatekeeper.

Sabine nodded at Pearl to indicate it was time. The Merfolk woman gave her a brilliant smile. Turning back toward the sea, Pearl opened her mouth and sang a wordless and haunting melody.

Water rushed through the chasm, lapping at the sand near Sabine's feet. Pearl stopped singing and laughed, reaching down to splash the cold water on her face. The other True Folk shouted their exultation and danced in the surf, cheering and splashing each other like children. Tears filled Sabine's eyes at the unrepressed joy these people had at once again being reunited with the sea.

Malek ran his thumb against her neck and murmured, "You did it. You really saved all of these people."

"Not everyone, but it's a beginning," she said and wrapped her arms around Malek.

He kissed her hair and murmured, "A very promising

beginning."

Pearl turned toward her and asked, "You have Ilwan's necklace?"

Sabine nodded and removed it from around her neck. She handed it to Pearl, and the woman closed her eyes. The necklace glowed, and Pearl turned back toward the waves, her eyes shining with unnamed emotion. "He comes."

They didn't have long to wait. Ilwan stepped out of the water in clothing similar to the style worn in Karga. Instead of his tail, he had two legs and very large feet.

"You're safe," Ilwan said with a wide grin.

Pearl laughed and leaped at him. He caught her midair, spun her around, and kissed her deeply.

"Well, I wasn't expecting that," Malek said with a chuckle.

"Me neither," Sabine admitted, watching the two Merfolk reconnect.

They broke apart, talking between themselves too quietly for Sabine to hear. Pearl gestured to the renegade True Folk and continued to speak. Ilwan asked a few questions but mostly appeared to be listening. After almost ten minutes, Ilwan wrapped his arm around Pearl and they walked toward her and Malek.

"You have held to your part of the bargain, and we will do the same. Your people will all be returned to you unharmed, as promised." He glanced at the people gathered nearby. "In exchange for reuniting our people with the sea, we will uphold the goddess's demand to sacrifice our Pearl of the Sea to you. With it, I hope you will continue to prove honorable by sealing the portal once and for all."

Sabine inclined her head. "We will make every effort to ensure another war doesn't happen ever again."

"Then my people shall bring it to the beach now, along with your friends. The remainder of the crew shall be delivered to your ship. Will this arrangement be acceptable?"

Relief surged through her, and she nodded. "Blossom, can you tell us what needs to be done to return these people to their true forms?"

Blossom flew in between them and said, "The goddess says once you've claimed the pearl for yourself, you'll have the ability to give them back their true forms. They need to be in the sea for the magic to work."

Pearl frowned. "Will they be able to change forms at will?"

"Yep, but not right away," Blossom replied with a grin. "The goddess wants them all to stay in the ocean for one lunar cycle. She says you need to teach them the true ways so this doesn't happen again. After that, they'll have the same ability as all your spellcasters."

Pearl's eyes widened, and she gripped Ilwan's arm tightly. "My love, you realize what this means?"

Ilwan appeared equally stunned, and he nodded. "She is returning a tremendous amount of our magic. With this gift of a new generation of spellcasters, we will be able to wrest control of the seas and ensure all the life within it will thrive."

Blossom polished her knuckles on her dress, looking entirely too pleased with herself. "All in a day's work."

Ilwan turned toward Sabine and said, "You have gone above and beyond to find a peaceful resolution, even insofar as putting yourself at risk. All the True Folk are in your debt."

The enormity of his words settled over Sabine, and she shook her head. "There is no debt between allies."

Ilwan gave her a brilliant smile. "Then allow me to give you a gift, in addition to a formal offer of an alliance between the True Folk and the Queen of the Unseelie and her subjects." He gestured toward the north, where Malek's ship was located. "I will send my people to assist in making the repairs to your ship. Once it is done, we will escort you to deeper waters and ensure you are troubled no further upon the seas."

Malek's eyes widened. "That's an extremely generous gift, and one which will help us arrive at our destination much sooner."

Sabine hesitated. "There's still a demon on board the ship. He's counted as my subject and one of my allies. Is that going to be an issue?"

Pearl arched her brow and then shook her head. "A dragon *and* a demon? I'm beginning to think we need to reassess our understanding of this world."

Sabine smiled at Malek. "I highly recommend it. I've found a different viewpoint to be extremely rewarding."

"Sabine? Is that you?"

Sabine turned and saw a tall, redheaded woman waving at her. Right behind her was Levin, along with one of the Merfolk.

"It's Esme!" Blossom shrieked and took off down the beach.

Sabine's breath hitched, and she released Malek to run toward her friend. Esmelle squealed and ran in their direction.

Tears sprang to her eyes, and Sabine hugged her tightly. "I was so worried about you. I can't tell you how glad I am to know you're okay."

Esmelle choked on a sob and managed to say, "I missed you so much. I knew if anyone could get me out of that mess, it was you. I told Levin you would figure out a way."

"It was a little touch and go for a while, but Blossom was a huge help."

"I was, Esme!" Blossom said eagerly, zipping around them. "You should have seen me. I saved hundreds of pixies. And I dusted a dragon. I got drunk off Faerie water. Oh, and I almost got eaten by a thontin."

Esmelle laughed and brushed away her tears. "I should have known you would be instrumental in saving us, Blossom. We'll have to see about growing a very special flower in your honor."

Blossom's eyes widened. "Oooh. Will you let me pick out what kind I want?"

"Of course."

Sabine scanned her witch friend up and down, but she looked exactly the same. It had only been a few days, but it felt like so much longer. If anything, Esmelle was glowing.

"You're not going to believe everything that happened," Esmelle said with a wide grin. "We got to see the Merfolk's underwater city. They live in this bubble place where they breathe actual air. It's crazy. Did you know in human form the Merfolk all have big feet so they can swim faster? The plants are incredible too. I found some new ones to make teas, and there were these little seahorses that would blow bubbles at me."

Sabine laughed. "And it doesn't look like the ocean messed up your hair."

Esmelle snorted. "Oh, you have no idea. I think I scared half the Merfolk with how it doubled in volume after it got wet." She leaned in close and whispered, "I've got to tell you all about what happened with me and Levin."

Sabine's eyes widened. "Really? You and Levin?"

Esmelle nodded. "Yep. I think we're going to have to do some cabin switching. Maybe then you'll actually give into your desires with Malek."

Blossom snickered. "They already did that."

Esmelle gaped at her, and Sabine merely smiled. Glancing at Malek, who was talking to Levin, she knew she'd end up giving into her desires again with the charismatic dragon. Unfortunately, getting Malek alone was going to have to wait.

"I think we're going to have to keep it to a girls' cabin for now. We've adopted a young seer who had to be smuggled out of Karga. Her name is Rika. She's sweet."

Esmelle arched her brow. "Oh? Sounds like you've had some adventures of your own. I'm particularly interested in the ones involving a certain dragon we know."

Sabine laughed and linked arms with Esmelle, and they walked back toward Malek and Levin. Ilwan, Pearl, and the Merfolk who had brought Esmelle and Levin to the beach were standing beside them talking. "We'll have to catch up later. There's a bit of unfinished business we need to handle first."

"I'm intrigued," Esmelle said with a grin.

Sabine released Esmelle and hugged Levin. She kissed the wyvern's cheek and said, "Glad to have you back with us."

"I'm very glad to be here," Levin replied and put his arm around Esmelle's shoulders. She smiled up at him with no small amount of adoration.

Pearl held out a small box inlaid with seashells. She smiled at Sabine and said, "To fulfill our terms of the agreement, we hereby sacrifice our Pearl of the Sea in exchange for the return of our people."

Sabine accepted the beautifully crafted box and lifted the lid. Inside was a large pearl, almost the size of a coin. She'd never seen one this big before. In the moonlight, it shimmered with swirls of color, a sign of its remarkable power.

Malek moved to stand beside her. "That's the Pearl of the Sea?"

Sabine nodded. "Will you hold the box for me?"

Malek took the box, and Sabine reached inside to touch the pearl. The moment her fingers came into contact with it, a rush of power swept up her arm, flowed through her, and surrounded her. It was alien and unlike anything she could comprehend. It was *wrong*. Some dormant part of her warned that this pearl had never been designed with her in mind. She knew what was needed to complete the claiming.

Lifting her head, she said, "A sacrifice is due."

Pearl nodded and held out her hand. Sabine handed her a knife, and Pearl cut her finger. Instead of blood, something appearing like seawater welled to the surface. She allowed a drop to fall upon the pearl and said, "I release you, by blood and magic."

Sabine held out her free hand, and Pearl cut her finger the same way. Sabine coated the pearl with her blood, sealing their magic together. Power infused her words as she repeated the oath whispered to her by the goddess when she'd accepted the first artifact.

"I claim you, by blood and magic. In tribute to the gods and the last sacrifice of the goddess Lachlina, I swear by all I am and the last of the magic of this world to uphold my family's oath in defense from those who would see this world destroyed."

The pearl warmed in her hand. Its shimmering surface illuminated and glowed brighter, until it was nearly blinding. It lifted into the air and hovered over her palm with a brilliance as powerful as the reflection of the moon. The sound of drums pounded in her temples, beating a staccato rhythm in time with her heartbeat.

As I will it, the pact is sealed.

Light and magic exploded from the pearl, dropping Sabine to her knees. Power rushed through her, racing up and down the marks on her skin as they glowed with renewed strength. A sharp pain lanced through her skin in the same location as the chalice mark she already wore. She gritted her teeth, struggling to breathe through the worst of it.

The marks she wore all became alive again as she accepted the pain of her sacrifice in exchange for this new power. When it subsided, only a faint pulse of magic remained along her skin, but she felt it strong and vibrant within her.

Sabine looked down at her wrist, staring at the new mark in shock. Instead of only a chalice, the image of a pearl was now embedded within it. The actual pearl was lying upon the sand, still shimmering in the moonlight. Sabine picked it up, staring at it in wonder. Like the chalice after she'd claimed its power, the pearl was now dormant.

She lifted her head and realized everyone had succumbed to the magical explosion when she'd claimed the pearl. Ilwan and Pearl were both on the ground, trying to shake off the effects in front of her. Malek was faring better, possibly a result of their new blood bond.

Blossom giggled. "Maybe we should start warning people before you do that."

"It would have been nice if I had known too," Sabine muttered and placed the pearl back in the box Malek had dropped when he'd fallen. She rose to her feet and brushed the sand off her dress. Malek stood, accepted the box, and reached down to help Levin and Esmelle back to their feet. Sabine turned to help Pearl and Ilwan, but they were already getting back up.

Ilwan shook his head, still appearing dazed. "You are truly touched by the goddess."

"It would seem so," Sabine replied, but she wasn't sure if that was a good thing. The power she'd accepted had changed something within her, but she didn't know what or how.

She turned and found the other True Folk still struggling to overcome the effects. They likely had never experienced such a large burst of magic before, and they would need a few more minutes to recover.

"You will be able to change them back?" Pearl asked,

moving to stand beside her.

Sabine nodded. "Yes. Once they've recovered, you'll need to take them all into the waves. Have them stand at least waist deep. When they're ready, I'll begin the change."

Pearl smiled. "Then let me say farewell now. We'll need to escort them back to our home once they shift. It may take a while for them to find their sea legs if they've never known them."

Sabine turned to face Pearl and said, "I hope one day soon we'll have a chance to visit together in Atlantia. This visit has demonstrated just how little we know about each other's people."

Pearl's smile deepened. "I would enjoy that. I would also like to learn how a Fae came to know such a diverse set of traveling companions."

"That's quite a long story," Sabine said with a laugh. She gestured toward Blossom and said, "If you ever need to reach me, simply leave word with one of the pixies in Atlantia. They'll be able to contact Blossom."

"I shall remember."

Ilwan moved to stand beside Pearl and said, "Before you leave, I need to give you a warning."

"What is it?"

Ilwan frowned and glanced in the direction of the sea. "The creatures of the sea are ours to command, and they've been bringing ominous tidings to us for more than a year. Your ship was encountered so close to shore because we were escorting some of our southern brethren to the northern seas for their protection. There are some strange occurrences to the south, and much of the ocean floor has been rendered inhabitable."

Malek tensed. "In the direction of Razadon?"

Ilwan nodded. "Foreign magic we haven't been able to identify has been leaking into the sea. It has been poisoning the fish and other wildlife. We don't know the cause or if it's also affecting the land creatures. We sent several of our people to investigate, but none have returned. We fear they've been lost forever."

Sabine exchanged a worried look with Malek. Both the entrance to the demonic volcano and the dwarven city were to the south. There were other lesser races which had access to magic, but none should be able to cripple the True Folk while they were in the sea. She couldn't help but wonder if this was tied to the portal collapsing. If so, they were running out of time to find the rest of the artifacts.

Malek placed his hand against her lower back. "We'll be careful, but we still need to travel south. One of the artifacts was reported to have been entrusted to the dwarves. We'll need to acquire it to ensure the portal remains sealed."

"Then we'll take you as far south as we dare, but we can't offer you safe passage through the poisoned water. Let us know when you are ready to depart," Ilwan said and bowed to both of them. He took Pearl's hand, and they headed toward their people and began directing them to the ocean.

Sabine froze, sensing a demonic presence rapidly approaching. She turned to stare in the direction of the ship and caught sight of Bane. Her heart pounded, and she ran toward him.

Bane scooped her up and lifted her into the air. She threw her arms around the demon, sending a wave of her power over him to cement his ties to the surface. He shuddered under her touch, and his arms tightened around her.

"I'm glad you're back and safe, little one," he murmured, still holding her tightly. "I was about to come hunting for you when I sensed you close to me. I see you managed to save the witch and the wyvern. You also picked up a few..." He narrowed his eyes. "Merfolk?"

She inhaled deeply, breathing in the scent of brimstone

she always associated with him. "Yes, but they're not staying with us. I'll have to tell you everything later. Did Rika make it to the ship safely?"

Bane frowned. "Yes, and I was surprised to learn you'd sent a baby seer for me to protect. The girl's been tripping over my damned heels every minute since she arrived. I finally managed to keep her busy by having her sew the ship's sails."

"Busy is good. Just make sure you don't scare her. She's had a rough time of it." Sabine glanced over and saw Malek walking up the beach toward them. More than half the True Folk had already recovered and were in the waves.

"There's something different about you," Bane said, leaning back and perusing her up and down. He froze, glancing back and forth between her and Malek. His eyes flashed silver, and he released her. Without a word, he leaped toward Malek with his claws extended.

"Bane!" she shouted as the pair tumbled in the sand, battling between them.

"I'll kill you for changing her!" Bane roared, swiping at Malek with his claws.

"Dammit, Bane," Malek muttered, narrowly avoiding a blow close to his eyes.

Sabine's jaw clenched, and she unleashed a sharp blast of her power. Bane went flying backward and landed in the sand a good distance away.

Sabine stalked toward him and snapped, "Explain yourself. Now."

Bane slowly rose to his feet. His eyes were still silvered, and he glared at Malek with enough venom to send a sliver of fear through her. "A blood bond, Sabine? What in the name of the underworld were you thinking?"

Sabine straightened, and she narrowed her eyes. "How dare you question me."

Bane closed the distance between them. "I swore fealty to the Queen of the Unseelie, not some Seelie puppet. If he tries to change your magic, I *will* end him."

Sabine froze. Her heart fell into her stomach, and she shook her head in stunned disbelief. In a voice barely above a whisper, she managed to say, "That shouldn't be possible."

Bane gave her a look of disgust. "I wanted you to bind him to you, not shackle yourself to an agent of the light. You're not nearly as strong as when you left me. Tell me you don't feel it."

Malek frowned and walked toward them. "What are you talking about?"

She swallowed. "Bane thinks our new connection changed my magic."

His head whipped toward her. "What? Is that possible?"

"I don't know," she whispered, turning back toward Bane. "I thought I'd just used a great deal of magic. You can sense a change?"

Bane's claws flexed, and his eyes reverted back to their normal amber. "Yes. We may be able to take steps to stop it from progressing, but we will need to find someone with more knowledge about Fae magic."

Sabine bit her lip. The Unseelie Elders had infused her blood into her skin to reinforce her ties to the Unseelie. "Do you know of someone who can help etch my skin? I don't think I can ask anyone in Faerie without them finding out what I've done."

Malek frowned. "Wait. You're saying our new bond or connection is dangerous to you?"

Sabine hesitated and then nodded. "In a manner of speaking, yes. My entire claim to the Unseelie throne rests on my magical alignment. If my Seelie magic grows too much and it upsets the balance, I'll become my father's subject."

Malek's brow furrowed. "Even though you don't live in

Faerie?"

Bane crossed his arms over his chest. "You're a fool. The Wild Hunt has acknowledged her as the Queen of the Unseelie. If she becomes a subject of the light, all of the Unseelie will be forced into servitude by her father. He'll be able to summon her to his side whenever he wants. He has quite a penchant for torture from what I've heard."

Sabine squeezed her eyes shut. Such a thing could never come to pass, no matter what sacrifice she'd need to make to ensure it didn't happen.

"Shit," Malek muttered, turning back toward Bane. "Do you know how we can remove the bond? Or even prevent such a thing from happening?"

"Other than killing you?" Bane rubbed his chin and shrugged. "There may be something in the dwarven archives. If not, my people have records pertaining to the Fae. They may have knowledge of an exiled Unseelie Fae who may be able to etch her skin to solidify her alignment."

Sabine took a shaky breath. There were no guarantees, but in the meantime, she'd need to be careful around Malek. The more they combined their magic, the faster the change would happen. "We'll look into it the first opportunity we get. For now, we need to return these people to their home."

Sabine turned toward the ocean, where the remainder of the True Folk were gathered. Ilwan approached her, frowned at Bane and Malek, and asked, "Is everything all right?"

Unwilling to answer, Sabine gestured at the ocean and asked, "Your people are ready?"

Ilwan nodded. "Yes. Once I join them in the sea, you may begin."

Sabine watched him walk away, catching sight of Esmelle, Levin, and Blossom, who were a short distance away. Blossom was still eagerly zipping around Esmelle, delighted to have her dryad friend back.

Ilwan held up his hand to indicate he was in position. Sabine took a deep breath, summoning her new magic to the surface. Since this was a foreign type of power, she wasn't concerned about being detected by her family.

A cold power welled up from the deepest recesses of her psyche, silent and heavy like the ocean's embrace. She gathered it within her, using the power of the land to keep it contained while it built in strength. Struggling to breathe under its staggering weight, she managed to take a breath and then spiraled it outward over those who sought to claim the sea for themselves.

At that moment, the sun crept over the horizon, blinding in its brilliance. The True Folk all glowed as well, eclipsing the light of the sun. Unable to keep watching, Sabine hid her eyes and looked away. In a flash, it was gone.

Sabine turned back toward the ocean, watching as the True Folk shouted in exultation, flicking their fins and splashing one another. They dove under the surface and then sputtered back up, the sight lightening the burdens on Sabine's heart. Malek placed his hand against her lower back and said, "It's a beautiful sight, isn't it?"

She nodded, unable to put her emotions into words. It was more than beautiful. What they were witnessing was the hopeful promise for a different future. Each of these people now had a choice, whether to return to their roots or seek out another path. And that was more precious than anything Sabine could imagine.

"Great," Bane muttered with a sigh. "More fish people."

Sabine smiled. "You suggested I make some alliances."

Bane harrumphed and crossed his arms over his chest. "Unless they're willing to drown your enemies, I don't see much point. Now the dwarves, they produce some rather fine weapons. I wouldn't mind an alliance with them."

Blossom came flying back, her wings fluttering in excitement. "Sabine! Don't forget your promise now that Bane's here. I want my reward!"

Bane's brow furrowed. "No one squished you yet? What reward is the bug talking about?"

Sabine paused and bit back a smile. Lifting her hand, she sent a powerful wave of magic over Blossom. Her image shimmered, and with a flash of light, she changed into a Fae-sized pixie.

Blossom's hair was glamoured yellow today with several long braids woven into an intricate style. Her matching dress was made from an impossibly thin gossamer-style material, and it sparkled like the morning's dew. Her wings twitched in excitement, and she grinned at Bane. "Surprise!"

"What the hell?" Bane scrambled backward, his eyes shifting to silver.

Blossom put her hands on her hips and stalked toward him. "Go ahead. Call me a bug again." She leaned forward and narrowed her eyes. "I dare you."

Sabine grinned at Bane's bemused expression. He'd think twice about tormenting the pixie for a while. Although, once the magic faded, it would be another story. But Blossom would get at least a full day's worth of enjoyment out of her new form.

Malek chuckled and put his arms around her. "Well, at least he'll learn to treat her with a bit more respect. The trip to Razadon should be interesting."

"I think you're right," Sabine said with a smile and leaned against him. They might need to be careful about fusing their magic together, but it didn't negate how much she'd grown to care for this dragon. Taking his hand in hers, she led him back toward the ship while silver fins danced in the waves behind them.

ABOUT THE AUTHOR

Jamie A. Waters is an award-winning writer of science fiction and fantasy romance. Her first novel, Beneath the Fallen City, was a winner of the Readers' Favorite Award in Science Fiction/Fantasy Romance and the CIPA EVVY Award in Science Fiction.

Jamie currently resides in Florida with a murder of crows in her backyard and two neurotic dogs who enjoy stealing socks. When she's not pursuing her passion of writing, she's usually trying to learn new and interesting random things (like how to pick locks or use the self-cleaning feature of the oven without setting off the fire alarm). In her downtime, she enjoys reading, playing computer games, painting, or acting as a referee between the dragons and fairies currently at war inside the closet. Learn more about her at: jamieawaters.com.

www.ingramcontent.com/pod-product-compliance
Lightning Source LLC
Chambersburg PA
CBHW032159180726
48284CB00001B/104